Praise for S

“It’s no surprise that *Saving Miss Oliver’s* is informed by a compassionate knowledge of the lives of all people who inhabit independent schools. After all, the book’s author spent years teaching at and leading this kind of institution, and later was one of the nation’s top school consultants. He knows the territory.

What may surprise, though, is that the book is such a strong, beautifully wrought, engaging novel. As one reads along, it becomes clear that Davenport writes much too well and feels far too deeply for his complex, passionately human characters to resort to the hype and melodrama that so often maim ‘school novels.’ Rather, he creates his figures and then lets them live, struggle, and develop in ways that are frequently moving and always honestly related.

In other words, the book steps beyond its genre. And in so doing it powerfully reminds us that real people are at the heart of any first-rate school. Their integrity, strength of character, hope for the world, and courage are the capital good schools are always built on. Davenport knows this. At the end of *Saving Miss Oliver’s*, so will you.”—Peter Tacy, Former Executive Director of the Association of Independent Schools and Head of the Marvelwood School, Kent, CT

“This book caught me by surprise—a surprise I would recommend to everyone. On the face of it, the story is about a difficult leadership transition in a well-established girls’ school that is experiencing hard times. It is much more. Mr. Davenport weaves an intricate tapestry of institutional and cultural history, and minefields in independent school leadership. His characters jump off the page and made me keep reading to find out what they were thinking, how they developed, and what they did next. I was enthralled by the stories within the story and moved to tears by the strength and bravery of the characters who so quickly became my friends and acquaintances. This is a story of struggle and disappointment, but most of all, it is a story about wisdom and hope.”—Jessie-Lea Abbott, Head of School, Katherine Delmar Burke School, San Francisco, CA

"Steve Davenport is a consummate schoolmaster and a gifted writer. In this splendid first novel, Davenport builds on all the other exceptional 'school' novels: *The Prime of Miss Jean Brodie*, *The Rector of Justin*, *The Headmaster's Papers* and *The River King*. *Saving Miss Oliver's* is a must read for anyone who appreciates the seasons of a school's life and the lives of people who make schools work."—Peter Buttenheim, Sanford School, Hockessin, DE

"Steve Davenport's novel is fast-paced, entertaining and singularly evocative of the pressure-cooker atmosphere of a boarding school. Steve knows schools, and he brings us face to face with their passions, their absurdities and their virtues—especially when it comes to schools for girls."—Rachel Belash, Former Head of Miss Porter's School, Farmington, CT

"*Saving Miss Oliver's* is a fascinating novel, a school story vibrant with personalities, crises, hopes, idealism, laughter, tears, struggle and soaring spirit. Anyone who has ever been a student or administrator or trustee or parent in a school will find the book riveting, and will stop again and again with recognition, shock and delight. The reader will care intensely about the persons and events in this book, the drama and comedy alive in it."—David Mallery, Seminar Leader and Consultant to Schools in the U.S. and Abroad

Saving
Miss Oliver's

Saving Miss Oliver's

A Novel

Stephen Davenport

This is a work of fiction. Any resemblance to real people or schools of any of the characters or schools in the novel is coincidental and unintended.

Library of Congress Cataloging-in-Publication Data

Names: Davenport, Stephen, author.
Title: Saving Miss Oliver's : a novel / by Stephen Davenport.
Description: Berkeley, CA : Graphic Arts Books, [2018]
Identifiers: LCCN 2018005418 | ISBN 9781513261317 (softcover)
| ISBN 9781513261324 (hardcover) | ISBN 9781513261331 (ebk.)
Subjects: LCSH: Women school principals--Fiction. | Boarding schools--Fiction.
| Teaching--Fiction. | Girls--Fiction.
Classification: LCC PS3604.A9427 S28 2018 | DDC 813/.6--dc23
LC record available at https://lccn.loc.gov/2018005418

Front Cover: Raymond Forbes LLC/Stocksy.com; P.Pine Photography/Shutterstock.com

Published by WestWinds Press®
An imprint of

GraphicArtsBooks.com

Printed in the U.S.A.

Proudly distributed by Ingram Publisher Services.

GRAPHIC ARTS BOOKS
Publishing Director: Jennifer Newens
Marketing Manager: Angela Zbornik
Editor: Olivia Ngai
Design & Production: Rachel Lopez Metzger

To Joanna

Book One: Summer

ONE

Even in that last year of her reign, Marjorie Boyd had insisted that the graduation exercise take place *exactly* at noon.

"When the sun is at the top of the sky!" she declared—as she had every year for the thirty-five years she had been headmistress of Miss Oliver's School for Girls. "Time stands still for just a little instant right then. And people notice things. They *see!* And what they see is the graduation of young women! Females! From a school founded by a woman, designed by women, run by a woman, with a curriculum that focuses on the way *women* learn! I want this celebration to take place exactly at noon, in the bright spangle of the June sunshine, so the world can see the superiority of the result!" Marjorie demanded once again, still dominant at the very end in spite of her dismissal. She would be the headmistress till July 1, when her contract expired. Until then, her will would prevail.

Even her opponents understood that it was Marjorie's vivid leadership that had made the school into a community so beloved of its students and alumnae (who were taking their seats now in the audience as the noon hour neared) that it had to be saved from the flaws of the very woman who had made it what it was. Founded by Miss Edith Oliver in 1928 and standing on ground once occupied by a Pequot Indian village in Fieldington, Connecticut, a complacent suburb twenty miles south of Hartford on the Connecticut River, the school that Marjorie created was a boarding school, a world apart, whose intense culture of academic and artistic richness was celebrated in idiosyncratic rituals sacred to its members.

"But it will be too hot at noon," the more practical-minded members of the faculty had objected once again in an argument that for senior faculty members Francis and Peggy Plummer had become an old refrain. They were like theatergoers watching a play whose ending they had memorized.

"No, it won't," Marjorie replied.

"How do you know it won't?"

"I just do," she said, standing up to end the meeting. For meetings always ended when Marjorie stood up—and began instantly when she sat down. Francis and Peggy understood that what Marjorie meant was that she would push the weather to be perfect for their beloved young women by the sheer power of her will. The weather had always been perfect for each of the thirty-three graduation ceremonies in which Peggy and Francis had been on the faculty—and that day, June 10, 1991, was no exception.

Now the clock in the library's steeple chimed the noon hour, and Marjorie Boyd was standing. She strode across the dais to the microphone. The graduating class sat in the honored position to the left of the dais, their white dresses glistening in the sunshine. The sky was an ethereal blue, cloudless, and under it the green lawns swept to the edge of the acres of forest that lined the river. Behind the dais a huge three-hundred-year-old maple spread its branches, and Francis imagined a family of Pequot Indians sitting in its shade. The scent of clipped grass rose. In the audience the mothers wore big multicolored hats against the sun, and behind them the gleaming white clapboards of the campus buildings formed an embracing circle.

Standing at the microphone, Marjorie didn't look much older to Peggy and Francis than when she had first hired them thirty-three years ago immediately after their marriage—Peggy as the school's librarian, and Francis as a teacher of math and soon after also of English—assigning them too as dorm parents in what was then a brand-new dormitory. Marjorie still wore her long brown hair, now streaked with gray, in a schoolmarmish bun at the back of her neck. Her reading glasses still rested on her bosom, suspended from a black string around her neck. "You *were* Oliver girls," they heard Marjorie say, and Francis reached to hold Peggy's hand. They knew what she was going to say next, and when she said it—"Now you are Oliver *women*!"—giving the word a glory, Peggy started to cry. She was surprised at her sudden melting. For up to this moment she had managed to assuage her grief over Marjorie's dismissal by reminding herself that she agreed with the board's decision.

But Francis wasn't crying! He was too angry to cry, wouldn't give his new enemies the satisfaction—for that's how he thought of those colleagues, old friends, whom he suspected of optimism over the dismissal of his beloved leader. He gripped Peggy's hand, squeezed hard, made her wince. *It's her school!* he wanted to shout. *Marjorie's! Not theirs!* He didn't want Peggy to cry; he wanted her to be angry, to be obstreperous at every opportunity, to express disgust at the notion that schools bore any resemblance to businesses, as he did; he wanted her to say rebellious things in faculty meetings, the way he'd been doing, surprising everyone, including himself, by seeming out of control.

Still sobbing, Peggy yanked her hand away. She'd been over this so many times before! *You can be loyal without being stupid*, she wanted to yell. *She was your boss, not your daddy.* But of course she didn't. It wasn't the time to tell her husband that maybe his ardent following of Marjorie was his way of escaping the dominance of a father who couldn't have been more different from Marjorie—he would have fired her years before this! She kept her mouth shut. It was bad enough that people saw her sobbing.

Marjorie sat quietly after exactly four minutes during which she told her audience that now *they* must take care of the school. All of her thirty-five graduation speeches had been exactly four minutes long. She practiced them, first in her bathroom. "I love to hear the words bouncing off the tile," she told Francis and Peggy every year when she started working on her speech weeks before the event. Francis and Peggy knew that she timed herself with the same stopwatch she brought to the track meets so that she could congratulate any girl who had improved her time. In this last year of her reign she had been taking the stopwatch to faculty meetings so she could time the windy ruminations of Gregory van Buren, head of the English Department, who, second in seniority only to Peggy and Francis, sat that day immediately to Peggy's right in the front row of the graduation audience, smirking as if he had discovered a grammatical error in Marjorie's speech. Gregory didn't even try anymore to disguise his joy at what he loved to call "Marjorie's expulsion"—or the "demise of the monarchy at Miss Oliver's School for Girls."

There was a second of silence after Marjorie sat, and then,

simultaneously, Francis and the graduating class stood up. In an instant Peggy was up too, taller than her husband. The audience rose. Their applause swelled. The block of undergraduates sitting right behind the faculty chanted, "Yay, Marjorie! Yay, Marjorie!" On the dais, the trustees stood too, their board chair, Alan Travelers, looking uncomfortable.

To Peggy's right, Gregory rose too slowly. She turned to him, grabbed his elbow, pulled him upward. "Stand straight, windbag!" she whispered through her sobbing. "Stand straight and clap!"

Gregory was too smart; he didn't even turn his head to her. He was gazing up over the podium as if he were watching a bird, his hands coming together so softly they didn't make a sound, and Peggy was amazed to hear herself hissing: "Louder, you *politician*! Louder! Or I swear to God I'll poke out both your eyes right here in front of everybody!"

For an instant as the words flew out, she felt wonderful, a prisoner released. But then stupid. This wasn't her. She didn't insult people, she had never been involved in the school's politics. And she didn't have Francis's talent for effective goofiness. She thought maybe she was going to lose control permanently, wondered if everything was falling apart: Marjorie's leaving and the resultant division in the faculty, and equally pressing, Francis's leaving the next day on a trip that would last all summer, the first time in their thirty-three-year marriage they would be apart for more than a week. It was the final straw. So she made up her mind: she'd stay in control. Not just for herself. For Francis too—until he was able to control himself again.

Gregory still didn't turn his face to her. He stared straight ahead, placed his right hand on Peggy's, lifted her hand from his elbow, placed it at her side as if he were putting something back in a drawer, and whispered: "I thought you understood, unlike your husband, who only understands the past. Actually, I *know* you understand."

Gregory was right. She did understand. It had been the newer members of the board who forced the issue. The era has passed, they had pointed out, when being a great educator is enough. No longer do certain kinds of families automatically send their children away to boarding school; and besides, just as boarding school grows too expensive for many families, single-sex education for women seems to be losing its allure. So pay more attention to the business side: to marketing scenarios, strategic plans, financial projections. That's the road to survival.

Peggy had tried hard to persuade her friend to pay attention; and when rumors began to fly that the school was so strapped that it might have to make the one decision no one could even dare imagine, the one that would destroy the reason for the school's existence—namely, to admit *boys*—to survive, she had barged right in to Marjorie's office and told her that if she, Peggy Plummer, the school's librarian for the past thirty-three years, were on the board, she would vote for Marjorie's dismissal in spite of their ancient friendship unless Marjorie changed her ways and started to act as if her profession, for all it was a calling, were a business too. But nobody gave Marjorie advice. It was the other way around. So Peggy hadn't been surprised when six months later the board, whose chair, Alan Travelers, was the first male board chair in the school's history, screwed its courage to the sticking place and demanded Marjorie's resignation.

Peggy stopped crying by the time she and her friend Eudora Easter, chair of the Art Department, had to go up front and confer the diploma on the first student. The order had been determined the night before when the president of the junior class picked the graduates' names out of the tall silk hat that was brought out of safekeeping once a year, according to ritual. The hat was rumored to have belonged to Daniel Webster. At Miss Oliver's it was a sign of loyalty to believe myths that lesser schools would scorn.

Facing the audience beside Eudora, Peggy was calm again. She was tall, slim, full breasted, her short black hair not covered by a hat, and she wore a trim business suit—librarian's clothes. Eudora was much shorter than Peggy, very round, her beautiful African features shadowed under a huge red hat, and her red slippers were pointed upward at the toes like a genie's. The students cheered her costume.

The ceremony went on for several hours. For the graduates the teachers recited poems, sang songs, performed dances, even put on little skits. Francis conferred the diploma on several girls by himself, and he and Peggy together did so for three girls who lived in their dorm. For each, Francis spun the amazing tale of their blossoming, thus blessing their parents. Gregory van Buren's one girl got a long poem that nobody understood. She tried hard not to show her disappointment. When Gregory hugged her, he bent his middle away from her, sticking his butt out behind as if he were wearing a bustle.

LATER THAT DAY in the desolate silence that overcame the school, when the last girl had left for the summer, Peggy roamed her empty dormitory. For the past four years at exactly this time, their son, Sidney, would return from college and she and Francis would focus on him all summer, feasting on his presence. But Siddy, who had finished college a year ago in June, left for Europe in September to wander for an indeterminate time. *He's figuring out who he is, what he wants to do with his life*, Peggy told herself over and over, seeking comfort. *All the young ones do that these days.* The mantra brought her no more comfort than knowing that young people didn't bother getting married anymore before they lived with each other. To Peggy, whose school was a home away from home for three hundred and forty-five students, wandering was anathema.

So, she asked herself, why did her husband insist on this trip that he would start tomorrow, the first day of summer vacation? He would be away not only from her for the entire summer but also from the new head who needed the senior teacher's help in getting acclimated—and had every right to expect it. Francis had a big responsibility to fulfill right here this summer, one that he could fulfill better than anyone. So why did he choose to wander? *He* was not just out of college; he was fifty-five, for goodness sake!

She knew Francis's response would be that he wouldn't be wandering. He'd be chaperoning a group of students from schools all over the East on an archaeological dig in California—what was wrong with that? Wasn't Miss Oliver's School famous for its anthropology courses; wasn't that what made them different from all those other schools? "If our girls can learn to look objectively at other cultures," he had reminded her, "then they can look at their own with open eyes, instead of the way they have been indoctrinated to see—by men. That's how we change the world! We're going to live in a reconstructed Ohlone Indian village on the shoulder of

Mount Alma while we do the dig to find the real village they lived in," he had told her—as if she hadn't known!

If he would just admit to himself the real reason, that he wanted to be like an Indian, she could object—and remind him that Indians made their vision quests when they were fourteen years old! For that's what Francis and his students were trying to do: be like Indians. Otherwise, why not just live in tents?

But chaperoning an exercise in anthropology? How could Peggy argue against that? She was the one who, thirty years ago, had started the tradition of cultural relativism that made Miss Oliver's unique. It was she who had discovered the jumble of Pequot Indian artifacts in a closet of the little house that then served as the school's library, and it was she who had persuaded Marjorie to raise the funds for a new library in which the Pequot artifacts, and several small bones of a young Pequot woman unearthed when the library's foundation was dug, were now respectfully displayed. It was lost on no one that the library—which many of the faculty thought of as Peggy's Library—was situated exactly at the center of the campus.

Peggy walked slowly down the hall of her dormitory, entering each girl's room as if it were ten-thirty in the middle of the school year and she were saying goodnight. Even though she knew the girls wouldn't be in their rooms to turn their faces to her as she stood in the door, she was surprised to discover how lonely she felt in the sudden barrenness where the sound of her footsteps echoed off the walls.

She moved from room to room. It didn't surprise her that Rebecca Burley had left the poster of Jimi Hendrix on the wall; she and Francis had told each other more than once that this kid needed to try on lots of different coats before it was too late, but further down the hall, when she discovered a well-used bong sitting squarely in the middle of the desk of Tracy Danforth—who had just graduated and was president of the Honor Council—she wanted to get Francis, bring him here to show him how Tracy had been trying to show them who she really was. But she didn't get Francis. Because he was too busy. Packing for his trip.

She thought: *He can't possibly pack for a whole summer without my help, he's helpless about such things, doesn't know where anything is, he'll go off with no underwear and ten pairs of pants.* She turned away from the empty dorm.

SHE FOUND FRANCIS in their bedroom. He was on the other side of the bed from where she stopped in the doorway the instant she saw him putting a big duffel bag on the bed. He was holding his hiking boots in his hands, about to stuff them in.

"Oh!" she said. "I've never seen those before."

"They're new."

"When'd you buy them?" They were ugly, she hated them.

He shrugged. "The other day."

"Oh!" she said again. She took one step back, almost out the door. Why did seeing him pack disturb her so? She wondered if she were going to cry for the second time that day.

He noticed the movement and stopped packing, his attention full on her. "I got them at Le Target." He pronounced it "targay," looking for her smile.

It didn't work. But his little joke did stop her retreat. "Maybe you should pack later, Francis," she said, taking several steps back into the room. "The reception for the new headmaster starts in half an hour." She knew it was dumb to think he'd change his plans and stay home where he belonged if he deferred packing until after the reception. Nevertheless, the thought flashed.

"I'm not going to the new head's reception," he said.

"Say that again." She was standing perfectly still now.

"I'm not going," he said again. But already he was beginning to relent. He knew how foolish it was to stay away, how churlish it would seem. But in Marjorie's house! *It's her home*, he wanted to say, *no one else's*. But of course it wasn't her house; it was the school's.

"Yes, you are, Francis," Peggy said. "You're going. You're not childish enough to stay away," and immediately she regretted using that word.

He dropped his gaze to the bed. Now he was tossing in his shaving things and his toothbrush and toothpaste. Loose. All jumbled up with everything else.

"Oh, for goodness sake!" she said. "You can't pack like this!" She reached in, pulled out a wad of shirts, tossed them over her shoulder. "Or this!" she said, tossing a crumpled pair of chinos in another direction. "Or this!" Three big paperback books went flying, their pages fluttering. She put her hand back in the bag again. She was going to empty the whole damn thing. She knew perfectly well she wasn't helping him pack, she was *un*packing him, and she was crying now, his clothes flying all over the room.

"Peg! I said I'll go!" He was gripping both her wrists now, one in each hand.

She let him hold her, keeping her hands still, and forced herself to stop crying. "You know," she said, "sometimes I think we're as married to the school as we are to each other." It was the first time she'd dared to put the thought into words.

"No," he said. "No way, Peg."

"So when you risk your place here, I wonder what other seams will start to tear."

"Peggy, I said I will go."

She felt a huge relief growing, as if maybe she didn't have so much to worry about after all. "You know, he's been very considerate," she said, speaking of the new head. She was looking at Francis again because now, with victory, she couldn't resist explaining her point. "He refused the invitation to speak at graduation."

"I know all about it," Francis said

She saw Francis trying not to look irritated and persisted anyway. She wanted so much to convince! "He said it was inappropriate. He said it was Marjorie's moment, not the new head's. That's pretty nice, you know."

"I don't want to talk about him," Francis said. "I'm not going to his reception for him. I'm going for you." She realized that the other part of her relief was that of the mourner who doesn't want the wake to end because then she'd be alone.

FIVE MINUTES BEFORE they left for the reception, Francis stood in front of the mirror above his bureau, putting on his tie. Peggy came up beside him, kissed him on the cheek. Leaning against him, she felt his body soften. "Indians don't wear ties," she said, trying for a joke. Right away she wished she could take the joke back when she felt his shoulders stiffen. He turned his head just slightly away so that her kiss didn't linger, and she stepped back, feeling her anger flame. *Why right now?* she suddenly wanted to ask again. To hell with jokes. On top of everything else! *Don't you know we're too old to believe in different things?* Francis moved away, leaving her framed in the mirror, and for an instant she didn't recognize the tense woman who stared back at her.

Francis still thought he was going on an archaeological dig, the face in the mirror told her. He's not ready to admit he's going on a vision quest. It's much too far out for Francis, too over the top, too *embarrassing*, to imagine himself, a middle-class white man in a tweed sports coat, a boarding school teacher, for goodness sake! chasing Indian visions. In California too, where everybody's weird! But that's what was happening. And she had thought for years that her vision and his were the same. She'd known almost from the day they met that Francis was a spiritual man. That was the deepest of the reasons she loved him so much. So it wasn't hard to believe that the reason he had asked her to join in his family's staunch Episcopal faith when they were married was that he believed in it. He thought so too, she understood, for the force of that belief was so strong in the family that he couldn't believe he was different enough not to share it. But what she knew now, better than he did, was that the real reason he had asked her this favor was that he couldn't imagine explaining to his father that he cared so little for his religion that he wouldn't ask his wife to join it. Even though she had none of her own to relinquish if she did.

I've been hoodwinked, she wanted to say, *hoodwinked and deserted*, thinking of how much she'd been rescued from the barrenness of her own disbelief by the religion she'd joined and now was nurtured by, how much she'd come to love her father-in-law for the belief she shared with him, how much she'd missed him since his death five years ago. *When you don't resolve things with your father, you live with his shadow until you die too*, she wanted to lecture Francis. *It makes you crazy*. She didn't say that either.

AT THE FRONT door of Marjorie's house, Francis hesitated. "This is Marjorie's house," he said. He'd walked through this door hundreds of times.

"It's the headmistress's house," she reminded him. Then corrected herself: "The headmaster's."

He turned to her then, gave her a look as if she has just slapped his face.

"Sorry."

"I can't," he said. "No way. Not in her house."

She took his hand, tugged it. "Come on, Fran, let's go."

He resisted.

"Grow up!" she said, tugging at his hand. "It's time."

When he still resisted, she dropped his hand, turned from him, went through the door. He hesitated, then, surrendering, followed her. He always stayed close to her at parties, using her vivacity as a cover for his shyness, but this time they moved to separate rooms in Marjorie's big house, which was loud with people talking.

Francis moved through the people in the foyer into the living room. It seemed bigger somehow, empty of something he couldn't put his finger on. He stopped walking. A surprising fear of the new largeness of Marjorie's living room rose in him. While anxiety took hold of him, Marcia Holmes, his young friend in the History Department, moved across the rug to him.

Smiling, she told him how much she liked hearing what he'd said about the girls he graduated. "You tell such wonderful stories," she told him, and went on to say how much she wished more girls liked her enough to invite her to graduate them, and suddenly, while part of him told her not to worry because next year would be easier, the second year always was, and another part of him watched her face, still another part watched the scene that suddenly appeared inside his head for the second or third time that week while he began to sweat and went on talking to this lovely young woman in her sexy summer dress as if everything were normal: the stern of a ship was moving away, he saw the froth by the propeller, going away from him, no one had seen him fall overboard, no one heard his shouts. Marjorie's big sofa was missing, he realized, coming back fully to his young friend, and the top three shelves of her bookcase were empty, and that was what he pointed out to her, as if it were a discovery of some amazing new scientific fact, interrupting her as she told him of her summer plans, and there was a funny look on her face—part worry and part a question, as if she were hoping that he was telling her a joke she didn't understand. "She's started to move out already," he said in a very matter-of-fact way.

"Yes," Marcia said. She was waiting for a punch line, but he couldn't think of anything else to say. She patted his arm—he couldn't tell if it was sympathy or just her way of excusing herself—and moved away.

FRED KINDLER, THE new headmaster, was standing by the fireplace in the center of Marjorie's living room. Marjorie stood next to him, a good six inches taller. They were talking calmly together—as if nothing had happened, as if everything was the same, and Francis remembered Marjorie telling him of her resolve to hide her bitterness. "These people, who wouldn't even have a school to be on the board of if it weren't for me, want me to pretend I yearn for retirement," she had told him. "Well, I'd rather yearn for death. But all this is for your ears only," she went on after a pause. "The last bitter statement I'm going to make. I'll take their advice. I'll say I want the time to take up—what, golf? My grandsons? You know, the truth of the matter is I'm not remotely interested in my grandsons," she murmured, speaking half to herself and half to Francis as if she'd just discovered this about herself. "This school is what interests me."

Francis was surprised again at the new head's red hair, the big red mustache, and the short, stocky, powerful body. For an instant, Francis, in his mind's eye, observed his own short, almost pudgy body, as if in a mirror, his round mild, unobtrusive face. He couldn't resist staring across the room at Kindler. *He's so* male! Francis thought, and then registered what he had seen instantly when he first saw Kindler standing next to Marjorie: that he was wearing the same brown polyester suit that he'd worn during his interviews. *Polyester!* Francis thought, shocked at himself that he even noticed. He'd always been proud that in the world of preppydom of which it was a part, Miss Oliver's School for Girls was studiously unpreppy, so why did he care what the man wore?

Kindler and Marjorie both noticed him. Francis saw Marjorie put her hand lightly on Kindler's wrist and Kindler move across the room toward him. He had an awkward gait; his feet pointed outward like Charley Chaplin's. For an instant, Francis felt sorry for him, imagined girls imitating that walk, every girl on campus walking like that everywhere they went, day after day, until the poor man had to leave.

Kindler's right hand was out. His left hand patted Francis on the shoulder. All Francis could see was the red of Kindler's hair and mustache. "Come see me tomorrow," Kindler said. "I'm here all day. Mrs. Boyd's lending me her office. I need all the advice I can get, and I want to start with the senior teacher. Want to collect the best ideas and get a running start when I come back."

Francis was appalled at the boyishness. He felt suddenly like a tutor. That's not what he wanted—parenting his own boss. "I'm leaving for the summer dig project tomorrow. Six a.m.," he said.

A waiter from the caterers came by with a tray of drinks. Francis plucked a glass of white wine. Without taking his eyes off Francis, frowning slightly, Kindler murmured to the waiter, "No, thank you," and then to Francis: "Oh? That so? You're going on that dig? Somebody told me that one of the teachers was going. I didn't realize it was you."

"I signed up way back in February," Francis said. He almost added *before you were appointed*, but he didn't feel like explaining himself.

"Well," said Kindler, "I could have used you around here this summer. But that's the way it has to be." His face brightened. "California, right?" Francis had the impression that the man had changed his expression on purpose to make him more comfortable.

Francis sensed Peggy watching him from across the room. "Right, California." He took a sip of his drink, noticed that several people were watching him and Kindler. *We're on stage*, he thought. *It's a big scene*, and now he was seeing himself as some kind of fulcrum. Took another sip, his hand was shaking, spilled some wine on his shirt, felt its cold.

Kindler handed him a napkin. "Mount Alma, right?"

"Yes," said Francis. "Mount Alma." He saw himself driving out across the flat Midwest, lonely without Peggy in the car. Then he saw the mountains, felt a little surge of joy, but his hand was still shaking, and he spilled some more.

"You all right?" Kindler asked.

For an instant, thinking the question was sardonic, the new head's first spear thrust, and Francis was relieved. Then looking at the man's too youthful face, he realized the question was sincere, uncomplicated, devoid of subtlety, and he was panic-stricken. "I'm all right," he managed. By now he was sure everybody was watching them.

"Look," Kindler said. "I understand." He was talking now very quietly so no one else could hear. "Why wouldn't you feel that way? You've served her for years. I've admired her too—just from a greater distance. Just the same, I'm sure we can work together."

"Well, as long as you don't change anything," Francis blurted. Then he realized what he'd said, how dumb it was. He managed a grin, a little chuckle, as if he'd been joking, as if he hadn't meant exactly what had come out of his mouth.

His camouflage seemed to work. Fred Kindler smiled. Francis saw the red mustache move. "Good," said Kindler. "I look forward to working with you." Then he moved away to mix with the others.

There! Francis thought, *I've managed to get through it. Now I can go home!* He looked for Peggy, saw her across the room, stared at her back until she turned. He signaled her with his eyes that he wanted to leave. But she turned her back to him to show she was engaged in the conversation. He felt empty, moved across the room to leave the house.

He figured if he could just get out the door . . .

But on the way, he overheard Milton Perkins telling one of his Polish jokes to a circle of uncomfortable-looking faculty members. Perkins, the recently retired president of one of the biggest insurance companies in the state, had been on the board a long time. Francis found himself slowing down on his way to the door, listening to the joke. He'd heard it before. Perkins was seldom able to resist baiting the faculty's liberalism and being politically incorrect in a loud voice whenever he got an audience of teachers. Francis had always forgiven the man, understanding that underneath, Perkins had a deep respect for the school and the people who taught in it—which he had shown by years of generosity. To Francis, who, if pressed, would admit he liked to make derogatory generalizations about businessmen, Perkins was merely a gambler in a fancy suit who was just smart enough to sense the inferiority of his vocation to that of teaching. So why should Francis be bothered by the old man's backwardness?

But now, listening to the story, knowing exactly how it would build to the punch line in rhythmic stupidities, Francis stopped walking toward the door, turned, stepped back toward Perkins and his group of embarrassed listeners. Francis knew what he was doing, knew he shouldn't, discovered that he'd been holding back these feelings for years in order to make things work for Marjorie, realized also that Perkins probably had been instrumental in Marjorie's dismissal. He took another step toward Perkins and his group of listeners and saw Rachel Bickham, the chair of the Science Department and director of Athletics, whom he admired, looking at him hard. She shook her head, an unobtrusive gesture meant just for him. *Don't*, she seemed to warn. *Just don't*. But he loved the release he was about to get. The room was very bright to him now, all its colors vivid.

"Why don't you shut up?" he heard himself saying to Perkins. "Why don't you just clam it?"

That's exactly what Perkins did—for an instant. He turned to face Francis. He clearly didn't know what to do. He was certainly not going to apologize! So he just turned his back on Francis and went on telling his story. That's what enraged Francis so—the dismissal! After all those years! He tapped Perkins on the shoulder, and when the man turned around, his face flaming, Francis told the same story back to him, substituting *Republican* for *Polack*. The group of teachers to whom Perkins had been telling his story glided away, so it was just Perkins now, and Francis, in the center of the room. Francis was pronouncing the name *Perkins* with the same clowning sarcasm with which Perkins had emphasized the final syllable *ski* of the Polish person in the joke.

They were center stage. Francis glimpsed Marjorie, who was still standing by her fireplace, staring across the room at him. Her expression was begging him to stop. Father Michael Woodward, the local Episcopal priest and part-time chaplain, one of Francis's and Peggy's best friends, was standing by the opposite wall making slicing motions at his throat.

Francis didn't see Peggy. He went on and on, building a vastly more complex story than Perkins's joke, a fantasy of ineptitude in which the absurdly Anglo-Saxon main character reached mythical idiocy. When a few of the people in the room couldn't resist laughing, he was even more inspired, felt the lovely release, and went on some more—until he realized that Eudora Easter was standing at his right side and Father Woodward at his left. Their hands were on his elbows. He shut up.

"Jeeeezus!" said Perkins into the sudden silence. "What in hell was *that* all about?"

Nobody answered because Eudora and Father Woodward were escorting Francis from the scene of the crime.

Two

The instant Fred Kindler saw the look on his secretary's face when she came into his office early on the morning of his first day as headmaster and caught him down on his knees giving thanks, he knew he'd made a big mistake. If she had found him working in his office in the nude she couldn't have looked more affronted.

Margaret Rice, a tall, large-boned, black-haired woman in her fifties, who to Fred's surprise was dressed in her summer vacation clothes—jeans and a man's shirt, rather than the more professional clothes he had expected and would have preferred—stood in the doorway looking down on her new boss; and still on his knees in his coat and tie, he suddenly saw himself in her eyes: the bumpkin, country clod, ex-farm boy ascended. He was out of style, and, to boot, a man in a woman's place. "Oh, my God!" Mrs. Rice whispered, then quickly correcting herself: "Excuse me; I should have knocked." But the look was still on her face: *Feminists don't get down on their knees,* it said. *We've been there too much already.*

Thank goodness he didn't ask her to join him, his first reaction. Instead, already rising from where he'd been kneeling beside his desk, he heard the apology in his voice, hating the sound of it. "I didn't know you came in so early." She was looking past him, her eyes scanning the walls as if she were looking for something—which he knew she was: Marjorie's paintings, each painted by an Oliver girl. All gone. Marjorie had taken them with her, and the walls were now bare and white. The office had a bright, clean, monastic look. He loved it, it energized him, and seeing in his secretary's eyes her resistance to this new sparseness, he felt his own stubbornness rising and was glad for it. No more apologies. *Just be yourself,* his wife had reminded him, and so, in his awkward way, had his own proud dad who never even finished high school. "I'm a lucky man," he found himself telling Mrs. Rice, his eyes focused on hers. But her eyes slid away, and he decided not to tell her how during his early morning run he'd been overcome with gratitude for his good fortune at being chosen as the headmaster of Miss Oliver's School for Girls.

"Marjorie always came in at eight o'clock," Mrs. Rice said. "I always came in at seven. It gave me time alone to get ready." Then she was out the door.

Alone now in the bright summer light pouring through the glass doors that looked out on the campus, he realized he was still standing in the exact spot beside his desk where he rose to after being caught on his knees by Mrs. Rice. His face was still burning. *So it's not cool to pray!* he thought, suddenly angry. "Well, you've never lost a child," he whispered to the door. "How do you know what to be grateful for?" He moved to his desk and sat down, already feeling just a little childish, unheadmasterly, to have allowed the words. He recalled his wife's reminder not to let their old wound tempt him to take elevated positions—as if losing a child makes one wiser than all the people who hadn't.

The day had already lost some of the luster it had when he'd walked into this office fifteen minutes ago at a quarter to seven, two weeks before he was required. His contract called for him to start on the first of July, but when Marjorie moved out of the head's house and cleaned out her office with surprising speed—"Who wants to die slowly?" she had asked—he was able to start earlier. He was too eager, too full of ideas, to sit around waiting. Now a piece of him wondered if he should have followed his wife's advice—or was it a request?—and taken two weeks' vacation. He shook his head, like a dog coming out of water. He would get on with his day.

His desk was bare, save for a framed photograph of his wife and the file of papers he had requested from Carl Vincent, the school's elderly business manager. He opened the file, turning directly to the projected budget for the fiscal year, soon to begin on July 1, 1991. Attached to the first page was a note from Vincent, dated just two days ago, telling him these were the latest projections "which the board has not seen because I'm presenting them to you first, according to protocol."

Fred felt a tickle of suspicion. Something was a little fishy about this note. But he put this aside and turned to the numbers. For several minutes the figures were a blur because his mind insisted on lingering over his awkward tête-à-tête with Mrs. Rice. Besides, he knew the gist of these numbers already; he'd been over them many times during his interviews and since his appointment.

He already knew there was a projected deficit of $245,000. So he didn't look at the bottom line. Instead he went right to the revenue figures. That's where the problem lay: the school had been under-enrolled for five years. And now there was a baby bust, a precipitous drop in the nation's teenage population. And even if that were not the case, the appeal of single-sex education for girls had been declining for reasons that only consultants pretended to understand. Large deficits had increased in each of those five years, culminating in this latest, biggest one. So now the accumulated operating deficit, on top of the capital deficit caused by the failure to raise enough money to fund the new theater, the last of Marjorie's pet projects, amounted to a total indebtedness of over two million dollars.

The way Carl Vincent had presented the numbers was hard to interpret. In fact, they were a mess. So it was a little while before Fred realized that these numbers were not the same as those he had studied so carefully just before he accepted the position, confident that the notion of single-sex education was so compelling to young women that all the school needed to fill again was a good marketing program. This budget he studied now, he realized, was keyed to nineteen *fewer* students than were predicted by the earlier version. Nineteen times the tuition of $18,600. That's $353,400! He averted his eyes from the bottom line. Then he noticed that the line item for salaries was bigger than it was in the last version, by $77,000. Even though there were fewer students to teach! Either this number was wrong, or the previous number was wrong. So he pulled out the compensation charts for the upcoming year and confirmed what his intuition was already loudly declaring: the latest was the correct number.

He couldn't keep his eye off the bottom line anymore, which he had already figured would show a deficit of $675,400 instead of only $245,000. He was right. If this rate of drain continued, the bank would surely call the loans, and there simply wouldn't be enough cash to run the school. He'd thought he had four years to turn things around. Now, on his very first day in office, he discovered he would be lucky to have two.

When Fred had accepted the board's offer, he did so on the basis of a very straightforward strategy that the board accepted: he would create an aggressive marketing campaign by which to rebuild the girls-only enrollment. He'd provided a schedule showing the targets for the addition of students each year. The board understood that failure to reach these targets even as soon as the first year was the signal to consider becoming coed, a strategy that some other single-sex schools and colleges were adopting. But it was best not to talk about this possibility, certainly not to write it into the formal plan. This specter looming in the background would enrage the alumnae, many of whom would rather the school close down than admit boys. In his own mind, though, Fred wouldn't even think about the possibility of closing the school. He'd admit boys before he did that. He knew something about the grief that follows a school's dying. That wasn't going to happen to Miss Oliver's. Not ever!

Fred spent the next half hour reviewing budgets for the previous five years, noting once again the consistent gap between the optimistic predictions and the disappointing results, and a few more minutes thinking very carefully about how he was going to handle his conversation with Carl Vincent. Then he remembered that Vincent had left for vacation. That was the reason for his timing in presenting the corrected budget: he didn't want to be around when everyone got the bad news and learned how inaccurate his projections had been. Fred felt sad for the old man.

All right, so the next thing to do was to talk with Nan White, the Admissions director, to see what the chances were of making up some of the lost enrollment over the summer. So, at exactly nine o'clock he was about to get up from his desk and walk down the hall to Nan's office when Margaret Rice opened his office door (without knocking, he observed), stepped a very small distance into his office, and announced that his eight-thirty appointment had arrived.

"Eight-thirty? It's already nine!"

"Hey, it's summertime," she said.

"From now on, Mrs. Rice—"

"*Ms.* Rice."

"Ms. Rice. Right. Sorry. From now on, I need you to keep me informed about the appointments you've made for me. I'd like to know a day ahead of time if it's possible."

"All right," shc said. "Fine. From now on."

"Who?" he asked.

"Who what?"

"Who is my appointment with? Whom, I mean."

"Three teachers."

"Mrs. Rice, please, who *are* the teachers? *Ms.* Rice, I mean."

"I bet they'll let you know when they get in here," she said, flushing.

He felt his face get hot too. She looked surprised, maybe even a little chagrined. "We're going to have to talk," he said, very quietly, very slowly. His sudden anger, always surprising to him, was a relief.

"There's just a way we do things around here, that's all." Ms. Rice's voice was almost conciliatory now, embarrassed. "Marjorie Boyd—"

"All right, Ms. Rice," he interrupted. "Later we'll talk. Right now, who are they?"

"Melissa and Samuel Andersen; she teaches French, he teaches history."

"I know what they teach," he said.

"They just got married last Christmas."

"Yes."

"Marjorie married them."

"Marjorie! Mrs. Boyd? *Married* them?"

"She performed the ceremony. It made some of the new trustees mad."

"Well, that's interesting. Who's the third teacher I'm about to see?"

But Ms. Rice went right on, her tone of voice almost friendly now: "Marjorie got one of those Universalist Church preacher's licenses that were created for COs in the Vietnam War. Since the alumnae learned about it, Marjorie's been asked to perform quite a few marriages."

"The third person?" he interrupted.

"Oh. The third person. That's Fredericka Walters. She teaches German."

"I know," he replied, feeling a further surge of worry. He'd made it a point, during his earlier study of the school, to know how many students each teacher instructed. Fredericka Walters was one of the highest-paid teachers on the faculty—with the fewest students. He was going to have to do something about that.

"Oh, that's right, you know what people teach," Ms. Rice said, and he immediately regretted cutting her off. It dawned on him that before doing anything else he should have had a long, relaxed talk with her.

"Some people call her Sam," Ms. Rice went on. "She likes men's names; and others call her Fred, of course." Then after a pause: "But don't worry. It won't be confusing. It will be a while before anybody's going to call *you* by your first name." Her face flooded with red again.

He forced himself to let that go, trying to believe she didn't even know that she was insulting him; she was just describing his situation. "Show them in please, Ms. Rice," he said as gently as he could.

Margaret Rice went out the door. In an instant, she returned. "They're not there."

"They're not there!"

"Right. They must have gone over to the faculty room to get some coffee. While you and I were talking."

"We only talked for a minute! The faculty room's clear on the other side of the campus."

Ms. Rice shrugged her shoulders again. "They'll be back."

"When's my next appointment?"

"Nine-fifteen. Mavis Ericksen and Charlotte Reynolds. Two of the new board members," she added, rolling her eyes.

I know; I met them during the hiring process, remember? Fred almost said. *So did my wife.* But he remembered what happened last time he told her he knew something.

"It's already five after nine," he said instead. "That only leaves ten minutes. So when the teachers get back from the faculty room, tell them I can't see them now. They can come back later."

Margaret Rice stood stock-still, staring at Fred for what seemed a very long moment. "You're joking!"

"No, I'm not joking. Tell them."

"You can't just cancel an appointment like that. They're teachers!"

"Yes, I can."

"They're going to be mad!"

Now it was his turn to shrug. As Ms. Rice started to leave, he said, "Let's leave the door open. I don't want anybody to think I'm hiding in here."

"WE HEARD THAT about making the teachers wait," Mavis Ericksen said. An alumna, she was a tall brunette, very pretty, in a red dress, stockings, high heels. She turned to Charlotte Reynolds for affirmation. Charlotte, also an alumna, and mother of an eighth, ninth, and tenth grader, was a stocky, thick-legged athlete in a short tennis dress. She nodded back at her friend. "Good for you, Fred," Mavis said. Both women sat down in the chairs he offered. He came from behind his desk and sat in a third chair facing them.

"Yes, good for you," said Charlotte, whom Fred found more comfortable to look at; that way he could keep his eyes off Mavis's heartbreaking legs.

"We're very glad you're here," said Mavis. "As a matter of fact, we are delighted! Welcome."

"*Delighted* is the perfect word," Charlotte pronounced. "How's everything going?"

"Fine," Fred fibbed, thinking of Carl Vincent's numbers filed right behind him in his desk.

"Really?" Mavis's eyes probed.

"Just diving in," Fred said, feeling suddenly guarded. He tried to make his voice sound enthusiastic. "There are a lot of things I need to learn about."

"One of the things you have probably already learned," Mavis said, "is that Charlotte and I are among the more recent appointments to the board. The result, I would say, of some. . . ." She hesitated, turning to her friend.

"Persistence," Charlotte supplied.

"Yes. Persistence," Mavis agreed.

"The school was getting pretty close to shutting down, you know," Charlotte said.

"I know. We will all work together to make what Marjorie built here permanent." He imagined himself apologizing to Marjorie for such a lame statement.

Mavis's eyes focused intently on his. "You're right. Respect for Mrs. Boyd. That's how we need to approach everything. But I refuse to let anyone make me feel guilty."

"I'm sure that's not what you meant," Charlotte murmured to Fred. Then more loudly: "How's Gail adjusting?"

"Quite well. Everybody has been very kind," he said, pushing out of his mind the fact that Peggy Plummer and Eudora Easter and Rachel Bickham, head of the Science Department, were the only teachers who have dropped in to say hello to his wife. "She's finishing hanging our pictures as we speak."

"Well," Mavis said, "we're sure you're busy, so we should get right to the point and tell you why we're here."

"Definitely," Charlotte murmured. "Time to get down to business."

"We're here to stand firmly behind you when you get rid of Joan Saffire," Mavis announced, looking straight into Fred's eyes. Joan Saffire was the assistant director of Development.

"Absolutely," Charlotte nodded vigorously. "We're right behind you."

"Uh . . . I'm afraid I don't understand," Fred said.

"There will be a rebellion, of course," Charlotte said, looking hard at Fred. "A huge fuss. Lots of the alumnae, virtually all of the faculty, and many of the board—all the trustees who voted for Mrs. Boyd to stay, as a matter of fact. That's almost fifty percent."

"Charlotte!" Mavis exclaimed.

"Oh, come on!" Charlotte said, not taking her eyes off Fred's. "He knows."

Fred felt little drops of sweat running down from his armpits inside his shirt. *No, I don't*, he wanted to say—for that was the truth.

"Don't you?" Charlotte asked him.

He still didn't answer. Because now, of course, he did know.

"If I remember correctly, we were talking about getting rid of

Joan Saffire," Mavis said.

Charlotte shrugged. "So we were."

"Well?" said Mavis to Fred.

"I don't want to appear not to be listening," he said trying to keep the tentativeness out of his voice. "Or reluctant to accept advice, but I, uh, I think I need to remind you that it is the head who makes these decisions."

"She's Marjorie's niece," said Charlotte. "You didn't know that?"

"Yes, I knew that."

"Charlotte, please." Mavis looked sternly at her friend. "That's not the reason. She's incompetent, that's why." Then turning to Fred: "The main thing is that she's always saying the wrong thing. She insults people."

"People like Joan Saffire need to keep their politics to themselves!" Charlotte blurted.

"Why don't you tell Fred about when your husband asked Aldous Enright if he would accelerate his pledge," Mavis said softly to Charlotte.

"Ladies," Fred asserted. "This isn't an appropriate way to evaluate—"

"You need to listen to this!" Mavis said.

Fred put both hands up, a double stop sign, but Charlotte was already talking. "When Gerald called for the appointment, Mr. Enright just exploded!"

"It seems that Marjorie's niece had already talked with him," Mavis interrupted. "She called on him to ask him to make a bigger pledge and to restrict it to financial aid."

"Financial aid!" Charlotte exclaimed. "From Aldous Enright? Everybody knows he doesn't believe in financial aid!"

"And when she talked with him, she talked about poor people in a way that made it look as if anybody with money is a fascist," Mavis said. "This woman, who everybody knows wouldn't even be here if she weren't Marjorie's niece, is lecturing Aldous Enright about financial aid!"

"So, not only did Mr. Enright not accelerate his gift, he canceled it," Charlotte announced.

There was a moment of silence while Fred thought of what to say.

He hadn't been in office for a morning yet, and already this! "Maybe Mr. Enright would have canceled it anyway," he tried.

"He would not!" Charlotte said. "I already said: people like her need to keep their political opinions to themselves."

"It's only one incident, though," said Fred. Then he cut himself off. That tack wouldn't work either.

"Of course one incident isn't enough!" Mavis was insulted. "We're only telling you one incident as an example. I don't believe in firing someone for one mistake any more than you do."

"I appreciate your concern," he said, desperate for an end to the conversation. "Very much. I will bring it up right away with Dorothy Strang."

"Dorothy is an excellent director of Development," Mavis said. "But what difference does it make what Dorothy Strang thinks of Joan Saffire? The board has no faith in Joan Saffire. That's what counts here. That is, the part of the board who raises money doesn't. The rest just loves everybody. So why are you trying to sell us on her?"

"I'm not selling, Mrs. Ericksen, I am insisting on ethical process." Fred hated the sanctimonious sound of his voice.

"This is no time for delicacy," Mavis warned.

"It certainly isn't," Charlotte said.

"And I resent being painted as the villain," Mavis said.

"Look, why don't we call on Aldous Enright again—give it another try," Fred said, "and in the meantime I guarantee you that I will make sure Mrs. Saffire's performance is evaluated. I could do more harm than good by appearing to fire people arbitrarily before anybody trusts me."

"If you want to earn my trust, Mr. Kindler, just do what you have to do, and do it right away."

"When is it going to happen?" Charlotte asked.

"I can't tell you that," Fred said.

"I tell you, you don't have the time to be so delicate!" Mavis's voice was quavering now. "Because if you don't get this place in order, they're going to let boys in here, and if that happens I don't care if the place does shut down!"

"I'm not even going to think about that," Charlotte murmured.

Mavis turned on Charlotte. "Maybe you're not," she said. "But

I am. Because all of a sudden, it feels like Marjorie Boyd all over again around here." Mavis's shoulders started to shake. "Oh, damn, just what I need, a crying jag!" She stood up, turned quickly around, and moved very fast out the door, slamming it behind her.

"She loves this school," Charlotte said, standing up too. "And she's awfully frustrated, you know. It's been a long struggle."

"I know it has," he said.

"Good," Charlotte said. She turned away from him and moved toward the door. With her hand on the knob, she turned back to him "It wouldn't be smart if you didn't," she said. Then she opened the door and left him.

IMMEDIATELY AFTER CHARLOTTE left, Margaret Rice took exactly one step into his office. "Karen Benjamin's here for her ten-o'clock appointment," she said. "She's the editor of the school newspaper."

"Good. Show her in." Fred's spirits rose. It was going to be fun to talk with a student after all these adults. He was glad that summer school would begin that week. When there were no students present, schools were dreary places.

"Uh-oh," Margaret said. "The three teachers are back. As a matter of fact, they got back right after those two ladies showed up. They've been waiting."

He said nothing.

"Well, don't you want to see them now?"

"How can I? It's ten o'clock. Karen's right on time. All the way from Boston."

Ms. Rice just stood there.

"Show her in, Ms. Rice."

"All right, if that's what you want." Ms. Rice stepped back out of the office. "Go on in, dear," he heard her say.

Karen Benjamin didn't walk into the room; she darted. Moving with quick, birdlike motions, she closed the door to the office and turned to shake Fred's hand. "I *hate* it when grown-ups call me 'dear.'" She was short, very slight, dressed in a white T-shirt with the front page of the *Clarion* printed on it, her thin legs in cutoff jeans. Her black hair was cropped, almost shaved, so that her head appeared as round as a ball on her thin neck. Her brown eyes seemed to flit all over the office, noticing everything as she sat down in the chair. Fred sat facing her.

"My mother calls me 'dear.' That's what mothers are for," she said, peering into her backpack. "Where are you, notebook? You're in here someplace." Then looking up at Fred, her intense eyes catching his: "But when other grown-ups do—"

Fred nodded, grinning, enjoying this.

She stirred around in her backpack some more. "Here it is!" she said, pulling out a notebook. "You're going to be featured on the front page of the *Clarion* in September. The first new headmaster in thirty-five years. Ta-da ta-da!"

"Something tells me there are some people who aren't happy about that," he blurted, surprised at himself.

"Something tells me you're right," she agreed brightly.

"Well," he said, grinning again, "nothing's perfect."

"Anyway, I've got some warm-up questions. You ready for that?" When he didn't answer immediately she said, "Tell me about your family. You've got children?" She poised her pencil over the notebook.

He hesitated, moving his eyes away from her face to the wall behind and above her head.

"Oh! I'm sorry. Did I ask—"

"It's all right. We have one child. Had one, rather. Sarah. She was killed in a car accident two years ago."

"I'm so sorry!" Her voice was soft now. "I should have known."

"No, you shouldn't. We asked that it not be part of the information about us. We didn't want people's first reaction to us to be feeling sorry for us. Of course there are people here who know. News travels. But there are still lots who don't, at least not yet."

Karen put her pencil down.

Naturally, Fred didn't mention that he and Gail had been trying to have another child. That was much too private—though it would have been a whole lot easier to tell this kid than anyone else who'd been in his office this morning, and he liked her so much already. "Sarah would have been a ninth grader," he said instead.

"Here?"

"Yes. Definitely. Right here!"

"Maybe that's the answer to that other question," she said quietly. "Why a male head for a girls' school? That you chose a school where your daughter would have thrived." And, after a pause in which that comment registered on him, she added, "I understand. It sort of makes up for her loss, doesn't it? Being with so many other girls the same age she would be."

He still didn't answer.

"So now I know what to say in the article."

"Please don't."

"Still too early?"

"Still too early."

"But it would help."

"Not the way I want help."

"Maybe you should take it any way you can get it."

"I'm not in that tough a spot."

She looked intently at his face and didn't answer.

"Evidently you don't agree."

"You're right. I don't. The students loved Mrs. Boyd. The only way they're going to know how to be loyal to her is not to like you. So she screwed up the money part. Who wants an accountant for a headmistress?"

"Yeah," Fred said. "Who does?"

Karen's face brightened now. "Time to change the subject," she announced. "Something light. Like why you wear such funny clothes."

Fred laughed. "You're kidding."

"Actually, now that I think about it, I'm serious. It's an important question."

"Not something light after all?"

Karen made a quick dismissive gesture with her hand. "Whatever."

"What's wrong with my clothes?"

"Your pants are shiny. And those shoes! They're weird."

"I'm just a farm boy, you know," he said, struggling not to appear taken aback. "Shiny pants are de rigueur on the farm."

"Yeah, but this is a prep school, not a farm. You'll get crucified!"

"I thought at Miss Oliver's we didn't place value on such things—how people dress. I thought we rose above that kind of judgment."

"We do for women. This is a *girls'* school, remember? Men we judge very harshly around here. My father says that Miss Oliver's is the most sexist environment he knows of."

"I hope not."

"Actually, I hope so. It's about time we had some sexism in the other direction."

"We are going to have to argue about that, you and I."

"Of course. I'd be disappointed if we didn't. You *are* the headmaster."

"Head of School," he corrected.

"No way. Mrs. Boyd was the head*mistress*, so you are the head*master*. You think you're going to hide your gender behind a PC name? Nobody's ever been able to hide anything at this school."

"All right," he said. "Headmaster."

"You really mean that?"

"Probably not. I dislike the term. But I like your point."

Karen bent over her notebook; he watched her mouth the words *Head of School* as she wrote. Then with that quick motion, she lifted her eyes and smiled. "So back to your clothes. Tell me. I'll write it down and win the Pulitzer."

"Cotton farming wrecks the land," he explained. "Sheep farming's not much better."

"But—"

"Everybody always says *but*. I'm getting a little tired of the word."

"Hey! All right!" She took another note.

"After all, we have very advanced technology and a sophisticated financial system to support it. Why not use that to make more and more unnatural"—he made quotation marks with his fingers—"things so we can leave nature alone? That's why I wear polyester."

"That's why? That's really why?"

"Either that or bad taste," he said. "Probably both."

"Well," Karen murmured, "that's different. Really different. Now we're getting somewhere!"

"Good!" said Fred. "Glad I'm not wasting your time."

"Okay," she said, ignoring his little joke. "So much for that. On to other topics. What happened at Mt. Gilead School?"

"It closed down."

"When you were the head?"

"Yes."

"It's another thing people are chalking up against you."

"Well, I was assistant head for six years there, and I fell in love with the place," he told her, very aware that Karen was writing now. "The head was a wonderful educator and I loved him, but he didn't pay attention to certain things."

"Like Mrs. Boyd?"

"Three things: marketing, finance, and asking people who were mediocre to go away."

"*Teachers?*"

"Yes, teachers."

"Oh, my God!"

"So, when things looked desperate, the board asked *him* to go and asked me to take over and see if I could turn things around."

"What happened?"

"I got started too late. That's my answer, anyway. I suppose some could say I screwed up, as you would put it."

"That's what a lot of people around here are saying."

"There a little bit of truth in that. I've learned some things. But mostly, and the board of Mt. Gilead believes this too, I got started too late. Things had already deteriorated so much that there was just too much hill to climb."

"Hill to climb," Karen repeated, writing fast. "I hope it sells. Now, one other question. Do you believe in censoring?"

"Censoring?"

"Mrs. Boyd didn't. She refused."

"You talking the *New York Times* or the *Clarion*?"

"I'm not dumb enough to talk about either of them separately. If I did, I would lose my argument."

"Which is? As if I didn't know."

Karen moved her head, up and down, slowly, several times. "Of course you know. Last year we had a full edition—all four pages—about drugs on campus, and before that we did a poll of the students to find out how many of their parents were alcoholics. Mrs. Boyd let us print them."

"I know. I read them all. They were very good articles."

"So you *don't* believe in censoring?"

"It all depends."

"So? What if I wanted to do a poll on our students' sex lives and write it up?"

"Well, your job is to make the *Clarion* as interesting as you can," Fred said. "And I'm sure that would be interesting."

"Yeah. So I'm still waiting for the punch line."

"And mine is to make sure that the public trusts this school enough to send their daughters to us."

"And to give us money," she added. "So who wins, as if I didn't know?"

"When, in my judgment, the two interests collide, I do, but in most cases I'm sure we could work it out."

"Work it out? Working it out's not the point, and you know it. The point's the principle."

"That's right," he said. "You're absolutely right. It's the principle."

"Well, this isn't going to help you at all," she said. "Not with the students anyway. This is another issue everybody's talking about. We all know it's one of the reasons Mrs. Boyd got blown away. The *Clarion*'s going to go right on trying to put the truth out, whatever it is."

"Good for you. I think you should."

"Yeah, good for me. But it's going to make your life all the harder. And that's too bad."

While he thought about how to respond to that remark, she surprised him by suddenly standing up. "Anyway, I've got to run," she announced. "Those teachers out there are going to go ballistic." Her eyes focused on his face even more intently. "I've enjoyed this. I'm surprised. I was prepared to think you were a jerk."

"Really? Then why is it that I liked you the minute you walked in the door?"

"And it took me until—?" Her thin shoulders went up and down. "Until whatever."

"That's right. Until whatever."

"Because you're a professional. You're a *teacher*. And I go to school here. My father says the same thing. He's a rabbi. He says he automatically starts to love anybody who joins his temple—the minute they join. He says if he couldn't do that, he couldn't be a rabbi."

"I'd like to meet your dad someday."

"You will," she promised. "You guys would like each other. But not till graduation, okay? This is my turf, not his." Then she was out the door.

"WE'VE BEEN WAITING for hours!" Melissa Andersen, the French teacher, complained, plopping her tall, thin body down in the chair Karen Benjamin had just been sitting in. Melissa's face was pale, drawn, and there were strands of gray in her blond hair. Fredericka Walters, her hair as red as Fred's, stood behind Melissa's chair, a tall, bulky woman wearing dark glasses, which obscured a lot of her face. Neither Melissa nor Fredericka made any gesture to shake Fred's hand.

"Take it easy, hon," Sam Andersen murmured. He was a burly man in his early thirties, with huge arms and bald already. He wore a red T-shirt and khaki pants. Turning to Fred, he put his hand out. "Welcome to our little world," he said. "How's it goin'?"

"Fine. Thanks."

Sam and Fredericka sat down on either side of Melissa, while Fred pulled his desk chair out from behind his desk so he could sit with them.

"We've come to find out what your agenda is," Melissa said.

"Hey hon, slow down," Sam said.

"Well?" Melissa asked.

"My agenda?" said Fred. "Maybe you could clarify—"

"Melissa believes in conspiracies," Sam said. "The Gulf War was started by Chevron. Seventeen reincarnated members of the Gestapo killed Kennedy." He was leaning back in his chair, grinning.

Melissa turned on her husband. "If you can't take this seriously, why don't you go home?"

Sam looked directly at Fred, arching his eyebrows so that the skin of his bald pate moved up and down. "We take things very seriously around here," he said. "Everybody knows this is the center of the universe."

Melissa was still staring at Sam. "I already asked once: If

everything's such a big joke, why are you here with us?"

"To find out if he plays tennis. Isn't that why you came? It's summer vacation, hon, for crying out loud!" Then turning to Fred: "I hope you do!"

"I do. I love to play tennis."

"That's a relief! I'm tired of playing with all these *females*! I need some competition." Sam's grin was bigger than ever. Fredericka took off her dark glasses and glowered at him.

Melissa ignored her husband's remark. She stared straight at Fred, leaning slightly forward, her body very tense. "Are you going to let boys in here?"

Fred felt his face flush.

"Whoops, that's a biggie!" said Sam. Fredericka put her dark glasses on again.

"Because it's better to let the school die than to have it be what it isn't," Melissa added, and Fred still didn't answer.

"Well, are you or aren't you?" Melissa insisted.

"I didn't come here to do that," Fred said.

Nobody responded. All three, even Sam, stared at Fred. "It's not my plan," Fred offered.

"You haven't answered the question," Melissa said.

"You know how to make God laugh?" Sam asked. "Tell Him your plans." When nobody even smiled, he shrugged his shoulders.

"I fervently believe in single-sex education for girls," Fred said.

"That's not my question," Melissa said.

"I think I've probably done as much research as anybody," Fred persisted, "more than anybody I know, as a matter of fact. I've read everything there is to read on the subject." Melissa started to say something, but he put his hand up. "How teachers call on boys more, how boys get in trouble more, disrupt more, disagree more so they get the attention. How most schools support the stereotype that girls can't do math or science and always try to think the way the teacher thinks. How in English curricula most of the authors are men and how history departments obsess over kings and generals. I could go on and on. Because I've worked in coed schools, you know, all my life."

"That's exactly my point," Melissa said.

"Well, it's not mine," he said, feeling the anger coming. "I'm the one who's seen how people show up to watch the boys play football and stay away in droves when the girls play softball, and I've watched the girls grow up much faster than the boys." Fred stopped suddenly, sensing he was talking too much. For an instant he saw the image of his daughter in his head and felt the old despair.

Sam turned to Melissa. "Honey, isn't that enough?"

"No, it isn't enough," Melissa said, and Sam turned his face away from her. He raised his eyebrows again to Fred.

"No, it isn't," Melissa repeated. "He's said what he believes in, not what he's going to do."

"Not fair," Sam murmured.

"Why isn't it fair?" Melissa persisted. "It's the question everybody is asking. It's the ultimate question: What will the new headmaster do if he thinks the only way to save the school is to let boys in? Why isn't that a fair question—since it's the one that everyone wants to know the answer to?"

"And you?" Fred said. "What would you do if you thought the only way to keep the school from closing down was to make it into a coed school?"

"I'd never think that," Melissa said. "I'd refuse to think that."

"Hon, now you're ducking the question," Sam said softly.

"I'm telling you, I'd never think that! How could anyone who's been here more than twenty minutes?" Melissa was close to yelling now. "The only point, the whole point, the only reason for Miss Oliver's, is that it is for *girls*. That's what the school is!"

"Let me tell you something," Fred blurted. "The one thing I'm not going to do is let this school be closed down!" He leaned way forward. He could feel the veins throbbing in his neck.

There was a silence. Sam and Melissa glanced at each other; Fred was sure he caught a told-you-so look on Melissa's face. Fredericka leaned forward, her face still inscrutable behind her dark glasses. "Well," said Melissa, standing up. "I've finally got my answer!" She moved toward the door. Sam stood but stayed near his chair, and Fredericka was motionless.

Near the door, Melissa turned and stared at Fred. "Don't you dare!" she said. "Don't you fucking *dare* let boys in here." Then she opened the door and disappeared, and Fred could hear her footsteps, almost running, as she crossed Ms. Rice's room to leave the building.

"Like I said, welcome to our little world," Sam said after a long pause. "Hang in there. I'll call you Sunday to see about tennis."

"Thanks," said Fred.

"Coming, Fredericka?" asked Sam.

"No," Fredericka replied, taking off her dark glasses. "I have one more question to ask."

Fred already knew what that question was.

"Hello," Fred said to Fredericka after Sam had left. As always, his anger had disappeared as fast as it arrived. "You didn't say a word."

"It wasn't necessary," Fredericka said. "It never is when Melissa's part of the conversation."

She was fidgety, clearly nervous, so he got right to the point. "I think I know what's on your mind."

"I'm sure you do."

"I really was going to address it, you know. I wasn't going to keep you on the hook. It just seemed a bit abrupt on my first day."

She looked as if she might start to cry.

"I thought we should get to know each other a little first."

She shook her head.

"And I wanted to see if we could find something else for you to do."

"Something else! Do you know how humiliating that would be?"

"Not necessarily," he urged.

"I'm a German teacher! Twenty-seven years I've been here."

"Yes. And a good one, too. I know your reputation," he said. For all she had after all those years was that good reputation. She certainly hadn't gotten rich.

"Marjorie promised me that I could stay until I retired. That's what she told me when everybody started taking Spanish instead of German. She promised."

"We have a huge deficit—"

"That's not my fault."

"No. It's not your fault," he said. *Not mine either*, he thought. Out loud, he said, speaking as gently as he knew how, "There are only nineteen students in the whole German program—all four levels—a full-time teacher with one of the biggest salaries, and a huge deficit.

We have to make some changes. Maybe you can be a dorm parent."

"I did that when I started! I'm not going to do that. I'm sixty years old."

"All right," he said, nodding his head, and the room went quiet while she looked at him, waiting for him to say something more. But he knew if he did, this would go on and on and make it worse for her. So he steeled himself and said nothing, and then she started to cry.

"I'm sorry," he murmured. She had her head bent down and waved her hand in front, as if to establish privacy. "I wish there were—"

"How old are you?" she interrupted, abruptly looking up at him.

The question caught him by surprise. "I'm thirty-seven. Why?"

"You were ten years old when I started here! A little boy! How do you think that makes me feel?" She turned her face away from him.

"Look," he said, standing up. "You need a chance to be alone. I won't need my office for a while. You stay as long as you need."

She waved her hand again and turned her shoulders so that her face was turned even further away, so that she would be facing completely away from him if the chair back would allow. Her shoulders were shaking very hard. He left her, closing the door of his office behind himself as quietly as he could.

HE USED THE time away from his office to consult with Nan White, the director of Admissions. He was sure there must be some way to recruit more students over the summer.

Nan greeted him warmly. They sat across from each other at a small table in the center of her office. She was a small woman, the single mother of three Oliver alumnae, in her late forties, brown hair gone slightly gray. He thought of her as calm, solid, honest. He had trusted her since his first interviews.

"Maybe we can get four or five new students before the end of summer," Nan told him.

"Four or five's nowhere near enough."

"The ones we get in the summer are the ones we tend to have to let go," she said.

"I know. It was the same at Mt. Gilead."

"Of course you know! You really are a risk taker, aren't you?" she said, thinking, *First he took on Mt. Gilead. Now here too.*

"That's what my wife says."

"Well, I'm glad."

"Thanks."

"But..." She hesitated. "These numbers aren't very accurate."

"Not accurate? Don't tell me they're worse! We're already nineteen fewer that I was told we'd be"

"They're worse, all right. Much worse."

"Jesus! Sorry."

Nan smiled. "You should hear some of the language I use when I look at these numbers."

"How much worse?"

"Maybe twice as many fewer than predicted. These are Marjorie's numbers, not mine."

"Vincent's," he corrected.

"Marjorie was the head," she replied softly.

He didn't respond to that.

"The truth is we'll be anywhere from thirty to forty kids down when we open in September. Guaranteed."

"Forty!"

"Fred," she said, "some of the board blames this on me. They think I must not be working hard enough. If having me around gives you a problem—"

"No way. Let's just figure out—"

"I don't have the slightest suspicion that it's my fault," she said. "That's not the point. The point is that if the board doesn't trust me, and you don't make me go away, they stop trusting you."

"I'm not about to start firing the good people," he said. "Let's just look together at your whole plan, all the ideas, where we can recruit, what alumnae are helping us, let's do that, and maybe we can come up with some ideas."

"God, I'd love to! When?"

"Right now."

"Wonderful! Somebody else besides me looking at this stuff."

"BOSTON, NEW YORK, Philadelphia, the D.C. area, Baltimore," Nan said, taking several folders out of a file. Neither of them was aware they'd skipped lunch. "That's one sector. In both New York and Baltimore, I have families lined up who have promised to host receptions for potential students."

"Great!" said Fred. "So you and I go down there, we get a few current students and their parents to attend, and we talk about the school."

"Exactly. I've got some dates ready."

"What about the other cities—Boston, Philly, and D.C.?"

"I had offers in each, but they reneged. Maybe if—"

"When?" he interrupted.

Nan hesitated.

"When they learned the new head wasn't a woman?"

"I'm afraid so," Nan murmured, and he liked her even more for not letting her eyes slide away. "But," she added, brightening, "maybe they just need some time to adjust. If you call them, I bet they'll change their mind."

"I'll call them. You bet I will!"

"And in the Southern sector, we have Richmond, Charleston, Atlanta, Fort Lauderdale. In the Midwestern, we have Cleveland. We've already got one family there, the Maynards, who've agreed to host a gathering, and then we have Chicago and Detroit. In the West we have Denver and San Francisco."

"San Francisco!" Fred interrupted. "Francis Plummer's out that way for the summer. Maybe he could join us—or maybe even save us the travel expense by speaking for us."

"I think not."

"Why not? Surely he'd be a draw for the alumnae."

"I just don't think we should," Nan said firmly.

"He's one of the ones who haven't adjusted yet?" he asked, remembering Plummer's little joke about not changing anything. He'd sensed the senior teacher's discomfort when they had interviewed each other during the search process and had received some subtle warnings from others about his resentment over Marjorie's dismissal. But he'd assumed that so intelligent a man, so celebrated a teacher, would have placed no blame for this on her successor.

"One of the ones," Nan answered.

"All right. I understand. When he gets back, though, and we get going in the new academic year—"

"I hope so," Nan said. "It's harder for some than for others."

They spent the rest of the day working on the plan and thinking of everything else they could do to improve the enrollment before school started again in September. When they were through, they figured that if everything went right, they could pick up ten or eleven new students instead of the five Nan had predicted. "That's all there is, there ain't no more," he announced. "But it's better than nothing."

"That's right," Nan agreed. "Better than nothing."

WHEN FRED GOT back to his office at five minutes to six, Ms. Rice was gone. Five minutes later, right at six o'clock as planned, Alan Travelers, the board chair, showed up. He was in his fifties, slightly taller than Fred, spare in body, pale skinned, with short, gray hair. He wore a dark business suit that even now, at the end of the day, was unwrinkled, as if he'd just put it on.

He didn't let Fred begin until he'd had his say. "Fred, I was about to call you this morning until my secretary reminded me we were going to meet instead. Just to welcome you. On your first day. No agenda. Just to say once again that I am delighted that you are our new head. Well, this is much better, face to face."

"Alan, thanks," Fred said, already feeling better.

"You're the kind of guy who will give it all he's got. That's why we're so delighted."

"Thanks. You can count on that." Fred pointed to the chair where Karen Benjamin had sat that morning—it seemed like days ago!—and took the chair facing Alan.

"By the way, Fred, Mavis Ericksen dropped in today," Alan began.

"She did?"

"She's really concerned about that Saffire woman, you know."

"I know. She dropped in to my office too."

"I know she did. What did you tell her?"

"I told her I'd look into it."

Alan nodded his head.

"This is my call, Alan."

"I know it is. I just wanted you to know there's a lot of heat involved in this one."

"There's a lot more in what I'm about to tell you," Fred said. Then he gave Alan the news.

After Fred finished, Alan sat very still, his face even paler. "Six hundred and seventy-five?" he asked at last. "You're absolutely sure?"

"Positive." Fred started to hand Alan the papers, Vincent's numbers and his own.

Alan put his hands up, shook his head. He didn't need to read them. "How in the world could we have fouled up so badly?" he murmured. He wasn't asking Fred; he was looking at the ceiling.

"He was the business manager," Fred offered, but Alan shook his head, refusing the excuse. Now Fred liked him even more. "I believed him too," Fred went on.

"Of course you did! Why wouldn't you? You weren't even here yet," Alan exclaimed. Then after a pause he added, "The deal's off if you want it to be."

"I don't understand," Fred said. Alan was looking hard at him, searching his face, and then it dawned on him what his board chair was getting at.

"You signed a contract thinking the situation was very different from what it is," Alan said mildly. "I'm not dishonorable enough to hold you to it."

"But I want this!" Fred blurted.

"Think about it," Alan insisted. "You owe it to yourself. You can tell me in the morning," and Fred was taken by surprise. Out of nowhere came this turning point! Now he was suddenly imagining himself backing out the door of this office, Alan's eyes still on him. He could feel the relief; he was floating, breathing easy in an enormous space. But the feeling only lasted an instant, and then he was overwhelmed by huge regret at throwing away his treasure. He imagined begging to be allowed to change his mind and come back.

"I'm here," he said. "No way I'm going away."

"I thought that's what you'd say." Alan was smiling now.

"If there comes a reason I should quit, I'll recognize it," Fred said.

But Alan paid no attention to that remark. Instead he was

making plans. "Okay, here's what we're going to do," he announced. "Executive committee meeting tomorrow. Noon sharp. We'll hold it at Milton Perkins's club, as usual, and he can buy us lunch, as usual. I'll call each of them tonight and tell them to be there, no matter what."

"You going to tell them what it's about?"

"Nope. Why ruin their sleep? They'll find out when you tell them, and we'll go from there."

"Yeah," said Fred, managing a grin, "why ruin their sleep."

Alan was standing now, shaking Fred's hand. "We'll be all right," he said. "We've got the right guy at the helm." Then he was out the door.

By the time Fred arrived at the head's house he realized he had had a booming headache for hours. He went through the house to the back, where he knew that Gail would be gardening in the evening's softening light.

"Hi," she said, getting up from her kneeling to greet him. She took her gardening gloves off and reached a hand to him.

He kissed her cheek.

"How was your day?" she said.

"Don't ask," he said.

Three

When Francis called Peggy from just east of the Mississippi River the day after Fred Kindler's first day in office, she didn't even ask where he was. He'd called to tell her how excited he was to be at the huge river, how much he wished she were with him so they could see it together, but she started right off before Francis hardly said a word. "He's already here!" she exclaimed. "He showed up yesterday. What do you think about that?"

"Who?" Francis asked. "Who's already there?"—as if he didn't know.

Peggy left a freighted silence. Then, wearily: "Come on, Francis. You know who," and now Francis wished he had traveled faster instead of spending four whole days at his college reunion in Ohio, two more at a friend's house in Indiana, and then a whole week in Chicago easing his conscience at a math teachers' conference. It didn't occur to him that maybe he'd been keeping himself on a short leash by stopping so often so he could turn around and go back to the school before it was too late. Nor did it occur to him that the reason for his taking his school clothes with him, his blue button-down shirt, striped tie, sports coat, and slacks, wasn't just the college reunion or the dinner at the end of the math conference; it was that these were his uniform, his identity. Instead, he thought that if he had escaped across the big divide of the Mississippi right away, he'd now be much further into the West and he wouldn't care where Fred Kindler was. He'd have room to breathe.

"Marjorie left early," he heard Peggy say. "She cleared out."

"Oh," he said. "So soon?" Then he realized he was not surprised. That was exactly what Marjorie would do.

But Peggy wasn't talking about Marjorie now; she was talking about the new guy. "Two whole weeks before he even needed to be here!" she said. He knew what she left unsaid for him to think about: *The new headmaster shows up early for his responsibilities—while you run away from yours.* But that's not what he was thinking about. What filled his brain instead was the picture of Fred Kindler actually ensconced in Marjorie's office, enthroned behind her desk, surrounded by the pictures her students made for her. The wrongness of the fit, its *impropriety*, astounded him. It was Marjorie's office!

"Well, what do you think of that?" Peggy asked again.

"Maybe he can't read a calendar," he said.

"Very funny, Francis."

"I didn't call you up to talk about him!"

"Oh, you didn't?" Peggy mocked. "All right, then. So forget about it."

He let a long silence go by, desperate for a way to rescue them from this. "Peg," he finally begged, "let's not fight."

That's right, she thought, *let's not.*

"How are you, Peg?"

I'm confused, she wanted to say, *and I'm scared we've lost each other*, but she was too angry to plead for sympathy. "I'm okay," she told him.

"Only okay, Peg?"

She shrugged her shoulders as if he were there to see. There was a long silence, while he waited for her to speak. "Where are you?" she finally asked.

"Just east of the Mississippi."

"That's nice," she said, failing to keep the sarcasm out of her voice. But she really did think it was nice that he was seeing the country and wished she were seeing it with him. And then it dawned on her that neither of them ever considered her joining him. The reasons for his trip were too foreign to her for that.

"All right, Peg," he sighed, hearing only the sarcasm. "I'll call you later."

"All right."

"I miss you, Peg."

"I miss you too," she admitted, "but if you were here we wouldn't have to miss each other."

Neither of them could think of what else to say. Francis hung up first and walked back to his old yellow Chevy, and started to drive again. In Denver, he would pick up Lila Smythe, next year's president of the student council, and give her a ride the rest of the way to California. Lila, one of Francis's and Peggy's favorite students, lived in the dorm they parented, and though Francis had been delighted when she decided to join the dig, he now regretted his promise. She'd want to talk to him, as faculty advisor to the student council, about the council's agenda for the coming year. He was much too preoccupied for that.

And Peggy lingered by the phone, willing Francis to call again. She'd speak more gently this time, she told herself. But he didn't call, and now she knew he was on the other side of the Mississippi, much farther away from her than he'd ever been. She'd never been in that part of the country and could only see it in her imagination as endless, empty space. And her husband was lost in it.

PEGGY LOOKED AT her watch. It was ten-thirty in the morning, and she had a meeting with Fred Kindler at quarter to eleven. She wanted to get there a little early because he'd told her that he had to leave at eleven-fifteen for a meeting downtown at noon. She was worried about how he'd react when, on only his second day in office, she would tell him about a problem that was going to make the budget crisis even worse. So she left the phone, stepped out of her house and across the thick green lawns of the campus toward the administration building. In the distance, at the campus edge, she saw the river gleaming in the sun.

The first thing she noticed about Fred Kindler's office was the big clock on the wall behind his desk, an imitation of a Mickey Mouse wristwatch, complete with huge leather wrist straps that reached from ceiling to floor. It hadn't been there yesterday when she glanced through the door. She smiled, getting his message right away, and wondered if Eudora Easter had had a hand in this. Maybe people would start getting to places on time now.

He smiled too, an easy greeting, and stepped from behind his desk with that ducklike, toes-out gait she knew she would never have noticed if Francis hadn't pointed it out to her. When Kindler put out his hand to shake hers, she realized again how formal and old-fashioned he seemed. They sat down in front of his desk, facing each other.

"How's Francis's trip going?" Fred asked her.

"He'll be in California by the end of the week."

"I hope he's having a great time."

"I hope so too," she said before she had time to think what this remark might reveal. She saw him look away from her for just an instant and knew that he was not hiding his surprise—there was no dissimulation in that not-very-handsome face—but being kind. *Whatever else he is, he is a good person*, she decided. One of the things she was proud of was her ability to size people up.

Fred wasn't sure whether it was surprise flashing across her face as Peggy's eyes met his and stayed longer than most people's—maybe that's why he already liked her so much—or whether she was about to ask him a question. If so, he knew what the question would be: *Are you considering allowing boys into this school?* He wished she would ask it. He guessed she was the kind of person he could think aloud in front of.

But he knew that of course she wouldn't ask. Not yet. She was too kind to ask so early. That she'd just admitted a hint of trouble between herself and Francis gave him a rush of sadness for her—and anxiety for himself. *I need your husband too*, he wanted to say. *He's the senior teacher. The most gifted on the faculty. Teaches both math and English beautifully. That makes him powerful. If he's against me, I'm dead.*

"We need more air conditioning in the Pequot Indian area," he heard Peggy say. "We had a consultant tell us that the displays would deteriorate."

"How much?"

"It's a lot. The estimate's for fifteen thousand." If he said yes, then she knew he understood how important the display was; it would mean he "got" Miss Oliver's School for Girls—and Francis would be wrong.

"Fifteen thousand!" Fred exclaimed; then to himself: *What the heck. What's another fifteen thousand to a deficit like ours?*

"I know it's not in the budget," Peggy said. "It's a lot to ask."

He made a little motion with his hand in front of his face as if to brush her comment away. "When we get the budget to where it should be, you won't have to ask."

"Won't have to ask?"

"Department heads'll have their own budgets. They'll have discretion," he explained, discovering how easy it was for him to share his ideas with her. He wished he could tell her about the emergency meeting with the board's executive committee that would start in just over an hour, where he was going to drop the bomb about the budget. He'd get her advice.

"Really? Discretion?" Peggy was surprised. "We always went to Marjorie for—"

"Well, anyway," he interrupted, "you've got it. Fifteen thousand."

"Really?" she said. "Wonderful!"

He saw relief flooding her face, felt her eyes on his. Then a worried frown.

"Where will we get the money?" she asked.

"I have no idea, but I do know what's indispensable and what is not."

Peggy sat very still, taking his comment in. *See, Francis, you're wrong*, she thought while it dawned on her how different this was from her meetings with Marjorie, how tired she'd grown of sitting side by side with her headmistress on a sofa, having her arm patted every time Marjorie made a point. For that's how it had always gone: Marjorie making the point, not the other way around. And now Peggy realized she had something else to say, she was going to make a point—because she knew he'd listen. "Just one more thing," she said. "I know you're busy."

"I've got time."

"Don't you bring it up. You'll get crucified if you do. Let the board do it."

"It?" he said. "You're being mysterious."

"No, I'm not. You know what I'm talking about. If we have to let boys in here, let it be the board's decision. Fight it. Even if you think it's right. Fight it anyway. For a while at least. Otherwise—"

"I've thought about that," he said, hearing again Melissa Andersen's *Don't you fucking dare*. "Still, it doesn't quite feel right."

"Of course it doesn't. Do it anyway!"

"You're a smart lady," he said. "I'll think about it."

"Good," she replied, standing up. He rose too and reached to shake her hand. "I'm glad you're here," she said, realizing she'd just done what Francis should be here to do: give advice. Show where the land mines were.

"Thanks," he said, tempted now to put his other hand out too, take her hands in both of his. But that was too forward; he hardly knew her.

Right after Peggy left, Fred made the call to Mavis Ericksen that he'd been dreading.

"Hello, this is Mavis." Her voice was cheerful.

"Good morning, Mavis, this is Fred Kindler."

Silence.

"How are you this morning?" he tried.

She still didn't answer, and it came to him that maybe she thought his question was sarcastic, as if to ask, *Are you still crying?* "I called to follow through on our conversation about Ms. Saffire," he said.

"I've been waiting," she said, making it clear she didn't like to wait.

Yes, for only twenty-four hours, Fred thought. "Earlier this morning I talked to Dorothy Strang—"

"I don't care what Dorothy—"

"Ms. Saffire reports to Dorothy Strang," he said. "Dorothy evaluated Ms. Saffire last November near the end of her first year as having done quite well. Like everyone else, she's been given some goals and will be evaluated again this November." Fred didn't tell Mavis that one of the goals assigned to Joan Saffire was learning how to handle certain kinds of people, and that when he had asked Dorothy, "What kind of people?" she had whispered, "Assholes," and then got red in the face and started to giggle. And then admitted that she shouldn't have sent a beginner to see Aldous Enright. She would have gone herself, but she was on vacation.

"November!" Mavis's voice was quivering. "It's only July!"

"Yes. November. It's an annual evaluation." There was another seemingly endless silence. Fred felt sweat running down the inside of his shirt. "You and I need to talk," he said. Maybe if he took her to lunch and they got to know each other, she would understand why it was important that the board not intrude on the head's domain. "Let's make an appointment," he began. Then he heard her hanging up.

How much safer he would be if Joan Saffire were incompetent and he could fire her, he thought—and immediately regretted the thought.

AN HOUR AND a half later in a private dining room of the River Club in Downtown Hartford, Alan Travelers got right to the point. "Our new headmaster's had a very busy first day," he told the executive committee. "Among other accomplishments, he discovered that we have a larger deficit than we thought we did." Impeccable in his blue suit, Travelers was standing at the head of the table. His tone sounded surprisingly cheerful to Fred.

"Yeah?" Milton Perkins growled. "So what else is new?"

"You're about to learn," Travelers said. "I think it'll get your attention." He sat down.

"Oh?" Perkins said. "How much?"

"Six hundred and seventy-five thousand."

Perkins sat back in his chair as if he'd been shoved in the chest. He stared at Travelers. Then he turned to Fred. "Tell me I didn't hear that right."

"You heard it right," Fred said, and from their frames along the oak-paneled wall opposite the tall windows overlooking the river, an array of nineteenth-century patriarchs, masters of New England thrift, looked sternly down at the room.

Fred handed out the papers he had prepared and proceeded to explain the difference between Carl Vincent's figures and his own, going slowly, line by line. While he talked, no one touched the raw oysters that Perkins, who has lived at the River Club ever since his wife had died five years earlier, had ordered for the lunch, and when he finished, the members continued to stare down at their papers. They couldn't bring themselves to look at each other. Perkins got up from the table, went to one of the windows, and stared at the river, his back to everybody.

"So much for the bad news," Alan said dismissively, breaking the silence. He knew he needed to get these people past their disappointment and, worse, their humiliation at having been so gulled by Vincent's numbers. "There's good news too. We've got a head who before he does anything else—on his very first day!—gets us to the truth. That's huge."

"Yes," said beautiful alumna Sonja McGarvey. "Finally some reality around here!" She turned to Fred, sent him a grateful—maybe even an admiring—look. She had black hair, blue eyes, pale skin, and her lipstick was very red. Only ten years out, Sonja was already rich. Marjorie had often pointed to her derring-do, entrepreneuring in software, as proof of the empowering effect of single-sex education on women, and Fred was already planning to ask her for the lead gift from the board this year.

"Exactly!" Alan said. He had to admit, he liked this challenge, since it gave him something to sink his teeth into, put some spice in his life. He'd won battles like this before. "We'll just go faster," he urged. "We'll just rebuild the enrollment in two years instead of four. We've got the right head finally. We'll just do it!"

But now Sonja McGarvey was shaking her head in disagreement. She leaned forward across the table toward Travelers, pent up, waiting to speak.

"Yes, that's exactly what we're going to do!" Travelers went on. "Revise the plan and move on."

"That's unrealistic," McGarvey snapped. "It's a pipe dream."

All eyes came off Travelers and moved to McGarvey, then back to Travelers, who was obviously surprised. He was not used to being contradicted, especially by a woman who was not yet thirty. He started to say something, but from the window Perkins beat him to it.

"So it's unrealistic," Perkins said. His back was still to the group, and he was still staring out the window, as if he were addressing the river. "When you don't have a choice, who cares?"

"What's he been smoking?" McGarvey asked the group. And when Perkins turned to face her, she asked him, "Can I have some too?"

Perkins left the window and, taking his seat again, leaned to McGarvey across the polished mahogany. "You could be right," he growled. "Bean counters are every once in a century. But maybe you aren't. Maybe we'll pull something out of a hat." He was grinning now, egging her on.

"Oh, for Christ's sake, here we go again!" she said.

"And if we don't," Perkins said, "the one thing we aren't going to do is let boys in here." He wasn't grinning anymore.

The room went silent once again. Everyone stared at Perkins, who was plunging a fork into an oyster now.

"Fred didn't say anything about letting boys in," Travelers said. His voice was tight. "Neither did I. Neither did anyone. That's not even on the table."

"Good," Perkins said, waving the fork with the oyster still on it. "We got that settled."

"Jesus!" from McGarvey. "Welcome to fantasyland!"

Perkins turned again to study her, miming a mild scientific interest at the source of such a strange remark. He extended the fork, the oyster he was about to eat still dripping on its tines, across the table to her. He raised his eyebrows, kept the oyster before her. It was a test: if she took it, then she was normal after all.

McGarvey, of course, was much too smart to rise to this. She hardly looked at the oyster—or at Perkins, turning instead to Travelers as if chastising the chairman for letting the meeting get out of hand. So Perkins shrugged, plopped the oyster into his mouth, nodded up and down, then broke into a grin and aimed it around the room.

On McGarvey's right, the elderly Ms. Harriet Richardson, who hadn't said a word, was too ladylike to acknowledge the animus that had just drenched the room. She nodded her birdlike head at Milton Perkins. "For once you and I agree," she murmured. Ms. Richardson, the former academic dean at one of New England's most prestigious women's colleges, stared intently across the table at Perkins, her tiny body very erect. "It would be a tragedy," she said. "An abandonment of the reason we exist."

Milton Perkins was grinning again. "You and I agreeing, that's a sign things are completely out of control," he told her. For Perkins, even to appear to agree with the likes of Ms. Richardson, a worshipful biographer of FDR, was more than he could stand.

"I'll say it again," Travelers said. "Nobody said anything about letting boys in."

"Not yet," McGarvey said.

"My dear, you aren't suggesting—?" Ms. Richardson's tremolo trailed off, while McGarvey put her blue eyes on Ms. Richardson's face and stared. Ms. Richardson tried again. "We have a vision to uphold!"

"It's not a vision. It's a hallucination!" McGarvey hissed. "We're supposed to know the difference." Ms. Richardson's face went pale, and McGarvey, who was trying to learn diplomacy and regretted her harshness, softened her voice. "Ms. Richardson, girls-only just doesn't sell anymore," she said.

"Sell! My dear, this isn't a store!"

So much for McGarvey's mildness. She reached across the table, tapped her bright-red nails on Ms. Richardson's copy of the papers Fred had distributed. "See where the number is below the bottom line on Carl Vincent's budget?"

Ms. Richardson took the bait. "Yes," she said. "I see."

"The one in parentheses?"

Ms. Richardson didn't answer.

"Now look at Fred's numbers; the figure in *parentheses* is bigger."

"Sonja McGarvey," said Ms. Richardson. "I can read."

"By almost three quarters of a million dollars."

"Six hundred and seventy-five," said Ms. Richardson.

"I can read too," said McGarvey. "I just like to round things off."

"Six hundred and seventy-five," Ms. Richardson insisted. "My dear, six hundred and seventy-five is not three quarters of a million; it is six hundred and seventy-five."

"People!" Travelers rapped his knuckles on the table. He was clearly irritated. McGarvey and Ms. Richardson stopped.

This was the opening Fred had been waiting for. "Even if it were three quarters of a million—a full million—it wouldn't make any difference to me," he told them. "I came here to help turn this thing around in four years. So now that we've only got two, we'll do it in two." Everyone's eyes were on him as he spoke, for the hunger for leadership was palpable among this board which, until the unseating of Marjorie, had been so dominated by her that they never developed the will, or the sophistication, to do their job. And he was doing what he came here to do—he was leading. He was giving them a solution to their problem in the cash-flow projections he'd put in front of them, which demonstrated that the addition of twenty-six girls, recruited during each of the next two academic years through aggressive marketing of the school's excellence and the efficacy of its single-sex mission, put him on the same pace to a balanced budget as the original plan, which had called for thirteen additional enrollments each year.

It's a good plan, he told himself, his confidence blossoming, because it provided him a fighting chance to save the school as single-sex, while leaving the option of admitting boys as a last resort if it became apparent the enrollment targets weren't being reached. Because the one thing he wouldn't do was close the school! Nor would he offer himself as sacrificial lamb by being the one to suggest bringing boys in. He remembered Peggy Plummer's advice. "I've given you new numbers," he said aloud. "They're challenging, but if we get the message out, we can do it."

"Good for you!" Perkins exclaimed. Then, "Whose numbers? Not Vincent's, I hope."

"No," Fred answered. "They're mine."

"Fred tells me he's going to let Mr. Vincent go as soon as he comes back from vacation," Travelers said very quietly.

"Carl! Gone?" Ms. Richardson asked, staring at Fred.

"Well, good for you," McGarvey murmured.

"Yeah," said Perkins. "Good for you. Poor old guy. Didn't know a number from a road sign."

"Well, anyway," said Travelers, "we're in trouble, and Fred's recommended a solution."

"We are not in so much trouble that we can let loyal, longtime employees go just like that." Ms. Richardson snapped her fingers.

"Jeez, he couldn't even count!" said Perkins. "As soon as he finishes getting Alzheimer's his IQ's going to double."

"That's enough, Milton!" Travelers said.

Ms. Richardson was still staring at Fred. "You mean you're firing him?"

"Oh, please!" said McGarvey.

"There's a principle here," Ms. Richardson said. "Mr. Vincent has been allowed to perform for years in this way, and suddenly he's dismissed? We don't interact that way at Miss Oliver's. I'm surprised at you, Mr. Kindler."

"Alan, for God's sake, we have an emergency!" McGarvey exclaimed before Fred could respond. "Can we deal with it?"

"We've already dealt with it," Perkins barked. "We're going with Fred's new plan."

"And if that doesn't work? What then?" McGarvey asked.

"We're going to close the school. That's what. Because if it's not going to be a girls' school, the hell with it. You think I'd let myself be bored to death in board meetings for a school where boys get all the attention so they can run the world while girls stay home and cook? I've got three daughters, and I know what they learned here. You might as well think it's going to snow in Florida in the middle of summer to think that boys are ever going to come in here. So why talk about it?"

"We're going to talk about it," McGarvey said. "I promise. Because the one thing I'm not going to let happen is closing the school. So if you people won't bring it up at the September board meeting, I will. I'll force the issue."

Once again the room went silent while everyone stared at her.

"Why in the world would you do that?" Travelers asked at last.

"To save the school, that's why."

"It's a terrible idea," Travelers said.

"It's being whispered everywhere," McGarvey persisted. Travelers leaned toward her shaking his head, but McGarvey held her ground and told him, "I'm going to put it to the board. Where it counts. And get some clarity."

"You put letting boys into the school on the table like that, how're you going to keep it quiet?" Perkins asked. He shoved his plate of oysters aside. Cracked ice spilled onto the table. "The board'll decide not to do it," he said. "They're not *that* crazy. But the story that'll come out in the first three seconds after the meeting anyhow is that right away we're going to admit seven hundred boys—all of them nine feet tall—and with extra big dicks. Fred here will have a crazy house on his hands."

The instant Perkins was finished with his harangue, McGarvey turned back to the chairman. It was as if to her Perkins wasn't even in the room. "Alan," she asked, "are you going to try to tell me I can't speak my mind at a board meeting?"

"No, Sonja, I'm not saying that. I don't have the right. But I wish you wouldn't."

"Good. Because if you were, I'd do it anyway."

"So that's what firing Mrs. Boyd was really about!" Ms. Richardson exclaimed.

Now it's Ms. Richardson's turn to be stared at.

"Where did *that* come from?" Travelers asked.

"You are very clever, Mr. Travelers," Miss Richardson said. "Far cleverer than I. But even I can see how this meeting has been contrived." She turned her stare on Perkins. "First Milton Perkins opens the door for all the posturing by saying the one thing we aren't going to do is admit boys," she said, then turning to McGarvey continued, "which of course gives Miss McGarvey the opportunity to propose that we should admit boys and that she will recommend admitting boys to the board of Miss Oliver's School for Girls. And you"—she aimed her glare at Alan again—"pretend that you can't stop her."

"You're out of line, Ms. Richardson," Travelers finally said. "You need to take that back."

But Ms. Richardson actually believed she had discovered the truth and wasn't about to take anything back. "All along I suspected," she said. "But I put my suspicions aside. I kept my faith." Her voice was a quaver, on the verge of weeping. "Now I see how naive I was. All along. A plot: prey on the school's misfortune, use it to pry Marjorie Boyd out of her office so we can bring in this *man* and open the doors to boys!"

"You couldn't be more wrong," Travelers said, clearly amazed.

"Oh, please, don't go on with this." Ms. Richardson's tiny shoulders were shaking. "It's out now! In the open! Why else would you fire the finest educator this school has ever had? I could never answer that question. Why fire the person who has made the school what it is?

"And *you*!" she turned on Fred when no one answered. "You have just confirmed my original suspicion, which I put aside because you seemed a gentleman and so sincere. Well, now I know. First, we get a male chairman of the board. Then a cabal under his direction gets rid of Mrs. Boyd to make room for you; then you, on your very first day, get rid of one of her most faithful colleagues, and then on the very next day it is proposed at the executive committee that the board of trustees contemplate the admission of boys. It's plain what's coming next. I won't be part of it. I'll resign."

"Ms. Richardson, you've misinterpreted everything," Fred said softly. He was devoid of anger. Instead, he was fascinated. For an instant he thought maybe he could unravel this for her.

"Oh? You deny it!" he heard her say, mocking surprise. "Then let me ask a question. Which one do you favor, Mr. Kindler?" She was not on the verge of weeping anymore. Her face had gone hard.

Fred saw the mine she was planting. Now he was irritated.

Alan stood up. "Harriet, stop!" He saw what was coming, and he didn't trust Fred to lie. "Just stop!"

But Ms. Richardson calmly went right on. "We did have two philosophies proposed this morning," she said, like a teacher reviewing the lesson for the dumbest student. "One that we should admit boys in order to keep the school in operation. The other that it would be better to close the school than to admit boys."

Fred's face flamed, his chest constricted; he felt everyone watching, and for an instant he could hardly see.

"Don't be angry," Ms. Richardson said. "Just answer the question."

"I'd close the school before I admitted boys," he said, lying deliberately and looking Ms. Richardson right in the eye.

It was very quiet in the room while she returned his stare. Then she said, "You don't lie as skillfully as you need to yet, Mr. Kindler, but I'm sure your performance will improve with time."

Travelers cut in. "Ms. Richardson—"

But she wasn't finished yet. She was still facing Fred, her back to Travelers. "The truth is, Mr. Kindler, even if you were an honorable person, you shouldn't be here."

"Harriet, you offered your resignation a minute ago," Travelers said.

"No, I didn't. I only threatened."

"Yes, you did, and it's accepted." He looked at Sonja McGarvey and Milton Perkins.

"Yup," said Perkins. "I heard her resign."

"Me too," said McGarvey. "Plain as day."

"It will be in the minutes," Travelers announced. "We'll take a short recess now. It will give you time to gather your things, Ms. Richardson."

She stayed in her chair. The frown on her pale face showed she was making a decision. Travelers had no legal right to remove her. She turned to Fred. "It was over for me as soon as Marjorie left," she said. "I could have saved you your little charade." She started to collect her copy of the financial papers.

"Not those," said Travelers. He reached to take them. "They're confidential. For board members only."

Harriet Richardson took a sudden breath, stared at Travelers, and held the papers in her tiny hand. Travelers wore a little smile, gave a tug; Ms. Richardson let out her breath, and now Travelers held the papers. Ms. Richardson sat very still for an instant. "You won't get away with this," she whispered, then got up, walked across the room. The big oaken doors didn't open for her, she was so little. Fred wondered if he should get up and open them. She pushed again, and the doors opened just enough, and then she was gone.

DURING THE RECESS Perkins murmured to Fred, "Just in case you're worried, I've told a few lies myself in my day. I'm kinda proud of them. They did more good than harm."

Then he handed Fred a note. It said: *Let's give old Vincent a little going-away present. I'll take care of it. Two years' salary. Anonymous. He obviously doesn't have any money.*

After they reconvened, Alan tried to persuade McGarvey not to bring her proposal to the board. She refused. "I have to do what I think right," she said. "Besides, the biggest problem isn't going to be the board. It's going to be the faculty. As soon as they find out the board's even toying with the idea of going coed, they'll be rabid. And the biggest problem on the faculty will be Francis Plummer. You think that little old lady who just resigned feels strongly?" she asked. "Wait till you see how our senior teacher reacts to the idea!"

"Whaddya expect?" Perkins grumbled. "He's loyal."

"He's loyal to Marjorie," McGarvey said. "You think he's going to be loyal to Fred here? And he's everybody's hero. The girls call him Clark Kent, you know, from before I was there. He's a loose cannon with a great big bang, and he's cracking up."

"He might be," Travelers said. "Look at the way he took you on, Milton—right in the middle of the reception for Fred."

"So I told a story and he told a better one." Perkins said. "Who cares? We were both playing games."

"Completely out of control," McGarvey said, and Fred remembered that Gregory van Buren, in one of his insistent appointments during the search process, mentioned sotto voce that he thought people who were cracking up were the most difficult to control because you don't know what they were going to do next. Fred also remembered hearing that Francis Plummer had taken to referring to Sonja McGarvey as Sonja Testosterone. He had laughed when he heard that. Now he had to be careful that the name wouldn't slip off his own tongue.

Goodness knows he was worried about Plummer. When he had interviewed with the senior teacher last January just before being appointed, Fred could tell how distraught Plummer was at Marjorie's dismissal. It was one of the many warning notes that would have told a more detached, analytical person how great a risk it was hitching his wagon to Miss Oliver's star. On Fred the warnings had had the opposite effect; he was inspired by the challenge. And Karen Benjamin was right: Miss Oliver's was the school he would have loved his daughter to attend. Why wouldn't he want to rescue it? So he had persuaded himself he could win Francis Plummer's loyalty. Surely a man so in love with his school as Plummer was would control himself, tamp down his anger, and join the new head in keeping the school alive. Now Fred wondered if the man really was out of control, really cracking up. What better way to get back at a board member who had helped get rid of the headmistress he loved than by taking him on in front of the faculty? Sometimes pretending to be out of control was a very good strategy. All Fred knew is that he needed Francis Plummer.

"You better reel him in, Fred," Travelers was saying. "Or else you'll have to get rid of him. I hate to say that. He's been a loyal teacher."

"There you go with loyal again!" McGarvey turned to Travelers. "He's loyal to what was. We are responsible for the future. If it were me, I'd reel him right out the door."

"You guys sound like Congress," Perkins growled. "I could get sick." He turned to Fred. "So, you want to know all this crap about Plummer or not?"

"Let me handle him," Fred said. "That's my job."

"I hope that's possible," McGarvey murmured.

THAT NIGHT AFTER dinner, Gail and Fred sat on the back porch, and Gail knew something bad had happened at the meeting, something he didn't want to talk about or else he would surely have told her at dinner, but he was so distracted it was as if she were not even in the room with him, and she waited and waited for him to tell her what was bothering him. Whatever it was, it must be worse than the budget fiasco he had told her about last night. "Don't ask," he had said. Which of course meant exactly the opposite, and even before they'd gone inside, he told her that the under-enrollment was exactly twice as large as he had thought and that he had only two years instead of four to save the school. So what was going on now, only a day later, that he was hiding from her?

"You're not telling me something," she said, sitting beside him in the twilight. "It's all over your face.

He prevaricated by telling her everything about the meeting, describing it blow by blow, except the part where Ms. Richardson turned on him. He didn't tell her that part. That's what had been bothering him. That's what he didn't want to talk about.

She saw right through this. "Come on, tell me," she urged when he'd finished. "What's really bothering you?" She knew the board bringing up the prospect of admitting boys, instead of him, wasn't bad. It was good. It took the heat off him, it was what he wanted.

He gave in finally and told her how Ms. Richardson had made him tell a lie. "How suddenly it all happened!" he exclaimed. "First she's a kind, elderly woman, then she's Machiavelli."

"You were right to lie to her, Fred," Gail said. "You're a realist. A grown-up. It's nice to be married to a grown-up."

They sat side by side in the squeaky wicker chairs. June bugs banged on the screen door, hungry for the light. Gail picked up Fred's hand and kissed it, held it to her cheek, then returned it to his knee. Neither of them spoke. After a while Gail stood up. "It's ten o'clock, I'm going to bed," she said, bending down to kiss his forehead. "Come on up when you think you can sleep."

He took her hand, held her back. He was still mulling over what she'd said. "A realist? You usually say idealist."

"That too. You're both. You're Don Quixote with a brain." He laughed and let go of her hand.

She wanted to add, *You could have chosen a school that didn't need to be rescued. That would have been just fine with me.* But she kept the thought to herself, bent to kiss him again, and went upstairs to bed.

He sat for a while, nowhere near ready to sleep, remembering the hollow sound of their voices in their house at Mt. Gilead after the furniture was taken out and put in the moving van. It was a relief that Gail's profession was portable. A graphic artist as good as she could be successful anywhere, make as much money here in Fieldington as she ever did—more than he did—and maybe, when she was ready, after she got her roots down, and he got things at school a little more squared away, whatever was keeping them from getting pregnant would stop happening, and they'd be parents again. "We're going to stay right here," he said to the empty porch. "This is the place for us."

After a while he went into the house, tried to read; when that didn't work, he turned on the TV, soothed himself with late-night blather, finally dozed in the chair. Near dawn when he went upstairs and got in the bed beside Gail, he found she was awake. He put his hand on her shoulder. That's when she started to cry.

"Hey!" he said. He put his arm around her, cradled her head. "You said yourself it's not so bad. And anyway, it isn't going to happen. They'll never let boys in here."

"That's not what I'm crying about," she said. "Besides, I'm stopping."

"I know," he whispered, kissing her cheek. "I know, I know." How safe things used to be, that's why she was crying. For that. Before he had decided to be a head. Before they had learned that a car accident could actually kill their daughter. *If I were a great teacher, a Francis Plummer,* he thought, *maybe I wouldn't be a head.*

"It's like you're out in space," Gail said. "All alone."

"But I'm not," he said. "I'm right here in bed. With you."

FAR WEST OF the Mississippi now, in the same dawn, Francis couldn't sleep either. In this huge landscape where there were no woods, no little hills to wall him in, he felt released but unanchored too, much too restless to sleep. So he drove instead, went faster and faster. It was four-thirty in the morning, fifteen hours after his phone call to Peggy, and there was no other car in sight. Just a big semi up ahead getting bigger and bigger.

He'd promised Peggy he wouldn't eat greasy breakfasts at roadside restaurants, so he was fasting, three cups of black coffee, that's all, and the caffeine was throbbing in his temples. He zoomed by the truck and waved to the fat guy, pasty faced, loaded on speed, NoDoze, everything but sleep, who from miles above waved back, then blasted the air horn, a crazed hello in the early morning.

Now Francis was going almost a hundred, the car was beginning to quiver, and he started to laugh. Once when he was a little kid crossing the living room, past the black-robed glowering of his ancestor's portrait above the mantel, and tripping on the rug, he heard his father mildly explain to a visitor, "Francis lacks coordination. And he's so dreamy, he doesn't always know where he's going." Francis, who at age fifty-five was still small, unathletic, and absentminded, remembered that now, so he pushed harder on the accelerator. Risk was the best revenge. When the car's shuddering increased, he laughed again, surprised that he was laughing, that he wasn't crying, wondered why he was speeding; he didn't ever know anymore how he was going to feel in the next moment. He thought maybe he was finally living up to the romance the girls had built up around him, living a secret life they insisted on believing.

Signs, telephone poles, fence posts blurred by, and after a while he found himself wondering how it would be to steer for one of them, smash his car and himself, and go to sleep. The image frightened him more than the midnight ocean into which he'd fallen overboard and was drowning all alone. So he slowed his car way down, gained control of it and of himself.

Now he had only several hundred miles to go until Denver, where he would pick up Lila Smythe. He felt less regretful now about his promise to give her a ride; he'd had enough of loneliness. And there was something comforting about keeping a promise to a student, something solid and practical and helpful, about saving her the money it would cost her to fly. He hung on to that.

Three hours later, he saw the front range of the Rockies up ahead. Soon he'd be in Denver.

FOUR

With Francis farther and farther away and Siddy wandering in Europe, Peggy was remembering what it was to be alone. She was thirteen again.

The pale winter light slid through the window, showing the grease lingering on the tiles behind the stove. The kitchen smelled of the old linoleum her mother hated, which wouldn't be there anymore if her mother hadn't died giving birth to the stillborn baby who would have been Peggy's little sister. Peggy peeled potatoes, alone. It was four o'clock, school was out, and her father wouldn't come home till seven.

They'll eat together, he'll ask her questions about her schoolwork, he'll wash the dishes, thanking her for making dinner, for being such a good daughter, then she'll go upstairs to her homework: gray geometry, Caesar dividing Gaul, a history text heavy with graffiti left to her by an anonymous predecessor: misshapen human forms, huge heads, penises that look like guns. Her father would be downstairs in the armchair across the fireplace from the matching empty one. Soon she'll hear his tread on the stairs, he'll come into her room, shyly kiss her on her cheek—she would know he wished he weren't so distant. Before going to bed, she'll hear him crying in his room.

Then she was twenty-two, newly married, standing on a warm thick carpet, the color of roses. The walls of the big room were a bright clean white, and Francis's father in a blue suit stood by the fireplace. He was smiling at her, standing under the portrait of John Plummer, Puritan Divine, black robe, white bib, round cheeks, stern, stable man, proud roots! The smell of roast lamb wafted from the kitchen. Francis's mother's in there with the black lady who helped, who called them by their last name while they called her by her first—all except Francis, who put a Mrs. before her last name, while his father rolled his eyes.

They'd just come from church. Peggy still felt bathed in the light from the rose window over the altar. Francis's father turned to her, he knew she'd listen, and he talked about the sermon. "Unless I believe as a child believes," he said, but she didn't hear the rest. It's not the words she wanted, she didn't need to understand. It's what's in his eyes. More than belief. More than confidence. More than knowledge. A vast beneficence had been granted! He smiled at her. He was tall, he's wearing a vest, there's a gold watch chain across the front. His blue eyes shined with his belief. She loved those blue eyes!

More than ever lately, Peggy found herself talking to her father-in-law. She couldn't see him, had no idea what the heaven she was sure he lived in looked like, but she knew all she had to do was open her mind to him. Their conversation was more intimate now than when he had lived in a real body on the edge of Long Island Sound in the house that Peggy loved so much. She was sure he knew now that the only reason Francis had begged her to join his family's Episcopal faith when they were married was to please him. "I didn't see that then," she told her father-in-law, "maybe because Francis didn't either. Or if he did understand, maybe it was kindness, he didn't want to hurt your feelings. What I really think, though, is how in the world could he have stood up to you?

"Because when Francis thinks of God, he thinks of *bears*," she explained, and *turtles*, and *fish*. "How's he supposed to tell you that? He told me once. I just laughed. He was joking then—before he knew it was true."

Peggy finally got so lonely on the night after Francis called her just before he crossed the Mississippi that she invited their dog, Levi, into their bed with her. Levi was a big brown mongrel who drooled a lot. His other name was Spit; he was lonely too. He stood by the bed as Peggy got ready, his rear end wagging with his tail, and when Peggy got in on one side, he leapt up onto the bed on the other, offering to lick Peggy's face, while Peggy pushed him away, and then he snuggled down beside her, groaning with satisfaction like an old man in a steam bath.

Levi was afflicted with fleas in the summertime, and so when his scratching reached an apogee in the small hours of the dark, the bed shook and Peggy woke up thinking for an instant that she was in California with Francis and there was an earthquake and they were both dying.

"But my dear," her friend Father Woodward said to her that afternoon when she went to his cluttered little office to tell him about her vivid dream, "Francis will be living in a reconstructed Indian village on Mount Alma. Nothing's there to fall on him." Father Woodward spoke in the faintly affected upper-class British accent he joked that he had learned by mistake in theological school. "Francis is going to live forever," he predicted.

The little priest sat opposite her in a chair to one side of his desk, his feet barely touching the floor, while the light from the window shined on his bald head. Before coming to Fieldington, he'd been a curate in a big New York City parish, and though she'd miss him terribly, Peggy thought he should return to the city's more eclectic scene. He had told her once that the bishop urged him to take the Fieldington parish ten years ago when the position opened. "He said living in suburbia would test my faith. He obviously suspected it wasn't very strong." But now the thought came to Peggy that maybe the bishop just had wanted him out of the way.

"Don't worry, my dear," Father Woodward murmured now, "Francis will be fine. He's exploring." She watched his little sandy mustache move up and down above his lip, which she found herself comparing to Fred Kindler's red one, and the thought struck her that she'd do better to go to Fred with her grief. She was sure his faith was not so damn supple as to allow the idea that what Francis was up to was exploring. She shook the treacherous thought away. How did she know what Kindler believed? Besides, he was her boss, not her priest.

She knew Woodward missed the point on purpose, so she pressed on. "Coming to Miss Oliver's was the best thing that could have happened to Francis and me. We found our calling. And now he risks it all," she said and went on to remind him that the only thing Francis knew about what he wanted to do with the rest of his life before Marjorie had hired them was that he didn't want to be a businessman. "Though he didn't have the foggiest idea what a businessman does," she said. "It was just what his father did."

"He knew you had to wear a suit." Father Woodward smiled. He was dwarfed by his chair, his tiny hands motionless in his lap. His knitting sat on the pile of papers on his desk in his dark little office, and she knew he was itching to get his hands on the needles. She'd advised him lots of times not to let his parishioners know he knitted.

"If it were fly tying or something, it would be okay," she said. "But knitting! You give your parishioners too much credit. This isn't San Francisco. It's New England. We're even less broadminded than you think."

Father Woodward's eyes flitted to his knitting, but he didn't move his hands. His eyes behind the owlish glasses focused on her. He didn't say anything. He was taking courses on how to counsel, Peggy thought. How to be like a shrink. But she didn't want his advice, let alone his therapy. She wanted his prayer.

She had no idea how hard her friend was working not to tell her what he thought she should discover for herself. *It's not just panic that is driving Francis*, he wanted to say. *It is also courage. Francis shouldn't have to defend his spiritual quest to anyone. It's his escaping, his running away, that's indefensible. He's going to have to figure out for himself that he can't do both at once.* But Peggy was not ready to hear this yet. So he waited.

"Francis has been having dreams too, all year," she told him. "I wonder if he's still having them way out there in the West, and if he is," she added, "I probably wouldn't understand them."

"That's not surprising," Father Woodward said. "If you could understand them, you would have gone with him."

"That's not fair," Peggy said, and Father Woodward shrugged his little shoulders. "And it's beside the point," she added.

"All right then, my dear, what is the point?"

"You tell me," she demanded. It was his last chance. Silently she was begging him, *Don't tell me he's questing. Tell me he's straying. Say* let us pray*!*

Father Woodward looked out the window to the bright sunshine on the lawn. "It's easier to explain than to understand," he murmured. "You could *explain* it. A Sioux medicine man could tell him what's really going on. But where are we going to find a Sioux?" Father

Woodward turned his face from the window and added, "One could claim they're the same. What Francis wants and what you believe."

Oh, please! Don't be so damn liberal! she wanted to yell. *I don't need a priest who believes in Everything.* Instead, she kept her face as expressionless as possible. He had enough problems without knowing how much he'd failed her.

Father Woodward shrugged. "Don't you two grow apart," he begged. "I couldn't bear it."

"It's time to go," she said, stretching the truth. She had plenty of time, and so did he. She stood, moved to his desk, leaned over it, and kissed him tenderly on his forehead like a sister—her forgiveness. His bald pate gleamed beneath her eyes. He kept his hands flat on the desk as if keeping it from flying away. His face was slightly flushed.

"I'll pray for you both," he murmured, and she went out into the bright summer light.

STRAIGHT TO EUDORA'S studio. If Father Woodward couldn't help her, surely Eudora could.

Peggy loved the smell of the studio: turpentine, clay, oil paints, dust. Her spirits lifted as soon as she was through the door. Ever since Marjorie had hired Eudora, a young artist, newly widowed and still thin, thirty-two years ago, just one year after she hired Peggy and Francis, Eudora had been the colleague whom Peggy trusted the most.

"I've lost him," Peggy began. And stopped when Eudora shook her head. "All right, an exaggeration," she admitted. "But it's how I feel."

"You don't lose them until they die. That's when they go away." Eudora tossed this off, a bright, encouraging matter of fact. She was not speaking from grief—her husband died years ago, two weeks after their honeymoon, drowned absurdly in a swamp on a reserve Marine Corps training exercise—but from memory of grief. She sat motionless in her red work smock in her chair across from Peggy's, more of a presence even than the mammoth wooden chairs she had inspired her students to create. Kinesthetic sculptures she called them, her latest enthusiasm. They dominated the space. And demonstrated

Miss Oliver's at its best. For here was one of the several areas in which the school had freed itself from the ant mentality that craved to departmentalize the curriculum of almost every school. As if life came in boxes! These creations surrounding Peggy in her colleague's studio were at once furniture and works of art and machines. And also jokes—as if to prove that, in the right atmosphere, teenagers could be counted on not to take themselves too seriously. The piece nearest Peggy was a red-white-and-blue throne, bright and arresting in the cracked and crazed enamel of its varnished paint, that played "The Star Spangled Banner" as soon as you sat in it—so that you had to stand up—and, of course, stopped playing as soon as you did. It was the sixth version; the first five had not been sufficient and were destroyed.

"Francis is doing what he needs to do," Eudora said.

"No, he's not. He's running away."

Eudora shook her head again. "Let's not talk about Francis. Let's talk about you and what you need to do."

"Like what?"

"See? I knew this wouldn't take long," Eudora smiled.

"Like what?" Peggy repeated.

"Like helping this new guy save the school. That's what you *need* to do."

"Of course. But what has that got to do—?"

"We save the school, we save everything."

"I already gave him some advice," Peggy murmured.

"And that's all you're going to do?"

Now Peggy was too restless to sit. She got up, moved around the room, stopped next to a larger-than-life sculpture, the one she loved best. It was Humpty Dumpty sitting on a wall, and in the center of his round, white stomach was a door that let you inside to sit on a bench where, when you pulled a lever, Humpty fell off the wall and came apart into exactly fifteen pieces. The students who had thought it up, designed it, and built it named the piece *Undefeated* because they, unlike the king's men, could put Humpty back together again—in a jiffy.

Peggy rubbed her hand over Humpty's smooth surface. She thought she knew what Eudora was going to say; it brought a little surge of joy.

"You can help him recruit," Eudora said. "Travel around the country selling the school with him and Gail and Nan. You'll be good at it. You'll be wonderful."

Peggy had no doubt that she could speak for the school, and she wanted to. But that's not what she needed to hear. For on the heels of her excitement about it came her anger. "That's what Francis should do!" she exclaimed. "It's his job."

"So you do it," Eudora said. "You're just as senior as Francis is. You be the head's right hand."

"Me?"

"Oh, baby!" Eudora murmured. "I've been counting on it." It was true; she'd seen this coming, as soon as she learned that Marjorie was fired.

Peggy knew how striking this exchange of roles would be. "What place will Francis have when he comes back?" she wondered aloud.

Eudora studied her and smiled. "You're catching on," she said.

"I don't want to catch on. I'm no politician."

"Yes, you are. Everybody is."

"It will create an even bigger separation between me and Francis."

"And this is the way to heal it. How else? Run after him and drag him back? Go out there with him and pretend to be an Indian?"

This was too much for Peggy all at once. She needed to be alone now. She needed time to think.

And besides, here came Mary Bradford, a tall, blond kid with coltish legs, a summer student, into the studio. Mary had been so eager to get away from her family in San Francisco, where she'd been for only a week since the school year ended, that here she was back on campus two days before summer school began. She was carrying a big black portfolio case. In spite of the bounce in her step, she had the drawn look teenagers get when they are tired and won't admit it. After flying in from the West Coast yesterday, she had stayed up most of the night to finish her drawings and couldn't wait to show them to Eudora.

"Hello, Mary," Peggy said, then turned to Eudora, smiled her goodbye, and started to move away. Mary was Eudora's business, not hers. Besides, she couldn't wait to be alone.

"No," Eudora urged. "Stay here with us." She wanted Peggy to see the drawings.

Eudora revered Mary's talent, which she knew was greater than her own; she was using all her skill and passion in nurturing it. That was what Miss Oliver's was all about. She wanted to confront Peggy with the result of her teaching, so clear in the blossoming of Mary's work. Maybe that would stir Peggy to acknowledge that if they save the school, they save everything she cared about, including her marriage. After all, the Plummers were as much married to the school as they were to each other—and what was wrong with that? She turned to Mary. "Let's show your work to Mrs. Plummer too."

Mary hesitated

"Mary, Mrs. Plummer is my friend."

That was all Eudora needed to say. For Eudora's claim to an adult affection, to loyalty and trust, named exactly what was absent in Mary's family—and the original reason for her having been sent away from home. "I'd love to have you see them," Mary said to Peggy, and now Peggy had no choice. Later, she would realize how clever Eudora was being.

Mary took her drawings out of the case and laid them side by side on a big table. Eudora studied them. A year ago, she would have praised all of Mary's work. But now, a year of hard work later, the stakes were up; she'd award no easy praise. She said nothing for the longest time, merely looked.

"It's a joke," Mary told Peggy, breaking the silence—and Eudora's rule: *Never explain. If it's not clear on the paper, do it again.* But she couldn't help it, she loved her idea too much to chance Peggy's not getting it. "It's a double computer," she said. "The place you put your feet is one keyboard—we'll use organ pedals with the letters painted on them—and the other's a wrap-around, so you can type with your feet and your hands at the same time, write two different books. And that's not all. We'll start with a hairdresser's chair. It'll have one of those weird old-fashioned hair dryer hoods so you can write two books and get a shampoo all at once!"

Eudora was still looking at the drawings, frowning now. It was as if she hadn't heard a word. "I'm sorry," Mary said to Eudora's back. "I broke the rule. But my parents are always bragging about how busy they are. Multitasking," she added. "How's that for a stupid word?"

Eudora ignored Mary's excuse and kept her back to her, still staring down at the drawings. She pointed with her left hand to the first picture in the sequence. "This one's good," she said. "Very good. These are even better." She pointed with her right hand to the next three in the sequence.

"Thanks," Mary said.

"Don't thank *me*, dear," Eudora answered. Then abruptly picking up the fifth drawing, holding it with both arms extended in front of her, she said, "What about this one?"

Mary hesitated.

"What about this one?" Eudora insisted.

"I was in a hurry."

"Do it again."

A tiny smile appeared on Mary's face. Peggy thought she looked relieved.

"Tomorrow?" Eudora asked.

"All right. I'll bring it in tomorrow," Mary said. Then, pointing to the sixth drawing: "What about this one?"

Now it was Eudora who was smiling. She shook her head back and forth and didn't answer. She knew that Mary understood: *We'll look at the sixth when the fifth one's as good as it can get.*

"That's what I thought," Mary said. She gathered her drawings into her case, slowly, deliberately, while Peggy and Eudora watched. Then she smiled at Peggy. "Thanks," she said, and turned to Eudora. "Same time tomorrow?"

Eudora nodded. "I'll be right here," she said, and Peggy thought, *Yes, and the next day too and the next and the next and the one after that*, and knew—as if there had ever been a time when she didn't!—how right Eudora was: *We save the school, we save everything!*

She followed Mary out the door and headed for Fred Kindler's office to tell him he needed *her* on his recruiting trips.

TWO THOUSAND MILES away on the outskirts of Denver, Lila Smythe and her mother, Tylor, waited at Tylor's house for Francis to pick up Lila for the trip to California and the dig. He'd been expected over an hour ago.

Mother and daughter were drinking their morning coffee at a little table on the patio. They were very much alike: tall, sturdy, their blond hair cut short. Tylor's was fading. She wore dark glasses against the glare. She glanced at her watch. "Where do you think he is?" she asked, hoping that Francis was still miles away so that she could extend this time with her daughter.

"He'll be here," Lila answered. She felt a rush of tenderness for her mother, knowing how lonely she was going to be. She kept her voice casual to hide her eagerness to get going. "He's absentminded. He's probably lost the directions."

"What do you think he'll do if—?" Tylor started to ask, and then stopped. She knew this worry irritated her daughter, but she couldn't leave it alone.

It was true. Lila had been home for two weeks, and almost every day her mother had brought up her worry that Miss Oliver's would abandon its single-sex mission. She'd never thought of her mother as a worrier before, and it was making her impatient. "Don't worry, Mom, we'd never let the school go coed," she had insisted each time. This time she didn't. She was tired of the subject, so she changed it. "Look, Mom." She moved her chair around the table, put her hands on her mother's shoulders, and turned her. Now they both stared at the side of the house. It caught the fierce light of the morning sun. The stucco glowed. "Light's so different out here!" she said. "You taught me that. Back east it's—"

"Pastel," her mother supplied the word. She turned her head back to Lila, grazing her daughter's cheek with her lips. "Thinner. Watery and vague. It's the first thing I noticed when I escaped out here."

That word: *escape*. Sometimes Lila envisioned her mother as if she were emblazoned with a sign: *I escaped. That's who I am.* Her mother's refrain: that she had divorced her husband fifteen years ago when she realized he would never think of her painting as anything more than a nice weekend hobby for a wife, and then picked Denver off the map as the place to live because she didn't have any family there to criticize her, especially not her father, who had refused to send her to college. He had paid her tuition to Katherine Gibbs instead so she could be a secretary. "Yes, I know," Lila would say.

"But you refused to go. You got yourself a full scholarship at Smith instead. And now you're a painter. A *professional.*" What she didn't say anymore to her mother—now that she knew how much it hurt—was that she wished she had a father.

Lila was grateful to her mother for sending her to a school where there were no males to paint over the picture of what she chose to become. Now she knew that when you can choose what to do with your life, *then what you do is who you are.* It scared her to know that. And made her happy. It was why she sucked up all the biographies of women that Gregory van Buren kept giving her to read, one after another. How did he know this was exactly what she needed?

And here was Francis Plummer coming around the corner of the house. He must have heard their voices. "Hello," he said. "Sorry I'm late. I got a little lost." Tylor was surprised to see how tired he looked.

He joined them at the table and told them what he'd seen on his journey, how flat the middle of the country was, how stunning his first sight of the Rockies was—but nothing of what he'd been thinking about.

Then there was a little silence, and Tylor said, "We were just wondering what you would do if Miss Oliver's went coed."

"You were, Mother. I wasn't," Lila said. "I wasn't even thinking about it."

"All right," Tylor acknowledged "I was. And I pay the tuition." She was looking intently at Francis, waiting for his answer.

"Well?" Tylor persisted, and Francis still didn't answer. "Evidently, I've hit a hot spot," Tylor said.

"Mother, please, it's not going to happen," Lila said, but Tylor's eyes were still on Francis.

"It's not a hot spot for me," Francis finally said. "Because Lila's right. It won't happen."

"A school can't change its mission?"

"It's not a mission; it's what we are," Francis said. "The alumnae won't let it happen." What was going to happen already had: Marjorie's being thrown out. The rest he couldn't imagine.

Tylor shook her head, not convinced.

"The students wouldn't either," Lila said, looking at Francis now, chastising him with her eyes for not including the students in the saving of the school.

"Don't be naive," her mother warned.

Lila smiled. *Naive is what I'm not,* she wanted to say, feeling a slight resentment that her mother couldn't see how much she'd changed. She wouldn't have to explain it to anyone at school. "I mean it, Mom, we'd burn the school down first."

Tylor wasn't going to answer hyperbole. Instead, she turned to Francis and asked her other question. "Why didn't they make you the headmaster?"

"Mother!" Lila exclaimed "For God's sake!"

Francis was too surprised to speak. The idea of his being the head had never crossed his mind. Tylor Smythe leaned slightly forward, waiting for an answer. Her dark glasses masked her eyes.

"Mother, he's a teacher!" Lila said.

Tylor kept her eyes on Francis. "Is that the answer?" she asked him.

"I've never thought of myself as a head," he answered, stunned to realize it.

"Shouldn't the best, most experienced teacher be the head? The one who understands the school the best?" Tylor's question was perfectly logical—for one who didn't understand how proud many teachers were to think of themselves as labor, and how preferable the act of teaching was to sitting, removed from students and the subject that you love, in an office worrying about diplomacy, budgets, trustees, and strategic planning. As if a school were merely a business!

Francis was still too stunned to answer. Tyler leaned back in her chair. "All right, I won't go there," she said. "I didn't mean to pry. I'm sorry."

"It's all right, Mother," Lila said. "It's just not who he is, that's all. It's hard to explain." Then she looked at her watch, glanced at Francis. "I've had enough coffee," she told him, getting up to leave. "I'm going to put my backpack in the car."

Tylor watched her daughter walk away. Francis saw the longing in her face. Lila disappeared inside the house, and Tylor turned her eyes back to Francis. "Did you notice how she said that?"

"What?" he asked, jolted by the sudden change of subject. He needed to linger over her question, why he wasn't the headmaster of Miss Oliver's School for Girls. It seemed that everything was happening much too fast.

"*The* car. If it were my car she would have said *your* car."

"Oh, I don't know—"

Tylor took off her dark glasses, studied his face. Now he could see her eyes. There were gray, little lines around them. "She never sees her father," Tylor said

"I know. She told me."

"Sometimes I think she fantasizes that you're her dad."

"Oh, no! She wouldn't do that."

"Why wouldn't she? You and your wife—married for years!—make a home for her where everything that's important to her happens. My home is just where she visits. It makes me sad."

Francis wanted to avert his eyes. He felt much too vulnerable to be getting into this.

She reached across the table, took his hand as if she'd known him for years. "I'm grateful. To you and your wife. In loco parentis. That's the phrase, isn't it? Can't do that and also find time to be the head. Maybe that's what Lila meant."

"Thank you," Francis murmured. He didn't know how to tell her it was not what Lila had meant.

"Well, give me a minute to say goodbye to my daughter." She let go of his hand, and stood and put her dark glasses on again. "Then join us in the driveway, and I'll wave goodbye to both of you."

She went out to the driveway to help her daughter put her things in the car. Lila was already finished when she got there. Lila closed the trunk of Francis's car and turned to hug her mother. "Thanks, Mom," she said. "Thanks for everything." She meant *thanks for escaping*. And *thanks for letting me go.*

Francis was coming down the driveway now. He said, "I guess we'd better say goodbye," and he and Lila got in the car and closed the doors, and her mother leaned in through the window and said goodbye again. Francis backed the car out of the driveway, and Lila waved to her mother, who lingered in the driveway. She knew her mother would go straight to her studio—and smother her loneliness with her work.

Hours and hours later, Lila barreled the dented yellow Chevy down Route 80 in Nevada, and Francis sat in the shotgun seat watching her out of the corner of his eye. Her two sturdy arms reached forward, her hands gripped the steering wheel, she stared straight down the road. She drove just like Marjorie Boyd, he thought; everything gets out of the way. She was going someplace, this kid, blasting forward toward some passion that she would ride on for a lifetime. He thought of Siddy, his son, so different, wandering in Europe, tasting everything, circling, and lonely suddenly, he riffed on the fantasy that Lila's mother had planted: that he and Peggy had adopted Lila too, Siddy's younger sister by five years, and the two kids were telepathic, they didn't need words to understand each other at the core.

He wondered if Lila remembered how much she had disapproved of herself when she arrived at the school three years ago—for her tallness, her thick legs, her braces. Now she liked her tallness, she thought her sturdy legs were just fine, and her braces were gone. In a coed school Lila would be one of the girls whom the boys didn't want to date. At Miss Oliver's she was president-elect of the student council; she would have more influence than many of the faculty.

"It's weird how things happen," Lila finally said without turning her head. Neither of them had said a word for miles. "If some little man, an archaeologist with a funny name, didn't show up at school in February and give a speech, I'd still be in Denver now with my mom instead of here."

"I didn't think it was a funny name," Francis said. "Livingstone Mendoza, what's so funny about that?"

Lila smiled at his little joke. "I knew the minute he started to talk that I was going to sign up," she said.

"Me too," Francis murmured, remembering the little man, almost as small as Father Woodward, standing at the lip of the stage, promising that they would find the remains of the village that was there on the side of the mountain for thousands of years before the Europeans came. "So they could see what the Ohlones saw," he had said, "maybe even dream their dreams." Blue work shirt, dark tie, brown corduroy pants, and hiking boots. Mendoza's intensity had made up for his small size, and his voice had filled the auditorium.

"How could I have spent three years at our school and passed up this chance?" Lila asked. "Three years thinking about, and then pass up this chance to be."

"I guessed that you would sign up," Francis said. "It didn't surprise me. Though quite a few of the people on the faculty thought he was a phony. Or a lunatic," he added, remembering Mendoza's telling them that the Ohlones were not just outnumbered by the animals but by every species of animal, and claiming in a kind of chant that "if we put one of you and one of them side by side in their world, you would see emptiness and would despair. They would see the majesty of First Things, the nearness of God."

For the first time, Lila took her eyes off the road, glanced at Francis. "But not you?" she asked. "You didn't think he was a phony?"

"No, not me."

"Why not? I mean, he was kind of intense. Sort of overboard."

Francis hesitated. He'd concede Mendoza's funny name, but he didn't think he was overboard at all.

"Like, you'll be three thousand miles away from home for two months, away from your wife and the school."

"Yeah, it's a long way."

"So why'd you come if it's so far away?"

"I'm only gone for the summer," he said, thinking of his conversation with her mother. "You're away from home from September to June."

Lila frowned, took one hand off the wheel to push her blond hair away from her forehead. "Now you're acting just like my mother," she said. "Whenever she doesn't want to tell me something I want to know, she changes the subject."

"All right," he said, giving in. "It's like this: Once when I was a little kid, I was fishing with my dad." He began to speak very fast now that he'd discovered he was going to tell her this amazing thing. "In a canoe. And a huge turtle swam up to the surface of the lake. Came right up beside me where I was in the bow of the canoe. He looked right at me, looked me right in the eyes." He stopped talking suddenly, aware of how foolish he sounded.

"And you looked back at him," Lila finished.

"Yes."

"And then he went away?" Lila's voice was very quiet.

"Yes. And then he went away."

"You recognized each other," she announced, and now he was surprised at how matter-of-fact her voice was. "He chose you," she said. "He's your totem. From out of the time when the earth was here and human beings were not." All Francis could think about was how different this kid's reaction was from Peggy's when he tried to tell her what this moment meant to him.

"Thanks for telling me. I know you better now," Lila said. "I've always wanted to know you. Now I do. Thanks."

Later, in a campground near Winnemucca, Lila waited for sleep to come. She'd rather have been out under the stars, but Francis had insisted she put up her tent and sleep in it. Afraid some crazy rapist would come through. "Who knows who comes to public places like this?" he'd asked. Speaking like a dad! He was in his tent too, not far from hers. She imagined she could hear his breathing over the noise of the big trucks on Route 80 half a mile away. She shivered with her happiness and hugged herself, and then she fell asleep.

FIVE

In Fred Kindler's office Peggy was saying, "I think I can help you," and wondering if he could hear the shyness in her voice. She still felt she was usurping Francis's place. "I think I'd be a good recruiter."

Fred didn't respond for several seconds that seemed like forever. *Forget it*, she wanted to say. *It was just an idea.*

In fact, he loved it. He was embarrassed that he had hesitated, caught assuming that Francis should be the one, not her. But he was sure she was right. "I should have thought of it myself," he said. "You've been here longer and know the school better than anyone."

"Except my husband," Peggy murmured She needed to let Fred know he was forgiven.

"Yes. Well, he's busy. He'd help if he could," Fred said, and Peggy thought, *Thanks. Thanks for saying that*, wondering if her new friend would be this diplomatic if he weren't the headmaster.

TWO DAYS LATER, the plane that Fred and Gail Kindler, Nan White, and Peggy took from Bradley Field to Hopkins Airport in Cleveland was two hours late; by the time they got across the airport and into their rented car for the drive to Shaker Heights, they knew the audience of potential students and their parents had already been gathered for half an hour in Steven and Sharon Maynard's house. They arrived at the Maynard's front porch at eight-thirty, feeling harried and rushed—an hour and fifteen minutes tardy, just as the summer sun was setting. Above them, draped from a second-story window, was a big American flag to celebrate the Fourth of July weekend, which would start in just two days.

Sharon Maynard greeted them in the spill of light from the front door of the big brick house, a tall, angular woman in her late forties, dressed in a white blouse and a floor-length blue skirt. Her faded blond hair was pulled severely back, her face was pale, and she wore no makeup; Peggy remembered a rounder face. But she felt warmly greeted when Sharon took her hand and smiled, then did the same with Nan. "It's lovely to see you again," Sharon said. "I'm glad you're still at the school." Nan let the comment go, and while Sharon was still holding her hand, Nan turned to the Kindlers, standing to her right, and introduced them. Very slowly, Sharon released Nan's hand and then proffered her own, only partway and limply, and just the end of her fingers, first to Gail, then to Fred, while looking at a space above their heads. The Kindlers pretended they didn't notice the slight.

Then they were in the house, and they heard the noise of conversation stop, and Steven Maynard was greeting them in the front hall. He was still in his brown business suit, a big man gone comfortably to roundness who wore a fifties crew cut. He took Gail's hand and held on. "Gail! Welcome to our house. Thanks for dropping your own work and coming all the way out here to be with us." Then he turned to Fred. "And Fred! We're glad you're here!" When he bent down to put his huge hand on Fred's shoulder, Peggy and Nan exchanged quick glances of gratitude, and Peg felt the impulse to hug this big, round bear. Behind Steven, through the archway into the living room, the guests were watching.

Steven put his long arms out as if to corral the four of them and shepherded them into the living room, leaving his wife in the doorway, and Peggy saw the surprise appear on Sharon's face. She watched the expression glide into a pout. Steven was not going to let her make the introductions! He had seen the way she greeted Fred and Gail. Peggy felt another rush of gratitude.

The furniture had been pulled to the sides of the Maynard's airy living room to make room for the folding chairs, where at least forty people sat. The walls were a stark white; an Oriental rug covered the center of the polished hardwood floor, and abstract paintings hung on the walls. Peggy thought they were ugly. It flashed through her mind that maybe Steven didn't like them either.

The four recruiters sat down in folding chairs at the front of the room facing the audience. Peggy scanned the room, looking at every face. There was no one here she didn't recognize. She knew everyone there! Couldn't remember everyone's name, but recognized every face. So everyone was either a parent of a present Oliver student, or an alumna, or a parent of an alumna. *Wait!* she thought. *There's been some mistake. Not one potential new family is present! Not a single girl of high school age is here!* She glanced across the room at Sharon Maynard, who stood in the archway to the living room, watching Peggy discover this. It dawned on Peggy then that maybe this wasn't a mistake. She stared at Sharon's eyes, burning in, until Sharon had to look away, and then Peggy knew: it *wasn't* a mistake.

She heard Steven introduce her first. But she didn't hear much of what he said because, along with her surprise at such treachery, she was aware that everyone in the audience was looking at her, not at Steven, while he talked. Their eyes pinned her to the wall as if to ask, *Whose side are you on?*

His, she wanted to answer, anger flooding. *That's right, his side. I'm loyal to him, this new guy, the man—and you better be too.* She wanted to jump up in the middle of Steven's little speech and explain to these people all the reasons why Marjorie had to go. Instead—for she would keep her cool—she forced herself to smile and nodded her head in acknowledgment of the warm applause for her that she knew Fred wouldn't get when he was introduced.

She needed to lean across Nan and Gail and whisper the news to Fred—make sure he understood no potential families were there to recruit, so he wouldn't make a fool of himself. Nan couldn't be sure; she hadn't been with the school long enough to know everyone in the room. But Steven had already begun his introduction, and Fred was already standing up. "I'm proud and delighted to introduce our new head," Steven said, doing his best to whip up enthusiasm. "We are fortunate to have a person of such high caliber." Peggy searched the crowd to see if others noticed *person* instead of *man*. Faces were stony, expressionless, the clapping halfhearted, so minimally polite as to be insulting, and Peggy was amazed at the fierceness of the feelings in the room, which burnt even fiercer now as Fred Kindler stood to make himself their target. It wasn't until these last few months since Marjorie was fired that Peggy had truly begun to learn, deep in her gut, not merely in her brain, just how volatile school communities are, how charged with emotion. She was getting another lesson right then and wondering where she'd been. The answer, of course, was that she'd never been at the head's right hand, let alone at this new one's, who had to follow in Marjorie Boyd's footsteps and do all the things she wouldn't do, and wasn't even the right gender. She wouldn't take Fred Kindler's job for a million dollars.

"Thank you for coming to hear about our school," Fred began, and Peggy's heart sunk. "And thanks also to you alumnae and parents who have brought friends so they can learn about our school," Fred went on, for he wasn't cynical enough—not yet—to believe this absence of school-age girls was the result of a dirty trick. In fact, the idea didn't even occur to him. He assumed instead that these parents wanted to check out the school—and him—on their own, before their daughters got interested. He would have preferred a less cautious approach, but he took what he could get and soldiered on. "And if what my colleagues and I say tonight inspires you enough, as I believe it will, to persuade your daughters and the daughters of your friends to hear more, we would be delighted to return and talk with them." But now, someone in the back row was laughing. And a surprised, embarrassed expression appeared on many of the faces, and Fred hesitated, and Peggy saw a look of confusion on his face.

Then she watched him guess the real reason why there were no Oliver-age girls in the audience. Steven Maynard, who had just taken his own seat in the front row, stood up again.

"I'm sorry, Fred" he said. "I assumed we had sent you the lists of who was coming and who wasn't." He glanced, appalled, at his wife, who was still standing in the archway.

Fred nodded an acknowledgment to Steven, turned back to his audience, didn't miss a beat. "Well, then," he offered, "since you obviously know the school, let's get to know each other." Peggy was awed at her new head's quick-footedness.

No response from the audience. Stony faces still, staring at Fred. They left him hanging.

Peggy watched Fred as he figured out what to say next. He wasn't quick enough. "Oh, it's all so slick!" a red-haired woman in the second row exclaimed. Peggy couldn't remember her name, who her daughter was. Next to her, her husband nodded his head in vehement assent. “A very professional spin job, your coming here,” the woman continued. She wore a red dress as if to match her hair. “But we didn’t come here to hear you talk. We came to ask you questions.”

“That’s right,” called from the back row. “We have questions.” It was Mrs. Johnstone. Peggy knew her well, the mother of Karen Johnstone, a terrific kid who lived in Peggy and Francis’s dorm. “Lots of them.” Mrs. Johnstone’s voice was brass. “We have lots of questions.”

“We’re angry!” the woman in the red dress exclaimed, looking as if she were about to cry, and Mr. Loyal Spouse next to her made a show of holding her hand while Peggy’s disgust blossomed. *Let your wife be angry all by herself, idiot!* she thought.

Now Carl Beecher stood up in the back row. He was short, very round, and bald. Peggy knew him, the father of two alumnae and a present senior. Her spirits rose; she knew *he’d* say the right things.

She was right. Carl looked directly at Fred: “Yes, there’s a lot of anger,” he admitted in a gentle voice. “But it’s certainly not your fault. *You* didn’t fire Marjorie. We need to move on.”

Thank you, Fred wanted to say, for he was certainly grateful, but decided he wouldn’t. That would make Carl’s statement of fact look like sop to a weak leader. So he merely nodded his head at Carl.

“That’s exactly right, we need to move on!” Steven Maynard said. He smiled at Carl, then stared at the woman in the red dress to shut her up. Then he turned to Fred: “So Fred, let’s hear your thoughts.”

“First *I* have question,” Carl announced before Fred had a chance to begin. Still standing in the back, he faced the archway and stared at Sharon. “It’s not for Mr. Kindler,” Carl added, and Sharon blanched, knowing what was coming. “Why didn’t you tell us this was a recruiting gathering?” Carl asked, speaking very slowly. Sharon’s tall frame stiffened, and she didn’t answer. “Instead of just a chance to meet the new head,” Carl continued. In the front, Steven turned to stare across the room at his wife. “You set him up,” Carl said to Sharon. “Didn’t you? You called us up, but you didn’t ask us to bring anyone. I bet you didn’t even call the list of families the school sent you.” Everyone’s eyes swung from Carl to Sharon, like people watching a tennis match.

“I’m right, aren’t I?” Carl persisted. “Aren’t I, Sharon. You set him up.” Steven Maynard was still staring at his wife. It was all over his face that he knew the answer.

Now Fred knew exactly what to do to be the leader. He would take them down a better track. "I don't think we need to pursue this," he said. "Let's not go down that road." Peggy was amazed again.

Carl turned away from Sharon, put his eyes on Fred. Steven did too, facing completely around, putting his back to his wife. His face was very pale as he sat down. In the back, Carl sat too. Sharon remained standing.

"I understand how people feel," Fred said into the silence. He moved his eyes around the room, seeking individual faces. "I'm glad you've put it on the table."

Hooray for you! Peggy thought. *You're running this thing, you're the boss!*

"I know the size of the shoes I have to fill," she heard Fred say next. "With your help, I'll fill them"—and suddenly she was very angry. *Oh, don't be so damn humble!* Peggy waned to yell, and the next thing she knew she was on her feet, and she was the one who was making a speech.

"Marjorie resigned of her own free will," she lied. "You need to know that. She decided on her own to quit," she heard herself saying. "She was tired. She knew the school needed new ideas." She looked into people's eyes, stared them down. "All right, I shouldn't have interrupted. But he"—nodding at Fred—"is too gracious to say it, and it needed to be said." *So get over it!* she wanted to add, *just get over it!* She felt Fred's eyes and turned from the audience to meet them, and sat down. Her knees were shaking; she felt empty, as if she'd been holding her breath.

In the silence that Peggy had created, Fred felt a surge of joy. He began to talk, listing the traits that made Miss Oliver's so special. The tension in the room began to melt—except for the lady in red, who whispered something to her husband. Fred went on, telling the audience what they needed to know—that he loved what they loved about the school.

He's proving me right, Peggy thought. *He knows what he's doing, understands what works.* She scanned the audience again. They were listening, at least. *Give this man a chance*, she wanted to say.

A few minute later, Fred finished and invited discussion. It was near the end of the meeting, and he was sure he was going to win this game. Steven Maynard stood, and everybody knew he was going to ask an easy question, throw a softball. But Steven didn't get a chance because the woman in red stood again. "You've been avoiding the subject all evening," she said. "Do you plan to admit boys, or don't you?"

"Why shouldn't I avoid it?" Fred snapped back. "Since it never crossed my mind." He felt another rush of joy: that he could lie so quickly!

"So?" Her voice rose. "You're telling us there is absolutely no circumstance—none whatsoever—under which you would consider admitting boys?"

Fred hesitated for just an instant, and Peggy waited, and Fred hesitated another instant—to draw breath, intending to blast this woman—but Peggy wasn't waiting any longer, she was on her feet again. "You heard him," she said, focusing on the woman as if there were no one else in the room. "You heard what he said. No boys. Ever. That's what he said. And he's the headmaster. Why do you even bring it up?"

Steven was looking at Fred. "Exactly!" Fred said. "Exactly why I didn't bring it up." He stared at the woman until she sat down. And then he realized: *This has to end right now.*

As if reading Fred's mind, Steven turned to the audience. "That's a good place to end this meeting," he announced. The audience was obviously surprised. There was a restless shuffling.

"Wait!" said Sharon from the archway. "We're not finished."

But Steven turned his back on his wife. His gesture was blatant, his disgust obvious. Then he stepped across to the front of the room and took Fred's hand in both of his and pumped it. "We're so glad you're here!" he boomed. "You're just what the school needs." Then, turning back to his guests: "Thanks so much for coming, everyone. Drive safely."

Still, the audience was in their seats. They turned to look at Sharon—like basketball players waiting for the second referee to reverse the call of the first. To no avail: she was not looking at the audience, she was clenching her fists, and trying not to cry, and staring at her husband, who had turned his back to her again. The guests wanted no part of this! They moved quickly to the door and out of the house.

Moments later, Steven stood in the doorway—conspicuously without his wife—saying goodbye to the four recruiters. He put his big hand lightly on Peggy's shoulder and said to Fred: "You've got some damn good people around you, don't you, Fred!"

"You bet," said Fred.

On the way back to the airport Gail drove; Fred sat next to her in the front. "I'm coming back someday," Nan announced from her seat in the back next to Peggy. "Mark my words, I'm coming back to exterminate Mrs. Sharon Maynard."

"I'll help," Gail said. "I'll bring the poison."

Neither Peggy nor Fred could bring themselves to speak. Peggy thought it was time to keep her mouth shut. She feared she'd made Fred look weak when she butted in and spoke up for him that second time, saying, "You heard what he said." As if he couldn't speak for himself.

And Fred was marveling at how quickly his lie had flown out of his mouth. He wasn't the slightest bit ashamed. He wanted to turn to explain to Peggy that he really hadn't needed her to stand up and save the day for him. But that would seem defensive and ungrateful. And then it dawned on him that his new friend *had* saved him, not from his reluctance to persevere in an untruth, but from his temper. He'd been drawing breath to blast the woman when Peggy stood up and blasted her for him, much more temperately than he would have. He would have told the red-headed woman to sit down and shut up and asked her who the hell she thought she was to argue with him. *That would have made a great impression!* he told himself.

"I'll check next time," Nan said. "I promise. I'll check the guest list myself. I won't give anybody another chance to be so treacherous."

"Please don't apologize," Fred said. "There's no way you could know that anyone would be like that."

"I do now," Nan said, and Peggy was struck again by how fascinating was the lesson she was getting about the leadership of schools. From now on when she would think of school politics she'd think of red cans of gasoline—and lit matches.

Thirty minutes later as Peggy and Gail got out of the same

side of the car at the rent-return, Gail put her hand on Peggy's arm. "Thanks," she murmured. "When he has to tell a fib, he needs lots of help." Gail didn't know how far her husband had progressed in the art of diplomacy since becoming the headmaster of Miss Oliver's School for Girls.

Peggy didn't answer right away. *Here's Gail,* she thought, *right here with her husband, while Francis and I are miles apart.* She thought about Steven Maynard turning his back on his wife, and the parallel between what the trauma of Miss Oliver's was doing to the Maynards' marriage and her own did not escape her. "Do you think they believed me?" she asked at last.

"Some of them. Maybe. Just a little. Anyway, it saved the day."

"That's good," Peggy said. To herself, she thought: *If Francis had been there—if he'd said it—they would have believed.*

MILES AND MILES away, across three time zones, Francis ate a paltry supper just outside the boundary of Mount Alma State Park, where Livingstone Mendoza's ardent little band was in the second week of its search for the Ohlone village. Francis, Lila, and the nine other students in his team sat in the long shadow of one of the huge oaks in the dry smell of oat grass that Mendoza had carefully explained didn't exist in the Indian days; it came with the oats the Spaniards fed their horses, which then shat the seeds over the hills, the horse food as new to the country as the horses were, as invasive, Mendoza accused, as their pale-skinned riders.

Francis and his companions refused to look east to where the tops of the hills were being scraped away, and south where already the exuberant vulgarity of a thousand steroid mansions spread like a rash to the horizon. Instead they looked only westward, down over the lion-colored hills toward an area where there were still no houses, where they sought the mounded earth that covered the thousand-year accumulation of ashes, bones, shells. Francis had been keeping to himself his growing conviction that the allotted time to find the village, between now and the end of August, was nowhere near enough. He was beginning to feel slightly absurd, embarrassed as if caught believing a gnat could conquer an elephant, to think that in all this space they could find the little village in so little time.

Now, just as the little band stood up from their supper to return to work, they saw Mendoza trudging up the hill toward them. He had an angry expression on his face.

"Greed!" exclaimed Mendoza, panting and waving his arms as he arrived. "Greed, irreverence, and intransigence. I've never seen so much!"

"What?" Francis interrupted.

"They just don't care!" Mendoza said.

"What?" Francis asked again. "Who doesn't care about what?" The last thing he wanted was to listen to Mendoza rant. There was only a little time before it would be too dark to work, and they needed every minute they could get.

"A thousand years!" Mendoza pointed his arm down the hill. "A thousand years they lived there."

The students studied Mendoza, warily. This distraught little person wasn't the same charismatic leader who had recruited them. Francis wondered if they were coming to the same conclusion he'd reluctantly been coming to: that Francis's colleagues were right. Mendoza *was* a phony and a screwup. How else to explain the man's inability to understand that much more time was needed?

Lila was the first of the students to recover from the shock of their leader's disarray. She put her hand out to touch Mendoza's, and Mendoza appeared to grow a little calmer. "It will be all right," Lila said softly. "You can tell us."

"We've only got till August first," Mendoza announced. "Not the end of August. August first!"

Nobody said a word.

"They just told me," Mendoza said after a long pause. He seemed to be shrinking to an even smaller size; the students towered over him.

"They can't do that!" a tall girl said. "No one can give people orders like that!" Lila looked at her as if she were three years old.

Mendoza didn't get a chance to answer the kid, because suddenly Francis was in his face. "Why in the world didn't you find out how much time we had before we came all the way out here?" he blurted. "How could you possibly not do that?"

"Officialdom! Rules, permits, lawyers!" Mendoza cried. Francis's question hadn't made a dent. "They don't give a damn what we're trying to do. All they think about is money!" he went on, and Francis realized it didn't occur to Mendoza that this disaster was his mistake. He thought it was caused by what he was trying to cure. He wasn't a phony at all; he was a total screwup.

Even if despite the little archaeologist's awesome incompetence they found the Ohlone village, it would be the result of mere demeaning luck, Francis realized. Win or lose, the whole venture a dreamer's folly. He heard again his colleagues' jeering and realized that he was not surprised—if not this disaster, then some other—and asked himself why hadn't he checked up on Mendoza, at least asked for a résumé and talked with his references, and knew the answer: he hadn't wanted to; he needed the cover. And this was good cover. For he really did need to do this spiritual exploring. Without that cover, he would have had to stay home and help the new head. It shamed him to realize he could be so sneaky, even with himself.

"That's when the developer comes in?" Lila asked Mendoza. "August first?" There was no indignation in her voice, no panic. She just wanted to know.

Mendoza nodded. He took a red kerchief out of his pocket and wiped his face.

Lila rested a calming hand on Mendoza's tiny shoulder while she turned her head to Francis. "So, Mr. P.," she asked him, "how do we fix this?"

"We could go to the developer and ask for an extension," he told her. He held back from saying, *It won't work, but we might as well give it a try.* These kids needed his faith to seem as strong as Lila's.

"Good idea!" said Mendoza, optimism flooding right back in. "I'm sure he'll agree!" Francis had to look away.

Lila was studying Francis, not Mendoza. "Whatever we have to do, we'll do," she said. Her voice was firm. She turned away and went down the hill to the site, the first to return to work.

When it was finally too dark to work, they returned to the huts they had made out of the tulle grass that Mendoza had somehow arranged to have gathered for them. Their replicated Ohlone village even had a sweat house, though they hadn't used it yet. There was an argument, proposed by Lila, that though only male Ohlones had used it, the women should also participate. As he tried to fall asleep in Mendoza's ersatz little village, Francis wondered at the purity of Lila's youthful heart.

The next day, a Saturday afternoon—less than a month before their time was up—Francis, Mendoza, and Lila (whom the students had elected as their representative) went together to the president of Mount Alma Improvement Company, Conrad Bullington, to ask for an extension. Bullington greeted them in his office, his obese body clad in a sky-blue warm-up suit.

All during the meeting, Francis wondered at Bullington's unfailing courtesy. He was far more respectful, less strident, Francis thought, than people who disagreed with each other on the Oliver faculty, who were quite given in their tweedy attire to offer polysyllabic insults to one another. Meanwhile, this gigantically unattractive man in his funny warm-up suit and greased hair remembered each of their names, offered them cool drinks, and explained very gently—but firmly—that it would drive up his costs prohibitively to leave the bulldozers and other heavy equipment idle beyond the agreed-on time. As if to alleviate their disappointment, Bullington offered to build a model of an Ohlone village. He would have it prefabricated and set up and prominently displayed once a year for the edification of the thousands of homeowners.

"Where would you put it, for crying out loud?" Lila exclaimed, leaning forward in her chair. Bullington leaned back in his, as if pushed. Francis thought maybe after the meeting he would advise Lila not to come on so strong.

But Bullington recovered immediately. "Why, I'd put it on this very commodious lawn in the center," he responded, pushing his huge body up out of his chair. He lumbered across the office to a map on the wall. The sun coming in through the window glistened on his shiny hair. "Right here. A very expansive lawn that fronts the central golf course, near the lake with the fountain."

"On a *lawn*?" asked Mendoza.

"Right here. We'll put it up every year at the same time we have the Concourse d'Elegance."

"But the Ohlones didn't have lawns," Mendoza objected.

Inspired by his idea, Bullington ignored Mendoza. "Thousands of people come to the Concourse," he said. Francis began to giggle. He turned his face away so Bullington couldn't see. He found that he didn't want to be impolite to this man. The giggling felt a little crazy. Scary—like maybe it would turn into something else.

"What in the world is a Concourse d'Elegance?" Lila imitated the developer's wooden French.

"Antique cars," Bullington answered. His voice took on a fatherly tone. "Very elegant automobiles: Rolls Royces, Pierce Arrows . . ."

"Next to a *lake*?" asked Mendoza.

"Daimlers, wonderful old Mercedes . . . "

"With a *fountain*?" Mendoza squeaked.

"A Stanley Steamer too. People will come for miles, pay a very significant entrance fee. The opportunity to view an authentic representation of how the Indians once lived here would be an extra draw. White Eagle would be delighted to place a commensurate portion of the proceeds with any archaeological project you identify."

"But surely we don't want to give the impression that we believe the Ohlones had lawns!" Mendoza exclaimed, leaning so far forward he was almost out of his chair.

"Not for a minute, sir," Bullington said, easing his body back toward his desk. Francis could feel the meeting coming to an end. "But I do think we could suggest that they would have enjoyed them," Bullington continued, and now Francis couldn't tell whether he was serious or just playing with them. "Why wouldn't they have enjoyed them? After all, people are people. If they could have mastered the technique of transporting water, as we have, then who knows, maybe they would have had lawns instead of ashes and old clam shells to put their dwellings on."

Mendoza was back in his seat. His mouth was open, but he wasn't saying anything.

"Why not put it in the area you're not going to develop?" Francis found himself suggesting. "The part designated for open land." *Maybe that would make Mendoza feel better*, he thought.

"By the chaparral?"

"Yes."

"Because nobody would go there to see it," said Conrad Bullington, standing up.

That afternoon, as if to put a capstone on Francis's sense of absurdity, two mammoth tractors, each dragging a trailer, labored up the hill to the replicated village. On each of the trailers were three well-used Porta Potties, which a band of workmen who had followed in a jeep removed from the trailers and placed in a ring around the little cluster of tulle huts, like the walls of a medieval town. The Porta Potties stood prominent under the ethereal California sky, a plastic Gothic; as they warmed in the yellow sunshine, they began to radiate a stink. Almaville's city manager, who would have of course preferred to sprinkle these fields with huge houses and hot tubs and lawns, explained to the enraged Mendoza, "You can't just go defecate in the fields like a bunch of Indians." Francis was sure that it was Bullington who had informed the city government that this was exactly what was happening and suggested the Porta Potties—and wondered if the gesture was an act of friendship or an insult. In either case, Francis disobeyed the city manager's edict, getting up at first light the next morning to climb further up the mountain, as he thought an Indian would. But when he returned, the ring of Porta Potties made him laugh, a disillusioned giggle. His sense of the absurd was now complete.

Later in the day, Francis got a message that Peggy had called. He hurried down the hill to Mendoza's tiny office in a trailer to phone her back. He was happy that Peggy called him and not the other way around; but he had no idea why she was calling, and by the time he was halfway there, he'd begun to worry that she was sick or that Siddy had an accident in Europe.

"You went to Cleveland!" he exclaimed after Peggy told him about her helping Fred Kindler with the recruiting. "With him?"

She didn't answer. Why should she? She'd already said it.

"Really?" he asked.

"Yes, and as a matter of fact, we're coming to recruit in San Francisco the last Monday of the month. About three weeks from now. You can offer to join us there and help. That's why I called you." She didn't tell him—why rub it in?—that she was sure the only reason Nan and Fred hadn't asked him to help at the meeting even though he was right next door was that they didn't trust him. The only reason she hadn't brought this up with them was that it was too embarrassing. That was why, just this morning, she had decided to call him on her own and ask him to call Fred Kindler and offer his help.

"Francis, we can both help him," she said. "We can get together and help make things work for our new boss. So will you come or not?"

"Yeah, I'll be there." In fact, he was delighted to have this chance to redeem himself. Before he even left California!

"Good! I knew you'd say that."

"You're coming out here! We can spend the night together."

"We're leaving right after the meeting," she said. "Night owl to Bradley. We're flying there to have another recruiting gathering on campus that night."

"Peg! Go in the early morning."

"I'll think about it. I'll ask Fred."

"Ask Fred!"

"Of course. Who else would I ask, Francis? He's the headmaster, remember?"

He heard her resentment rising again, so he held himself in check, as if he were counting to ten. "We've been away from each other for weeks," he said at last.

"And whose fault is that?" she asked. Then, "I'm sorry. I shouldn't have gone back to that." She was so tired of being resentful. "Just join us in San Francisco, Francis," she pleaded. "Just come and help him. Just do the work, all right?"

"Of course I'll come. I already said I would."

"Fine," Peggy said, her voice softening. "Call him and tell him."

"I'll call Nan White."

"I think you should call him. He's the headmaster."

"I'll call Nan," he insisted. "She's the Admissions director. I'm not going over her head."

She knew this wasn't the real reason. He'd never cared much for such niceties. Now she was resentful again.

He waited for her to respond, ready to relent. What the hell, he'd just grit his teeth and call Fred Kindler. He knew perfectly well he didn't have to like the guy, didn't even have to approve of him; all he had to do was work for him. But when Peggy didn't say anything, he dropped that idea and changed the subject. He wanted to make love to her, was what he wanted. "How are you, Peg?" he began.

"You know what? Let's wait until you're home to tell each other how we are. Over the phone it just makes me angry."

"All right, but I still miss you."

"Me too," she confessed.

"Maybe after San Francisco you won't be angry anymore."

"That would be nice, Francis."

"Then we'll spend that night together. There's no way I'll let you fly away that night."

"Maybe," she said. "Anyway, I'll see you in three weeks." Then she hung up. Right away she regretted this ending. "Of course I'll stay the night," she whispered to see how the words would sound, and thought of calling him back—she knew he was waiting for just that. But she kept hearing him refuse to call Fred Kindler. How childish! He could square things with Fred with one simple call. She loved Francis one minute and was furious the next. How tired she was of going up and down with all these feelings!

Francis stayed by the phone, hoping. After a while he knew Peggy wasn't going to call. So he picked up the phone again and put in a call to Nan White. It was Saturday. Back east it was three hours later, and even Nan had gone home. Unless she came in on Sunday too, she wouldn't get the message until Monday morning. Nevertheless, he left the message on her voicemail that he would attend the San Francisco recruiting meeting and asked her to call back with details. Then he hurried up the hill to the dig and got back to work. They still had a few hours before it got dark. Tonight, thinking of his chance to redeem himself, he would sleep better than he had since leaving Connecticut.

When Nan White came to work on Monday morning and heard Francis's message on her voicemail, she had no idea that Peggy had called him and urged him to attend the recruiting event. She assumed instead that Francis had known about it all along. Who more than the senior teacher to know such things? She forgot that the plan had been made after Francis had left. So she stuck to the original decision that Fred had made on her advice not to include Francis Plummer. She wasn't going to ask Fred to make the same decision twice. If Francis Plummer was angry about this, let him be angry at her.

So she picked up her phone and left a message for Francis on Mendoza's tape. If she had waited a little longer she would have realized her mistake. But she had a rule: whenever you have something unpleasant to do, do it right away. "Thank you, but our plans are all set," she recorded at seven-thirty in the morning in Connecticut, while in California Francis was still asleep. "We have a very specific design," she added to make the message less insulting. Then she put Francis out of mind. She had a million things to do.

At breakfast, Mendoza handed Francis the note in which he had transcribed the message Nan left on voicemail. "Thank you, but our plans are all set," Francis read.

Mendoza saw the shock on Francis's face. "Anything wrong?" he asked. His voice was kind, worried.

Still looking down at the note, Francis shook his head. "We have a very specific design." He had no idea, of course, that these words weren't Kindler's and had been added by Nan White to alleviate the insult. They had exactly the opposite effect. For who else but the head of school made such decisions? *Specific* meant without him. Kindler had slapped his face.

"I sure hope everything's all right at home," Mendoza said.

"I have to go make a phone call," Francis said. "I'll be back in half an hour." He was going to call Kindler, interrupt whatever he was doing—he'd call even if it were the middle of the fucking night, he was so mad. "What do you think, I'm not going to help get kids into the school?" he said to the air around him. But as he walked down the hill, he began to change his mind, and by the time he was in the office he had decided: he wouldn't stoop to argue with Kindler about his worthiness to represent the school—after all these years! It was humiliating enough already without his begging. And the insult to Peggy after she'd already invited him. Let Kindler do his own recruiting.

Mendoza was surprised to see him returning so soon. He sent Francis another worried look. "Everything's fine," Francis lied. He was tempted to tell Mendoza what was happening and everything that had led up to it. After all, Mendoza was a kind of priest, a medicine man, but Francis rejected the idea as just as crazy as Mendoza.

By the middle of her day, Nan woke up to what a dumb mistake she'd made. Of course Francis would tell Peggy that he offered to come to the meeting and was refused. She was not about to let this insult to Peggy happen. She would just have to call Francis right away before he told Peggy and invite him after all. She would make up something about how excited they were about that specific design, but now that they've had time to think about it. . . . And she would make sure Francis understood the whole thing was her mistake, not Fred's. So she picked up the phone and left her new message.

But this message, which Francis listened to in Mendoza's office during the lunch break, didn't assuage his feelings even a little. Instead, it made him even angrier. And though he'd been thinking that maybe he would show up at the event after all—what right had Kindler to tell him he couldn't participate?—now he was ten times more resolved not to attend. Not for one minute did he believe that the original refusal of his offer had come from Nan. Why would she do that? They'd known each other for years. He knew damn well she was the kind of person who didn't pass the buck. So she was taking the heat for Kindler because he wouldn't take it for himself. And what enraged him further was his assumption that the only reason for this recanting was Peggy's going to Kindler. Begging! She, a favored subject, kneeling to the king on behalf of her unworthy husband. *How do you think that makes me feel?* he wanted to ask her. But he was so deeply insulted he knew he wouldn't ever be able to bring it up with her. There were some things between husband and wife best not talked about, and this was one of them. And another thing he knew: he was not even going to respond to Nan's recanted disinvitation. It didn't deserve an answer.

MENDOZA'S CREW WORKED fervently for the next two weeks to find the Ohlone village. Francis committed entirely to the cause, discarding as much as he could his sense of absurdity and disbelief and working harder than everyone except Lila, whose energy and passion he couldn't begin to equal. If the dig succeeded, his Western adventure would not be merely an escape.

Two Sundays later, with only six days left before their August first deadline, they had still found nothing. Mendoza stayed up all night searching for an idea to rescue them, and at dawn, confusing desperation with inspiration, he decided that impurity of resolve was the reason for the failure to find the village. "We haven't truly walked in the shoes of the Ohlones," he explained, and so he resolved the argument about whether only males should use the sweat house by declaring that they all would imitate the Ohlone purification ritual. They would stay most of the night in the sweat house, scraping the sweat off their bodies with willow sticks, building the heat to the fainting point then building it more, until the present melted and they saw visions. They would make themselves worthy by sweating out of their bodies the evil that caused them their blindness. While Mendoza urged fervently, Francis started to giggle again as he had in Bullington's office. But when Lila reached out from where she sat across the circle to touch his hand, he realized that she was not doing so to join him in his laughter but to calm him down, and when he turned back toward Mendoza's voice, the little professor gave him such a pleading look that Francis agreed to the ritual.

Francis joined the others in helping Mendoza prepare the sweat house. He worked hard, trying not to admit that every once in a while in the last few days he'd found himself wondering if he really wanted to find the village. The relentless searching had made him begin to feel it would be an invasion of the privacy of defenseless strangers to probe around in what they had left behind—especially if they found the burial ground. And then it was not much of a jump for him to understand that he was going to feel the same way when he got home and stood in front of the Pequot display in Peggy's library. Maybe, deep down, he'd always felt this way. He didn't even want to think about that.

He tried, also unsuccessfully, to keep his mind from the fact that a crucial recruiting event for Miss Oliver's School for Girls was going to take place without him tomorrow night just across the bay. As the afternoon went by, he sensed Mendoza's spirits lifting. "We won't let them sweep everything away, we'll protect their village, we'll protect their bones," Mendoza urged in his mesmerizing chant. "They are in the ground because they were the lesser-ranking members of the tribe and they didn't rank the honor of a funeral pyre," he added, as if to prove that the meek shall inherit the earth.

That evening, twenty-four hours before the recruiting event in San Francisco that Francis had decided to spurn, the group assembled in the sweat house after the sun went down.

They sat, male and female, in a tight circle, in their underwear, a completely asexual near-nakedness. Mendoza had pushed for complete nakedness. "To be like Indians," he'd said. But Francis had talked him out of it, over Lila's objections. "We don't have to go that far," he'd said. Now in the fading light, he saw Lila's face across from him, her eyes closed, sweat faintly glistening on her shoulders. He and she both knew that Mendoza hadn't even got this right: the fire to heat the rocks still burned, and there was a hole in the domed roof to let the smoke out, but the Indians had used rocks heated earlier by a fire and there should be no hole above. Nevertheless, Lila had given herself completely, unselfconsciously, to the ritual, entirely serious, and Francis was envious of youth, regretful of his common sense.

His almost-naked butt itched where it pressed against the scraped earth; he suspected there were bugs down there exploring; it got hotter in the little hut; he was already wondering if he'd make it. To his left, one of the male students groaned. "Shut up!" the girl next to him whispered, and from his right another girl said, "Are you sure we're doing this right?"

"Hush!" said Mendoza. His face was uplifted. Sweat was running down his neck toward the black hairs on his puny chest. Francis looked longingly at the tiny closed doorway, imagining the spacious night outside, the cool evening air. Mendoza started to chant.

It grew hotter. Without stopping his chant, Mendoza leaned forward, stirred the fire. The lodge was full of smoke. Above, through the hole in the roof, blurred a single star. The rocks in the center gleamed red in the coals.

The guttural syllables of Mendoza's chant rose in volume. Several of the students joined him. Francis couldn't bring himself to join the chanting, though after a while it began to sound more authentic. Different from the psalms that Peggy loved. He was glad

Peggy couldn't see what he was doing. He saw two Francis Plummers simultaneously: one was dressed in a sports coat and gray flannels and was talking convincingly to a group of teenage girls and their parents about Miss Oliver's School for Girls; the other sat almost naked, on the ground in a fake Indian hut, listening to Mendoza's chant while an army of bugs crawled up his ass.

As an antidote, he tried to keep his promise to Mendoza—and to himself—to see with Indian eyes. But no vision arrived. He saw only his little group of students and Mendoza in the blazing weather of the tiny hut. He was much further away from an Indian consciousness than he ever was back home—where the Oliver campus overlay an ancient Pequot village from which, sometimes, some hint seeped up into his brain—and where he knew he was needed.

Nevertheless, he started to chant, forcing himself to get into it. In the red glow of the rocks, he saw Mendoza glancing at him in thanks. Mendoza stirred the coals with a long stick. The rocks grew redder. The end of the stick flamed, lighting the hut. Shadows flickered. Lila was pouring sweat. Francis was dizzy, short of breath.

The chant seemed strangely beautiful suddenly, the rhythm more accentuated. He felt the heavy frightening beating of his heart. It was much hotter now. The girl next to him moaned softly. Mendoza stirred the fire again. Francis's heart was a loud drum. He started to faint, felt himself falling away.

Then, in the acme of the heat, Mendoza made a little motion with his hand and stopped chanting. A syllable later, so did everyone else. Francis heard moaning, and one of the boy students, giving up, scooted out through the doorway. Lila leaned, put the tulle mat the boy had kicked aside back over the doorway.

"Another hour," said Mendoza. "One more hour."

"Whatever it takes," Lila whispered. "A day, a week, a year, whatever it takes."

Half swooning in this furnace, his brain melting, Francis despaired. Still, no new visions had arrived; instead he heard himself babbling to Peggy about church, stale territory, and he was trying to make her laugh. "When the priest says, 'Lift up your hearts,'" he told her, "I see this huge red giblet I'm holding above me and it's dripping on my head." But she wasn't laughing.

"Hotter," he heard Lila saying. "Make it hotter!" He could hardly see her across the little space. A vague figure, disembodied, she hung in air. Mendoza's airy body leaned forward as he stirred the fire.

"And when he says, 'It is meet and right so to do,'" Francis went on in his unreadiness, "I always imagine 'It's meat and rice, LUUNCH TIME!' because by that time I'm so hungry! But the service goes on and on." Peggy was looking at him as if he were a little kid.

And then, as if he were outside himself, he listened, horrified, to his brain decide to try one more thing. He would tell a joke to *this* congregation. That would take the heat off; you can't fail if it's only a joke. "What's the difference between a BMW and a porcupine?" he asked. Mendoza stared across the fire at him, disgust written all over his face, Lila looked away, and no one else seemed to hear. "With a porcupine, the pricks are on the outside," Francis announced.

"All right, enough!" Mendoza shouted, giving up. He started to get up on his knees to crawl out the little door, then fainted. Lila reached to support him. Francis did too, but Lila pushed his hand away. Mendoza stirred, got back onto his knees, pushed aside the tulle mat, and crawled out. Everyone followed. Outside the little hut in the cool of the starry night, Francis was as embarrassed as he had ever been. He couldn't wait to escape to his hut.

"There's one more thing," said Mendoza, looking straight at Francis. "We'll give you one more chance." Mendoza, Lila, and Francis were standing now by the entrance to Mendoza's hut. The others had drifted off to bed. They'd just finished hosing themselves down in the stink of the Porta Potties from the water truck parked between two of the them. "Because there are no creeks left," Mendoza explained, after they were back near his hut, away from the stink. "In those days, before the white man destroyed the water table, these hills were traced with creeks. The country was actually wet." He swept his hand. The windless night was domed with stars. Behind them, Mount Alma's dark shape loomed, the smell of dew on dry adobe ground.

"One more thing," Mendoza said again, then disappeared into his hut. "For those who dare," he said, reappearing and looking again straight at Francis. Mendoza was carrying a canvas bag. He pulled out a plastic tarp and spread it on the ground. Then he pulled out an Atlas jar with something white inside. "Lime," he said. "I made it myself. Ground up seashells." Then a canvas pouch. "Tobacco. The final step in the purification process was this." He dumped a little pile of lime on the tarp, knelt down, and mixed in the tobacco. "The Ohlones grew tobacco on these hillsides," he explained.

"You can't smoke lime," Francis said. Lila gave him another funny look.

"Wasn't going to," Mendoza said, dividing the mess into three parts. "Going to eat it." He stood up, one pile cupped in his two hands, and held them out to Lila. "Ladies first," he said. Lila put her hands out, cupped like Mendoza's, and received.

"Eat it?" Francis heard the squeak in his voice.

"That's right. We eat it."

"What for?" he said, as if he were curious and wanted to understand.

"It's an emetic," said Mendoza, holding his cupped hands out to Francis.

"Emetic?"

"A cleanser."

"Do we do it here?" Lila asked.

"You take it to someplace you want to be alone," Mendoza answered. "It's a very private experience."

"How do you know, you ever done it?" Francis asked. His hands were down by his sides. Mendoza's hands were still held out to him, offering.

"I read about it," Mendoza said. "Makes you clean. Empty, like after fasting."

"You mean you puke?" asked Francis.

"Well, if you want to talk about it that way."

"I don't like to puke." Then trying to be funny again: "It comes out my nose." He glanced at Lila. She was looking hard at him. Not smiling.

"It's different," he heard Mendoza saying. "You get convulsions, go in and out of consciousness. You don't get sick and then get well. You go in one place and come out another."

Francis's hands were still down at his sides. Mendoza looked hard at his eyes, dropped his outstretched arms, shrugged, and walked away, taking the offering for himself. He left the third portion on the tarp by Francis's feet. Francis stared down at it. When he looked up, he could see Lila walking away through the dark. He knew where she was going: a ridgetop on which he had watched her sitting in the early morning waiting for the sun. He left the powder on the tarp and went to his hut.

But, of course, he didn't sleep.

He lay on his cot hearing the wind that rose now, riffling the walls of his hut. In his head, he watched again as Lila walked away toward her ridgetop and saw himself spurning Mendoza's offering hands, and it came to him that now that they knew the dig was going to fail, it would be his fault, not Mendoza's. He knew the thought didn't make any sense—it was Mendoza's bungling that doomed the venture—but it wouldn't go away, and he spent the few hours remaining in the night tortured by it. In the morning as the group returned dispiritedly to work, the students avoided his eyes.

At the lunch break he sat down next to Lila. He wanted to apologize and explain to her that he was not as free as she was to be like an Indian; he had too much history in another role. Before he could even begin, she got up and moved away.

It's not hard to understand how insulted Lila was, how abandoned she felt, by what she could only interpret as Francis's irreverence, the apogee of which was his dumb joke in the sweat house. For it was Lila who had listened to the story his wife never wanted to hear and gravely explained its meaning. It was she who had legitimized his spiritual hunger, who said, "He's your totem," speaking with no hesitation of the turtle who chose to appear to Francis "from out of the time when the world was here and human beings were not." A few years hence, Lila would lighten her disappointment with a helpful dose of irony. Right then she and her passion were too young; and, after all, she had thought she'd found in Francis an adult soul mate, something very rare, and a surrogate dad—and now she thought he was neither.

And on Francis's part, he couldn't see the legitimacy of his spiritual hunger anymore—though it was just as legitimate as it always was. Not after this summer's chain of events he couldn't, for all he could see was the farce of his Western adventure: the Porta

Potties, Mendoza's bungling, Bullington's greasy infallibility, his own sacrilegious delirium in the sweat house. That and the embarrassing fact that he'd been running away from his responsibilities. And so, right there and then, he declared to himself that he was through with all that. All spiritual questing from then on was going to be in tune with Peggy's, he told himself, forgetting that he had tried that for years and had always been hungry.

And he would return to his responsibilities, his legitimate role at the head's right hand. On this, at least, he was on solid ground. For there *was* a school to save. And he was the senior teacher.

The first step was to show up tomorrow night at the San Francisco recruiting event. So what if he was not wanted? Fred Kindler, mere upstart, had no right to keep him away.

LATE IN THE afternoon of the next day, Francis walked down the hill to where his yellow Chevy was parked, opened the trunk, pulled out his suitcase, extricated his gray flannels, his tweed sports coat, his blue button-down shirt and striped tie. He put them on in the shade of an oak tree, and now he was in uniform again. Then he got in the car and combed his hair in the rearview mirror. Francis started to drive.

Catherine Jackson, class of 1956 (the first year of the reign of Marjorie Boyd), was the hostess of the event. Francis got to her big Victorian in Pacific Heights too early. He wanted to arrive after most of the guests had assembled so he could enter unobtrusively and take a seat in the back after Kindler had begun to talk. Less of a scene that way. Then, after the talk, he would mingle with the guests and say the things about his beloved school that brought the families in. He didn't even think about what he'd say to Kindler and Peggy after the meeting was over.

To kill time, he drove the several blocks to Divisadero to find a place to park. Then he sat in the car, listening to the news. George Bush was giving a news conference. Usually whenever Bush said anything, Francis talked back to the radio or TV screen, loudly explaining all the ways he was sure the president was wrong; but tonight he was so keyed up he barely listened. At eight-fifteen he got out of the car and started to walk. From high up on Divisadero hill, he could see the water in the bay shading to purple in the sunset. The air was cold and sharp. In this, one the most beautiful cities in the world, Francis was hungry for the smell of his New England woods, the sight of his river.

Fifteen minutes later, he climbed the steps, crossed the porch, and stopped at the door. For an instant he thought he'd turn around; he'd never gone anywhere he was not wanted before. Then he pushed on the heavy door, and now he was standing in the foyer and to his left through the opening to the living room he saw the backs of about eighteen people, three of whom, he noticed immediately, were teenage girls. Some of the guests were sitting on sofas, some in folding chairs, and Fred Kindler was standing there facing them. Fred saw him first as he tried to tiptoe in. Their eyes met and held. Kindler stopped talking.

And everyone turned around to see who was coming in the door.

In the front row, Gail and Nan and Peggy turned too. At first, all he could see was Peggy. Her face was lit with relief. "Hello," she mouthed to him, and Fred Kindler smiled and said aloud, disguising his surprise, "Here's Mr. Plummer, everybody, our senior teacher. I'm so glad he's here."

All the alumnae and parents of present students knew Francis, of course. They stood up to greet him, so that only the three families who were being recruited remained in their seats; and in the back row of folding chairs nearest him, Marcia Bradford, whom he'd known since she entered the school twenty-one years ago and whose daughter, Mary, was Eudora's kinesthetic furniture student, reached for his hands and held them while her husband slapped his shoulders. "Why, it's Francis Plummer," she loudly exclaimed. "My favorite teacher! It's so good to see you!"

"I didn't mean to interrupt," Francis said to the room, speaking the truth and stepping gently back from the Bradfords. This glaring entrance was exactly what he didn't want.

"That's all right, I've finished," Kindler said. But he really hadn't. He had a few more things to say—that now he couldn't say because it would be too awkward to start again.

And anyway, nobody was even looking at him anymore.

"Mr. Plummer, give us your thoughts. Come on up here and tell us what you think makes this school so special," Fred urged, forcing himself to smile. What else could he do in front of all these people? He was wary, thinking of how little Nan trusted this guy and remembering Cleveland, Sharon Maynard's treachery, and the woman in the red dress. Just the same, Plummer was here, he must have come to help, Fred told himself and glanced at his teammates. Gail was frowning. Nan looked worried. But Peggy was smiling at Francis. *She wants her husband to come up front and stand beside me*, Fred thought. *So maybe it's going to be all right*. He beckoned to Francis.

"No. Really, I didn't mean to interrupt," Francis insisted.

But that's just what you did! Fred thought. *You came in late and made a showy entrance.* He felt small for even thinking this way. Just the same, he'd never do what Plummer had just done if it were the other way around. He beckoned again. Peggy nodded across the chairs to Francis, urging him.

"Come on, Clark, talk to us!" Marcia Bradford said.

"All right, I'll just say a few words from here," Francis said, relenting—he knew how churlish it would appear for him to keep on refusing. But he was not about to go up front and be even more obtrusive. And besides, he wasn't going to stand beside Kindler and help the man pretend he was glad to see him. When he had to be forced to invite him!

But Francis's attempt not to draw attention to himself had the opposite effect. All the guests turned completely around in their chairs to face him. Some, in the folding chairs, even turned the chairs themselves around. Now all their backs were to Fred. He might as well not have been in the room. Nan watched Gail's face. *Do you see what I see?* she wanted to ask her. *He's sucking the power right out of the room and to himself, the egotistical little bastard! He's cutting your husband's legs right out from under him.*

Francis was only going to say a few things because he felt like the bull in a china shop. He roved his eyes around the room, thinking what to say. He looked at each of the three potential students. Affluenza, he thought, the symptoms printed on their faces—entitlement warring with the unacknowledged hunger to have their desires resisted—and started to talk directly to them as if they were the only ones in the room. "I'd think carefully before I signed up for Miss Oliver's School for Girls," he started. "You need to be sure that's what you really want to do. Don't say we didn't warn you." And then he told them why: "Because there's never enough time at Miss Oliver's School for Girls.

"Something in the air of Oliver's demands that limits be pushed. It's just the way we are, it's a crazy kind of place. When you write a paper for an Oliver teacher, you'll always get it back, it won't be good enough, you'll always do it again. Are you ready for that? If you think you're weak in math or science, don't worry: we'll pile on the math and science until you know you aren't. Same with history. Same with art. Nobody gets enough sleep at Miss Oliver's School for Girls." He went on like this, much longer than he had intended, strewing hyperbole to make his point. He never showed them the top of the mountain he was inviting them to climb, only how hard the climb. That was what grabbed these kids' attention, focused their minds, changed what they want. If they had needed to see something else about the school he loved, he would have shown them that.

He knew only great teachers could bore into someone else's mind like this—only they have that kind of power. Maybe that's why teachers were paid so little: what they earn has more power than money.

When he stopped, there was silence. And then there was applause and Fred Kindler announced that the formal part of the evening was over—for anything more would be anticlimax—and the guests got up from their seats, and the next thing Francis knew was that at least ten of the guests were moving to him. They surrounded him, virtually backing him against the wall, thanking him for his talk, telling him stories about when they were in school, asking questions, and Marcia Bradford was hugging him. Over her shoulder he saw Fred and Gail talking with exactly one guest. The three potential students were gathered around Nan and Peggy. Francis extricated himself as soon as he could, pretending to be dying for a glass of white wine, moved to the table that served as a bar, poured himself a glass, and then, as soon as he saw that Nan and the three girls had drifted away from her, he moved to Peggy and stood beside her. He sensed her body stiffening. "Hello," he said under his breath.

She didn't turn to him, stared straight ahead.

"Hello," he said again. She still didn't answer. He saw Kindler glance at them from the other side of the room, then look away. "Hey," he murmured to Peggy, "this is a recruiting session, isn't it? Well, I recruited." He pointed with his chin to where, on the other side of the room, Nan was handing folders to each of the three girls. "That's the application packet," he said. "How much you want to bet they sign up?"

"We'll talk later," she said, and moved away.

He started to follow, putting his hand out to hers to hold her back. Then he changed his mind and let her go, watching her as she moved across the room to where Gail and Nan were talking to some parents.

A few minutes later, the guests began to leave. Fred Kindler and Catherine Jackson stood at the front door to say goodbye. Nan, Gail, Peggy, and Francis stayed in the living room. Soon most of the guests were gone, but the conversation drifted in through the open door from the front porch where people were lingering. Just as the last guest went out the door, Francis heard an angry voice. It was clearly Mr. Bradford's, Marcia's husband, Mary's father, and it was loud enough to for everyone inside the house to hear: "Why didn't they make *him* the head, Francis Plummer, for Christ's sake, can anybody answer that?"

After a little moment, Fred moved from the foyer where he'd been standing with Catherine by the door, toward the living room. He stopped in the archway and looked right at Francis Plummer.

"Look," Francis began. "I didn't mean—"

"I know you didn't," Fred cut him off. It was true; he could see what had happened. The guy had gifts, that's all. Just the same, Fred was furious.

Francis tried again. "Really, I came to help."

"Fine. Thanks," Fred said. He was not going to talk about it. Not in front of all these people. Maybe never. Gail moved across the room and stood beside him.

"I think you people could use a drink," Catherine offered. "How about it? Anyone want to join me?" She moved toward the bar.

"Thanks, but we have to get back to the airport," Nan said.

They all moved toward the front door now where Catherine stood saying goodbye. Then out on the porch, Fred turned to Peggy. "Goodbye, Peg. I'll see you tomorrow." He gave her a hug. "Thanks for all you do," he added. "You're wonderful." Then he turned to Plummer and shook his hand. "I'm glad you came," he said, and forced himself to add, "We probably will enroll those three girls. It was your speech that did it." What else could he do in this situation but hide his resentment and blossoming mistrust and be gracious? He knew he'd be hearing that Bradford person asking his question over and over, probably for the rest of his life.

"We all did it, not just me," Francis said, and Kindler gave him a look of contempt and Francis understood that Kindler knew he was lying—because it *was* his speech that had nailed those kids—and now he felt his own anger rising. Everyone was blaming this on him! *Learn how to make your own fucking speeches*, he wanted to say. He kept his gaze on Kindler's eyes. Maybe the guy would read his mind. Then Gail and Nan hugged Peggy too, and nodded coldly to Francis, and Gail put her hand through her husband's crooked arm, and the three walked down the steps, leaving Peggy and Francis alone on the porch.

"So," he said, "you're staying."

Peggy sighed. "I made a reservation at the Hilton. I changed my flight to tomorrow morning."

"Good." That's all he was going to say. He was wary. It was her move. When Peggy didn't respond, he said, "Wait here, I'll bring the car around so you don't have to carry your bag." He went down the steps and headed for Divisadero.

"I wouldn't have if I'd known what you were going to do," she murmured. He pretended he didn't hear.

ON THE WAY to the hotel they kept their distance, hardly talked at all. Francis was sure that when he was alone with her in their hotel she would admit she understood that what had happened at Catherine's house was the farthest thing in the world from what he'd intended. And he would confess that, yes, maybe whether or not he approved of the new headmaster he should have stayed home to help him.

I'm through with all that, he was going to say. *I'm going to put that quest aside, beat those feelings down, and rush home as soon as the dig is over at the end of the week, do my job. My head's on straight again,* he was going to promise her. *And there's a school to save.*

Fifteen minutes later, alone with her in their hotel room, he started by trying for a hug.

"I'm tired," she said. She put her hand on his chest, holding him off, then stepped back from him.

"It's only eleven o'clock."

"It's two o'clock my time, and I got up at six."

He turned his back, went to the mirror over the bureau, and started to take off his tie. "What was I supposed to do?" he asked. "Give a lousy talk? Bore 'em to death?"

"Don't be funny, Francis."

"What then?"

She didn't answer.

"What, Peggy?"

"I don't want to talk about it."

"Maybe he just doesn't have it, Peg," he said. He knew he shouldn't—especially right after making up his mind to help the guy—but he felt the hurt of her pushing him away, and now he wanted to hurt. "Is that why you don't want to talk about it? Maybe your hero's the wrong guy for the job."

That got her. She came up behind him. He could see her face in the mirror, to the right of his. "How would you know?" she asked. "You've talked with him for exactly ten minutes at a cocktail party, for goodness sake!"

"Yeah, the first two minutes were enough."

"Just before you made an ass of yourself by insulting Milton Perkins."

"I wasn't making an ass of myself, Peg. I'm supposed to insult him. He's a Republican! That's what they're for."

"And then you run away and come sauntering back a month later, and barge right in the middle of his speech and make him look bad."

"Yeah. It was so easy I couldn't resist."

He watched her face in the mirror. She stared back over his shoulder. He thought he saw her expression slide from anger to contempt—and then to sadness.

"Make all the jokes you want," she said. "He's worth six of you!"

"Oh, he is? Then marry him!"

"You bastard!" She crossed to her suitcase, got her pajamas and her kit with her toothbrush in it, and went into the bathroom and shut the door. When she came out, she got into bed. He got ready in the bathroom too, then came out and got in the other side. They lay miles apart, listening to each other breathe, each waiting for the other to take the words back. They wouldn't hurt so much if they were true. Neither of them spoke, and finally they fell asleep. Early in the morning, when Peggy left for the airport and Francis left for Mount Alma, they barely said goodbye and didn't touch each other.

Four days later at noon, when there was only one afternoon remaining to Mendoza's allotted time and it became absolute that the dig would fail, Lila looked Francis steadily in the eye, not trying very hard to hide her disillusionment, and told him she wouldn't be going home with him, she'd go by air instead, and he pretended he really did believe she wanted to get home in a hurry. The next morning the bulldozers came, and Francis started his long ride home, alone.

Six

Francis was on Route 80, zooming eastward. Still in California, he already felt the homeward end of the long cement, a string on which he was gladly nowhere, here and there at the same time. He drove on and on, planning not to stop. Climbed the Sierra, cranked the windows shut, turned on the air conditioning so he couldn't smell the world. He was in a tunnel shooting home.

But when he came down the steep eastern slope where the evening light washed the Nevada desert, he gave up because he couldn't resist what was outside his car any longer. He opened the window, killed the air conditioning, swam in the rushing air—and got off Route 80 west of Winnemucca onto a thin, pocked, blacktop road so he could be closer to the land.

The road followed the shape of the earth, up rounded brown hills and down, while the sky grew red then faded to the deepest blue then died, and through the windshield he could see the stars. The space between him and the bright pinpricks in the black and this space on the solid were the same.

Francis stopped the car, got out into the caressing night, walked down the side bank. When he looked back over his shoulder, nervous about getting lost, he saw the car silhouetted above him; so he walked farther away, up over a hill, until when he looked back his car was gone. He sat down on the ground, wrapped in the cooling air, the smells of dry earth, cactus, sage. He heard a scrabbling behind him. Maybe a gopher? Maybe a fox?

No people, no buildings. No churches, no schools. No meetings, no books. No theories. If he stayed here long enough, refrained from thinking, casted off his memories, fasting, he would become part of this, he told Siddy in his mind, feeling a little crazy and longing for the presence of his son. Maybe Mendoza had been wrong, his offered potion wasn't Francis's last chance after all, maybe this potential hermitage is yet another.

"Jeez, Dad, get a life!" said Siddy, red-faced with embarrassment, and then melted, and now Francis wondered if he could find his car, remembering stories about people dying in the desert. He waited, recalling what Peggy would say about being open to the grace that comes, for isn't that what happens in the desert, the spirit's livening as the body struggles not to die? But grace didn't come and all he felt was agitation. He couldn't sit still. He gave up, rose, trudged, found the side bank immediately, discovered the disappointment of the lost fear, the car looming above him in the dark. As he neared it he heard the ticking of the cooling metal.

In an hour, Francis was in Winnemucca: red neon, smell of frying meat, yellow glow that tried to dim the stars, straight streets that ended. He was falling asleep, couldn't drive anymore. So he gave up.

The motel room was pink. The double bed was reflected in a mirror that covered one wall, there was a condom machine in the bathroom, it took him forever to peel the plastic wrap from the plastic glass so he could have a drink, the taste of chlorine mixed with the smell of the disinfectant they'd cleaned the room with, the air conditioner hummed full blast, and it was freezing in the room. It wasn't in him to understand that he could adjust the temperature on the air conditioner, so he got on the bed with all his clothes on, pulled the polyester blankets up to his chin, noticing the tiny sparks they gave off when they rubbed against his hands, and fell asleep.

And dreamed: his ancestor, semi-famous Divine, the founder of a town, the beginning of a line—a man whose portrait Francis's father had loved, and stood below to lecture him—had come weirdly down out of his frame above the mantelpiece from where his eyes followed wherever you went and stood now glowering over the bed in this pink motel room in Nevada. His pudgy, sanctimonious hands lay there, one on a Bible, the other lying open on his rounded stomach. He wanted to know what Francis was doing acting like a naked redskin savage in a sweat house miles from home and wife and work.

Francis opened one eye and winked. "If you have to ask, you'll never know," he said, quoting Louis Armstrong, and woke up laughing.

Bolt upright on the bed, he was amazed at his answer—and stunned by the lightness he felt. He'd made the right decision: he was rushing home to heal his marriage, protect his reputation, and save the school. He didn't have to defend himself to anyone! In the very early morning he started driving again.

THREE NIGHTS LATER, past midnight, Peggy opened the door to Francis's knock. He was standing in the doorway, a suitcase in each hand. Levi was standing on his hind legs, trying to lick his face.

Peggy grabbed Levi's collar and tugged him back into the house. "Hi," she said. "Come in." Like welcoming a neighbor who'd come across the lawn to borrow a cup of sugar.

He was in the house now, the two suitcases side by side where he'd left them on the welcome mat. "Peg," he said and reached out. But his arms were tentative and she stayed back.

"Have you eaten?" she asked.

"Not hungry."

"Sure you are," she said. "It's the middle of the night. You have to be." If she could be busy making a sandwich and he busy eating it, it would make this easier. She went into the kitchen and he followed, almost tripping over Levi, who was banging against his legs.

Peggy opened the refrigerator door, bent down, looked in. "I'm really not hungry," he insisted. She stood up, holding a plate of cold cuts in one hand and faced him. He stepped across the little space between them, touched her face and hugged her. She put one arm around his shoulder but kept her other stiff, still holding the plate.

"Half a hug is all I get?"

She didn't answer. She didn't put the plate down either. *For now*, she thought. It wasn't just that she was angry; it wasn't just that she was sad. *I don't know what I'm supposed to do*, she wanted to say. *I don't know how to act when I feel like this.*

She was relieved when Levi didn't follow them into the bedroom. She didn't want Francis to know where their dog had been sleeping. They turned their backs to each other when they undressed. Then Francis lay down stiffly next to her on the bed. She turned the light out. He didn't move, and neither did she. "Peg," he said into the dark. "I'm sorry."

She didn't answer. He hadn't turned to her; he'd said the words straight up at the ceiling.

"I'm home, Peg. It's all right now. And tomorrow, I'll go see Fred Kindler. I'll work it out with him."

She heard him draw a breath, was sure he was going to explain. "Good," she said. "I'm glad of that. And I'm glad you're home, I really am. But don't ever try to tell me why you went away. What you were looking for. I'd rather have my head in the sand." Then she waited in the silence, hoping he'd insist on explaining anyway.

"I wasn't going to try," he said at last.

She knew he didn't want to turn his back to her, and neither did she to him. So they both lay on their backs, not touching, and after a while she drifted off to sleep.

Seven

The first thing Francis did early the next morning was call Fred Kindler's office and ask for a meeting. He was surprised when Kindler answered instead of Margaret Rice. He didn't know yet that now the headmaster got in before the secretary.

"Wait a sec," Kindler said, "you don't mean today. You're in California!"

"No, I'm not. I'm home."

"Really! You're home? What happened? You all right?"

"Yes, I'm all right."

Silence from Kindler

"Really, I'm fine."

"And you want to talk?"

"Yes."

"Good!"

"I mean it," Francis persevered, assuming that Kindler was being sarcastic. "I want to talk."

"So do I." Kindler responded. Francis was taken aback. He was wrong: there was no sarcasm in Kindler's tone.

"Mr. Plummer?" Fred said softly. He'd had time since San Francisco to think about what had happened there. He'd explained to himself that Francis Plummer was just a better speaker than he was, that's all. And he hadn't arrived late because he wanted to show the new headmaster up; he was late because he'd been at Miss Oliver's all his life, where everybody was always late, and then he stayed in the back of the room because he was embarrassed. Fred's resentment still boiled when he heard inside his head Mr. Bradford's loud question: *Why didn't they make* him *the head, for Christ's sake*? But Fred was a grown-up; he understood these things. He'd tamped his resentment down so he could receive the message: *If people think Francis*

Plummer should be the headmaster, then make Francis Plummer his partner. "Mr. Plummer, you there?" he asked again.

"I'll be right over," Francis told him.

With Fred Kindler's surprisingly friendly tone ringing in his head, Francis was full of hope as he crossed the campus toward Kindler's office. Francis Plummer, aka Clark Kent, was home again where he belonged, and where he'd always known exactly what to do.

But the first thing he saw as he entered the headmaster's office was a huge Mickey Mouse wristwatch on the wall behind Fred Kindler's desk. Its fake straps extended all the way from the ceiling to the big, round figure of Mickey in the middle and then down to the floor. And next to this dipsy timepiece was a floor-to-ceiling computer printout of an exclamation point.

For all his good intentions, Francis was appalled. He couldn't remember a time before he had started to hate this cornball little rodent and all his cutesy friends, romance stealers of his youth. In his boyhood he'd been a Phantom freak, a Batman worshiper. Who could want a mouse? He knew it was silly to be so put off by a mere office decoration, but there was a certain style at Miss Oliver's, a certain way of being that said what the school was in ways that words could never say. And this just wasn't it!

Fred Kindler stood up quickly, came around his desk toward Francis, stuck his hand out. "Welcome back, Mr. Plummer. It's good to see you."

They shook. Kindler's hand was very firm. "I really appreciate your wanting to talk," he said, and they sat down, facing each other in the two chairs in front of Kindler's desk. Francis squelched the urge to make the space between himself and Kindler bigger.

"I'd like to get something off my chest right away," Kindler said.

Francis was sure that Kindler was going to tell him it was wrong of him to go to California when he was needed at school. *I'll agree*, Francis thought. *I won't defend myself.*

"That was a great speech you made," Fred Kindler said. Francis was too surprised to answer. "Thanks to that speech, we got the three girls who attended."

"We did?" Francis said, pretending surprise.

"Yes, we did. We didn't get any in Chicago, and we didn't get any in St. Louis. Philadelphia netted exactly one, and Boston two, and I'm sure Peggy's told you what happened in Cleveland."

Francis kept his face blank. Kindler was the last person in the world he wanted to know how little he and Peg were talking. He didn't have the foggiest idea what had happened in Cleveland.

"She did tell you what happened?"

"Not yet. I just got home."

Fred nodded to cover his surprise, then realized he was *not* surprised. But he was embarrassed: he hadn't meant to look as if he were prying. As briefly as he could, he told Plummer what had happened in the Maynards' house in Shaker Heights. He skipped the part about how Peggy got up and told everyone that Marjorie Boyd left of her own free will. That would just make Plummer angry. But he did want to warm Plummer up by telling him how much he admired his wife. So he made it very clear how thoroughly Peggy had blown the lady in the red dress right out of the water when she asked if he were going to let boys in. "She saved the day," Fred said. "She was wonderful."

What Francis heard was miles away from Fred Kindler's intent. He thought Kindler was rubbing it in how much more admirably Peggy had been acting than he had. Francis was ready to admit he should have stayed home. But he wasn't ready to hear Kindler go on and on about it. Now the humiliation of Peggy's having to beg Kindler to let him participate in San Francisco rankled more than ever. Just thinking about it made him angry all over again.

"I wish we had some more recruiting events to do," Kindler went on. "If I'd known you were coming home so early, I would have scheduled at least two of them for later."

"Now that you know I'm not a traitor?" Francis blurted.

Fred was surprised. *Where did that come from?* "No. Now that I know how good a recruiter you are."

Francis waited for Kindler to say more. He wanted to hear Kindler apologize for making Peggy beg.

"I never thought you were a traitor," Fred said.

Francis still waited.

But Fred, who didn't have even an inkling that Francis assumed Peggy had to beg for him, wasn't about to let Francis know that the person he should be angry with was Nan White, not him, first for advising him not to invite Francis, then for standing by the decision, then for changing her mind. Fred Kindler was the head. He didn't pass the buck. "*Traitor's* not the word," he said. "I could get a little irritated for your suggesting that I thought it was."

All right, Francis thought. *He's not going to do it; he just doesn't have the guts to clear the air.*

"As a matter of fact, I could get more than a little irritated," Fred Kindler said, because clearing the air was exactly what he was trying to do. "It was perfectly reasonable for me to assume that having been here for thirty-three years, intensely loyal to Mrs. Boyd and as her right-hand person, you might well have been a little too uncomfortable with the change."

"To be a good recruiter," Francis finished bitterly.

"That's right," Fred Kindler agreed. His tone was mild and matter-of-fact. "That's what I thought. I'm glad I changed my mind."

Francis heard the generosity of that remark and forced himself to accept it. "Well, I'm home now. I'm here." He needed this meeting to succeed as much as Kindler did.

"I'm glad you are," Fred said, and then added, "I hope everything's all right."

"It is and it isn't. I'm glad to be home. But the dig failed," Francis said, sharing his news to nurture this friendly tone—though he didn't share that he was beginning to feel relieved that they didn't find the village, especially the burial ground. What would they have done with the bones? "We ran out of time," he said.

"So soon!"

So Francis told the story of what had happened. He said nothing about his spiritual quest that he'd abandoned for his marriage's sake; and he downplayed Mendoza's incompetence as much as he could. He felt a surprising loyalty to Mendoza, wanted to protect him.

Fred saw right through Francis's defense of Mendoza—and liked him for it. "Poor Mendoza," he said. "Such an interesting man. All he needed was a little administrative help."

Once again, Francis had been slapped in the face. He assumed that Kindler was telling him that not only did he fail as the head's right-hand man but as Mendoza's too.

Fred had no idea that he'd insulted Francis. It never even crossed his mind to think of Francis as an administrator. "Well, anyway, I hope you had an interesting time," he said.

"It was a good experience," Francis lied.

"That's one of the things I miss from when I was a teacher," Kindler said, "the long summer."

Francis nodded again.

"But by the time the summer was half over, I was always itchy to get back."

"Yes, that happens," Francis murmured.

"I had a nice talk with your wife about that just that a week or so ago," Fred said, still trying hard. *God, this guy was hard to talk to!*

Francis nodded again. "That's nice" was all he could think of to say. He tried hard to focus, but he soon lost track of what Kindler was saying because he was still burning about Kindler's administrator remark. And besides, he was still waiting for the chance to say what he came here to say: that he knew it was a mistake to go away; that he really was back on track, ready to go, he could be counted on. If he could get that off his chest, he'd be fine again. He saw Kindler's lips move under the red mustache, heard his voice, but the shape of the words was indistinct and distant. Like the far-off quacking of ducks.

"Of course, we weren't really talking about her because she was quite busy here all summer," Fred said, and immediately regretted it. Plummer would take it as a dig. *Maybe it is a dig*, he thought. *Maybe I can't help it.*

"Who?" asked Francis. When he saw the surprise on Kindler's face, he caught on. He knew now, but it was too late.

"Why, your wife," Kindler said. "Peggy. That's who we were talking about."

"Oh! Of course," Francis mumbled. *Whom*, he wanted to say. *Whom we were talking about.* "Yes, she was very busy," he said out loud.

"May I get you a cup of coffee?" Fred asked, drifting now from irritation to worry. Maybe Plummer *was* cracking up. Plummer shook his head. "Tea? Water? Anything?"

"No, thanks. I'm fine."

There was a silence, and then Fred resumed. "Well, you certainly weren't bored either. Can't wait to hear you talk to the students about it. You and Lila Smythe."

"She did better than I," Francis confessed. "She threw herself into it."

"Oh?" Fred Kindler leaned forward in his chair. Now their knees were almost touching. "It must have been tough not to find the village. Especially for Lila." Fred was genuinely interested. He'd finally gotten this conversation rolling!

"For her it was," Francis said. "She never doubted until the end. While I just felt silly a lot of the time."

Fred leaned even further forward, frowning slightly, intently interested. "I think I understand," he said. He sensed the hunger in Francis, how unassuaged it was, and discovered a deepening respect. It was a good surprise.

On the verge of intimacy, Francis hesitated. He wanted to spill his feelings, get them outside himself, find their validation—the way he could with Father Woodward, and could with Lila, who, before he lost her, understood him instantly. But he was not ready to share with Kindler what he couldn't even explain to Peggy. He shrugged his shoulders and looked away.

Fred leaned back in his chair, disappointed. "Some other time, maybe," he murmured. "I'd really be very interested." He looked at his watch. "Right now let's talk."

"All right. Let's," Francis agreed. The moment for sharing was gone. He already regretted that.

"Now that Mrs. Boyd is gone, you are the embodiment of this school," Fred began. "You symbolize it for everybody, the alumnae, the students. More than anybody. Surely more than me—the newcomer."

Francis looked past Kindler to the monstrous watch on the wall. *More than I*, he thought. *Not* me. *I.*

"I need your help. We need to work together, it's as plain as that."

"Listen," Francis interrupted. "That's what I came in here to say. I want to work with you—and you didn't have to ask. That's why I came home so fast—that and to be with my wife. I will do anything you want except—" Francis wanted to say it: *Except help you bring in boys*, but he hesitated, and Kindler cut him off.

"Let's not get to the exceptions," he said. "Not now. Because if we do this right, there won't be any."

"All right," Francis said.

"Good," Fred said. Then, softening his voice: "I think I understand how difficult this change must be for you. I really do."

"That's not the point," Francis declared. He didn't want excuses for himself.

"It's one of them. You've been here for thirty-three years. I'm only thirty-seven years old, for goodness sake!"

"I can handle it," Francis said.

"All those years serving one person! I know how much you depended on each other."

"I can *handle* it," Francis repeated.

"Well, I'm not sure *I* could," Kindler said even more softly. "Not without some help."

Francis stared. "Help? What do you mean, help?"

Kindler was looking him right in the eye. "I simply mean there's a lot of stress. A huge amount in a change situation like this."

Francis turned his head ninety degrees away from Kindler's gaze.

"All right, I've overstepped," Kindler said. "All I meant is that if you, or anyone else on the faculty, wanted some counseling, some advice about dealing with the kind of strong emotions that come with this kind of change, I want it known that over the summer I got the board to extend the insurance to cover it. But I intruded on your privacy. I should have waited. I'm sorry."

Francis wasn't hearing Kindler talking about the predictable, normal stress that organizational change engenders; he was hearing his new boss, Marjorie's usurper, telling him he was sick. He started to stand up.

"Please, Mr. Kent. I apologize."

Francis was standing now, staring down at Fred Kindler.

"Could you sit down? Please. I really want us to talk."

"Mr. Kent? My name is Plummer!"

"Slip of the tongue," Kindler murmured, touching the fingers of his left hand to his forehead. "I seem to be really fouling up this meeting." He paused, then shrugged. "It happens," he said. "You'll have to forgive me. When I heard that the girls call you by that name—Clark Kent—it put the name into my head. It makes me happy that I have a teacher on my faculty who the girls admire so much he becomes a myth." Kindler was almost smiling now. "So, please sit down. You should be very proud."

Francis made no move to sit down. "It's a tradition that the adults in this school never mention the secret names," he said, voice quivering. *The guy thinks I need a shrink! And he mocks my name!* "Only the girls ever mention those names," he preached, forgetting that Marjorie had been the one exception. "That's the tradition."

"Oh? Then forgive me," Kindler said very quietly. He was silent for a moment, frowning; then he said, "I'm still learning. I'll not make that mistake again."

Francis started to say, "Just the same, you shouldn't—" then realizing how foolish he sounded, he stopped.

"Just the same I shouldn't what?"

"I was just going to explain," Francis murmured. How did he let himself get into this? He really did want to explain the traditions that Kindler needed to know.

Now Kindler was standing too. It was very sudden. Francis saw again how small the man's body was—just as small as his own. The anger on his face was clear, a kind of hardness.

"Well now, I'm suddenly not in the mood for explanations." Fred's voice was quiet; the words came slowly. In the back of his mind he was aware he should be controlling this sudden rage. But he couldn't—or wouldn't—he didn't care which. "In our next meeting, *I* will do the explaining," he announced. "I'm sure it will be more productive than this one—which is over."

"Wait a sec! I didn't mean—"

"You heard me, Mr. Plummer. Our meeting's over."

Francis still stood there. "You're actually kicking me out of your office?"

Kindler didn't answer.

"All right. But I'll be back," Francis promised.

"WELL, HOW DID your nice little talk with our new headmaster go?" Margaret Rice asked as Francis walked through her office on his way out of the administration building. She had come in while he and Kindler were talking.

"Fine."

"I bet!"

Suddenly Francis wanted to talk to his old friend. He sat down on the loveseat, where visiting parents had always sat when waiting to see the headmistress. Now, before walking through Margaret's office, they waited in a special room that was full of shiny school brochures that had appeared over the summer. When, at breakfast this morning, he had looked through one of the brochures Peggy had brought home, Francis had a strange feeling that he was reading about a school he'd never seen.

"Well, what was so fine about it?" Margaret asked belligerently.

"It ended quickly."

Margaret laughed. She sat very still behind her desk, a large woman in a yellow sweater the same color as the leaves on the aspen trees in the Rockies he was still seeing inside his head. She and her ex-husband, Bob Rice, whom Francis remembered as maybe the only male he had ever loved the way one might love a twin, used to invite Peggy and him and Siddy every Thanksgiving to their place in New Hampshire near Mount Chocorua. He remembered the five of them walking down abandoned roads through leaves that lay deep as their ankles on the frosted ground.

But one day, Bob told Francis, "I just can't stand it here anymore." Francis knew that Bob meant he couldn't tolerate the idea that only a few of his students would become full-time professional artists. His fine teaching made them see themselves as artists, but Bob had learned that in many parents' view, one of the unspoken aims of so expensive an education was to insulate their children from such disturbing adventures of the spirit. Bob Rice had received more than one call from an agitated parent suggesting that he be not too inspiring, that perhaps being a lawyer was a sounder goal for a student. Or a stockbroker. Even an old-fashioned, full-time mother. But an artist? Only on weekends. "I've awakened to reality," he told Francis on the day he went away. "I've finally faced it, and I can't stand it anymore."

Margaret followed him to their place near Chocorua, where he still eked out his living as a sculptor, but after several years she had come back. She didn't like living all alone, the wife of a man so obsessed he didn't have any needs other than his work. Francis marveled at his friend's courage to have discovered, at so much cost, who he really was. *Discovery and grief are the same thing*, he had thought to himself, smiling that faraway smile that inspired the girls to imagine he was reliving his exploits as Superman.

Peggy had viewed Bob Rice's departure in a different light. "He just gave up," she had said. "Why should every parent immediately agree with him? Besides, if he really were obsessed as a sculptor, he'd be in New York City—not hiding out on a farm he inherited."

Margaret broke into his thoughts. "How old are you now, Fran?"

"You know my age as well as you know your own. I'll be fifty-six in January."

"Plenty of time left. Nine years, at the very least. You'll outlast him."

"Maybe. And maybe not," he said. "And besides, that's not the point."

"Oh, yes it is, Fran. Very much the point. And don't worry. We'll both be here long after he's gone."

"What makes you so sure?"

"Because his mustache looks funny," Margaret said with a straight face. "That's the one thing they didn't teach him at the New Heads' Workshop: when your mustache looks like it should be under your armpit, you need to shave it off." Margaret grinned.

Just then the door to the new headmaster's office opened, and Fred Kindler's red hair appeared. He looked surprised when he noticed Francis sitting on the sofa. Francis forced himself to meet Kindler's eyes. Then Kindler turned to Margaret. "I need you for a moment, Ms. Rice," he said. "Please bring the calendar." He closed the door and disappeared.

Margaret turned back to Francis as he stood up. She was smiling again. "Good thing he can't hear through that door." It was obvious she wanted some reaction to her armpit joke. He failed to respond, didn't return her grin. That was not how he wanted to defend the school, making jokes about the new guy's funny mustache; he wanted some higher ground than that. If Kindler tried to bring boys in, he wouldn't owe him any support. But he did owe him support.

He saw a worried look in Margaret's eyes. "You'll be all right," she murmured. "Say hello to Peg."

CROSSING THE CAMPUS back to his apartment, Francis remembered how happy he'd always been this time in the summer when the grass on the school lawns smelled like hay and the leaves on the big copper beech tree in front of the Administration Building were already shimmering with faint traces of red, and the new school year was going to begin in just a couple of weeks. Marjorie used to remind him all the time that he was in love with the school. That's why she had trusted him. He knew she meant in love the way a man loves a woman. "Schools are just like people," she had said. "They go through stages and are even more complicated." He used to wonder if Marjorie thought that Peggy loved the school the way a woman loves a man.

Peggy was still home when he arrived. She was usually in her library by this time in the morning. "How did your meeting with Fred Kindler go just now?" she asked.

"Who?"

"Don't be funny, Francis. Fred Kindler. Your new boss."

"He told me I need a shrink."

She waited for Francis to say more. She so wanted Francis and Fred Kindler to be friends!

But Francis didn't want her to know how badly the meeting had gone. "That's what he told me: I need a shrink," he repeated, trying to make it seem like a joke.

She saw right through this. Her heart sank. And she was angry again. "Well, maybe he's right," she said as she left for her library.

Eight

When the phone rang in her Cambridge apartment at supper time on August 18, two weeks before the September board meeting and just a few days before the opening of the new school year, Ms. Harriet Richardson, late of the Oliver board of trustees, knew who was calling. She sighed, disappointed with herself for her procrastination. It would be Sandra Petrie, an Oliver board member. Sandra always called two Tuesdays before the board meetings to offer Ms. Richardson a ride. It seemed strange to Harriet that so volatile a personality could be so rigidly organized.

If she had just written a note right after the summer executive committee meeting to tell Sandra that she wouldn't be needing a ride to the September board meeting in Sandra's Mercedes, Sandra would have forgotten to call and ask why. But now she would probe, Harriet thought, reaching for the phone. If she figured it out before the board meeting . . .

"Hello, Sandra," Harriet said. She hoped knowing who's on the phone before Sandra even said a word would shock Sandra into forgetting to ask why she didn't need a ride.

It didn't work. "You don't?" said Sandra, sounding disappointed. It took her less than a minute to tease out of Ms. Richardson that the reason she didn't need a ride was that she had resigned. She wanted to know why.

"The reasons are personal, Sandra," Harriet said.

"Personal?"

"I'm getting on, you know. I will be seventy-seven years old in November. It's time for younger blood."

"I don't believe a word you're saying."

"Really," Harriet insisted. "Seventy-seven is getting on."

"They're letting boys in, aren't they? That's what happening.

They're letting boys in!"

"No, we are not." Then remembering: "I mean, they are not. You're on the board, Sandra; they wouldn't make such a decision without you."

"Oh, my goodness! They're letting boys in!"

"Sandra, they've made no such decision."

"I knew it! I just knew this would happen!"

"Sandra! Listen to me! Please! They have not made that decision."

Silence again; then softly: "Oh? What decision *did* they make?"

"They merely agreed to let one of the members bring it up at the board meeting."

"Merely! No wonder you quit!"

"Sandra. Please. Keep this to yourself. Deal with it at the meeting. But don't tell anyone. Let the board deal with the issue."

"Let the board deal with the issue," Sandra mocked. "Are you crazy? You think it's just an issue? You sound like Alan Travelers. Or Sonja whatshername. I'm going to deal with the issue!"

"Sandra, be careful."

"I'll be careful, all right. Very careful! Careful to do whatever I feel like doing. That's what you should have done. You should have stayed on the board to vote against it."

"I thought if I threatened to quit, it would change their minds," Harriet said very quietly. "I thought it would shock them to see how I felt about it."

"Well, it didn't work, did it!"

After Sandra hung up, Harriet tried to guess what Sandra was going to do. Whatever it was, it would cause trouble. Harriet had to admit she was glad. But she decided not to put off calling Alan Travelers and warning him that the cat was out of the bag. She owed him that much. Let him try to guess where Sandra was going to strike!

By the time Harriet had moved to the sideboard to pour herself a sherry—just one glass to calm her nerves—she had changed her mind. Why should she help that man and his new headmaster ruin the school? Whatever Sandra was going to do would make it harder to bring boys in. "No," she said aloud to herself, "I'll keep mum. That's the least I can do." This was a first for her, she'd always been known for her integrity. She took a sip of sherry, felt its warmth. "But this is different; they're the enemy, and I don't owe them anything. Not after what they did to Marjorie."

Book Two: Fall Term

Nine

On August 20, the second anniversary of her daughter's death, Gail Kindler woke up crying and turned to reach for her husband and found the bed empty. So she turned her back, away from the place he'd left, and cried all by herself.

Fred was up, dressed, and in his office. This was the day the faculty reconvened to prepare for the new school year, which would start in several days.

Gail, though, with no new job to run to, stayed in their bed and again saw herself standing on the front porch of their house on the Mt. Gilead campus while her husband ran across the campus to her to get the news. She had phoned him to come home so she could tell him face to face. "I need to tell you something," she had said. "Something bad has happened." She still hadn't believed it when she said it over the phone—and didn't believe it until she saw his face as he came up the porch steps and understood that he had guessed. "Sarah's dead," she'd said.

She'd never dreamed she would ever see a face so crushed as Fred's, so melted, a perfect stranger's face, and they didn't dare touch each other, not a hand clasp or an embrace to share their pain, for all the hours and hours it took to call their relatives and tell them; they knew that if they gave in to their need to comfort each other, they would break down completely and never finish the phoning. She'd read in lots of places since then that for many marriages the loss of a child is the end. *But not for us*, she thought, *we wouldn't, either of us, do that to the other, or to Sarah. Our bond's too strong for that.*

She stood up and took off her nightgown. She might as well get dressed. She was almost glad that he'd forgotten, the grief spread out to every day, for what difference did it make which day she died on? She was dead every day, and today was a special day in a very different way. Nevertheless, Gail hated this place, this house that belonged to someone else. It was like living on an iceberg.

She turned now to get to the chair where her clothes awaited her and saw him standing in the doorway. "You forgot," she said.

"I only started to." And then he was across the room and hugging her, and she was crying again, harder than she'd ever cried, as if the last pieces in the hollow insides of her were shattering again to even smaller shards, and he picked her up, right off her feet, and put her in the bed and got in beside her in his sports coat, his tie, and his flannel trousers. His shoes, muddy from running to her across the garden, made a smear on the sheets, and now he was crying too. "Oh, it hurts!" she said. "It hurts. It hurts." And after a while they went to sleep.

They didn't wake up until five minutes to nine—and he had to run to the meeting.

PEGGY PLUMMER WAS walking across the campus toward the meeting with a springy step. Under her new headmaster, the new school year really was a tabula rasa, a brand-new chance to do things right and save the school. Next to her, Francis, who had relived his disastrous meeting with Fred Kindler a thousand times, was more subdued. He'd promised himself that in future meetings he would try to see through Kindler's eyes—and be alert to Kindler's sudden storms of temper.

They were headed to the exact center of the campus, to the library where the full faculty had always met in the big central room. Sometimes it made Francis just a little jealous that so much of the school's life was centered in the library.

In the library, Peggy and Francis sat next to each other at the same place at the same table where they had always sat. He was calm enough. He touched Peggy's hand beneath the table, where no one else could see, to show her he was going to make this work.

Fred Kindler stood to open the meeting, and Francis saw again how much shorter than Marjorie this new guy was. He didn't fill the space around him the way Marjorie had. There was something subdued in the man—except when he was angry!—some hint of sadness that Francis hadn't noticed before and didn't seem right in someone so young.

The first thing Kindler did was point out that the meeting had started ten minutes late.

"At nine o'clock, our starting time, I took a head count," he announced. "And discovered that about a dozen of us hadn't arrived yet or were just coming in the door." He paused for an instant and then resumed. "So I waited to start the meeting because I wanted all of us to be together." Kindler's voice was calm, the only person in the room who was not embarrassed. "I won't wait again to start a meeting," Kindler went on. He let his eyes rest on Francis's face, and waited. It was clear to everyone that Fred Kindler was waiting for the senior teacher to say something in support of the new emphasis on punctuality; but there was something Francis wanted to add. He wanted to explain that Oliver lateness was a function not of carelessness but of intensity: the need to say one more thing in class, to finish up a conversation with a student. *We're here all day*, he wanted to say, *we're not on a treadmill. Oliver people aren't going to be dominated by anything, let alone a schedule.* What he didn't understand, of course, was that he was not defending the faculty's bad habit with this flimsy argument. He was defending Marjorie. He couldn't help feeling that every change the new head made insulted his predecessor and demeaned the past.

His hesitation lasted too long. With a barely perceptible shrug of the shoulders, Fred Kindler moved his eyes away from Francis. "Let's start making Oliver Time mean On Time," he said. The man's voice was pleasant, and he was smiling, but Francis heard his stubbornness.

Then Kindler gave a little talk to start the year. He told the faculty how honored he was to be the headmaster of Miss Oliver's School for Girls, how much he admired the school and how strongly he believed that, working together, they could regain for the school its historical position as the premier all-girls school in the nation. It was an appropriate talk, Francis was ready to admit, measured, respectful, and not self-centered. But for Francis, there was an ebullience missing that he was trained to expect, and there was that trace of sadness again, as if a little piece of Kindler's mind were someplace else. It made Francis feel sad too, in a vague way he couldn't account for.

Next, Kindler gave the faculty the bad news about the budget. Having been so shocked himself when he had perceived this news at the beginning of the summer, he was hardly surprised when he saw how shocked the faculty was. What he didn't know was that part of what stunned the teachers was they were actually being told, and he was using specific numbers. Marjorie had never shared financial realities in any specificity with the faculty. For she and they were *educators*, and in her mind educators didn't involve themselves with such mundane matters as budgets. These were to be relegated to the lower orders: the business manager and bookkeeper and the members of the finance committee.

But the truth of the matter was that even the board's finance committee had had little to say about the finances of Miss Oliver's School for Girls, for Marjorie actually had run the board. She had run everything—until the revolution, initiated sadly and as kindly as possible by Milton Perkins and less kindly by Sonja McGarvey, which had brought in new board members, including Alan Travelers, to save the school from the very person who had made it so worth saving. How many times and in how many different kinds of organizations has this story been played out!

Fred was careful to disguise how badly Carl Vincent had fouled up, and he was glad he was being truthful when he made it clear that Vincent retired of his own free will. For it was true that as soon as the ancient business manager had learned of Milton Perkins's anonymous gift to his retirement fund, he couldn't wait to quit.

Fred knew better than to linger on the bad news. So he moved quickly to his plan for recouping the enrollment. Admittedly, there were no strategies unknown to other schools in his plan. There were only so many ways a school could be marketed. What was new and what lifted his spirits as he talked was the energy, the care, the discipline, and attention to detail the school would invest. Near the end, he passed around the new brochure, designed pro bono by his wife, which emphasized the school's academic rigor and de-emphasized its idiosyncratic culture (one of the reasons Francis felt it described some other school) and which, in Fred's and Nan White's opinion, was better written, printed on better stock, and more graphically sophisticated than its predecessor. He ended by inviting the faculty not to think of enrollment as exclusively Nan White's province but as theirs too, urging them to reach out to every visitor to campus.

The faculty listened intently to Fred's talk. All were aware that his entire emphasis had been on the recruitment of *girls*. Thus the specter of boys invading the school faded—at least for the moment. Looking around the room as he finished, Fred felt satisfied with this beginning.

Near adjournment time, he said, "At one of our next meetings, I'd like you to come prepared to think about the way our students dress. I would have put it on the agenda for today if there had been time for it."

No response.

Fred looked around the room, rested his eyes on Plummer's face again. Then he looked away, much sooner than he had before. "I think if the students look more presentable it will be easier to sell the school," he said.

Several teachers were nodding their heads in agreement. Francis turned, as if by instinct, to see how Gregory van Buren was reacting. Gregory was looking around the room to see how others were reacting. The son of a bitch was counting votes! Francis watched while Gregory's eyes went all around the room. Then Gregory put his hand up.

Most of the time, Marjorie would try to ignore Gregory's upraised hand. But Kindler called on him right away.

"You don't actually intend us to incur the students' wrath?" Gregory asked, looking directly at Kindler. "You don't really think that we should actually invade the sacred teenage right to emulate the appearance of sexual perverts, freaks, and criminals?" and Francis realized this wasn't going to be the usual windy sermon. Gregory wasn't putting his hands together as if in prayer, just beneath his nose, as he usually did, and he was not pursing his lips between sentences, and he was not nodding his head in assent to his own wisdom, and he was not speaking very slowly to allow his listeners time to comprehend the elegant thoughts he was assembling in his ponderous syntax. He was not doing any of these things! He was waving his hands! And being sarcastic! And speaking very fast. He'd been pent up for years on this subject. Kindler had uncorked the bottle.

"You are not daring, sir, I hope, to ask us to ignore the increasingly alarming fact that no one outside this hermetic little enclave understands our misbegotten allegiance to the concept that it is a good idea—a meritorious educational strategy, in fact—to allow girls studiously to take on the appearance of female garbage collectors or drunken agriculturists—when they don't manage instead to look like strippers nearing the climax of their dance. Surely you don't actually believe that it is difficult to explain to parents that our allegiance to this arcane concept is one we hold on purpose, that it is a considered choice among other options, such as occasionally requiring our students to look like normal persons."

While Gregory paused to refill his lungs, Fred Kindler tried to cut him off. Marjorie used to say: "Never mind, Greg, we already know how you feel on this subject." But Kindler was too polite, or not quick enough, and Gregory rushed on. "Failing to understand our strange philosophy, these outsiders who, I take this opportunity to remind us, constitute our market," Gregory added. "That's correct, our market—a blasphemous word in these elevated precincts—thinks we don't give a damn about how our students look. Or perhaps they think we can't *see* the children who have been committed to our care, that one of the important filters through which candidates must pass in order to be awarded the privilege of teaching here is that they be *blind*. How else could they explain such self-destructive eccentricity?"

"You make your point quite clearly," Fred finally managed, with just a hint of irony. "Thank you, Mr. van Buren."

"My point is that we are under-enrolled, sir. We are dying!"

Fred looked around the room to see if anyone else wanted to speak.

But Gregory still wasn't finished. "Thank you, sir, for bringing the subject of student attire up," he said, his tone gliding now from passion to his customary unction. After all the years with Marjorie, he could be forgiven for not understanding that with this new head he didn't need to act as if addressing royalty. "Mrs. Boyd—who couldn't bring herself to censor the students' writing in the school newspaper—wouldn't allow the faculty to discuss how students dress. I am delighted that we finally have a leader who—"

"Marjorie Boyd was right," Francis heard himself blurting. Gregory shut up, and everyone stared at Francis and then turned to Kindler to see his reaction. He was clearly surprised. But Francis wasn't even thinking about the new head's opinion; he was just saying, automatically, what he deeply believed. And besides, he was not going to let anyone criticize Marjorie, especially not Gregory van Buren. "She never would have put it on the agenda," he said; then he realized that hadn't come out right, he didn't want to say the new head couldn't bring up whatever he wanted to bring up, and he went on because he really did want to explain, he really did have a reasonable point to make. "Marjorie and I figured out a long time ago that you can't talk to a teenage kid about how she should dress without sounding like an idiot to her."

"Really?" Kindler asked, and Francis had no idea whether or not he was being sarcastic.

"So then you can't talk to her about the really important things," Francis explained. "You have to choose how you're going to use your ammunition. You only have so much."

Gregory took his eyes off Francis's face and looked across the room at Kindler, and waited. The room was silent. Peggy slid her chair a few inches further away from Francis. "Well, I certainly don't want any of us to sound like an idiot," Kindler finally said. His face was blank. Everybody, except Peggy, who was looking down at her hands in her lap, was glancing back and forth between Francis and Kindler. Suddenly Kindler's face wasn't blank anymore. He was smiling. Everybody understood: *He'd decided to smile.* "It's noon," Kindler announced. "The time I promised this meeting would end. We will start meetings on time. And we will end them when we say we will end them. So we'll bring this up another time. The meeting's adjourned." No one stirred. "We will bring the subject up again," Kindler added. "I assure you. In the meantime, have a productive afternoon." Then he stood up to end the meeting.

A WEEK LATER, on the last day of new-student orientation before classes began, one of the six new students, a junior, Julie Lapham, from Norwich, Vermont, walked by herself back to her dorm after the evening meal. She was too unhappy to want company. She already knew it was a big mistake to have persuaded her parents to let her enroll at Miss Oliver's School for Girls.

Closer to the dorm, she noticed an old, beat-up Subaru just like her brother's in the dorm parking lot and felt even lonelier. She wished it really were her brother's car. But Charley was a sophomore at Trinity College in Hartford, an hour away, and he was very busy and had his own life to lead, and she'd only been away from home a few days. So why would he come see her? Just two months before in July, Julie's parents had told Charley and her that after Charley was born, they'd spent three years trying to have another child, and when they realized they couldn't, they'd adopted Julie. Right up to that instant, neither Julie nor Charley had had any idea that she wasn't their parents' biological daughter. "We waited to tell you till we thought you were both old enough to know and we could tell you together," their father said. And then their mother turned to Charley and said, "We thought you'd like a sister." As if he was the one who needed comforting.

Julie's first reaction had been that she needed to go away to find a place where she could have a family of her own. She chose Miss Oliver's because Julie's best friend's mother, who had graduated from Miss Oliver's in 1965, always said the school was like a family. Well, it didn't feel like a family to Julie. She missed her real family and would have given anything to be helping her parents in their construction business in the afternoons after high school got out, instead of being stuck at a boarding school. But she couldn't go home. Her parents, who at first had refused to enroll her at Miss Oliver's, finally relented under the proviso that she promised to stick it out, whether she liked it or not, through her junior and senior years and graduate from Miss Oliver's. Julie had made that promise eagerly at the time, and now she'd rather die than come crawling home, begging to be released from it, admitting she was wrong. It was a mantra in her family that you finish what you start.

A few yards closer to the dorm, she realized it *was* Charley. She saw his blond head. He saw her too and blew the horn. She quickened her pace. He leaned and opened the passenger door for her. He was in jeans and moccasins with no socks; the sleeves of his T-shirt were tight around his arms. His summer work with their parents had provided him with enough money to pay for his college expenses and his car and made him strong. Julie was almost as tall, but as if to advertise their different genes, she was much thinner than he, and her hair was brown.

"I just thought I'd come by and see how you're doing," he said. They were shy with each other and didn't hug. They'd not always been the best of friends.

"Thanks." She didn't want to give away how happy she was that he'd taken this trouble.

"Well, how are you?" He made it sound like a challenge. He didn't want her getting sentimental.

"I'm okay."

"That's what I thought," he said. "What's wrong? You don't like it here?"

She shook her head.

"Give it time. It's only been a few days." But she knew that's not what he really thought. He wasn't surprised she was unhappy here. He had argued with her when she told her mother and father—right after she learned they weren't her mother and father—that she wanted to go away to school. Charley had known better. "You'll feel even more lost," he'd said. "Stay home and get used to the idea." But he hadn't known how it felt when the people who were your mother and father all of a sudden told you that they were not.

"Thanks for not saying, 'I told you so,'" she told him now.

"I just wish they'd kept it a secret," Charley said.

She shook her head. They'd been over this before. She thought it would be wrong not to know and wanted to defend her parents. "It's not like them to hide the truth," she said. "That's not Mom and Dad."

"Hey, I hope you heard the words you just used? I hope I didn't hear them wrong?" He looked away. That shyness again! It was new between them, and surprising. As if he were embarrassed to have it confirmed that he had a different status in the family than she did.

"Well, what should I call them? Mr. and Mrs. Lapham?"

"Don't talk like that!"

"Maybe they should charge me rent, since I'm really only a guest."

"Come on! Cut it out. You know they love you just as much as me." There. He'd said it. They had been avoiding this subject for years, since long before they learned that Julie was adopted. "That's what you're worried about, isn't it?" he said. "Well, it's crazy. We're still brother and sister."

"We're not brother and sister, we're not even related. If I were eighteen, we could fuck and it wouldn't even be illegal."

He stared at her. *There she goes again*, he thought. Saying outrageous things to get attention. It was not his fault she didn't take the pains to make life easy for herself by acting the way Mother and Father expected. That was why they were always on her case and not on his. He remembered how, even when she was still in middle school, Julie had loved to eat the greasy hamburgers in the school cafeteria because her parents, dedicated vegetarians, were heavy into animal rights, and she'd always sworn a lot because her parents hated profanity, and he knew the reason that she had worked so hard to win the high school rhetoric prize when she was still a sophomore with an essay "proving" the rightness of the Vietnam War was that their parents were pacifists.

Charley understood too that, until a year or so ago, her orneriness didn't disturb their parents. They understood it as her way of establishing her identity, finding it amusing, sometimes even endearing. But now as she approached adulthood, she really did have an identity, which her father especially found less than endearing, because he suspected that she smoked and drank and did drugs with her friends and was maybe even getting sexually involved. (All of which, in fact, she had so far abstained from, mostly to be different.) And, maybe even more irritating to her father, she could now best him in their arguments—which he thought she started and she thought he started—successfully demolishing what she described as his thoroughly unstudied liberal positions with facts and statistics Charley suspected she made up as she needed them. Charley knew damn well that if their father were a conservative, Julie would be a liberal, rather than the other way around. "You're too smart for your own good," he told her now, "and you're a pain in the ass."

Just the same, he wondered how he'd feel if he were the one to learn what Julie had learned just a few weeks ago, and he remembered he had come here to see how she was doing. "Let's go for a ride," he said. "Maybe that'll cheer you up."

"I can't," she said, looking at her watch. "I'm supposed to be in the dorm by eight o'clock. It's five of. They check you in." She'd learned how carefully Mr. van Buren, her dorm parent, took attendance.

"What is this, a school or a prison?" he asked.

"Both," she said, but they both knew it wasn't Miss Oliver's that was the prison; it was her pledge to stick it out there.

"But on weekends it's different. I can check out," she told Charley. She'd already heard the stories about how tricky some of the girls were in convincing the teachers on weekend duty that they were invited to somebody's parents' house where adults would take responsibility: forged letters of invitation, friends pretending to be parents over the phone. And sometimes they just sneaked out after the final check-in at ten.

"Yeah, we have some big-time parties you could come to," Charley said, his voice brightening at this reminder of his release from the strictures of home. It was not partying, the booze and the drugs so much more accessible than at home, that excited him. He'd already felt a tinge of boredom at the parties, which all seemed exactly the same. It was that he didn't have to lie to his parents when he got home.

"Promise?" she asked. "You'll invite me?"

He shrugged and made a gesture that said of course he would, she didn't have to ask, and she leaned to hug him, her resentment flying away.

But as soon as she was out of the car, waving goodbye to him as he drove off, she felt depressed again.

When she got to her dorm, Mr. van Buren was already coming down the hall, checking the girls in. Clarissa Longstreet, Julie's roommate, from Riverdale, just north of Manhattan, was sitting at her desk when Julie entered their room. She looked up from her book and said to Julie, "Where've you been? I was worried." Clarissa was very small with a dark, round face and dyed blond hair and glasses whom Julie, who towered over her, had decided that she liked.

"You don't want to get on the wrong side of Mr. van Buren," Clarissa warned.

Julie shrugged. Maybe that was exactly what she wanted to do. She lay down on her bed.

Clarissa shook her head. "Really," she said. "You don't." Clarissa wrote for the *Clarion*, to which Mr. van Buren was faculty advisor. She knew how sharp his tongue could get when you didn't do things on time and do them well.

The door opened then, and Mr. van Buren was standing in it. It was eight o'clock at night and he was still wearing a blue blazer, white shirt, dark tie, and flannel trousers. He glanced quickly at Clarissa and nodded his head. "Reading ahead," he said. "Very smart."

Then he turned to Julie lying on the bed and stared. Clearly, he didn't like that she was lying down. "You were almost late," he said mildly. She couldn't read the tone of his voice or the slight smile on his face, had no idea whether he was angry or simply stating a fact. "It would be advisable, I think, not to be almost late again," Mr. van Buren said. Then, turning to leave, he looked back over his shoulder and raised his eyebrows at Julie as if to show how seriously she should take his advice. Then he closed the door and was gone.

"Pretty weird, huh?" Clarissa said. "But wait till you have him in class. He's the best English teacher in the world."

Julie had only been at Miss Oliver's for a few days, and already she had heard how some students argued, as Clarissa did, that Mr. van Buren was the best and others that nobody could be better than Mr. Plummer, aka Clark Kent. Right then, if she cared enough to have an opinion, Julie would have agreed with Clarissa. She liked it that Mr. van Buren didn't harangue her about lying down while he was talking to her, the way her father would have. She would have sat up, if he'd not left so soon. And she admired the ironic way he used the word *almost*.

But he was a teacher, and she was still in his presence at eight o'clock at night and would be again in half an hour when he presided over a dorm meeting "to get properly organized for the year." For Julie, school has always been a scene she was released from to a larger world at three o'clock in the afternoon.

Now she was sealed in twenty-four hours a day, and there was no relief. She could hardly breathe.

On the first day of classes, the students entering the dining hall for breakfast found a stack of the *Clarion* on each table, two pages of which were filled with Karen's article on the new headmaster. To be greeted early in the morning of their first day of classes by a feature about the new headmaster made them even more resentful of Mrs. Boyd's dismissal. They wanted to be greeted by Mrs. Boyd. For all their intelligence and good education, what many of the students took away from the article was that the new headmaster had ripped down all the pictures that students had given to Mrs. Boyd and that he was going to take away the freedom of press that Mrs. Boyd had championed.

Only her close friends would learn that Karen, who had spent an hour with Mr. Kindler, was well disposed to him. If Karen had wanted to express her personal opinion in the *Clarion*, she would have written an editorial supporting the new headmaster, instead of an objective report of an interview. But she wouldn't do that; it would look to the students as if the new headmaster had manipulated her and make him even more contemptible in their eyes. There was nothing she could do to make Mr. Kindler popular. He was on his own.

This first morning of classes, Francis got to his classroom long before his students. He taught both his math and English classes there, where he also had his office; lighted by big windows that looked out on the campus, it was his seat of power, a little kingdom. It was one of the perks of his seniority that no other teacher used it. The front wall and the wall opposite the windows were covered by blackboards, and on that day the back wall, behind the big model of the Globe Theater created by a student years ago, was covered by a collection of black-and-white photographs of comely New England farmhouses that Bob Rice had sent him because he knew that Francis taught a lot of Robert Frost. The floor was covered by a thick rug. The tables in the classroom had been put together to form a three-sided square whose open side faced the front, where Francis's desk was placed. He never sat at it when he was teaching.

This morning, as he entered the empty classroom, the first thing

Francis saw was *A FIRST DAY OF SCHOOL GIFT FOR MR. P!* emblazoned on the blackboard. Under this greeting, the big slate was covered with a math problem that went on and on, over the front blackboard and around the corner onto the one on the adjoining wall. He saw that the problem was worked two ways with two different answers. *AND THEY'RE BOTH RIGHT!!! CAN YOU PROVE THEY'RE NOT? HUH, CLARK, HUH, I BET YOU CAN'T!* Whoever had snuck out of the dorm in the middle of the night and spent hours in here doing this had used her nondominant hand. The figures were a little child's; she wanted him to guess who she was.

Francis smiled, his spirits lifting. He decided to leave the problem up there on the board for the advanced calculus class that would troop in to the classroom in a half an hour. That was the way to start a day! Math's a game, play is the mind at work, and he was going to get the bagels and coffee ready.

But he only got a minute or two to himself because there was a knock on the door, and he opened it, and there stood Lila Smythe. His heart skipped a little beat. Next to Lila, but shyly standing half a step behind, one of the new ninth graders faced him.

"This is Sara Warrior," Lila said. "She's a ninth grader. She wants to talk with you." Lila stood stiffly, unsmiling, in the doorway.

She didn't even say hello, Francis thought. "All right," he said. "Come in."

Sara hesitated. Lila turned and smiled to her. "He won't bite," she said. He couldn't tell if she was being sarcastic, and then the two were in the room, and he was motioning them to seats at one of the tables and took a third, facing them. "Sara's Indian," Lila announced. "Pequot. That's why she wants to talk to you."

"Native American," he corrected. He'd read the admissions folder. Sara, who could trace her Pequot ancestry all the way back to the 1870 census, lived in Stonington.

"All right, say it the PC way." Lila shrugged. "Who cares?" And for an instant Francis thought he would ask Sara to excuse herself and have a talk with Lila. But he changed his mind. That wouldn't be fair to Sara.

Sara was a small girl, dressed more formally than the Oliver custom in a simple green skirt, a white, long-sleeved blouse. She looked at him, studying his eyes. He couldn't read her face. But he did know she was the first Pequot citizen to be enrolled at Miss Oliver's School for Girls. He found himself wanting to apologize for that. "Welcome, Sara. We're very glad to have you," he said.

"Thank you." The first words she'd said.

"Are you glad to be here?"

"I don't know," Sara said. Because she really didn't. She remembered how glad she had been at first, and how kind Mr. and Mrs. Kindler were at the reception for new students and their parents. Her mother and dad had driven her to school and were going to leave right after the reception, and she was already homesick, but the little red-headed man with the funny walk who she was surprised to learn was the headmaster crossed the room to greet them. Her father and he seemed to like each other right away as they shook hands. They were the only two men in the room who were wearing suits, the headmaster in a funny brown one, her father in his pinstripe blue. That had made her glad. She knew the headmaster wore a suit for the same reason her dad did: to show respect.

But now, after what she had discovered in the school library yesterday, she felt like a stranger. And she knew why the student who toured her around when she was visiting as a candidate skipped over the library, claiming she had a class to get to.

Sara also remembered how excited she was when her middle school English teacher, a tall, thin black man with dreadlocks in his first year of teaching, who she had sensed felt just as out of place as she did—and on whom she had a crush—persuaded her to think seriously about attending Miss Oliver's. "They make you work," he'd said. "They actually want you to think for yourself." He'd heard about the school when had he reached out to the Mashantucket Pequot Tribal Government, just a few miles away, to see if he could arrange some interaction between the tribe and his class in order to broaden his students' view of the world, which, to his disillusionment, he'd found to be exceedingly narrow. He was soon after chastised for including in his curriculum material something incapable of being reduced to a standardized test—but that's another story.

"Sara's seen the Collection in the library," Lila said.

"Good!" Francis said brightly.

Lila turned her head away, stared out the window, and then it dawned on him what Sara was going to say. Her eyes were full on his.

"It's wrong!" Sara said.

He didn't want to think about this. He didn't need it between him and Peggy.

"Sara's right, isn't, she? If it were white people's bones, they'd be in a graveyard, wouldn't they?" Lila said. "Not in a display in a private school library."

"Yes, I suppose so," he murmured.

Lila just watched him.

"But it's mostly artifacts: clothing and tools and weapons," he said halfheartedly. "There's only a small piece of one femur." Sara Warrior was still studying him.

"Is that what we would have done if we had found the Ohlone village?" Lila asked.

"I've been thinking about that," he admitted.

"I never thought about it at all," Lila said, "but then Sara came to me."

"I asked her how you got them," Sara said. "I asked if they were given to you."

"But of course she already knew the answer," Lila said.

"I was hoping they were gifts," Sara said. "That you hadn't taken them."

"I see," said Francis.

"It was my new school," Sara said. "That's why I was hoping."

"There are two ways to look at this," Francis began. He owed it to Peggy to defend what she believed: that the display was a presence that students didn't just read about but see. It put the understanding in their gut, not just their brain, of how many ways there were to be human.

But Sara cut him off. "Not if they weren't given to you," she said. "Not if you took them. Then there's only one way."

We didn't take them, he wanted to say. *We found them.* But he knew that was lame because they weren't given, and he couldn't think of anything else to say. *Let Peggy try*, he thought.

"What do you think?" Lila asked. "You're the advisor." He heard the accusation in her tone: that he was going to back off this time too.

He hesitated again.

"All right, I'll decide," Lila said "We'll bring it to the school. The student council. In Morning Meeting. Won't we, Mr. Plummer?" Lila prodded. And now they were both silent, because he was thinking about how this issue, if it got in the papers, could hurt the school, and she was thinking here was another time when he couldn't take the heat.

"All right," he said at last. It was the Oliver tradition when an issue came up: the student council aired it in an open discussion in Morning Meeting. It was one of the things he loved about the school.

"You don't have to sit on stage. We can break that tradition," Lila said.

"You think I'm going to hide?"

"You think I came in here to embarrass you? You've already said there are two ways to look at it. Suppose Mrs. Plummer wants to defend the other way?"

"I'll be on stage," he said. "I'm not about to break the tradition. Besides, my wife is a reasonable person. And I'll let her know what's going to happen so she won't be surprised."

"Good for you," Lila said There was no bitterness in her voice. Maybe he'd earned back a glimmer of her respect.

"I'll introduce the issue," Lila said. "Then we'll put Sara on, and she'll make her proposal."

"Proposal? I thought it was going to be a discussion."

"Tell him, Sara," Lila said.

"To give it back to its rightful owners," Sara said. "Of course. To get it off this campus right away."

"Otherwise it might be hard for her to stay here, don't you think?" Lila said. Though her tone was mild, he was a little irritated. He knew what her rhetorical question meant: if you're going to be inclusive, you have to adjust to the ways the people you include see the world. Well, he didn't need a lecture. *You're so much nicer when you're not being sanctimonious*, he wanted to say. But of course he didn't. He'd lost the chance to be her guide.

The bell for first period rang. Francis's advanced calculus class, waiting outside the classroom door, knew his closed door meant he was having a private talk. They wouldn't come in until he opened it. "Thank you for listening," Sara said, and both girls stood up and left. Then his students trooped in. They talked quietly, sleepy in the early morning; their chairs scraped against the floor as they took their seats, and Francis made a mental note to go to Fred Kindler's office first thing after classes. Kindler needed to know this issue was coming up. Right after that, he would tell Peggy.

What Francis didn't know was that Sam Andersen, the history teacher whose sense of humor Francis liked so much and whom he had seen playing tennis with Fred Kindler, was designing a new course that he would teach later in the year in the spring term. It fit right in with the Oliver emphasis on experiential education: an archaeological dig right here on the campus, where certainly there were many artifacts still to be found. Sam wondered why in the world no one had thought of this before. He'd shared his idea with Peggy Plummer—who thought it was wonderful.

TEN

In the same morning that Lila and Sara confronted Francis about the Pequot display, Fred arrived at the River Club parking lot a few minutes before his first full board meeting. All during the drive from Fieldington he had heard, over and over again, Ms. Richardson say, "You won't get away with this," and now he wished Alan Travelers hadn't persuaded him that Ms. Richardson would never stoop so low as to tell people that Sonja McGarvey was going to propose the admission of boys at the board meeting. "Ms. Richardson would never break a confidence, I don't care how angry she is, and if I'm wrong the worst part for me won't be holding the meeting in public," Alan had said. "It will be my disappointment in a friend." He went on to say he'd be damned if he were going to sneak around and hold the meeting at a secret time and in a secret place. "We'll just handle it, if it happens," he said to Fred. "You and I. We'll take it as an interesting challenge."

Through the windshield, Fred stared at the river, just yards from the edge of the parking lot. How peaceful it would be just to sit here all morning watching the unresisting water flow! He shook his head to jettison the thought, got out of the car, and entered the building.

As he approached the oak doors he heard the sound of angry voices, and when he entered the room, he saw right away that most of the people sitting at the table weren't board members—he recognized very few of them—while the legitimate members, their places usurped, stood with embarrassed and angry looks on their faces among the crowd that surrounded the table, taking up all the space between the table and the walls. It was obvious to him that these invaders had made sure to arrive very early, before the board members, and had commandeered the seats.

The room went silent as he stopped in the doorway, and everyone turned to look at him. *We have the power, not you*, the invaders' expressions said. *You can't do anything we don't want you to do.* He saw this on their faces, that they could riot to get what they wanted, and his nervousness flew away. He was suddenly calmer than he'd ever be staring at the river. And even more surprising, he was happy. This is exactly what he wanted: a fight! *Oh, yes, I can!* he thought, *I will do exactly what I want.*

"Good morning," he said. No response.

No matter: waiting for an answer provided an instant in which to think. He was grateful also to discover that Alan Travelers was one of the few board members who were at the table; he was sitting calmly at the chairman's place at the end of the table opposite where Fred was standing. His eyes met Fred's.

Milton Perkins was also at the table, next to Travelers. Fred knew right away he would be the first to speak. He was right. Perkins's voice was a whisper, intended only for Fred, but it was nevertheless loud: "We've got a traitor in our midst!" Fred heard irony and chagrin in Perkins's voice, but the crowd did not, and there were boos and hisses. "Well, damn it, we do!" Perkins said, this time not in a whisper, and now there was laughter. Fred's gorge rose even more: that these people would ridicule the old man! The students would never be so unkind.

Fred kept his face perfectly calm, almost expressionless, as if he were about to go to sleep. He put his hands up to the people who stood to his right and left along the wall. The laughter stopped. He gazed around the room, looking into people's eyes while he let his anger flood him. He didn't see the oak walls behind the people, was oblivious to the array of Hartford's patriarchs in their golden frames, and didn't notice that the sun, breaking through the clouds and sparkling on the river just outside the windows, had lit up the room. He only saw each face, and stared, and sent his message—*now you have to deal with me! So don't you ever mock a human being again!*—wondering all the while: *Where the hell did I learn to do this*? The room went very quiet.

He turned his gaze steadily on Alan Travelers, who instantly stood up. Now Fred and Alan, at opposite ends of the table, were the only ones at the table who were standing.

"It seems that all of a sudden there is a lot of interest in what goes on at board meetings," Alan said, speaking as if no one other than Fred were in the room with him.

"Clearly," said Fred.

"It's about time!" someone yelled from the crowd to Fred's left. He didn't want to take his eyes off Alan to find her. "We should have been watching you all along!"

Now another young woman was waving her arms. She was in the crowd near the other end of the table, directly behind Travelers. "What are these men doing on the board, is what I want to know," she shouted. "We never had men before. This is a girls' school!"

Suddenly everyone—except the board members—was talking at once. Fred waited for Travelers to get control. It would be wrong for the head of school to presume to do so. This was a board meeting. So he was relieved when Travelers put both hands up above his head. When the noise level descended just barely enough for him to be heard, Travelers spoke in a loud voice: "Your attention, everybody. Please. Your attention." Above the noise Travelers shouted—though, to Fred's admiration, he kept his calm. "Would the members of the board who are standing please take seats at the table, and will those guests who are at the table please give their places to board members."

Several board members stepped forward from the crowd along the walls. But no one at the table moved. The noise level rose even higher. The standing board members hesitated, clearly embarrassed, then stepped back. Someone in the crowd yelled, "No men!" It quickly became a chant: "No men! No men! No men!" Fred looked around the room to see who was not chanting. Many were refraining. He could see their embarrassment; several were trying to help Travelers get order. Across the room Mavis Ericksen stared at Fred with an expression that seemed to say: *See what you've done?* The chant continued. The noise bounced off the walls. Fred thought of standing on a chair and shouting for order.

Instead, Milton Perkins stood up. His hands were shaking. The noise subsided, and into the relative silence he yelled: "Shut up! Just shut up and get away from the damn table!"

There was an immediate silence, a kind of gasp. "Sit down, Mr. Perkins," Travelers said very calmly into that silence. Perkins sat down. It grew even quieter.

When a woman on Fred's left stepped forward into that silence, Fred knew instinctively that she was going to grab the power back, if Travelers gave her time. "Oh!" she wailed. "*I am so outraged!*" She stamped her foot, and Fred's heart sunk; Travelers wasn't going to be quick enough. The man hadn't been to enough faculty meetings. "Not for me!" the woman wailed. "It's not for me that I am outraged. I'm used to abasement." Fred knew she was the perfect person to play this part. He hated himself for noticing how unattractive she was, a tiny woman in mud-brown slacks, a blouse that looked as if it should have been worn by a third grader, oily brown hair, and wire-rimmed glasses. Behind her, Charlotte Reynolds was nodding her head encouragingly. "But for all the women in the world!" The mousy lady writhed her hips and shoulders as if somehow the motion would pump even more volume out. "All of them who have been slaves to men from the beginning of time! All of them in every country, in every century, who have labored while men have rested, who have nurtured the children whom men have ignored, who have stayed home while their brothers went to school."

"Hear, hear," someone yelled.

"Jesus, all of a sudden we're in England!" Sonja McGarvey said.

"And now it will happen again. Men will enter our sanctuary and take the spoils. So I am especially outraged. I am violated. I am raped by the thought that our young women of Miss Oliver's School for Girls, our hope of victory, of transcendence, will once again—" Here she hesitated, overcome; she looked around the room, her mouth opening and closing as if she were still speaking, but no words were coming out. Now the majority of people in the room were clearly embarrassed. "Once again," she was finally able to say. "Once again." Then she stopped.

"So whadda we do now?" Milton Perkins asked in a loud voice, "Hold hands and sing 'We Shall Overcome'?"

In the silence that followed, a few titters. Then more.

"At a board meeting, for cryin' out loud!" Perkins said. Travelers reached his hand out to Perkins's shoulder. Perkins pushed it away. "Who's got a violin?" he asked.

That's when the mousy lady began to cry. Fred knew instantly it was a mistake. She was taking it much too far, he thought, much relieved. She hadn't been in faculty meetings either! While the woman sobbed, some watched, some looked away. But one very young alumna came all the way around the table with her arms outstretched so far in front of herself she looked as if she might fall down, and put them around the weeping woman. The two of them swayed together for what seemed an eternity. Perkins wore an expression as if he were watching a freak show. Fred prayed he would keep his mouth shut.

When the weeping subsided and the hug ended, Travelers spoke and Fred marveled at his grace. "Thank you, Ms. Aguire," Travelers said very gently. "We deeply appreciate your great concern."

Fred watched the woman's face lose it staginess. "Thank you," she murmured, her hand flying up to her mouth in her surprise that her feelings had been affirmed and her name known.

"Now," Travelers said in the same gentle tone, "I do hope that we can make places for every board member at this table." As he spoke, he moved to a place just behind the nearest chair occupied by a non-board member, and placed his hand at the top of the chair back. The woman sitting in it glanced up at him and rose as Alan Travelers, with a graceful gesture, pulled her chair back to ease her standing. Then he turned to the nearest board member who stood next to the wall and invited her to the empty chair with an equally graceful gesture of his open hand. The woman took the chair, and Travelers moved toward the next chair in which a non-board member sat. But he didn't have to. Simultaneously each of the usurpers gave up their seats. The last board member to sit down was Mavis Ericksen.

When all were seated, Travelers said, "Now we'll begin. May I have a motion that the minutes of our last meeting be approved?"

"Just a minute," Fred said. Travelers stared down the table.

"We're missing one of our members." Fred announced. He was staring now at Sandra Petrie, who had remained with the crowd against the wall.

"So we are," said Travelers. His tone of voice made it clear that he too had suddenly figured out who had broken the confidence and started this riot. Harriet Richardson must have told her what Sonja McGarvey was going to propose today. Why else would she remain standing at the wall?

Petrie's face was pale. "I'm resigning," she whispered.

"There's a process for that," Travelers said. "Not appropriate in the middle of a board meeting. I insist that you join us."

Petrie shook her head, remained standing. Travelers stared and waited, and Petrie finally sat down, just to get out of the limelight. She averted her eyes from the other board members.

"The motion to accept the minutes, please," Travelers said.

"How about you, Mrs. Petrie," Fred said. "Wouldn't you like to make the motion to accept the minutes?"

Sandra Petrie flashed him a confused look. Now that she was sitting down, she seemed much shorter than when she had stood by the wall; all her height had to be in her legs. Her face was thin, very pale—almost pretty, Fred thought, if it weren't for the frown.

"Ms. Petrie?" Fred said.

"All right, I move the minutes be approved." Her voice was tentative.

"What about the misspellings?" Fred asked.

"I don't understand," said Petrie.

"The misspellings."

"Where?" she said.

"I don't know," he said. "You're the one who's approving the minutes."

"Fred, please," Travelers said.

"Don't you think we should spell things right at Miss Oliver's School for Girls?" Fred asked, looking directly at Petrie.

Her face was very pale.

"Well?" Fred insisted.

Petrie looked down at the table, hunching her shoulders. Clearly she wasn't going to speak.

"She only talks when she's standing up," Fred announced across the table to Alan Travelers, who looked at him as if he'd never met him before.

"I move the minutes be accepted," said Reginald Griffin, a new board member. He was struggling not to laugh.

"Second," Sonja McGarvey said.

Travelers chaired the rest of the meeting through every committee report, none of which had anything to do with the subject that had brought the intruders. After a while, some of them left. Those who stayed grew increasingly restless. "When are you going to get to the real question?" asked a tall woman in a green dress from where she stood by the wall.

"Madam, we've been dealing with real questions all morning," Travelers responded innocently.

Fifteen minutes later when the old business was finished, Travelers opened the meeting to new business. Sonja McGarvey was the first to raise her hand. Travelers recognized her.

"We have a fiscal crisis," McGarvey said. "Everybody knows it. We are going to go under unless we make a change." She stopped there while every person in the room stared at her. "Therefore, in order to ensure the continuing existence of our school, I move that we accept boys."

Silence in the room. Then "bitch traitor!" from a woman standing by the wall. A murmur started to rise.

Travelers was fast. "Is there a second?" he said. The room went quiet again. No one at the table raised a hand.

"The motion fails," Travelers announced, and the tension left the room, like air through a window.

"All right, I'll make another motion then," McGarvey said.

"No more, bitch!" the same woman hissed.

Travelers called on McGarvey.

"I move the admission of boys as an alternate strategy to closing down when we reach a point where it is obvious that the goals in the headmaster's schedule for rebuilding the girls-only enrollment cannot be reached." The board members stayed quiet. The angry murmur rose again among the standees.

"Will you accept a change from *when* to *if*?" Travelers asked. The room went quiet again.

"Oh, all right," McGarvey said, and repeated word for word her previous motion except that she changed *when* to *if*. She turned away from Travelers then and put her eyes on Fred. He thought he saw a hint of a smile on her determined face. *Thank you*, he wanted to say. *If* was exactly what he needed!

"We need a second," Travelers said.

No one put up a hand.

"The motion fails," Travelers said.

"Well, I've done my best," McGarvey said. "Let the school commit suicide if it wants to."

"So we've just decided we'd close the school down before we let boys in?" Reginald Griffin asked. "We've painted ourselves into a corner?"

"We haven't decided anything," Travelers said. "The motions weren't seconded. We didn't vote."

"All right then, I move that *if* the school gets into financial extremis, we *consider* the option of admitting boys," Reginald Griffin declared.

"Second!" Sonja McGarvey said. Then under her breath, "Chicken shit's better than nothing."

Travelers stood up. "Any discussion?" He frowned. It was clear that if anyone raised a hand, he'd kill. And anyway, the members couldn't wait to get out of there, off that stage. "Good," he said. "We'll vote by secret ballot." He handed a tablet of paper down the table.

The room was quiet while the board members wrote either *yes* or *no* on their ballots and handed them back to Travelers. Fred was not a board member, so he didn't have a vote. Travelers made two piles on the table in front of him. Then he counted each of them. Twice. "There are twelve *ayes* and eleven *nays* and two abstentions," he announced calmly, and Fred knew right away that if the members had been asked to raise their hands in front of their audience, there would have been only two ayes, one of them Sonja McGarvey's and the other, he was fairly sure, Travelers's, though Alan hated the idea of going coed.

"So you've voted to let boys in!" one of the invading alumnae declared. In her forties, blond hair gone mostly to gray, the woman was clearly trying to keep her voice calm in spite of her agitation. She had been glancing at her watch for the last hour.

"We have not," Travelers responded. "We've simply included it among the options to consider if we're in extremis. And in the meantime, we are going to do everything possible, under the leadership of our new head of school, Fred Kindler here, to rebuild our all-girls enrollment."

"I wish I could believe it won't happen," the alumna said.

"Trust us to try," Travelers said, standing up. Then turning back to the table, he said, "A motion to adjourn, please."

"So move," said Reginald Griffin.

"Second," said McGarvey, standing up.

"One more question, please," from the gray-haired alumna.

"Madam, we have an adjournment motion."

"For Mr. Kindler," the alumna said.

Alan knew that she was up to something, so he ignored her. "All in favor of the motion to adjourn," he said to the table, and all the board members raised hands. "This meeting is adjourned," he declared. The board members rose quickly from the table, and so did Fred.

But he didn't escape. The woman and about ten others surrounded him as soon as he stepped away from the table. "Surely, you're not going to refuse to talk to us," she said.

"No, of course I'm not." Fred glanced at Alan, who had seen what was happening and was listening hard.

"Mr. Kindler, my name is Elizabeth Preston, class of '61."

"How do you do, Mrs. Preston," Fred said gravely.

"I have a daughter in the class of '93. I don't suppose you've had time to get to know her yet," she added sarcastically. Her implication was clear: he'd been so busy plotting to let boys in that he'd had no time to get to know the students.

"I'm looking forward to getting acquainted with every student, Mrs. Preston."

Preston nodded, leaving a loaded silence. Then she said, "My question is where do you stand on this issue?"

Now Travelers was by Fred's side. "Mrs. Preston, in the first place, it was a secret ballot, and in the second, he doesn't have a vote."

"I'm not talking about a vote, Mr. Travelers. I know he doesn't have a vote, and I know why: so you can protect him. But that won't work, will it? I mean, we're grown-ups here, and he is the leader, isn't he?"

"Madam, it's a board position."

"Oh, please, Mr. Travelers. He's the headmaster."

"Mrs. Preston," Fred interrupted. "Believe me—" Then he saw

the trap she was laying and stopped. He had to support whatever position the board took—or resign.

"I'll do my best," Preston murmured.

Fred took a breath. He stared at her.

Preston shrugged her shoulders, didn't flinch. "Just as I thought," she said. "You'll do whatever you're told to do. The board's little patsy."

"Let's go, Fred," Alan said, tugging at Fred's elbow. "There's no point in this."

"We would have preferred someone with conviction!" Preston said.

Fred resisted Alan's tugging. "I'm not going to lower myself to respond to that," he said.

"I wouldn't care if you did," Preston said. Then she turned her back and walked away, and her supporters dutifully followed.

"She's smart," Alan said to Fred after the room was empty. "She's crazy, but she's smart. You say you're against letting boys in and the board votes to do that, you have to leave. I could have killed her."

"How do they get so good at smelling blood?" Fred wondered aloud. "Instinct? Or a plan?"

"We'll never know," Alan said. "She probably doesn't either."

Eleven

Now Fred Kindler was in a rush. He needed to get back to campus as fast as he could and be the bearer of this news: *The board is willing to consider admitting boys.* Otherwise, someone else would bear it. If he didn't get there first and do things right, Perkins's prediction would come true: he'd have a crazy house on his hands. Fred's walk across the parking lot to his car became a jog, and then a run.

First tell the faculty, Fred decided. That's protocol, that's courtesy. That put them on his team. He'd call a meeting right away and tell them, sculpting the news, keeping it to its truthful context—*only* if the only other choice was to close the school. Then together, they'll call a meeting of the school and he'll tell the students. And he'll call Alan and ask him to write a letter, today, from the board to all the parents and alumnae. It was a matter of getting the news out first, calmly, from the people in charge, before the crazy people did.

Then—brilliant thought—the way to do this thing *exactly* right: tell Francis Plummer first, the senior teacher. *That's* the protocol; *then* go to the faculty. Plummer would appreciate that. So would the faculty. He'd take five minutes, do that first, make it clear to Plummer that for all their problems he's still the senior teacher. Honor that, and Fred would be honored back. Stick to protocol. In a crisis, do everything right.

That plan made, Fred had room in his mind to think over what had happened as he rushed back to school. He had to admit he was irritated at Alan Travelers for trusting that Ms. Richardson would honor the principle of confidentiality, and then being so careful of his own integrity that he wouldn't consider moving the meeting to a secret place and another date just in case she did break the principle, which now it was clear she did. That had been Travelers's first mistake.

His second was not pulling Sonja McGarvey aside before he started the meeting and telling her to hold her proposal to admit boys for another time when the board would meet in private and have the time to figure out how to let the community know what was being considered and how to manage the reaction. Maybe Travelers had assumed McGarvey would make her proposal anyway, being the kind of person she was. McGarvey would scorn any approach that seemed roundabout, convinced that the only road to salvation was the quickest and most direct. Maybe she hadn't trusted her colleagues ever to muster the courage, at least not until after it was too late, if she didn't force the issue.

By the time Fred arrived on campus, his irritation had melted. Who was he to judge this board, still virgin in the heated politics of school after having been so long a rubber stamp, vassal to a royal head, for making his job even harder? He could have turned the job down; it was not as if he hadn't known the risks. He knew how bored he would have been tamely managing the status quo of an untroubled school. Besides, he'd known he could fall in love with Miss Oliver's School for Girls, and there had been the subliminal push from his dead daughter. He still wanted to lead the school that he was sure she would have loved.

Francis got the message in the middle of a class. He could tell it made the students as nervous as it made him. Teachers being summoned to the head's office in the middle of a class? That had never happened before. The only reason he could think of for Kindler's wanting so urgently to see him is that he'd gotten wind of the student council's plan and needed to talk with the faculty advisor about it. That issue would have made even Marjorie nervous. Maybe Lila had paid Kindler the courtesy of telling him what she and Sara Warrior and the advisor to the student council had decided this morning. Good for her if she did, he thought, but he had wanted to be the one to tell Kindler. He had planned to go to Kindler's office right after classes, not only because Kindler really needed to know, but also so it wouldn't look as if he were withholding information to catch Kindler unaware. Francis wished he had told Lila that he would bring the information to the new headmaster.

He'd forgotten—maybe he hadn't even known—that Kindler

had been off campus at a board meeting all morning, and so no one could have warned him about this delicate issue that was going to complicate both their lives.

When Francis stepped through the door to the head's office, he saw the tension on Kindler's face. Kindler stood up, reached across his desk to shake Francis's hand, then sat down behind his desk. This time he wasn't going to come around his desk and sit near Francis. "Sit down, please, Mr. Plummer," Kindler said, motioning to one of the chairs in front of his desk. Francis sat. Behind Kindler the crazy wristwatch loomed.

Francis didn't wait for Kindler to start the conversation. "I'm sorry that I didn't get to you earlier with this news," he said. "But I had classes."

Fred stared at this little man sitting across the desk from him. "What?" he said. "You knew?" He started to stand up.

"Only since this morning," Francis answered. He tried to keep the defensiveness out of his voice.

"This morning was early enough. The board meeting didn't start till nine o'clock." Fred was standing up now. He was so angry he could hardly see. It didn't occur to him that there wasn't much he could have done if Plummer had told him as late as this morning that people were going to invade the meeting and actually sit in board members' places. Actually take their places! All Fred knew was just how little he trusted this bastard. Conniving with Sandra Petrie! *And I was going to tell him first?*

"Wait a second!" Francis said. "So Lila got to you by nine o'clock? Good for her. I had classes. I'll be goddamned if I'm going to skip classes to tell you something you don't need to know right away. The student council isn't going to do anything for a couple of days at least. What the hell are you standing up for, for Christ's sake?"

"Get out of here!" Fred Kindler said. "Just get out."

"No," said Francis very calmly. "No, I won't get out."

Kindler was still standing, gripping the edge of his desk with both hands. Francis saw how white the backs of Kindler's hands were.

"You called me in to talk about the student council proposal," Francis said. He was sure now this guy shouldn't be the head of Miss Oliver's School for Girls. He was out of control, you never knew what was going to set him off. "So let's talk about that," he went on. "Not about the fact that I didn't sprint across the campus to tell you in the first three seconds after I found out."

"What student council proposal?"

Francis didn't answer for a second. "Oh?" he said. "That's not what I'm here about?"

"What student council proposal?" Fred Kindler asked again.

"To give the bones back," Francis said.

"The bones back," Fred repeated. He was still standing, and he was frowning, but the anger was beginning to leave his face.

"The bones and the whole display. They think it's blasphemous."

"Who thinks what's blasphemous, Mr. Plummer?"

"Sara Warrior. She's Pequot."

"I know who Sara Warrior is, Mr. Plummer." Fred sat down.

Francis shrugged.

"All right," Fred said. "I shouldn't have told you to get out. I'm glad you resisted." But just the same, his mistrust lingered.

"Sara Warrior came to Lila, since she's president of the student council," Francis explained as Fred looked at his watch. "And Lila brought her to me."

"And then what happened?"

"The decision to bring the proposal to the students in Morning Meeting."

"To give the display away?"

Francis nodded. "If you want to put it that way," he said.

"That's what you decided?"

"Hell no, that's what *they* decided."

"They! Well, tell them no! We just spent fifteen thousand dollars we don't have on—"

"I can't tell them no," Francis interrupted. *Don't you think I'd like to?* he wanted to ask. *The librarian's my wife.*

Fred stared at him. "You're the advisor, for goodness sake, tell them no."

"You don't really mean that," Francis said. "That the student council can't bring up an issue at Morning Meeting?" That Kindler could even think of the idea proved he wasn't the right head.

"Let's drop this for now." Fred looked at his watch again. "I've got something really important I want to talk to you about. I'm going to need your help."

"But this is important! Discussing issues in Morning Meeting is a tradition."

Fred's face went red again. "Oh," he murmured "you're going to give me another lecture about tradition."

Margaret Rice stepped into the office right then, without knocking. There was a new, satisfied look on her face. "We're talking," Fred said.

Margaret arched her eyebrows, shrugged her shoulders. "Okay," she said, and left.

"Let's start all over again," Fred sighed to Francis.

"All right," Francis said. "Good."

Fred looked relieved. "This morning at the board meeting—" he began.

Then Margaret was back in the office. "She says it's urgent."

"Who?" asked Fred.

"Peggy Plummer," Margaret said, looking straight at Francis.

"Wait a second," Francis said. "I haven't talked to her about what the student council's going to do."

"You haven't?" said Fred, looking at him even more sharply. Then turning to Margaret: "Urgent? Somebody hurt?"

Margaret didn't have time to answer because by then Peggy was in the office. She didn't even look at Francis. "You need to be in the auditorium, Fred," she said.

"The auditorium?"

Peggy nodded her head. "The whole school's gathering there right now. As we speak. A board member came on campus just a half hour ago. She went to every class. Announced in each one that the board has just voted to go coed. She's leading the meeting. I think you've got a riot on your hands."

"Who?" Fred asked, standing up.

"Why, Sandra Petrie," Margaret Rice said gleefully. "Who else?"

TWELVE

Fred stood up so fast he knocked his chair over. He took two steps toward the door, tripped over the edge of the rug, and almost fell into Plummer's lap—which he prevented by throwing his hand out to brace himself against Plummer's chair. He missed, hitting Plummer in the shoulder instead, hard, as if he were punching him. Better if he'd hit him in the face! He was out the door and gone before Francis even stood up.

Fred sprinted up the steps to the auditorium two at a time. On the big green front doors someone had posted a placard:

Estrogen Yes!
Testosterone No!

Inside, at the back of the auditorium, the first thing he saw was Sandra Petrie up on stage, standing at a podium. He'd noticed the podium before, stored offstage. She must have moved it onstage to make herself seem authoritative. Petrie saw him right away. He stopped in his tracks to stare at her. She stared back, and he felt her anger as if it were a weight pushing him back, right out the doors he'd just come through. This wasn't the same woman who'd been so embarrassed by what she'd done that she had obeyed Travelers's command to join the board at the table just to get out of the limelight. And for her this wasn't just about letting boys in anymore; it was about Fred Kindler too—for having kept that limelight on her, showing his contempt for her with that business about the minutes. If he hadn't stirred her anger so, she wouldn't be here, doing this.

Fred would realize this later, with time to reflect. But he was not reflecting then—he was walking up the aisle toward the stage, and everyone in the audience was turning to look to where Petrie was staring. He walked very slowly toward Petrie, who stood at the podium, as if she were waiting for him at the altar, and, as if he were outside himself, watching, he found himself whispering to a girl on the aisle, "Here comes the bride!" But his little joke was wasted on her. The only sound in the auditorium was the sound of his walking.

As he climbed the steps onto the stage, someone in the audience shouted: "We don't want boys! We want Marjorie. Give us Marjorie back! Marjorie and no boys!" By the time he reached the podium, the chant had swelled: "Boys no, Marjorie yes! Boys no! Marjorie yes!"

Petrie didn't budge from the podium. Inside his head Fred watched a movie of himself bodily picking her up—though she was taller than he —lifting her off the stage floor, and dropping her over the edge.

Instead he stood next to her at the podium and looked out over the chanting crowd, keeping his face blank, as if he were watching an uninteresting phenomenon that had nothing to do with him. He would simply wait for them to stop. After a little while, after they had expressed their feelings, they'd catch on to how discourteous they were being. Without turning his face from the crowd, he said, just loud enough for Petrie to hear, "This is not your podium, Mrs. Petrie. You should sit down."

"It doesn't appear to be yours either," she hissed.

He didn't answer, just kept waiting. There was now a rhythmic stamping of feet to accompany the chant. But quite a few of the girls had stopped; maybe they never had started. Petrie's daughter, Melissa, sat at the outer edge of the last row on his left, very close to a side exit door, her face averted from the front. He looked for the faculty, discovering that many of them were not there, and felt a rush of respect at their refusal to be a part of this. The rest were spread out through the audience. Rachel Bickham sat in the back row. He was surprised that she was there. She seemed much too, well, noble to participate in something like this. He looked into her dark, handsome face, and she looked right back. What bothered him the most was Gregory van Buren's presence in the front row. *I thought you were for letting boys in*, he wanted to say, then realized, as van Buren continued to avert his eyes, that maybe van Buren was there in the front row to be supportive of him. It would have been nice to know.

The noise slightly subsided. However angry they were, the girls were too sensitive not to get the message implied by his calm standing there, waiting. One of the girls in the front row stood up and faced the crowd, shouting, "Give me an M!" She got only a halfhearted reply from fewer than half the girls. "Give me an A!" the girl yelled—to which even fewer students responded, one of whom added with a disgusted shrug: "In all my subjects, so I can get into my daddy's college." That's when Rachel Bickham stood up in the back row.

Sandra Petrie pointed to Bickham, and Bickham started to speak. "This is outrageous!" Bickham was very tall; her voice was quiet, but it filled the room. The chanting stopped.

"Yeah, he wants to let boys in," someone said.

"Maybe he does," Bickham said.

"Maybe?" Sandra Petrie interrupted. "You know very well he does! That's why I called this meeting."

Bickham's beautiful, long-fingered hand was up, signaling silence. "Don't embarrass yourself anymore," she said to Petrie.

"But," said Petrie, "I—"

Bickham shook her head back and forth, a subtle gesture, and Petrie said no more. When a student rose, starting to speak without raising her hand, it was Fred who pointed to Bickham. "I believe Ms. Bickham has the floor," he declared.

"When the other team shoots fouls shots, we don't make any noise," Bickham said. "That's the Oliver way. Fairness. This would be the worst time to abandon it." Then she sat down. The auditorium was suddenly much quieter.

So, thanks to Rachel Bickham, Fred had the floor. He stepped forward toward the lip of the stage to explain what the board had actually decided. Then he noticed Francis Plummer at the back of the auditorium, and he had a better idea.

"Good morning, Mr. Plummer," Fred called loudly across the auditorium. "I assume you've come because you heard some noise and thought we might need your help." His voice was loaded with sarcasm. He didn't care how much the girls liked this sneaky little creep who—it was as plain as day—had kept him in his office on purpose with another one of his lectures about tradition so there'd be time for a riot to get started behind his back. He was going to take him on right here, right now!

Francis said nothing.

"Mr. Plummer, you have no answers for us this morning," Fred said, and as soon as Francis opened his mouth to speak, Fred cut him off. "Well, anyway, thanks for dropping by. You're just the right person to help us out." Ignoring the several girls four rows back who were silently mouthing an exaggerated imitation of his every word, he kept on. "I think I'm right in saying that it's the Oliver custom"—*Oliver custom*, now a whole row was mouthing his words—"that the student council is the body that calls special all-school meetings."

Still no answer from Francis, who was trying to figure out what was happening. "Well, then, maybe the president of the student council can tell us," Fred said. He looked around the audience, peering, as if he didn't know where Lila Smythe was sitting. "Lila?"

"That's right," said Lila, her voice tentative for once.

"Fine. It is also the head of school's prerogative." He couldn't keep his eyes away from the mute imitators, but he refused to react. "So, since this meeting was called with neither my authority nor the student council's, I'm treating it as if it hasn't happened. It was a non-meeting. So, Lila, would you like to call a *real* meeting for tomorrow morning so we can discuss our situation, or do you want me to call it?"

Lila hesitated.

"Lila?"

"I'll call it," said Lila.

"Good. What time?"

Lila turned toward Francis at the back of the auditorium.

"Your decision, Lila," Fred said.

"First period?" said Lila.

"Good. Will you run the meeting?"

"Yes."

"Excellent. And since this is a non-meeting, I'm canceling it as of now. We've missed a whole class period. Funny how something that doesn't happen can take up time. That's not a problem though. Mr. Plummer here can figure out the best time for us to make it up." There were a few hisses from the audience at this, but Fred went right on, riding his anger. "What do you think, Mr. Plummer, would this Sunday or the Sunday after be better?" Some more hisses. Francis started to say something, but again Fred cut him off. "Give yourself time to figure it out," he said. Then, addressing the whole crowd: "Have a good morning, everybody. Mr. Plummer will let us know." He turned to Petrie, raised his eyebrows at her, stepped away from the podium, and walked down the steps to the orchestra and up the aisle.

Behind him, he heard Sandra Petrie say, "All right. He's left. Now let's continue." He heard someone else say, "Tomorrow." By the time he neared the doors at the back of the auditorium, he could hear people getting up to leave. He was not surprised. He'd always known that whether they liked you or not, teenagers responded to the grown-up who's willing to risk, to put it all out there—to be a little crazy when it counts.

As he passed Francis, who was still standing in the doorway, Fred said, "Be in my office in exactly five minutes."

Francis entered the head's office and took a chair.

"I didn't invite you to sit down," Kindler said.

Francis didn't believe the man was serious and continued to sit.

"Stand up," Kindler said.

So, not knowing what else to do, how to act in the presence of this man who was so obviously out of control, Francis stood up.

"This won't take long. I've only got two things to say," Kindler announced. "Listen carefully to both of them."

Francis said nothing.

"The first—as you would have already learned from me without our little riot—is the board has decided that under extreme conditions it would consider whether or not it is in the school's best interest to become a coed school."

"Consider? Or actually decide?" Francis asked carefully. His own rage was rising now, a counter to Kindler's—if he could control it.

"What do you think, Mr. Plummer?"

"Just tell me," Francis said. "This isn't a quiz show."

"Consider, Mr. Plummer, merely consider. And I expect you to treat their consideration with respect. That's the second thing."

Francis started to say how crazy it was even to think about this, how it would never happen, no matter who was running the school, but Kindler started talking again before Francis got a word out. "If you had behaved yourself, you wouldn't have had to ask. I would have told you," he said, staring at Francis.

Francis opened his mouth to speak, but Kindler put his hand up and waved it back and forth in that gesture that drove Francis crazy. "Not now, Mr. Plummer. And not to me. I'm not interested in your opinion anymore. And won't be until you get your act together."

"My act together?" Francis repeated, realizing suddenly: *He thinks I knew! He thinks while he was talking with me in the office I knew there was a riot getting started. He thinks I set him up!* He'd forgotten the coed issue. All he could think of was this.

"If you fail to do whatever you have to do to get yourself back on track, I'll fire you," Kindler said.

"Whatever I have to do? What does that mean?"

"I've suggested therapy already, Mr. Plummer," Fred said, aware that last time he had called it counseling. "Do I have to again?"

Francis opened his mouth, but no words came out. If Kindler had stood up, reached across his desk, and punched him in the face, it wouldn't have felt any worse.

"Well, do I?" Kindler said.

Francis still couldn't speak. He was dizzy with anger; Kindler's face was a blur.

"I guess so," Kindler said.

"Don't you ever say that to me again," Francis said at last. "Do you hear? Ever."

Kindler just shrugged.

"Or you'll *fire* me? Who do you think you are?"

"Be careful, Mr. Plummer. Or I'll show you who I am."

"I'll resign then," Francis blurted thinking, *I'll be goddamned if I'm going to get down on my knees and tell him that I didn't even know what was happening! I was already in here when Sandra came on campus.*

Kindler put his hands on his desk, leaned forward. "You think I'd let you resign? You even begin to, and I'll fire you. I won't give you that to hide in. I'll fire you publicly. I'll announce it in the school newspaper. I'll write an article in the alumnae magazine. I don't care what kind of hornet's nest it stirs up. If it weren't for my respect for your wife, I could even enjoy such a fight. That's how you win fights, you know. The ones you get in just for the hell of it are the ones you always win."

"My wife's none of your business, Mr. Kindler."

"Except for the fact that she's the best damn librarian in the business, you're right."

"This fight's just between you and me."

Francis watched Kindler's body tense. He thought for a moment he'd won, the man was going to lose it completely, go totally out of control. He was wrong. Kindler spoke very slowly. "It doesn't have a damn thing to do with either you or me," he said. "It's about the school. Why don't you grow up?

"Think about that," Kindler added. "This meeting's over."

THAT EVENING IMMEDIATELY after dinner, Peggy had an appointment with the ninth graders to teach them how to use the library. She went straight there from the dining hall. The minute she'd finished she would hurry home. She needed to talk with Francis.

She was still hearing the bitterness in Fred Kindler's voice that morning as he mocked Francis in front of the whole school, telling him to pick the Sunday for making up the classes, and cutting him off when he tried to speak. There had been something irredeemable in that very public insult, something much too reckless. How could he retreat from that, she wondered. How could Francis forgive him?

She remembered the stony expression on Fred's face as he walked down the aisle, stopped and said something to Francis, and then went out the door. Only minutes later, she'd seen Francis heading for the administration building and was sure he was going to Fred's office. She needed to know what had happened there.

Francis went home after dinner and waited for Peggy to finish with the ninth graders. As soon as she got home, he would tell her about the student council's proposal to give the Collection to the Pequots. He didn't want her to be taken by surprise when it came up in Morning Meeting. He had wanted to tell her right after morning classes to be sure she'd hear it from him rather than someone else. But then there had been the riot in the auditorium and Kindler attacking him in public and threatening to fire him in his office, and the Pequot issue had gone clean out of his mind.

While he waited for her, he had two sets of compositions to comment on and grade. It was a rule of his own to obey: every paper will be returned within forty-eight hours. Gregory van Buren almost never kept papers longer than that, and Francis wasn't about to be bested by him. But it wasn't long before Francis found that he was going to have to disobey his rule, because he couldn't keep his mind on the students' writing. He was too full of the pain of everything that had happened that morning. All day he'd been hearing the new headmaster say, "I'll fire you publicly" and "I'll write an article in the alumnae magazine." He'd have to tell Peggy about it someday, though right then that was too humiliating even to imagine. His new boss, half his age, leaning across his desk and asking him why he doesn't grow up!

Francis gave up and went out into the dorm, poked his head into each girl's room to say hello. His spirits lifted a little when Lila Smythe asked for advice about an essay she had written for Gregory van Buren's celebrated course: "Tragedy from *Oedipus Rex* to *Death of a Salesman*." Gregory had told her to do the essay over because there was a subtle flaw in the logic of her argument that she needed to find on her own, and on his first reading Francis couldn't see it either. When he did catch on to Gregory's point, he asked her some leading questions to help her discover it on her own and watched her understanding dawn. "Thanks, Mr. P.," she told him. "You've helped a lot." He was grateful for this warmth from Lila, and forgot for a moment his trouble with Kindler; but he understood that he never would have caught Lila's error; he would have given her an A. And just the other day, Rachel Bickham had casually suggested to Gregory and Francis that they do what the teachers in her department do and visit each other's classes. Of course that's what they should have been doing all along: learning from each other, like grown-ups.

Peggy finished with the ninth graders quickly. After all, there were only nine of them. Then she hurried across the campus and found Francis in the dorm just as he'd finished helping Lila. "I need to talk to you," she said, motioning toward the door to their apartment.

Naturally, he thought she'd heard about the proposal through the grapevine and wanted to know why he hadn't told her. He should kill himself.

He was wrong. She hadn't gotten wind of the proposal. The near-riot in the auditorium, the specter of boys at Miss Oliver's, those had shoved all thoughts of the Collection out of everyone's mind. The council members weren't thinking about it right now, and they weren't telling anybody about it, and if they were, no one would have paid attention.

In their apartment, Levi came across the room to welcome them, wagging his tail, his toenails clicking on the floor. They ignored him. "What happened?" she asked before they even sat down.

"I'm sorry," he said. "I meant to tell you before anyone else did."

She shook her head to tell him no. Of course Fred Kindler hadn't told her what had happened between him and Francis in his office. How could Francis think he would?

He thought she meant no, forgetting's no excuse. "Well, I think you would have forgotten too," he said, a little angry now.

"Francis, please," she begged. "What happened? Between you and Fred Kindler today." Both of them were still standing up.

"Oh, that's what we're talking about!"

"Francis!"

He was stunned, realizing that maybe he wasn't ever going to tell her what Kindler said to him today. So now he felt guilty about that too. "Which time? I had two meetings with him," he said. Anything to postpone having to admit to this disgrace.

"After the auditorium. I saw you heading for his office."

"Yeah," he said. "You did. That's where I went."

She waited.

"He threatened to fire me," he said at last, and added, "That's all, nothing important," as if it were a joke.

"That's what I thought," she said, discovering that it was true, though until he'd said it, she hadn't dared think it. She looked away. She couldn't bear to look at him, he was so chagrined.

"He thinks I set him up. He thinks I knew Sandra was on campus."

"Oh, come on. He wouldn't think that."

"Yes, he does, I could tell. He thinks I kept him in his office to give her time to get the meeting started without him."

"You?" she asked. "How could he?" Even if Francis were devious enough, he didn't have that kind of cunning.

Because he goes out of control at the drop of a hat, Francis wanted to answer her. *Because he gets angry and acts before he thinks.* But he wouldn't say that. She would just leap to Kindler's defense.

He was right; she would. But she had seen Fred Kindler attack the school's most beloved teacher this morning, right in front of everyone, and then, another reckless act, just leave the auditorium, just walk away. How did he know Sandra Petrie wouldn't get the power back?

"Peggy, I'm going to keep my promise. I'm going to do my job and help him, whatever he does."

"Don't say that, Francis."

"What?"

"Whatever he does. As if he were an idiot."

"That's not what I meant, Peg. I think you know it."

"All right," she sighed, "it's not how you meant it."

"Good," he said. He was dying to change this subject. And he wanted to tell her about the student council proposal before ten o'clock when they always went through the dorm again to say goodnight to the girls. "Lila Smythe came to me this morning—" he began.

She interrupted him. "Francis, why can't you and Fred be friends?" As soon as the words were out of her mouth, she knew how naive they sounded.

That stopped him. It had never occurred to him that he and Kindler could be friends.

"It would save everything," Peggy said. Naive or not, it was true. *Not just our school, but our marriage too*, she thought, remembering Eudora's "we save the school, we save everything." She tried to imagine Francis getting fired and teaching at another school and couldn't. But she wondered nevertheless if she would stay at Miss Oliver's or go with him. It amazed her that she couldn't answer the question.

"I don't have to be his friend to work for him," Francis said.

"Maybe not, but you better explain to him, Francis. You need to go back and tell him you had no idea that Sandra was on campus. He'll never trust you otherwise."

"Maybe," Francis said, "I'll try," and knew he wouldn't. He was not going to watch Fred Kindler decide that he was a liar as well as a sneak. Peggy watched him. His answer was not enough for her. But before he could think of the words to convince her he's going to be loyal to Fred Kindler whatever Fred Kindler thought, the clock in the library's steeple rang ten times.

It was a relief. They could retreat from this problem between them into the routine that had been there for them to escape to all the years of their marriage. They went through their dorm, chatting with the girls, checking them in. When they got back to their apartment at eleven o'clock, Francis remembered the uncorrected papers on his desk. He thought he'd get up at five in the morning to get them done, then rejected the idea. He knew how tired he would be. So he sat down at his desk and went to work. Peggy went to bed.

When he finished the papers at two o'clock in the morning and got in bed beside her, she stirred in her sleep. He turned to her and kissed her cheek. She didn't awaken, and anyway, he didn't know what he'd say to her. Maybe if it were not for the pile of papers he'd had to correct in the middle of the night he would have remembered to warn her about the proposal to give away the Collection. And yet there was nothing unusual about his staying up until early morning correcting papers. It was more likely that if Fred Kindler hadn't threatened to fire him that morning, he would have remembered. And if Peggy had woken when he kissed her again in her sleep, he might have remembered. They would have talked about it then and gone in the morning to Kindler's office with their ideas about how to respond. But she didn't wake up, and then he fell sleep.

By ten minutes after eight the next morning, five minutes before the beginning of first period, all three hundred and forty-five students were seated in the auditorium. Fred sat at the right-hand end of the first row, near the same steps he'd climbed up onto the stage the day before to the deafening chant of *Marjorie and no boys!* Today the auditorium was tomblike. The twelve members of the student council—three from each class—sat in chairs on stage. As tradition dictated, Francis Plummer sat with them, looking uncomfortable.

President Lila Smythe rose from her chair, next to Francis, and slowly walked to the podium at the front of the stage. She stood there for a moment, prolonging the silence, much more poised than Sandra Petrie had been the day before.

Lila's voice was clear. "The student council has called this meeting." She pushed the microphone, still off, to one side of the podium. She didn't need a mike; she was a presence. Her voice carried. "Our head of school has an announcement."

The steps squeaked as Fred climbed onstage. The girls studied his awkward gait as he crossed to the podium. By the time he got there, Lila was sitting down. "Thank you, Lila," Fred said as he stepped behind the podium.

The thing came almost up past his shoulders, dwarfing him. It had been built for Marjorie Boyd! Why hadn't he noticed that and stayed away from the damn thing? Yesterday when Petrie stood behind the podium she'd been plenty tall enough, but now that he was behind it, it was obvious he wasn't. It dawned on him what the girls were seeing: only his head. A titter rose somewhere in the silence, began to grow, and for a crazy instant he had the idea that he would play with this absurdity. He'd bend his knees to make himself even shorter, disappear completely, clown around. That's how some people he knew could handle this: join the laughter, relieve the tension, win the war. But that was not who he was, he knew—a fleeting regret—and he knew he couldn't pull it off. He stepped around the podium and stood in front of it. The laughter stopped.

"It is a little more than an announcement," he said. He was silent again. He wanted them to know that for him this was heavy too, he wasn't trying to slide it by.

Then, careful not to speak down to the students, he laid out the whole situation: the baby bust, the national trends that had begun several years before away both from boarding schools and from single-sex schools for girls. "In spite of our school's excellence," he went on to say, "the result has been a serious under-enrollment, and the result of that has been a very disturbing deficit. We have less money in revenues than in expenses. When that happens several years in a row, schools get into serious trouble." He stopped there, hoping for some reaction, some questions he could answer. To get them involved was to enlist their help in saving the school.

No one raised her hand; no one said a word. He was speaking to a sea of stony faces.

He soldiered on, spoke passionately about his commitment to rebuilding the girls-only enrollment, described the efforts made over the summer, and turned the disappointment of the meager result—only six new students, other than the ninth grade—into positive news by exclaiming how wonderful all the new students were, what excellence he expected of them. For this, but for nothing else, he received a mild applause.

He didn't realize how foreign a territory he was describing. How could he? Francis Plummer could have helped him understand that Marjorie was even less inclined to share the realities of the financial situation with the students than she was with the faculty. But Francis Plummer and Fred Kindler weren't talking to each other; and even if they were, Francis was probably not ready yet to recognize this characteristic of Marjorie's leadership as a weakness. Instead, he would explain it—maybe even proudly—as "just how we do things at Miss Oliver's." So now, when Kindler invoked such terms as *deficit*, *revenue*, and *budget* rather than the school's glory, because he assumed that especially at Miss Oliver's, financial realities, the way things actually worked, should be part of the curriculum, he became for the students even more the interloper, the man who didn't belong.

Sitting on the stage behind Kindler and staring at his back, Francis could hear in his tone how passionately he wanted to build the girls-only enrollment, and for all his anger and his conviction that Kindler was the wrong person for this job, Francis was relieved. It was then that he realized that his meeting with the new headmaster yesterday had almost nothing to do with admitting boys. They had been so angry with each other, they had gone by the issue. Their fight had been merely personal, he was ashamed to realize. Neither had been doing his job.

Finally, near the end of his talk, Fred actually had to say it, to put it out there: "Therefore the board of directors, at its last meeting, decided that it was its responsibility to the school to consider admitting boys if our effort to build girls-only enrollment doesn't produce enough revenue." He almost said, *instead of shutting down.* He caught himself just in time. Those words, released to the air, would have been too much reality all at once.

"Please understand, the board hasn't decided to admit boys, only to consider it under certain circumstances, which I believe will never develop." He hesitated again. "And of course, if that did happen, they would have to look at the fundamental question: Is there any point in being Miss Oliver's if we are not for girls only."

Silence.

"I'd like to hear your thoughts," he said. He still hoped to entice them, get them involved, make them part of the rescue.

No one raised a hand.

"This school is known for facing problems square on. We can discuss this."

Still no response. Everyone in the audience was watching him. No one said a word.

After what seemed forever, he heard Lila's voice behind him. "Here is our answer." Then she was standing next to him, handing him a sheaf of papers. The heading of the top page was *DECLARATION.* He read:

> *We, the undersigned members of the student body, declare our undivided loyalty to Miss Oliver's School for Girls, and are adamant that this school remain for girls only. We also declare that we will not attend any school that admits male students, and that if Miss Oliver's School for Girls decides to admit boys, each one of us will leave this campus permanently.*

Underneath, and on the next three pages, were the signatures.

"There are three hundred and forty-five students," Lila told Fred in a clear voice, which everyone could hear, "and three hundred and twenty-eight signatures. I understand there is a similar declaration going around the faculty."

Fred stood, holding the sheaf of papers in his hand, saying

nothing. He made no effort to disguise the fact that he was stunned. "Oh! Well, thank you, Lila," he finally managed. "I'll pass this on to the board."

"Good," said Lila. "So this meeting's over, right?"

"Seems to be," Fred said, though now that he was over his surprise, it was dawning on him that he was proud of these kids for their resistance. Later, he would realize that he should have turned back to the audience then and told the students so, praised them for their conviction and their faith, and thanked them. But he was too stunned and didn't think fast enough.

If Lila had known what was going through Mr. Kindler's mind she would have waited to adjourn the meeting so Mr. Kindler could express his thoughts, tell the students how proud of them he was. It could have saved the day for him. But Lila couldn't know, and she was already at the lip of the platform. "This meeting is adjourned," she declared. "Time for classes." In silence, the girls stood, their faces impassive. As they left, Fred joined them, walking down the aisle.

No one looked at him.

THIRTEEN

The last thing either Francis Plummer or Fred Kindler needed was to be face to face with each other. But that was exactly what was about to happen a day later as Francis hurried across campus to his classroom and Fred Kindler walked on the same path in the opposite direction to his office. They both considered stepping off the path to avoid one another. But of course they rejected the idea. They were grown men, after all.

Francis forced himself not to look away from Kindler's face as they approached each other. Fred Kindler did the same: he kept his eyes up, full on his senior teacher's face. *Let him cringe*, he thought. He'd already crossed Francis Plummer off his list. He was hurrying to a meeting with Rachel Bickham. He could trust her advice. And Peggy Plummer's too. And there were others, maybe, to help him steer the course.

Nevertheless, it made him sad to think how good it would have been if this Plummer were a different kind of guy and he could have had him for a partner. When Fred had visited Plummer's English and math classes during his visits as a candidate, he'd seen the demands Plummer was able to make of his students, the standard to which he raised them. It was a revelation for Fred. He was sure that if he and Plummer were working hand in hand, they'd be able to turn the Declaration Lila presented to him yesterday into a victory for both of them and the school. *The four of us*, he thought. *Gail and me and the Plummers.* That would have made a home.

"Good morning." Francis tried to say it first, but they both said it together—a kind of unison. The irony would occur to Francis later. Right then, all he was aware of was that every interaction he'd had with Kindler had been a disaster.

And then they were past each other, and he wondered if he should have stopped, put his hand on Kindler's elbow, said something to give them both a chance to start again. But he didn't know what he could say to make that happen. He could be a mentor to Fred Kindler if Kindler needed some advice as to how to run some other school. But here? Following Marjorie? How could that be! Kindler didn't look like the head of this school, he didn't talk like the head of this school. And he didn't think like the head of that school. *How could he not see how wrong he is for us?*

Nevertheless, Francis would keep his opinion to himself, let others have their own.

On the other side of campus, Fred's spirits lifted. He was looking forward to this meeting with Rachel Bickham. The high standards to which she held herself intimidated some of her colleagues, but they delighted him.

Chair of the Science Department, teacher of physics, head of athletics, and coach of the varsity basketball team, Rachel Bickham was six feet tall, thirty-four years old. Her stately presence drew one's gaze when she entered a room. Her face was more handsome than beautiful, her voice quiet enough so you had to pay close attention to hear what she was saying, and when she taught, she moved her graceful hands through the air to express her passion for her subject. "The study of science reveals how elegantly the world works," she would tell her students. "What could be more inspiring than that?"

Five years earlier, Marjorie Boyd had recruited Rachel by pointing out that a major goal was the annihilation of the female stereotype as weak in math and science. One of the first things Rachel had done as chair of the Science Department was to announce to Marjorie, who almost never could bring herself to fire anyone, that the teachers who had been teaching science at the school for years were good—but not good enough. She hadn't waited for Marjorie to get up the nerve; instead, against ancient protocol, Rachel took it upon herself to inform the least effective teacher that she no longer had a job as of the end of the winter term, and gave the rest of the department one academic year to find other schools at which to teach. Then, by making it clear that her standards would be extraordinarily high and her demands on them relentless, she succeeded in luring away from other schools three gifted teachers, each of whom had graduated from a single-sex college for women. And she did all this with enough directness and courtesy that the dismissed teachers left causing much less furor than Marjorie had predicted, their self-esteem reasonably intact.

"I think you may have chosen a consequence that doesn't quite work," Rachel told Fred, her long legs taking up much of the space between their chairs. "Taking their Sunday for a class. It doesn't feel right."

"Well, now, it doesn't feel right to me either," Fred agreed. "Besides, the girls could refuse. Just stay in their dorms, and then where would we be? It was much too arbitrary, but you know, I was just riding with whatever came to mind."

"I could see that," Rachel smiled. "So could everyone else! Riding hard, too. No one was going to get in the way."

"And that's what came to mind: Sunday class. Dumb idea."

"Clearly off the cuff. But thanks for not getting steamrolled. I would have hated to see that."

"I might have," Fred admitted, "without your remark about foul shots. Thanks."

"No way. You were doing fine. Besides, if it weren't me, it would have been somebody else."

"I hope."

"Anyway, our kids just needed a little reminder. They know how to behave."

"Signing that Declaration is behaving right, you think?"

"For the students? Yes, I do."

"So do I," Fred said "It's what I would have done too."

Rachel studied Fred's face but didn't say anything.

"What about you?" Fred asked. "If we went coed, what would you do?"

"I'd leave."

Fred nodded in agreement. "That's why you signed the faculty's declaration?"

"You don't know? You didn't read it?"

"I did not. I wasn't about to pretend that the faculty's declaration had any weight. It's not that I don't care; it's just that it doesn't make any difference. We're either broke or solvent."

"That's why I didn't sign it," Rachel said very quietly.

"You didn't?"

"Hell no."

"Sorry. I shouldn't have assumed."

"Some other teachers didn't sign it either."

Fred nodded. "Speaking of grown-ups."

"Yes. Some are. Some aren't. What about the board, did they read it?"

"Don't know yet. I sent it to the chair with a strong note suggesting he send it back, unread."

"You did?"

"I did."

"My goodness!"

Fred waited.

"I kind of hope he doesn't take your advice," she said.

"I kind of hope so too," Fred said. "Now that I've had time to think about it."

"Well, anyway," Rachel continued after a little silence. "Back to that Sunday. I have an idea."

"First I have a different question," Fred said, realizing how much he wanted her advice.

Rachel looked surprised. She waited.

"What is your opinion of the appropriateness of our Indian display?"

"Oh," said Rachel. "That."

"Yes. That."

"I wouldn't go there if I were you."

"Suppose I don't have a choice? Suppose the student council brings it up and says it's wrong?"

"Yes, I hear rumors that will happen."

"It is going to happen."

Rachel nodded. "Well, when it does, I'd say they're right."

"You would? Really?"

Rachel shook her head. "No, I guess I wouldn't. It's what I believe, but it would be wrong to say it."

"Wrong? If you believe it?"

"Not for me. For you. The head. We've had the display for years.

It would sound disrespectful of the past."

"Including Mrs. Boyd?"

Rachel nodded. "When you speak, yes. Especially Marjorie."

"Just what I need right now," he said, and wished right away he could have those words back; they sounded too much like whining.

But Rachel didn't seem to notice. "The idea has come up before," she told him. "Five years ago, in my first year. It didn't have much heat around it. Nobody was using words like *blasphemy* and *racism*, so Peggy Plummer wasn't offended. And Marjorie just let the controversy die. She liked the Collection right where it was, and besides, it would have taken a fair amount of work to reach out and make the arrangements with the Pequot authorities, whom, I regret to say, we've never had anything to do with; and maybe she was afraid that when the Pequots realized we've had these things for years, they'd accuse us of racism and disrespect, which, of course, would be all over the news."

"All right," he said. "I'll just let the discussion happen. I won't take sides, at least not at first." He didn't say—because he'd already sounded like a whiner—that sometimes the person with the most responsibility is the one with the least power. Instead, he murmured out loud, "It's going to be tricky."

"Very," Rachel said. Then after a little pause: "Sometime I wonder if I could do your job."

"Sometimes I wonder if I can do it," Fred said, smiling.

Rachel smiled too. "You're doing fine. Just keep at it. Anyway, back to my idea."

"I could use one!"

"Yes, you could." Rachel grinned. "And here it is. Instead of classes on a Sunday, we do a service project. That way you still make your point."

"What about my just calling the whole thing off, just admit I was off base?"

"Don't you dare!"

"That's what I thought you'd say."

"They'll feel useful," Rachel pointed out. "You don't want to use classes for punishment. Besides, it will be good publicity."

"It's a fine idea," Fred declared. "Let's get the student council to choose the project."

"Good idea."

"Why in the world didn't *I* think of this?" Fred asked himself out loud.

Rachel reached out, patted his hand. "Maybe because you're human," she said. "I'll tell Francis."

"That will help," said Fred, not quite succeeding in keeping the sarcasm out of his voice.

Rachel stood up to leave. He could see she'd heard the sarcasm, but, good politician that she was, she ignored it. "Just one more thing," she said, "an afterthought. I'm sure you've thought of it already."

"Don't count on it," he grinned.

She smiled. One of the things she liked about this guy was his self-deprecation. "Bring Francis and Peggy Plummer in together to discuss the council's idea," she advised. "So they can work it out between themselves and you before it's dropped on her in public."

"I will," he said. "Of course."

AND, ON THE other side of campus, in the classroom that had been his for thirty-three years, Francis's spirits also began to lift. He was about to do what he did best.

The bell had just rung. The students in his ninth-grade English class trooped in and took seats along the outer edges of the three-sided square of tables. Francis stood at the front of the classroom, just inside the square, like an actor in a theater whose stage projected out into the audience. "Home Burial," he said, "by Robert Frost." It was one of the poems he had assigned for them to read last night. The girls opened their books to the page and followed him as he recited this poem from memory about the young New England husband who from the bottom of the stairs catches his wife staring from the landing above him, out the window at the little graveyard behind the house, where their firstborn lies.

He didn't try to hide how much he loved this poem he'd been teaching for years, how it really was by *heart*. For Francis (who didn't know the Kindlers' secret) there could have been no greater draw on his compassion than a parent who had lost a child.

It took him several minutes to recite this long poem, and when he finished there was silence, which he allowed to linger. He knew that many of these kids, whose programmed childhoods had been thicketed with expensive lessons in tennis, soccer, yoga, piano, gymnastics, martial arts—and the skills of outdoing less affluent people in the taking of standardized tests—seldom heard poems recited from memory. For who among their parents had the time or the inclination to memorize a poem? He wondered if Sara Warrior, who had been watching him intently from the back of the room, was an exception. Her head had not been down in her book like the other girls. Was that because she didn't need to follow with her eyes, she could listen? Maybe her people didn't hold their stories at arm's length as if borrowing them for only a little while. Maybe they took them into memory, drawing them up inside themselves, and owning them.

But next to Sara, what Amy Leveret was intent on was showing how disengaged she was. She was slouching as far back from the table as she could get at the rear of the room without knocking the Globe Theatre off its table. Black pants, black leather jacket on this hot September day, black hair dyed even blacker and spiked straight up. Still intent on improving the students' attire, Fred Kindler had told Amy to take the ring out of her nose on her first day of school. She'd been looking for revenge ever since.

"Well, Amy, what do you think of the poem?" Francis asked her. He usually stayed away from such open-ended questions for their tendency to engender uncritical, self-reflective answers. But if he didn't smoke Amy's distemper out into the open, it would subvert the class for the rest of the period.

Amy slouched still further. "I think it's boring," she said.

"Why do you say that?" As if he didn't know the answer: because he was yet another adult who professed to know what was good for her, what clothes she should wear, what poetry she should love as much as he did. If she were to be seduced by this poem, the anger she'd been nurturing for months would begin to melt, and then who would she be?

"Because you asked," Amy said.

"Boring?" he repeated.

"Yeah. Boring."

"How do you know, Amy?" There was no challenge to the question. He just wanted to know.

"Because I was bored," Amy said. "How else would I know?"

"Well, Amy, that's one way to find out," he said. He was smiling, relaxed. He was not going to blame her but the entitled upbringing that made her answer by talking about herself. Besides, he liked her nervy quickness. He was glad the low enrollment had given Nan White an excuse to accept this kid.

Because he wouldn't fight, she didn't know how to respond to him. She looked around. Her classmates weren't looking at her; they were looking at Francis. "But it's the one I like the best!" Francesca Burke objected. She sat up very straight to the left of Francis, her back to the blackboard, her red hair lightened by the windows across the room. She leaned forward, her arms on the table, her feet wiggling nervously beneath it. Francis knew she was going to explain why she liked the poem. That's exactly what he didn't want.

He put his hand up to Francesca, smiling gently. "Wait," he said. Francesca returned his smile, thinking he'd asked her to hold up long enough for the others to understand what he and she already did.

"Do any of you live in a house like the one in the poem?" he asked the class.

No one raised her hand. "No one?" he repeated. Usually there were several.

"I do," Joanna Perrine finally admitted. Her voice was tentative and shy.

He knew from reading Nan White's notes to the faculty about incoming students that Joanna had lost her brother in a skiing accident a few years before. "We live in New Hampshire too," she added. She sat to Francis's right, by the windows, across from Francesca. Under the table, her long legs reached out toward the empty space in the center of the room; she was almost as tall as Rachel Bickham. Everybody knew she was from New Hampshire; it's not what she was trying to say. "The front door is at the foot of the stairs in our house too," Joanna murmured.

He needed to keep this safe for her; he had better be careful. But if she didn't want to engage with this poem about a loss so like her own, from a house just like the one she lived in, she wouldn't have raised her hand to answer his question. Maybe she'd found some solace in the poem, which she wanted to secure more deeply. At any rate, his heart went out to her. He would help her engage. He would bring her up to the front to help him teach. "Can you draw it for us, Joanna?" he asked.

Joanna hesitated, not sure what he wanted.

"The way the scene in the poem is laid out," he explained. He turned, stepped to the blackboard behind him, took a piece of chalk from the tray beneath it, and held it up, inviting her, and she got up from her place at the table, moved across the space to him, took the chalk, turned her back to the class, and started to draw. She made a perpendicular line on the board and labeled it *front door*—as far away from the graveyard as she could get, Francis thought. Then, just to the right, a side view of a staircase ascending to the right. She labeled the top step *landing*. Then to the right of that, another perpendicular line, with a break in it, which she labeled *window*. To the right and below that window, she drew four gravestones, and next to them a little mound of earth—a child's new grave without a headstone yet. She didn't label those. Then she put the chalk into the tray beneath the blackboard and turned to him.

"Exactly!" Francis said, and recited again:

He saw her from the bottom of the stairs
Before she saw him. She was starting down,
Looking back over her shoulder at some fear.

Joanna took a little step away from the front, from all these eyes watching her, toward her seat at the side of the room. He put his hand lightly on her elbow. "So, Joanna. Does the young husband stay at the bottom of the stairs?"

"No, he goes up the stairs to her."

"To find out what she's looking at?"

"Yes."

"And does he find out?"

"Yes. The grave where their child is buried in the family graveyard."

"Their only child, you think?"

She nodded her head.

"What makes you think so?" he asked her.

"Because it's so sad."

"All right." Ordinarily he wouldn't accept this answer; he'd make her go to the text, where the facts were. He'd make her find the words *baby* and *first child* as evidence that the young couple's loss was complete. But she'd brought her own grief to the poem. So he said, "Yes, it's very sad. They only have each other now." He hoped she would take some comfort that though she no longer had her brother, she had her parents and her parents had her.

"And does she stay at the top of the stairs?" he asked.

"For a while, that's all."

"Just for a while, yes, and then what?"

"She ducks beneath his arm and goes downstairs."

"Where he was at the beginning?"

"More than that," Joanna said. "She goes right out the house."

"Hey, Joanna!" he said. "You're a good reader." He let go of her elbow.

"Thanks." She smiled shyly, and moved back to her seat. She was glad he had given her a second chance to raise her hand.

He turned to the class then and asked, "What's the husband's reaction when he discovers what his wife's been looking at?"

Angela Nash had her hand up before he'd finished asking the question. She had black, curly hair and pale skin and looked younger than her fourteen years. "Angela," he said, "you're going to tell us?"

"He's kind of amazed," Angela answered.

"Amazed, yes, you're right. It's in the way he speaks, isn't it? It's in the tone of his words," he said, rewarding her for leaping in, taking a chance with half an answer—the way a boy would. Angela smiled and nodded, proud of her success.

"Amazed at what?" he pursued. "What is he amazed at? Surely he knew the graveyard was out back and his child was in it."

Angela hesitated.

"Read the words," Francis told her. Angela looked down at her book. She scanned the poem, looking for the passage, didn't find it right away. Now a lot of hands were up. One of them was

Sara Warrior's. He called on her.

"The wonder is I didn't see at once," Sara read. Her voice was quiet.

I never noticed it from here before.
I must be wonted to it—that's the reason.
The little graveyard where my people are!
So small the window frames the whole of it.
Not so much larger than a bedroom, is it?
There are three stones of slate and one of marble,
Broad-shouldered little slabs there in the sunlight
On the sidehill. We haven't to mind those.
But I understand: it's not the stones,
But the child's mound—

Sara stopped reading, looked up from the book. He couldn't read the expression on her face, had no idea what's she was thinking.

He was tempted to read the passage over aloud, because Sara had read it so quietly. But he wouldn't risk her taking that as a put-down, for she was fragile too, a stranger in a foreign place. Instead he said, "Thank you, Sara," and asked the question again, this time to the whole class. "What is it exactly that he is amazed at?"

Several hands went up. One of them was Amy's, though she only put it up halfway—and took it down as soon as she remembered how bored she was.

"Amy!" he said. "Tell us."

Amy sighed.

"You don't know?" he said, laying his little trap: if she didn't answer, she wouldn't appear above this; she'd just look dumb.

"He's amazed that he had to look out the window to find out, that he didn't know all along what his wife keeps looking at," she finally answered.

Francis waited for more.

"He wonders why he didn't look out the window too every time he went by it."

"Your evidence?" he asked. "The line?"

"I must be wonted to it," Amy quoted, quick as a flash, without looking at her book.

"And how does his wife feel?"

"That he shouldn't be amazed. I mean, his kid is dead," Amy said, and almost added "for Christ's sake" to get back to being negative, but she didn't dare.

Francis didn't answer, just stood there and waited as if she hadn't answered yet. Now she was thinking hard in spite of herself. He looked away from her to ask someone else, and then, just in time, it came to her, the precision he was demanding. "Oh, all right," she said, as if he were just quibbling. "Her point's not that he shouldn't be amazed. Her point is he shouldn't get used to his kid being dead."

"Good catch, Amy," Francis said.

"Well, it's obvious," she said, and checked out again, returning to her slouch.

Francis scanned the room and asked another question: "What does the wife do now, the woman named Amy?"

Sara answered. "His wife, Amy, tells him to stop talking, and then she ducks under his arm and goes down to the bottom of the stairs." Francis nodded and recited aloud to confirm her answer:

"Don't, don't, don't," she cried.
She withdrew, shrinking from beneath his arm
That rested on the banister, and slid downstairs;
And turned on him with such a daunting look,
He said twice over before he knew himself:
"Can't a man speak of his own child he's lost?"

As he recited, he moved across the space in the center of the room to where Bridget Younger sat at the right-hand row of tables, blond head down, taking notes. She'd written pages of notes in the classes they'd had so far but hardly said a word. He reached across the table and pointed to the lines in Bridget's book in which the husband answers his own question:

God, what a woman! And it's come to this,
A man can't speak of his own child that's dead.

He said the lines out loud while he kept his finger on them. Now Bridget couldn't write in her notebook because his arm was across it. "Bridget," he asked, "can you read her answer?"

Bridget looked up at him. He could see how anxious she was, how afraid of failing, and knew she hadn't even begun to know the pain of the young couple in the poem; all she knew was that if she wrote down everything her teacher said, she would be safe. And all he knew was that he wanted to give her poetry, the skill of reading it that engenders the love of it that would last the whole of her life. "Give it a try, Bridget."

"You can't because you don't know how to speak," Bridget read.

"Right!" he said and her face brightened just a little, some of the anxiety melting. "So go on."

Bridget read:

You could sit there with the stain on your shoes
Of the fresh earth from your own baby's grave
And talk about your everyday concerns.
You had stood the spade up against the wall
Outside there in the entry, for I saw it.

Francis interrupted her here and said the husband's lines:

I shall laugh the worst laugh I ever laughed.
I'm cursed. God, if I don't believe I'm cursed.

Bridget looked up at Francis, encouraged. She resumed:

I can repeat the very words you were saying.
"Three foggy mornings and one rainy day
Will rot the best birch fence a man can build."
Think of it, talk like that at such a time!
What had how long it takes a birch to rot
To do with what was in the darkened parlor?
You couldn't *care!*

He stopped her there. "Good work, Bridget," he said. "So what is it exactly that Amy finds indefensible in her husband's behavior?" he asked her, throwing her this softball to build her confidence.

Lots of hands went up. But not Bridget's. Her hand was holding her pen above her notebook, poised to write down whichever of her classmates' answers Francis would approve. "Bridget?" he said.

Bridget looked up at him but didn't answer, and now Francesca was waving her hand, dying to answer. "Bridget will answer," Francis said. He reached across the table, put his fingers around Bridget's pen, gently removed it from her hand. He held it in his own and waited. He repeated the question. "What does she object to, Bridget?"

"That he can think of things like birch rotting when his child's just dead?" She was still eyeing her pen in Francis's hand.

"You tell me," he said.

"All right. That's what she doesn't like."

"You're absolutely right," he said, and Bridget smiled. He put the pen down on the table in front of her. But when she reached for it, he put his hand over it until she took her hand away, and left the pen alone. Then he turned to the class. "Let's see how it comes out," he said. "We'll act it out." He wanted them to see how dynamic the poem was, the action, the movement up and down the stairs, the changing of places. "Yes, we'll act it out," he said. He was looking straight at Amy.

She shook her head; she knew what was coming next.

"Amy?"

Amy didn't answer.

"We need you to play the young mother's part," he said. "You've got the same name as she does."

Amy put the collar of her jacket up. "Not me," she said.

He waited.

Amy shook her head again, scrunched her chin even further down in her collar.

He moved his gaze to Joanna.

"You want me to be the wife?" Joanna asked. She thought he'd given up on Amy.

He shook his head. "I want you to be the husband."

"No, you," Joanna answered. "You're the only man in the room."

"That's immaterial," he said. "You can take another's part."

"I'll be the narrator," Francesca said. Her hand was way up, waving again.

"Good, Francesca!" For he wouldn't refuse her again. He was delighted that she understood how different this was from many poems in which the poet does all the talking. He would get them to think about that tomorrow. "You can read the narration from your chair," he went on. "But I'll not be the husband," he added, hoping that Joanna would relent. To give her time, he told the class how he loved to walk in New England woods, where a hundred years ago there was pasture, and find the little graveyards behind the cellar holes.

"Can we do the poem now?" Francesca interrupted.

"Oh, all right, I'll do it!" Amy announced, relenting, as if she were doing the class a favor, and stood from her chair, moved around the square of tables to the front of the room.

"All right, Amy!" Francis said. "Joanna?"

But Francesca couldn't wait any longer. She cleared her throat. "Home Burial," she announced.

"Wait a minute, we need the husband," Amy said, looking at Joanna. Francesca stopped.

"Okay, I'll be the husband," Joanna said.

Francesca was so eager she started again before Joanna got to the front of the room:

He saw her from the bottom of the stairs
Before she saw him. She was starting down,
Looking back over her shoulder at some fear.

"So where's the window I'm looking out of?" Amy interrupted.

Francis didn't answer. He just raised his eyebrows, and then left the front of the room, moved to the seat that Joanna had occupied, and sat down.

"Behind you," Joanna said, standing next to Amy. She took Amy's hand, and turned her so that her back was to the windows of the classroom. "You're on the landing now," she said. "And here's the window you are looking through back over your shoulder to the graveyard." She pointed to the classroom windows. Then she backed away from Amy, facing her, toward the other side of the room. "Here's the foot of the stairs," she said, "and the door is right behind me." Her staging mirrored her drawing on the blackboard. She reached behind herself to touch an imaginary doorknob. Francis allowed himself a smile as Francesca began to read:

She took a doubtful step and then undid it
To raise herself and look again. He spoke
Advancing toward her:

Then Joanna read the husband's question:

"What is it you see
From up there always—for I want to know."

And Joanna, the young husband now, took her hand off the latch of the door behind her, tilting her head up toward Amy on the stairs, and everyone saw the young husband moving up the stairs to his wife, then climb past her to the window and discover the grave she'd been staring at.

The three students rode the poem until, near the end, Amy's hand was on the latch. She read the wife's concluding lines:

Friends make pretense of following to the grave,
But before one is in it, their minds are turned
And making the best of their way back to life
And living people, and things they understand.
But the world's evil. I won't have grief so
If I can change it. Oh, I won't, I won't!

Then Amy mimed pushing the door wider open, stepping backward, away from her husband and out of the house, and Joanna read the last line:

I'll follow and bring you back by force. I will*!*

And then it was over. The stairs melted away, the front door disappeared. The two stood, looking at each other, surprised to be who they used to be again, and sensing they were not.

After a while someone asked, "Do you think she ever comes back?"

The students looked to Francis, waiting for him to answer. But of course he didn't. He was still in Joanna's seat, as if he were one of the students. Joanna and Amy still stood up front. It was their class now, more than his.

"Naturally she comes back," Joanna said. "You think he's going to just let her walk away?" She was very sure. After all, she ought to know, she had just played the part. "It says right here: he's making the best of his way back to life and living people and things they understand."

"And that's good, you think?" Francis asked. "That's what he should do?"

"Oh, yes," Joanna said.

"I do too!" he said.

Nevertheless, an argument ensued about whether Amy comes back. Some of the girls insisted the poem was too sad for a happy ending. Finally, one of them asked Amy: "How'd you feel just now, when you played Amy in the poem?"

"I don't know," Amy said, shrugging to show she didn't give a damn, wanted to get back to her disengagement. None of her classmates believed her. They stared and waited.

"Answer the question, Amy," Francis said from Joanna's seat.

Amy turned to Francis, keeping her mouth shut. She wasn't used to being ordered around.

"Your opinion, Amy," Francis demanded again. He'd keep her there forever if he had to, to make her answer.

"She comes home," Amy said, giving in.

"Why?"

"Because she has no other place to go," Amy said, thinking quickly. For she was damned if she was going to admit she thought the bereaved young mother comes back to her husband out of love. "The woman needs a house like everybody else," she said. "She has to eat." Amy knew damn well marriage as an economic contract and a trap wasn't what Frost was getting at, but it was a smart answer. She could tell by the look on her classmates' faces she was the only one who had thought of it. Now she had her persona back to go with her black clothes and spiked hair. Francis had to admit he liked her answer; it showed how smart she was.

Nevertheless, he wouldn't let her get away with this. "I don't think that's what you think at all," he said.

"How do you know?"

"It's not in the poem," he told her. "There's not one word to suggest it is. You're too smart to think there is."

She didn't answer.

"And besides, it's not how you read the part," he said.

That stopped her. She had no answer now. Everyone in the room had seen how much of herself she had put into the other Amy. She looked out the window, and he let her go. They'd made enough inroads for one day.

A few minutes later, in the middle of a discussion—in which he hardly said a word—of all the meanings of *home* that shimmer in the poem, the time ran out. When the bell rang to end the period, the conversation went on. He had to order the students to leave.

There are bad days when no matter what you try, nothing works; and there are good days when everything you try is magic. This had been one of the good days. No one in this class would ever be the same again.

FRANCIS DIDN'T HAVE much time to savor his satisfaction. The phone rang on his desk before the last ninth grader was out of his classroom. It was Margaret Rice telling him the new headmaster wanted to see him right away. "I know it's just exactly how you want to spend your free period," she said.

"Oh, really?" he asked, matching her sarcasm. "What does he want this time?" She didn't half know how much he didn't want this.

"How would I know?" Margaret answered. "We don't talk a lot, remember?"

But by the time Francis was halfway across campus, he had guessed. It was the business about the Pequot Collection.

And he hadn't told Peggy yet!

So now Peggy would have heard through the grapevine, rather than from him, that the student council he advised would give the Collection away to some people who had never asked for it and probably didn't even know it existed. He needed to apologize to her.

He needed to bring this subject up with her before she brought it up with him—and certainly before Kindler brought it up with her. Even Kindler was sensitive enough not to want to do that. So Francis would explain the issue fully to Kindler now, and then right afterward talk with Peggy. He'd even skip a class if he had to. Then he and Peggy together would plan with Fred Kindler for how they should react to the council's proposal.

"Go right on in," Margaret told him a minute later, waving him to Fred Kindler's office. "They've already begun to talk."

"They?" He was relieved he wouldn't be alone with Kindler. Margaret didn't answer. Just looked at him as if he ought to know. He guessed it was Rachel Bickham. She was one of the people he'd go to for advice if he were the head.

He opened the door to Fred Kindler's office on that meager burst of optimism, and it took an instant for him to realize who was sitting, her back to him, in the chair in front of Kindler's desk. It wasn't Rachel. He stopped dumbfounded, staring at Peggy's back. She was facing Fred Kindler, who stared past her at him.

She turned around in her chair to face him. "Hello," she said. He couldn't read what was in her voice, and Kindler didn't say a word, just pointed to a third chair. Francis entered the office and sat. They were in a circle, Kindler to his left, Peggy to his right. Their three pairs of knees were almost touching.

"We're talking about what the student council wants to do," Peggy said to Francis. He couldn't tell if she was chastising him or just letting him know that the meeting was about a subject delicate for both of them.

"Peggy, I'm sorry," he said. "I just forgot to tell you." He was about to go on and tell her why he forgot: because everything that had happened yesterday had pushed it right out of his mind. But Kindler was watching him, and he couldn't make the words come out. He wouldn't apologize to his wife in this office in front of Marjorie, for Christ's sake, let alone Fred Kindler.

"It's all right, Francis," Peggy said. "I understand." She didn't want to have this apology here in front of Fred Kindler any more than he did. And she did understand how Kindler's threat to fire him would make him forget. But the damage was done: he'd already apologized to her in front of Kindler. Francis felt naked under Kindler's eye, as if the man had caught him in some perverted act. He turned on Kindler. "You should have talked with me first about this," he said.

"Well, I'm glad I didn't," Fred Kindler said. "She might never have found out."

Francis was stunned. "Say that again."

"I think you heard me," Fred Kindler said.

"You mean you told her? She didn't know when she came in here?"

"Francis," Peggy said softly. "Please. What difference does it make?"

It made so much difference to Francis he couldn't speak. *Kindler doing what I should have done. How intrusive can this bastard get?*

"I didn't want her to be kept out of the loop," Kindler said. He didn't even try to keep the contempt out of his voice. He had been shocked to have figured out from the way Peggy reacted in their conversation just now before Francis had entered that Francis hadn't even mentioned this to her. "Or perhaps you don't think the person in charge of the Collection should be the first to know it might disappear," Kindler added. Then regretted his bitter words. Here he was, taking sides between a husband and a wife, butting into a private place. And he was the head, for goodness sake!

Peggy watched as these two men looked at each other then away, and she saw nothing but potential disaster: the dissolution of her marriage, the school's succumbing, Fred Kindler's defeat. Worse than this, and more surprising, she felt a sudden disgust for both of them. That scared her more than anything. She'd do whatever had to be done to erase that feeling. "Let's get on with this meeting," she said. "What are we trying to get done?"

Fred sent her a look of thanks. He would answer her question and be a pro again instead of just an angry man. "I brought us together so that there would be no surprises for any one of the three of us tomorrow when the student council makes its proposal," he said. He was already feeling a little calmer. "I want you to know how I intend to react and why. And give you a chance to do the same."

"Fine," Peggy said. "Thank you." Francis, feeling wary, said nothing.

Then Fred finished. "I'm aware there could be some difficult feelings, some tough emotions around this situation. I thought we could put them on the table here in this privacy so they would be easier to deal with in public tomorrow." He looked straight at Peg.

Francis was appalled. *Oh, Jeeez!* he thought. *It's touchy-feely time.* He felt the same as when Kindler had told him he should go to a shrink. He'd always cringed when the younger teachers wanted to "share their feelings"—in faculty meetings, for crying out loud!—and was always grateful to Marjorie for cutting them off. He turned to Peggy. He knew how she'd react. She always felt the same way. She wasn't about to share her feelings. She'd rather get undressed in public.

"All right, I'll start," Peggy said.

"You'll *what*?" Francis said.

She turned to him. "I'll clear the air."

Now he wondered if she was going to change her mind and chew him out for forgetting to tell her. Right there in public. If she said just one word of that, he'd leave the room.

"I know you weren't trying to surprise me," she said. What else could she do but change her mind and talk about this now? She couldn't turn to Fred Kindler and talk about Francis as if he weren't in the room. But Fred had to know that Francis wouldn't ever try to pull a fast one. "I know you just forgot to tell me," she said. "I know you didn't want me to walk into the auditorium tomorrow and see you up on stage and learn that the—"

Francis looked out the window. He had to struggle not to flee, and Peggy saw how deeply she'd insulted him.

"I'm sorry," she said. "I shouldn't have said that you would think—"

"Don't even say it!" Francis interrupted.

"All right, I won't," Peggy said, but really, she'd already said it.

"Fair enough," Fred Kindler said, keeping his eyes on Peggy. He didn't want her to know how much he distrusted her husband.

He needed to change the subject and get the focus on tomorrow. "I'm going to be neutral," he said. "I'm not going to be for or against. I'm going to let the discussion happen. You need to know that." He was looking straight at Peggy. "I hope you're okay with that."

"I'm not, I hate it." Peggy said.

Fred was taken aback.

"You asked," she said.

"All right," he said, and turned to Francis. "And you?"

You think I'm going to disagree with my wife in front of you? Francis thought. Out loud, he lied, "I hate it too."

"Well, we've got a problem," Kindler said.

Peggy leaned back in her chair, she was not sure why—to distance herself from both of them? Let them figure it out. Why should she? The silence went on until she heard herself say, "No, we don't. Not much of a problem, anyway. I'm not crazy. I can see both sides." She really could, and besides, she was here to save the day.

Fred was too relieved to think of what to say. Francis wasn't sure he believed her.

"But if anybody even begins to spout PC theology, if anyone even utters the words *blasphemy* or *sacrilege*, I'm going to fight back," Peggy said. "And if we don't find the right Pequot authorities and they don't guarantee they'll take care of it, I won't let it out of my sight."

"Me too," Francis said, feeling a little better now.

"Believe me, we won't give it away to just anybody—if we give it away at all," Fred said.

Now there was a silence. No one knew what to say.

"Is there anything else we need to bring up?" Fred asked.

Francis shook his head. Later, when it would be too late, he would understand what a big mistake he'd made, but right now all he wanted was for this meeting to end.

"Just this ironic fact," Peggy said. "That it's the Collection in our midst that inspired the moral development in the girls to make them not want to keep it in our midst."

"Will you say that tomorrow?" Fred asked.

"If no one else does," Peggy answered.

"Good," Fred said, and Peggy waited for him to say more, some recognition of how much she had surrendered, but he kept his mouth shut. He wanted to tell her how much he agreed with her, how he loved the paradox she'd named, but he was damned if he would engage in a philosophical conversation with Francis Plummer in the room. "Anything else?" he asked.

"I can't think of anything," Peggy said.

"Well, that didn't take so long," Fred said.

Francis could see Kindler was trying to end the meeting on a strong note. He wasn't going to hang around for that. He stood up and turned his back on Kindler. "Let's go, Peggy," he said, and moved to the door.

Peggy hesitated. Fred said nothing. He wasn't going to rise to the insult of Plummer turning his back on him.

Peggy watched Fred make that decision. Francis waited for her by the door. They'd leave together, side by side. But she made a little gesture with her hand, refusing him. He understood: right then she was more Fred Kindler's right-hand person than Francis Plummer's wife! She didn't move from her chair until Francis left.

When she got back to her library, she would stop in front of the Collection and look at it as if maybe she'd never have another chance.

THE NEXT MORNING, the auditorium was loud with conversation as the students trooped in and Francis and the student council took seats on the stage. Peggy took a seat near the front right behind Sam Andersen.

Lila stood up, moved to the front of the stage. The room grew quiet. "Some of you already know Sara Warrior, our new ninth grader," Lila said. She gestured to where Sara sat in the front row of the audience. "As you know, Sara's Native American, Pequot," Lila went on. "She wants to talk to you."

Sara stood up and moved toward the stage and climbed the same steps that Fred Kindler had climbed the other day. She looked small and frightened.

"Listen carefully," Lila said. "Sara is going to make a proposal." Then she stepped away from the mike and went back to her seat. The students applauded. It was the Oliver custom to make new students feel at home.

But Peggy was not applauding. Francis hadn't told her Sara was going to make the proposal. He hadn't even told her that Sara was the one who had brought the issue up. The student council was bringing up this issue, and Sara was not on the student council. Peggy stared past Sara to where Francis sat right next to Lila Smythe at the back of the stage. How could he do this to this kid? How could he use her so? A fourteen-year-old child, a Native American to boot, who was homesick and lonely and needed to be nurtured. Put her up there on stage and see who dared present the other side. *Francis, you bastard!* Peggy thought. *We said there'd be no surprises!*

The microphone was much too tall for Sara. She looked for the screw that she could turn to telescope it down, and for the longest time couldn't find it, then finally did and started to talk. But her voice didn't carry; it was hard to hear her. Peggy wanted to rush up there and mother the kid, put her arms around her and take her offstage where she'd be safe. Lila got up from her seat and rescued Sara. She put one hand on Sara's shoulder while the other turned the switch to activate the mike, then she smiled at Sara and went back to her seat.

"It kind of bothers me that I'm the one who has to tell you this," Sara said. Her voice quavered, and she looked as if she might start to cry. She looked back at Lila, who nodded her head.

"Go ahead," Lila whispered. "You're the one to do this."

"All right," Sara said, and began. "There were twenty-six villages along the Connecticut and Rhode Island shore and up and down the river. In 1630 the captain of a white man's merchant ship kidnapped the chief and demanded six thousand feet of wampumpeag for ransom, and when they got it, they killed him and put his body into a canoe and floated it into the harbor where now New London is." Sara spoke with more assurance now as she recited this history she knew so well and that enraged her. "They killed the warriors and burned the villages and murdered the mothers and the children, and then they stole the land."

Some of the older students were restless in their seats. They resented this talk. They had studied this history, and they felt guilty and had no power to undo the injustice. *If it had been the other way around, you would have done it too*, they wanted to say.

"And you shouldn't act like them," Sara said, and immediately understood she'd made a mistake, and paused. She was flustered now. She knew these kids didn't murder people, didn't invade and kill women and children. "I didn't mean it like that," she said. "I didn't mean that you would do it." She tried to find the words to say what she did mean. But her mind was all a jumble now, and she couldn't find the words, because she was only fourteen and she was up there all alone with all these people looking at her, and she'd never made a speech before.

Then she saw the headmaster standing in the back of the room. He was the one who should be doing this. And he was the one who could help her. The students turned to see where Sara was looking. There was a lot of silence. Everyone in the auditorium could see that Sara wanted Fred Kindler to say something so she could be a ninth grader, not a prophet, and everybody was waiting to see how he'd respond. But he'd already decided he wouldn't take sides. He restrained himself, and the moment passed. Sara, even more alone and disillusioned, tried to speak.

She was supposed to make the proposal. Then she could sit down. She drew a breath. "We should give it back," she said, not the words she had been going to say, the elaborate ones Lila had helped her with. She soldiered on. "It's not right to put the things of people who your ancestors murdered in a case just so you can study them. And pieces of a person's body in a case too so you can stare and stare and stare." Then she remembered what Lila had said. "That's sacrilege," she said. "That's blasphemous."

Now Peggy was on her feet. Sara looked her way and stopped talking.

"I think you misunderstand," Peggy said. "Let's talk, Sara. Please. Later."

Sara stared at her, and Sam Andersen turned around in his seat in front of Peggy. He found her eyes, and shook his head, a gesture he hoped only she could notice. She understood and wished she could have the last ten seconds back. "I'm sorry, Sara," she murmured, and sat down, even more furious now at Francis for what she thought was his part in putting Sara onstage.

Sara was crying. How could she not be? First her fear of public speaking, then her outrage, and then the headmaster not pitching in for her, and finally this woman challenging her. This woman who pretended to be a mother in the dorm and was the guardian of the bones, standing up in front of everybody and saying Sara didn't understand. What was there not to understand?

Lila came downstage and put an arm around Sara, kissed her cheek. That's all the signal that was needed: the students stood and clapped for Sara's bravery, her fierce conviction. Shaken, Sara left the stage and took a seat in the audience.

Then Lila made the announcement that Sara had been going to make. "On your behalf, the student council will petition the headmaster and the board of trustees for the immediate return of the Collection to the rightful owners, the Pequot people," she said. "We'll make the petition in our next meeting and send it around. You can decide for yourselves whether to sign it. I hope you will."

There was a long silence then in the audience. Everyone's eyes moved up front and went back and forth between Peggy in the second row and Francis up on the stage. Everyone was waiting for Peggy to speak. But she would not. She was not going to say anything about her opinion that there were two sides to this issue, or mention the paradox she named yesterday in Fred Kindler's office. She wouldn't even defend the Collection from the accusation of sacrilege and blasphemy. Not with Sara in the room. Because Sara was the one who uttered those words, and she was the one who needed protection.

Fred Kindler watched Peggy. He guessed why she wasn't talking. Nevertheless, an idea came to him, bringing a surge of excitement. As one more strategy to save the school, he would reach out to the Pequot Nation, recruit their children (he wondered why that hadn't been done before), invite several of their parents to join the board, and instead of returning the Collection, thus looking guilty and suspiciously correct, persuade the Pequot Nation to create an even more significant Collection to honor their tradition right here at Miss Oliver's School for Girls—of every hue—where once a Pequot village had thrived. And the Pequots would participate in the dig that Sam Andersen was going to organize. Thus turn a potential public relations disaster into a victory. That's how to build a school: reach out, bring in, include, make layers, build strength.

Then the bell rang, and Lila adjourned the meeting. Feeling vaguely dissatisfied because they still wanted to know what Mrs. Plummer thought, the students moved out of the auditorium and to their classes. Karen Benjamin, stringer for the *Hartford Courant*'s weekly column that covered teenage concerns in Capital Area schools, skipped her class to phone the story in.

THAT EVENING IT seemed to Francis that he waited for hours and hours for Peggy to come home from the library. He wasn't going to let one minute go by before he cleared the air with her. He was not sure she really did forgive him for not telling her about the proposal before Fred Kindler did. And he was not sure she really could see both sides of the issue. Why should she after all these years? But it didn't even cross his mind that she could think that the reason Sara had been chosen to make the proposal was to shut Peggy up. Sara had been chosen because she was the one to object to the Collection. What could be more obvious than that?

He was surprised when suddenly the door connecting their apartment to the dormitory opened, and there Peggy was, framed in the doorway, and frowning at him, instead of at their front door where he'd been listening for her. He realized she'd been touring their dormitory before coming home, avoiding his company as long as she could. For thirty-three years they'd made a point of visiting with the girls together in the evening. He felt a wisp of anger rising, stuffed it down beside the hurt, and stood up from the chair he'd been sitting in. "Hello, Peg," he said.

She stopped just through the doorway. She could tell from the way he was looking at her that he'd been sitting there waiting for her, about to pounce on her with excuses and reasons before she even drew a breath. There was no way she's going to listen. "I need some tea," she announced and went to the kitchen.

All right, I'll wait out here, he decided, and sat down again. She needed a little space. Besides, he was not going to follow her like some faithful puppy. He heard the water gush into the kettle, heard her crossing to the stove and putting the kettle on it, even heard the click of the handle for the gas. As the minutes passed his sadness blossomed.

"So now you're politically correct?" she said at last through the doorway, speaking the term as if describing vermin. "How stylish!" She'd misinterpreted his staying in the living room, thought he was going to act as if nothing had happened. No way. She needed to fight.

He kept his mouth shut. He wasn't going to rise to crap like that.

"You sure your name isn't van Buren? Francis van Buren, politician?" She imagined his face getting red.

He sat there. He wasn't going to say one word to this.

"No, I guess not. You're just twins. Two of a kind."

Now he stood up. But he wasn't headed for the kitchen. He was headed for the front door. Fuck this. He'd just leave. She could talk to air.

"You could kiss and make up," she said. "You and Gregory. He could be up on stage too. He could sit in your lap."

He whirled around. Now he was the one who needed to fight. He went through the kitchen door. She was facing him, her back to the stove. "You need to watch your mouth," he said.

"Really? Like when you blurted out in the middle of the first faculty meeting of the year that the new headmaster shouldn't even talk about how the kids dress because Marjorie wouldn't?" she asked, grabbing at the opening he'd given with his comment about watching her mouth. She didn't care how crazy this was, how off the subject. The way he'd behaved in that meeting—in front of everybody! "Is that how you watch your mouth?" she asked him.

"Why are you talking about that?" he asked her. "Speaking of running at the mouth."

"Because he had to save your butt, that's why. He had to stop the meeting just so the senior teacher wouldn't go on acting like the biggest asshole in the world in front of everybody."

"What else, Peggy?" He took a step forward. He was in her face, almost yelling. "What else? Think of everything. Make a big fucking list."

She stared at him. Then very quietly she said, "We don't have much in common anymore, do we, Francis?"

She didn't wait for his answer. Instead, she took a step toward him, put her hand on his chest, pushed past him, and walked out of the kitchen, through their living room, toward the front door. He followed past her, reached the door before she did, put his hand on the knob. "Open the door, Francis," she commanded. "I'm going to the library to work."

"That's a relief," he said. She reached for the knob. He let it go and stepped back, made a big sweeping gesture with his arm to usher her out. "Don't hurry back," he said, more hurt than he'd ever been.

Outside, she turned back to him. "Using that little girl that way," she said. "Preying on her feelings. Putting her up on the stage like that so nobody could argue. How could you let that happen!"

"Oh!"

"Don't act surprised, Francis. After we told each other there would be no surprises."

"Oh, my God, so that's what this is about!"

She stared at him. "Well, what did you think it was about?" she asked. Then she turned and walked away.

FOURTEEN

Fred was relieved a few days after Sara Warrior's talk to discover in the *Hartford Courant* that Karen Benjamin's report on the student council proposal was only one short paragraph in the Teen section, buried in the middle of a series of reports from several schools. He was grateful for the *Courant* editor's preference for banal stories featuring football stars and pretty cheerleaders. If Fred had been the editor, he would have featured the controversy over the Pequot Collection. It was exactly the kind of issue that students and their teachers should confront.

But Fred, who had almost never read a newspaper article about an independent school that hadn't used the word *exclusive*, knew how inclined the public was to stereotype schools like Miss Oliver's as arrogant. Even a very objective article on this issue would have fed the stereotype, which was exactly what he didn't need.

He had reason to be worried: not only had the summer recruiting effort only managed to garner a mere six additional students for the sophomore and junior classes, and the smallest ninth grade in the school's history, but so far, in September, there had only been three requests for information from families exploring schools for the next school year, the second in Fred's programmed two-year race against the growing deficit. Nan White had told him that even in the previous year's dearth there had been fifteen such requests by this time, the second week in September.

It wouldn't occur to Fred until much later that maybe Karen had had the same worry that he had and wrote a boring article on purpose.

However unimportant to the public, the proposal to give away the Collection was momentous to the school, and Gregory van Buren, faculty advisor to the *Clarion*, hoped that it would require enough of Karen's editorial attention for her to abandon her article on the sex lives of the seniors, a project he despised. There was huge opportunity in the Collection story. On the day her sparse report appeared in the *Courant*, he called her in to his classroom to ask her how she proposed to cover it in the *Clarion*.

"I've given it to Clarissa Longstreet," Karen told him.

"Very amusing," he murmured.

"Really. I have," she said, and now he was staring at her. "Aren't you proud of me? I'm delegating. I'm giving away the plums instead of taking them for myself," she said, keeping a straight face. She knew what he was trying to do, and she was tired of his indirection.

"All of it?" he asked. "Karen, there are at least three features in this story."

"Let Clarissa decide how many features. She's probably going to be editor in chief next year."

"The scene in the auditorium with the Warrior girl's talk," Gregory said, interrupting to list the features. He counted them on his fingers. "The place of the Collection in the development of the school. An editorial on the rightness, or wrongness, of giving it away or keeping it." He knew that Karen understood all this. Clarissa too, he'd taught them both. But he was trying so hard to lure Karen into this story and away from the article she wanted to write! Just thinking about celebrating adolescent sex by writing about it in the school's newspaper offended him.

Perhaps one source of Gregory's feelings on this subject was simple envy—his own sex life seemed to be finished. But Gregory, forty-five, divorced twenty years before, stuck with a monkish life because he really did believe that sex without love and lifelong commitment degraded humanity, and Gregory was too absorbed by Miss Oliver's intense, inward-looking scene to have the time to fall in love again. Maybe the reason Gregory seemed so pompous and anachronistic was that, though surrounded by irony on every side, he took himself seriously enough to believe he had an eternal, precious soul that could be stained by fornication. He knew because he'd felt that stain a few times when, during his summer travels in foreign places, he'd fallen off the wagon, punctured his celibacy with some other lonely person, and then suffered weeks of remorse. At any rate, he took his students just as seriously as he took himself. They had souls too, just as eternal as his. That was really why he taught. If he had thought otherwise, he wouldn't have bothered.

And he was one of the reasons Miss Oliver's went against the tide. At Miss Oliver's, Gregory van Buren was cool precisely because he wasn't.

"The whole subject?" he asked again. "Karen, you're still the chief!"

"I've got other fish to fry," Karen said.

"I know you do, and it's wrong!"

Well, why didn't you just say that at the beginning? she thought. Out loud she said, "I'm sorry you feel that way." She really was. She was grateful for how tough he'd been on her, making her revise everything over and over until she got it right. Now she did that for herself. She knew Mr. van Buren disapproved of her article on moral grounds and also because it would be bad publicity for the school. Well, the headmaster had already told her that if he thought the article would harm the school, he wouldn't let her publish it.

"I can't tell you not to do the interviews," he said, as if reading her mind. "You can talk about anything you want. But you know the new headmaster won't let you publish the article, so why do you persist in wasting your time? Mr. Kindler has more sense than his predecessor about such things," he added, giving in to his sudden urge to goad her. Karen got his goat. He'd always been able to control his editors until this one came along. And she was the one he admired the most!

"Well, then," she said, "if the new headmaster won't let me publish it, what are you so worried about?" It didn't occur to either of them that Gregory would be the one to make the decision to ban the article. The school had been trained by Marjorie, who had made all the decisions.

"Because it's wrong. It's perverse and degrading. That is what disturbs me, not the PR that the head worries about."

Karen wanted to say that there was nothing degrading about telling the truth, but she knew him well enough to know he would say that there was no such thing as objectivity, that just writing about teenagers having sex with each other without saying it's wrong would make it seem to teenagers that it was right. Well, she didn't agree. She didn't think it was right, and she was a teenager.

"I'm sorry you don't agree with me that it's wrong," he murmured, giving up. He stood to show the conversation was over.

Karen stayed in her chair. She wanted to say something more, but it didn't come to her, so she stood up. "Clarissa will do fine," she said. "I promise."

He nodded his head to affirm he knew that was true and sat down again, and feeling very sad, he watched her walk out the door.

When she was halfway across campus heading to a class, she realized that one reason she wanted to write article was to earn Mr. van Buren's praise. For once she wanted to write a piece that was so good he couldn't find one thing to criticize. She'd come close lots of times, but there was always something. He'd taught her how to work, and she wanted to prove to him she'd learned. Just trying to make him admit that this one, which would be harder to do well than all the others, and that he hated, was as good as it could get, was worth the risk that the headmaster wouldn't allow it to be printed.

THAT AFTERNOON, FRED had an appointment with the officers of the student council. Lila arrived at his office before the others, bringing a greeting that had nothing personal in it, neither of animosity nor of affection—a mere "hi" as she came through the door. He sensed that she hadn't written him off like most of the students.

"Good morning, Lila," he said warmly and gestured to one of the chairs in front of his desk. Sitting down, she never took her eyes off his face.

"Well, I guess you know what this is about," she said.

"Well, I'd be pretty dumb if I didn't," he said and smiled.

But Lila, with too much on her mind to catch his playfulness, pushed on with her agenda. "I've asked Sara Warrior to come too," she told him. "Even though she's not on the council. Since it was her idea, I thought I should."

"That's fine," he said, though it wasn't; it would make the meeting tenser.

"Thank you."

"You okay?" he asked. He was worried about her. He saw how

pale she was, how tired, this eighteen-year-old, the force behind the Declaration, the person who took responsibility for Sara's claim. She had more pressure on her than many of the faculty.

"I'm okay."

"Just okay?"

She didn't know how to answer. If it had been later in the year they would have known each other better, and she could explain how Mr. Plummer had disappointed her, and Fred might observe that finding out her hero had clay feet showed she was outgrowing Miss Oliver's School for Girls, as she should in her senior year. But they were too unknown to each other for such a conversation, so she simply nodded her head to insist she was feeling fine.

And besides, here came the other girls.

Angela Nash had been picked by lottery because nobody knew the ninth graders well enough yet to vote for one. She was so eager to get this job permanently when her classmates would vote in January that she tripped on the rug and almost fell down while making sure she got the chair nearest Fred. He had to turn away to hide his smile. *Take it easy*, he wanted to say to her. *I don't have a vote.*

Sara sat down beside Angela, her eyes cast down so she didn't have to look at Fred. Marie Safford, a junior, was taller than Lila and stately, a young black woman wearing dreadlocks and studious glasses. She stalked, as if entering dangerous territory, to a chair on the other side of Lila from Fred, clutching a manila folder.

"We have a proposal," Lila said.

"I figured you did." He smiled. "Let's hear it."

Lila nodded to Marie. Marie looked at Angela and moved the folder toward her, offering it. "No, you," said Angela. "Go ahead." The quirky way she held her head when she said this reminded Fred of his daughter, and now, suddenly more than ever, he didn't want their proposal between him and them. He would have given anything just to sit and chat with these kids, just pass the time of day.

Marie opened the folder. "We, the student council of Miss Oliver's School for Girls . . ."

"Please," said Fred. "Don't read it. Just talk it through with me."

Marie shook her head. "Why not?" Angela asked. "We'll explain it as we go."

"No," Marie said. "I want to read it. This is not a conversation; it's a proposal."

Lila looked at Fred. "Go ahead, read," he said to Marie. So she did:

> *We, the student council of Miss Oliver's School for Girls, require the administration and the board of trustees officially to return the artifacts, sacred to the memory of the Pequot culture, to their rightful owners, along with the human remains of a member of that tribe for burial in accordance with their sacred customs, and moreover, that the school, now and forever, relinquish all claims of ownership to these items currently on display in the school library.*

Jeepers! Fred thought, trying hard not to giggle. *How about some iambic pentameter to dress it up?* Out loud he said softly, "Don't say *require*. Say *request*."

"Why?" Lila asked.

"Because you'll get further. That's the way the world works."

"I'm not sure I like the way the world works," Lila said.

Angela put her hand on Lila's knee, but Marie just rolled her eyes. "Lila's been studying history again," she explained to the ceiling. "She's just now learning about racism." Sara, stiff with tension, didn't said a word. Fred tried to catch her eyes, but she looked away.

"Well, I have an alternative proposal," Fred said and told them of his idea of rendering the ownership of the Collection to the Pequots while keeping it on campus in the library. He grew even more enthusiastic as he saw Lila's expression brighten. Why shouldn't she like it since everyone would win? "We'll build another wing," he went on. "It will be their Collection, honoring their history on ground where their village was situated, and we'll invite members of their nation to be on our board and recruit their children—"

"Oh!" Angela interrupted, smiling, and sitting up even straighter. "What a wonderful idea!"

"It stinks," said Marie

"Well, I don't think it stinks," Fred said.

"It stinks of compromise."

"Compromise is how the world works," Fred said, then wished he hadn't.

"Oh, let's stop pretending!" Marie exclaimed. "This isn't a Pequot village. It's a school for rich white girls."

Marie, please, what color are you? Fred thought.

"That's right, *white*," Marie said, as if reading his mind. "We live in Greenwich, for God's sake! My father's a lawyer for Exxon; my mother belongs to the Junior League. They're whiter than you are."

"Well, why shouldn't they live in Greenwich if they want to?" Angela asked, and Marie looked at her as if she were three years old.

"Hey, Marie," Fred said softly, feeling a sudden flood of empathy for her parents, whom he hadn't even met. "We need to talk." He knew she wanted to know why the school could be so proud of its diversity—all those skin colors living together—when hardly anyone came from neighborhoods where kids got shot and the only stores were liquor stores. *That bothers me too*, he'd tell her. *It's one of the things I want to fix.*

"Okay, we'll talk," Marie said, shrugging her shoulders. "Sometime. Maybe."

So now Fred turned to Lila. "Well, Lila, what do you think of my idea?" he asked, and then the room was very quiet and everyone was looking at Lila, and right away Fred realized what a lousy thing he'd done. Sara was staring at Lila's face, counting on her to answer. And he was the one who was worried about the pressure on Lila, and now he did this to her! *Forget it, don't answer that*, he wanted to say.

He didn't need to, because Marie was too heated by this issue to wait for Lila's answer. Or maybe she was trying to save Sara from the disillusion of Lila's deserting her. She was certainly not trying to take the pressure off Lila. "It doesn't make any difference what you think, or what Lila thinks or what I think," she said to Fred, and he could feel her anger filling the room. Marie's rage at injustice was inflamed by her thinking she'd been cheated out of the hurt of it because her family was rich. She thought she'd never have a chance to be as passionate as those other young people who before her time had sat scared to death at white lunch counters to try to make the world the way it ought to be. "The only person in this room who has any right to an opinion about this is Sara," she said.

"That's not fair," Angela blurted.

Marie ignored her, keeping her eyes on Fred. "I ask you: Who are you to decide what should be done with the Collection? The only jurisdiction you have is that it's in your possession." *And that you're white and male and the headmaster*, she was tempted to add. But she was too smart to go that far. "We need to not be the owners anymore," she said instead. "We need to give the stuff back to the rightful owners. If they want to put it back here in our library, that's their decision."

"Oh, you're just splitting hairs!" Angela exclaimed.

"No, she isn't," Fred said. "She's being precise. That's a good way to be." Then turning to Marie, he said, "I like your approach. I like it a lot. But you have to know I like mine better."

"Why?" she wanted to know.

"Because more good comes from it," Fred answered, and Marie shut up. She sensed how stubborn he was, how fixed in his plan. There was another way for her to win: collect a ton of signatures on the petition. Let him deal with those.

Sara still hadn't spoken. Lila felt the weight of her gaze. How to explain to Sara that she liked Mr. Kindler's idea? And how to explain how much she wished she didn't? She envied the purity of Marie's belief, the single-mindedness of it.

"Anyway, Marie," Fred said, "I think the proposal's fine, and I admire it. But I like mine better. So I'll deliver both to the board of trustees at the November meeting."

"Well, we already know which proposal they'll take, don't we," Marie said. "You're the headmaster."

Yup, you're right, Fred was tempted to say. *That's the way the world works.*

Instead he didn't say anything, and that was all the signal that Sara needed. She stood up and fled the room.

Fred stood too, all his instincts pushing him to follow her. He wanted to put his arm around her, he wanted to explain, but he knew that wouldn't work. He'd end up chasing her through the building, making her feel even worse, so he stood still behind his desk. Marie and Lila and Angela stood now too. All three were looking at the door.

"Yes," he said. "Take care of Sara." The girls moved to the door.

"Right," Marie said bitterly, "We'll make sure she's learned her lesson."

"What lesson is that, Marie?" he challenged.

"How the world works," she answered over her shoulder as she went through the door. "Isn't that how you put it?"

Fifteen

"The Lord bless you and keep you," Father Michael Woodward said to his congregation as the service ended this first Sunday in October. "The Lord make his face to shine upon you and be gracious unto you." He made the sign of the cross. "The Lord lift his countenance upon you and give you peace." As he said this benediction, he looked straight at Francis and Peggy, and saw Francis inching his way closer to the aisle so he could be the first to get out of there. *Well, good for you, anyway, for trying to conform,* Father Woodward wanted to say to Francis, though the last thing he would pray for when he prayed for them both and for their marriage would be that Francis succeed in this pretense. Instead, Father Woodward (who had annoyed the vestry at last month's meeting by suggesting only half in jest that the road to world peace was to give everyone who believes in a God a lobotomy to make them forget the differences in their beliefs—and then proceeded to go to sleep during the finance committee report) would pray for Peggy's belief to broaden to embrace her husband's too, rather than just the other way around.

In fact, there was another reason, besides his alienation from the service, for Francis's haste to leave the church. This was the Sunday the student council chose for the service projects Rachel Bickham had suggested to Fred Kindler instead of Sunday classes as a consequence of those missed during the Petrie invasion. So right after church, Francis hurried to join Rachel to lead a group of students in the cleanup of a salt marsh near the mouth of the river. When he got to the bus that would take them to the marsh, Rachel and the students were already there, waiting for him.

On the way south to the marsh, Rachel reminded the students how wondrously complex an estuarine marsh was, how like blood was the mix of salt and fresh water that came and went over it, the marsh itself was like a womb where many of the creatures that lived in the ocean were born.

They spent the afternoon walking in line abreast back and forth across the marsh, picking up discarded tires, bottles, cans, plastic bags that, floating in the ocean, choke turtles to death because they think they're jellyfish. The students wondered at the many different kinds of crabs they saw, the balls of matted fur and crushed bones shat out by birds of prey, the variety of birds, grasses, animal tracks.

When they were finished, they walked back to the bus in the slanted sunlight of the autumn afternoon, and just before they climbed on, Rachel told them that each acre of a healthy salt marsh delivered an average of sixty-two tons of foodstuffs to the food chain every year. "Without one hour of human labor," she told them. "No farm in the world can match that, no human ingenuity needed. We could disappear off the earth, and it would still happen," Rachel said, echoing Lila's words last summer when she had told Francis that his turtle appeared to him from out of the time when the world was here and human beings were not. Francis was struck by how similar Rachel's words were to those Livingstone Mendoza had spoken when he came to the school last February and inspired Francis and Lila to follow him out west. Yes, inspire, Francis admitted, for it really was about the breath of life that Mendoza had been talking. It dawned on him that his efficient colleague, Rachel Bickham of the orderly mind, gifted teacher, able administrator, destined for the highest posts, would not have been as embarrassed as he, Francis, had been playing Indian for a childlike Livingstone Mendoza. Rachel and Mendoza would have recognized in each other that openness to the grace that comes, as Peggy put it. For to be as a child—full of wonder—is to be full of grace.

Standing on the narrow black tar road just before he climbed back up into the bus, October's woods flaming behind him, Francis looked out over the brown grass and living mud of the salt marsh to the sea beyond it, and seeing, he hoped, with Indian eyes, as Mendoza had offered, he wondered if he would be able to keep his promise that from then on his spiritual yearnings would be in tune with Peggy's.

A WEEK LATER, just home from church, he was still in doubt, though the words of peace in Father Woodward's benediction echoed in his head. He wondered if he should bring the subject up with Peggy, ease their pain by talking about it. But he didn't get this chance, because the doorbell rang. Peggy got there first. She opened it, flooding the apartment with golden light, and there, framed in the doorway, stood a tall woman who was smiling and reaching out for a hug.

Looking into the visitor's face from where he was standing behind Peg, Francis knew exactly who she was, who her friends were, what her mother and dad were like, the exact year she had graduated—but he couldn't remember her name, and he was in his ocean again. He'd always remembered the names before; it was the young teachers who forgot. All this in an instant, a little spear of panic, and then Peggy said, "Why, Hannah! Hannah Fingerman!" and Francis, rescued, couldn't even imagine the moment a second ago when her name hadn't existed in his brain. "Come in!" Peg said. "It's wonderful to see you!"

Hannah was the same tall person she had been twenty years ago, though now the blackness of her hair was fake and she was a little thicker in the middle. Francis remembered she hadn't been one of the "smart" ones, hadn't succeeded in getting in to any of the colleges to which her friends had been admitted. The faculty had given her the benefit of the doubt when they graded her final exams in her senior year so she could graduate. "And why shouldn't they?" Marjorie had applauded. "Everyone knows that the kids who flounder in classrooms are the ones designed to shine later." That's what Marjorie had been trying to say when she had irritated the trustees year after year by refusing to publicize the invariably impressive list of the most competitive colleges to which the seniors had gained acceptance. "That's not how we measure success," Marjorie would say, while Francis's heart flamed with pride and Gregory van Buren shook his head.

Hannah stepped through the door and fended off Levi, who was trying to put his nose up under her dress. "You guys never change!" she said. "You had a dog like that twenty years ago!" Now she was in the middle of the room, and Francis was kissing her cheek. "God!" she said. "You don't look any different."

"Being around kids keeps you young," he said.

"Yeah, lucky you." Hannah tossed her hair—a familiar gesture, but it didn't look the same. Somehow, she was too old for it. "What was that dog's name?" she asked.

"Levi," said Peg, smiling.

"Levi? Oh, yes. I remember! What's this one's name?" She reached down now to pat Levi, whose whole rear end was wagging. "God, it's good to see you guys! It feels like ten minutes ago. Lots of water over the dam."

"And you're going to tell us all about it," said Peg.

"Levi," said Francis. "The dog's name is Levi."

Hannah looked up from her patting, searched Francis's face. "You're kidding."

"The one you knew was Levi One. This one's Levi Two," he said.

Hannah was grinning now. She sat down on the sofa.

"Really," said Peg.

Hannah, playing along, asked, "Is he Jewish?"

Peg looked at Francis.

"Yup," said Francis. "He's Jewish, all right."

"Now I really feel at home," Hannah said, grinning even wider now.

"Hannah," Peggy said, "tell us where you've been."

Hannah shook her head. "I love it when things don't change," she said.

"Well, we could talk about that!" Francis said.

"Hannah, catch us up," said Peg.

"I've made a bunch of money," Hannah announced. "Surprise! Surprise!"

"We're not surprised," said Francis.

Hannah told them she had married a Canadian whose health club in Montreal was failing, and, offering to help him, she had taken it over bit by bit, discovering an instinctive talent. "It's the right brain," she informed them. "As long as I don't think too hard about things, I always get them right. He was just the opposite. He planned everything so much he never got around to doing anything. Too much business school, not enough guts. Well, we're divorced now. He couldn't stand it that his wife was better at something than he was, poor thing. Hell, I'm better at everything than he is, and now I have three clubs in Montreal, one in Toronto, and two in Vancouver. I'm national! Also, I'm a free woman. Being single is almost as much fun as being rich!"

"That's wonderful, Hannah!" Peggy said. "We're very happy for—"

"Yeah, and I hear you might go coed," Hannah interrupted. She leaned forward, her voice suddenly harsh. She could never have done that to a conversation as a kid. "If we hadn't been just girls when I was here, I'd still be an assistant club manager and married to a wimp."

"Right!" said Francis.

"It's not definite," Peggy said. "A long way from being definite. The girls—"

"Yeah, yeah, I know, but I have a way to guarantee it won't happen."

"What's that?" Francis asked.

"Money!" Hannah leaned back, spread her arms along the back of the sofa, taking up as much space as any man would.

"You're going to make a donation." Peg's tone was matter-of-fact.

"That's right." Hannah kept her arms spread, her head tilted back, relaxed, as if she did this every day. "You bet! A big one."

"Hey! Hey! Hey!" said Francis. "Hannah baby!"

"How big?" Peggy asked.

"Two. Two big ones," Hannah grinned.

Francis and Peg looked at each other, disappointed. Two thousand? What good is that? Peg started to get up to get Hannah some coffee.

"Two million," said Hannah. "How's that?"

"Two million!" said Francis.

"Two million," Peggy repeated, as if testing the sound.

"That's it!" Hannah leaned forward again. "Two million to buy the deficit until the school builds the enrollment back up. And I mean the enrollment without any boys around. Just girls!" She leaned further forward still, gesturing with her hands in front of her, projecting herself, filling the room.

"Just girls," Hannah repeated. "No boys. We keep the old school, just the way it always was. That's the whole point of the place, right?

I make a deal: the school agrees to stay for girls only, and I cover the deficit while it builds the girls-only enrollment up again."

"We can do that," said Peg.

"We better!" Hannah said. "No compromises."

"Right," said Francis.

"Besides which, I go on the board," Hannah declared.

"Of course!" said Francis.

"When's this going to happen?" asked Peggy.

"Soon as my lawyers finish squashing my ex-husband's attempt to get some of this dough."

"Oh," said Peggy. Already she'd lost heart. She started to get up again.

Hannah gestured to Peg to stay seated, she didn't come for coffee. "Don't worry. I mean it. It's close to a done deal. Two months at most. I wouldn't have come to you about this until it was actually done, except the board needs to know about this before it goes and does something stupid."

"Really?" asked Peg.

"Count on it."

"Okay," said Francis. "We're counting on it!" His mind was full of schemes. If he took this gift right now, it would put him in charge. Whose gun was going to make a bigger bang than this?

There was a little moment of silence while Francis thought of this, and none of them spoke, and the Sunday morning dormitory sounds of showers running on and on, padding feet, sleepy voices drifted into the apartment. "Ah, Sunday morning," Hannah said. "The only day we could sleep."

"Yeah, we keep 'em busy," Francis said.

"That was the hardest thing for me to get used to," Hannah remembered, "Saturday classes. You know, Mr. van Buren would harp on that, quoting from Thoreau all the time: 'Simplify! Simplify! Simplify!' I loved the guy, but on this he was full of crap. That's not what this school is about."

"So what is it about?" said Peg.

"Why, intensify, of course," Hannah said, spreading her hands. "Anybody can see that. Intensify! Intensify! Intensify!"

Francis thought: *You were never dumb. We just asked you the wrong questions.*

"Well, Hannah," Peggy said, "I'm sure you're right. We can count on your gift. It's wonderful! How marvelous! I hope you'll march right over to Fred Kindler's house right now and tell him. It will make his day!"

"Fuck him!" Hannah said.

Peg moved back in her seat, as if she'd been slapped.

"All right then, screw him, is that a little better?"

"No. It's not a little better," Peggy said.

"He's trying to ruin the school. He's a traitor."

"Peggy's never liked swearing," Francis offered.

"And you always have?" said Peggy turning to him.

Hannah's eyes went back and forth between them. She looked like someone trying to figure what the weather's going to do. Peggy looked at Francis, waiting. "*Traitor*'s not the right word," he told Hannah, speaking softly. *But* outsider *is*, he wanted to add.

Hannah looked directly at him. "So? What is the right word?"

"Headmaster," Peg said.

"Head of school," said Francis. "For Christ's sake!"

"You do like to swear, don't you?" Peggy said.

"What's going on here?" Hannah's voice was alarmed. She paused, waiting for an answer. Then getting none, she said, "The guy's a traitor." Her voice was harsh again, but her question lingered in the air. "If he gets credit for this gift, he gets power," she went on. "We want to get rid of him, not make him stronger."

Peg reached out her hand to touch Hannah's. For a second, Hannah started to pull her hand away, but changed her mind. "Hannah," said Peg softly, "your gift is going to save the school. We'll always be just for girls. That's what counts."

"So you'll take it?"

"No, Fred Kindler will. He's the head."

Hannah turned to Francis.

"That's right," Francis murmured after a little hesitation. "He's the head."

Hannah pulled her hand gently away from Peg. "That's the deal?"

"That's the deal," Peggy murmured, and when Hannah didn't reply, "You will go see him, won't you?" And after another little pause: "Won't you, Hannah?"

"All right," said Hannah. "With just a little added proviso."

"What?" Peggy asked warily.

"To honor you. He gets the gift, but you get the honor."

Peggy shook her head; she didn't understand.

"I'll specify," Hannah said. "The two million bucks will be specifically to support the specialness of the curriculum. The whole anthropological thrust, or whatever it is. I'll get a lawyer to think up the words. The whole anthropological thrust that makes Miss Oliver's the best damn school in the world, the idea you started in your library. How about that?"

"I think it's just fine!" Francis said.

"Wait a second," Peg blurted. "It's not my library."

"Oh yes, it is," Hannah said. "If Kindler gets to receive the gift, you get the honor. He'll have to stand up in front of everybody and read the words." She looked intently at both their faces. Francis thought for a minute she was going to ask again what was going on between him and Peggy, but he knew she didn't need to. He could see the disillusion in her eyes. Hannah stood up. "We've got a deal," she announced.

Francis stood up too. "Don't go. Stay a while. We'll have lunch."

"I'm going. Going to see Miss Oliver's School for Girls' boy headmaster. See if he wants a couple million bucks."

"Thank you," said Peggy. "Just don't put my name in, all right? Mention the curriculum, the library, but not me."

Hannah shrugged her shoulders.

"Promise?"

"All right," Hannah said.

Peggy stood, pulled Hannah into a hug, and over Peggy's shoulder Hannah winked at Francis to tell him, *Of course we're going to put Peggy's name in.*

His world saved, Francis couldn't wait to be alone with Peg. He was going to put his arms around her, celebrate.

"See you guys later," Hannah said.

"I'm coming partway with you," Peg said. "I'm on my way to the library." And then they were both out the door.

THAT NIGHT, FROM her side of the bed, Peg said to him. "You would have taken it, wouldn't you? You would have played that kind of game."

"No," he responded, saying the words straight up to the ceiling in the dark. "Not after I thought about it, I wouldn't. You made me think about it. I'll give you that."

"Well that's something." She was turned away from him, speaking her words to the wall. "That's something, anyway."

After a while, he said to the ceiling, "And you? You would have risked the gift, wouldn't you? You would have just let it go if she didn't agree to take it to Kindler."

"Yes, I would have risked it."

"Well, now I know," he said.

"Because I'm sick of the past," she said. "Marjorie's past. All her worn-out preciousness that she made into a theology you cling to."

"Peggy, be careful."

"It's too late to be careful, Francis. Because suddenly I don't care whether Fred Kindler brings in boys or not." It was true: she didn't care, it's not what was important. The realization came to her as she spoke. "I don't give a damn as long as the school's thriving and he is running it."

Francis didn't know how to answer that. He didn't really believe her.

"As a matter of fact, I don't care if the school becomes all boys!" she said, exaggerating out of her loyalty to Kindler.

Well, now I know, he said to himself. He wouldn't say it aloud again. He closed his eyes, as if he could sleep.

SIXTEEN

It's only November now, Gail Kindler thought as she watched her husband get into bed beside her. Two weeks to go before he got a break at Thanksgiving recess, and after that, eight whole months of the school year left, and already he looked as tired as if it were March. *We hardly have time for each other; and when we do, he's so distracted it's as if he were miles away.*

But not tonight, she decided. *Tonight I'm going to get his attention.* She snuggled up so that her head rested on the same pillow as his. He was flat on his back with his eyes closed. "Hey!" she said and draped her arm over his chest. His distracted "hey" in return was mere reflex, she knew, his mind far away from this bed, this dark, this heat. It surprised her that he couldn't take his mind off the school even after a lovely windfall of two million dollars to underwrite the deficit! Plenty of time now to build the girls-only enrollment back up. He should be as optimistic as the board was when he told them the news.

She cupped her hand against the other side of his face, turned his head to hers, kissed him on the lips.

"You're supposed to kiss back," she whispered. "Those are the rules."

"Yeah," he said. "I'm sorry."

So she flicked on her bedside lamp, then turned back, propping her head on her hand, seeing him squint against the sudden light. "Relax," she said. "Just try."

"Yeah. Relax."

"This," she said, touching his forehead with the tip of her finger. "Not that." She pointed downward.

He grinned. "Turn over," she commanded, and as he did she got up on him as if riding a horse, straddling his hips, and began to massage the back of his neck, the tops of his shoulders. "It's a wonder your head doesn't break off in a wind," she said, "your neck's so stiff with tension." She bent down, kissed the back of his neck, nuzzled her tongue behind his ear. "It's nighttime!" she said. "You're not in your office. It's not school! It's us!"

"Sure doesn't feel like the office," he said.

"Everything's fixed now," Gail said. "With that Fingerman woman and her big gift."

"Yeah," he acknowledged. "Maybe. A little further down, okay? By the shoulder blades?" She moved her hands further down his back, pressed hard, leaning in with her weight. "Ah," he sighed. "Perfect. How much an hour you get for this?"

"I don't do it for anybody who has to pay for it. What do you mean, maybe?"

"Just maybe. Why don't we do this tomorrow in my office? We'll take our clothes off, I'll lie down on the floor and dictate to Ms.—did you get that *Ms.*?—Rice while you massage."

"I'm busy tomorrow. Maybe Ms. Rice could learn."

"Uh-uh. She can only do one thing at a time."

"Well, now, that's a relief. So why can't you count on the Fingerman gift?"

"Because I think maybe her ex-husband has a very long arm," he said. Then after a pause: "Besides, even with the gift, I'm still not Marjorie."

"Well, screw them!" She wanted to bang her fists on his shoulder blades. He was worth a thousand Marjories!

"Hey," he said. "Gail! What's got into you?"

"Nothing." She forced the anger out of her voice, let her hands relax. "That's just the trouble," she added softly after a pause. "Nothing, lately." She tapped her finger on his back. "That's what I've been trying to tell you."

"I can fix that." He turned over while she turned out the light.

Above him in the ardent dark, she tried to see his face, was full of him, remembering in a wave of sadness that they used to wonder if their daughter heard them when they were doing this from her bed in the next room, on the other side of the thin wall, in the assistant headmaster's house of Mt. Gilead school in Ohio—in the long ago. *You really want to make a baby?* she yearned to ask. For that's what she really had meant, she realized now, by "nothing": nothing's inside her—or outside her either—to replace their daughter. *Then focus on it*, she wanted to say. *First things first. Quit your job. I'll make the money. Because I don't become my work the way you do. Quit your job. We'll make love all day.*

Afterward, while she held him, it was her mind this time that wandered: she was in her office again with the baby-faced client, the momma's boy, his suit, his leather briefcase stamped with his initials, the pretty tassels on his shoes, who was so sure he knew more about her profession than she did. *All right*, she thought, *I'll design the damn brochure your way instead of the way I just explained to you three times already that would save you lots of money and do a better job. I'll take your money. And laugh behind your back.*

Why can't you laugh like that about your job? she wanted to ask her husband. But of course she didn't. She wouldn't even if he were still awake. Besides, she knew the answer: he didn't think of it as a job. It never crossed his mind that he was making a living—though she would have liked to charge about three million dollars a day for feeling suffocated in this hermetic little fiefdom he wanted to save. And then the thought arrived, a discovery filling her mind with a too-bright light: soon this time in their life would be over. He didn't know how lucky he was that it wasn't going to work; Miss Oliver's School for Girls would never be Fred Kindler's school—and he would be free to move on. She felt another wave of sadness. "Whither thou goest," she murmured. "Whoever you try to become."

In his sleep, he pressed tightly against her.

SEVERAL HOURS AFTER Gregory van Buren went through his dorm, checking the girls in for the night and saying goodnight to each of them, Julie Lapham climbed out the window of her first-floor room to sneak across the campus to the place where her brother had agreed to meet her in his Subaru. "We're not going to a party," he had told her. "We'll just have a few beers and talk." Julie was relieved and glad for this chance to be alone with Charley. She trusted him, now more than she trusted her parents, to know how she felt. In her bed on the other side of the room, Clarissa pretended to be asleep.

Outside in the moonless November night, Julie shivered in the cold. She sneaked across the lawns, covered with fallen leaves, and stopped behind a faculty house where through an upstairs window she saw a lighted room. A bookcase filled one wall, a fireplace another. Above it, on the mantel, stood a vase of flowers, some photographs Julie couldn't make out from the distance, and a pair of candles. Then a woman moved soundlessly across the window in the warm yellow light and outside in the cold dark, Julie felt as if an arrow had struck her in the heart. She started to run.

She climbed over a stone wall and crossed a field on the southern edge of the campus. She could just make out the shape of Charley's car, parked up ahead on a narrow dirt road that led to the river. Soon she was at the car. "Charley!" she said. He was behind the wheel smiling at her through the open window. She ran around the front of the car to the passenger door, opened it, and put her face only inches from the face of a girl who looked up at Julie from the seat where Julie had expected to sit. "Surprise! Surprise!" the girl said. She held a bottle of tequila. There were empty beer cans on the floor by her feet. The girl's face lurched into a crooked smile, and Julie knew she was drunk.

"Get in the back!" Charley whispered. Julie opened the back door and jumped in on the right-hand side and slammed the door as Charley started the engine. Then the car was bumping over the dirt road toward the river, and she sensed someone was in the backseat with her she hadn't seen when she jumped in. She turned to look at him. He was as far away from her as he could get, scrunched up against the door. She saw big shoulders, made out a leather jacket in the dark and a white baseball cap.

"That's Robin," the drunk girl said. "Of linebacker fame. Or is it backliner? Is it backliner, Robin? I can never get it straight. Sports are so boring I can never remember."

"Penny," Robin said, "please, just shut your mouth."

"Now you know my name is Penny," the drunk girl said to Julie. "Now everybody knows everybody." Her voice went up and down as the car hit the bumps. Charley was driving much too fast. Low branches scraped against the roof.

"Charley, slow down," Robin said.

"He can't slow down, he's drunk," Penny said.

"Charley, slow down," Robin said again.

"Drunk with love for me," Penny said.

Charley giggled, drove even faster. Julie could smell the wet, marshy odor, like rotting leaves, of the river. She wondered if Charley knew how close it was. He might drive right over the bank!

"Charley, stop!" Robin said.

And now Julie was sure they were going to drive right over the bank. "Charley! Please!" she yelled.

Charley giggled again and went even faster and then suddenly slammed on the brakes, and the car slithered sideways in the loose dirt of the road and stopped. He turned the engine off. In the sudden silence they could hear the rushing of the river.

"What the hell's gotten into you, Charley?" Robin said. He was still scrunched as far away from Julie as he could get. She was grateful for that.

"I've gotten in to him, that's what." Penny said. "Maybe soon it'll be the other way around. Him and lots of tequila," and Charley laughed. Penny slid closer to him, put her arm around him, pulled him to her, kissed him on the mouth.

Robin got out of the car, and now Julie was alone in the back.

Penny turned back to Julie. "You want to watch us make out?" she asked.

"Charley, take me home, please," Julie said.

"Oh, in a little bit," Penny murmured. She put the bottle down on the floor, spilling it, and the smell of tequila filled the car, and then she pulled Charley's head into her chest so his face nuzzled her breasts. Julie looked away and saw Robin by her door. It swung open. "Let's go," he said. "I'll walk you home." She hesitated. "Really. You'll be safe."

"Oh, you'll be safe all right," Penny said. "That's the trouble with Robin."

Robin reached into the car, took Julie's hand, and tugged. She got out of the car, her hand in Robin's, and they started to walk away from the river. They walked quite a few paces before they realized they were still holding hands. Embarrassed, they let go of each other and walked side by side. He seemed huge to her, his shoulders miles above hers as they walked, and it was so dark she could hardly see his face.

After a while Robin said, "Your brother was coming to see you. So Penny and I thought we'd come too. We bought the beer and tequila on the way. Then Penny got drunk and got up in the front with your brother. She can be a pain in the ass when she wants to be."

"My brother got drunk too."

"Your brother gets drunk a lot," Robin said, and then stopped walking. "Wait a sec, I just thought of something."

"What?" But before he answered, she thought of it too. "He's too drunk to drive," she said.

"Yeah, he'll kill everybody," Robin said, taking her hand again, giving it that same little tug he'd used to get her out of the car, and they walked back toward the Subaru. This time he didn't let go.

When they got back to the car, Charley was not in it. Penny was passed out in the front seat.

"Oh, shit!" Robin said. "Where's that crazy bastard gone?" He reached into the car, shook Penny's shoulder. "Where the hell is he?" he yelled. Penny didn't stir. Julie felt panic rising: Charley had fallen down the bank into the river, he was drowning!

"Charley!" she yelled.

"Over here," Charley called. They turned to find him, but it was too dark to see. They stumbled through the bushes toward the sound and found him sitting on a boulder. "Where the hell were you?" Charley said.

"Let's go, Charley." Robin put his hand under Charley's arm, lifted and steadied him. Julie got on Charley's other side and steadied him too. They walked him to the car, opened the back door, and pushed him into the seat. Julie walked around to the other side of the car and got in beside Charley, and Robin got in the driver's seat, turned the ignition, and started to drive. Penny was still passed out beside him.

Julie turned to her brother and said, "Put your seatbelt on." He didn't stir. She reached across him to find the belt, and her face was close to his. His arms came up around her in a brotherly hug. She fixed his belt, then leaned to kiss him on the forehead, but he smelled like tequila and there was lipstick all over his face, and she felt a wave of disgust and lifted his arms away from her. His eyes were open, watching hers, and he tried to keep her in the hug, but he was too drunk and his arms flopped down at his sides, and Julie moved across the seat as far from him as she could get. In the glow of the dashboard that lighted the rearview mirror she saw Robin's eyes. They met hers and then looked away.

Minutes later, Robin stopped the car near the edge of campus where there were no lights. "Thanks, Robin," she said to the back of his head. She wanted to say more, but she couldn't think of the words.

He turned to look at her. "Take care of yourself." She got out of the car and headed for her dorm. This time she wasn't sneaking. If she got caught, she got caught. Then she heard the Subaru move away and realized that Robin had waited. He'd been watching her, hoping she got back without getting caught. She hoped that Charley had been watching too.

When Julie climbed through the window into her room, she could tell by Clarissa's breathing that she was still only pretending to sleep. She let Clarissa know she didn't believe her by being nowhere near as quiet as she would have been if Clarissa really were asleep. She rummaged around on her bureau for her toothbrush, then stomped out of the room to go to the bathroom, and when she came back, she closed the door with a bang.

Clarissa went right on pretending. Her way of letting Julie know she didn't want to deal with her tonight. She thought Julie had been partying with the Park Avenue crowd, Clarissa's name for the kids who got wasted almost every night. They bored her to death. She opened her eyes just enough to see in the dim light coming through the window that Julie was throwing her clothes on the floor as she took them off to get in her bed.

Now Clarissa was too furious to pretend any longer. "Pick your clothes up," she commanded in the dark. She knew Julie was just trying to get her goat by strewing her clothes all over the floor. They'd fought about this before. Clarissa was a neatnik, Julie a slob. "Hang them in the closet," Clarissa said.

Julie turned on the light.

"Like you promised me you would," Clarissa said. She sat up. She was wearing her green pajamas, pressed and neat, her initials embossed on them, her mother's gift to begin the year.

Julie picked up her clothes and hung them in the closet, making a parody of being very neat, folding her T-shirt three times to get it right, creasing her jeans, and hanging each on a separate hanger. "I knew you were awake," she said.

"You better be careful," Clarissa said. "Van Buren's got eyes in the back of his head."

Julie didn't respond

Clarissa sat up even straighter in her bed. She didn't want a roommate who didn't like it here. Too much like she felt at home trying to explain to all her friends why she loved this school. They just thought she was weird. "Why not just quit and go home if you don't like it here?" she asked.

"My parents have paid the tuition; I'm not about to waste it." Julie turned from the closet and sat on the edge of her bed.

"All right. Then stop taking chances."

"And anyway, I wasn't doing what you think I was doing."

Clarissa shrugged. She wasn't the Gestapo. What did she care? Getting caught out of the dorm was trouble enough.

"I was with my brother," Julie said. She didn't have to defend herself, it was nobody's fucking business what she did or didn't do, she just wanted Clarissa to know about her escapade, that's all, she felt like telling her. So she told Clarissa about what she had been really doing when she snuck out. She liked Clarissa, liked her green pajamas, the way she studied so hard. She had heard the story about how last year Clarissa had refused to take van Buren's final exam because there was an essay question on it about Huck Finn. And hadn't argued when van Buren flunked her, not because she misinterpreted the book, an assertion he wouldn't make because he had no essay to assess, but because civil disobedience has no meaning if it doesn't have a price. How can you help not liking that?

"Robin sounds like a nice guy," Clarissa said when Julie finished. "I'm glad he was there for you." Her voice was soft, her irritation gone. She turned out the light and lay down.

Julie got in her bed. "Thanks for listening," she said in the dark. She liked hearing Clarissa's breathing across the room from her. *This is how it must be for sisters*, she thought.

Just the same, she couldn't figure out what it was about Miss Oliver's that Clarissa was so loyal to and loved so much. How could she care whether or not boys were admitted; what was all the fuss about? What's so special about going to school with only half the human race? And to have a whole meeting about whether to give that stuff back to some Indians? The Indians hadn't even asked for it! She wanted to get up on stage in Morning Meeting and tell everybody to get a life. She wanted just not to be there.

TEN DAYS LATER, on the Monday morning of Thanksgiving week, Fred Kindler saw right away how upbeat the board members were when they gathered for the meeting at the River Club. There was good reason for their happiness: just last week the school's lawyers, who had been working closely with Hannah's, reported that they couldn't find any way by which Hannah's ex-husband could stop her from making the gift. It was Hannah's money, they had declared, and as soon as Hannah's ex realized he was wasting his meager resources trying to prove it wasn't, the school would get the gift. It was a sure thing, and it would be wrapped up in only a couple of months.

So now the school had much more time in its race against the deficit!

Fred barely acknowledged this happy news as he started his report to the board. He moved instead immediately to the grim recruitment statistics. He was a conservative man. The money wasn't in the bank yet. Nevertheless, a new attitude, of optimism tempered by realism, of faith in good organization and specific plans, started to grow around the mahogany table as the meeting progressed. Alan Travelers sensed this optimism as he moved through the agenda, acknowledging it to Fred with a subtle glance.

Near the end of the agenda came an important item under new business: the student council's petition to the board, signed by more than two-thirds of the students, to return the Collection to the Pequots. There was a little silence when everyone was finished reading. The members all looked at Alan. How to deal with this?

But Milton Perkins stared at Fred. "Why are you bringing us this crap, Fred?" he asked. "First they threaten us with the Declaration. Which, I gotta admit, I liked the nerve that took. But then they bring us this! Has nothing to do with building the enrollment, or even letting boys in, or any other price of eggs. Just tell them no, for crying out loud, and let's get back to running the damn place!"

"He's probably already told them no, and they're still there," Sonja McGarvey said. "That's why he's bringing us this 'crap,' as you so elegantly put it."

"Process!" Perkins exploded. "Jesus, process again! Petitions. Protests. Even Hitler couldn't run this nuthouse!"

"Try Eva Braun," McGarvey suggested. "Hitler's the wrong gender."

"When I first got on this board," Perkins remembered out loud, "nobody argued with the head. And they never even saw the board."

"Was that before the glacier," McGarvey asked, "or after?"

"That was when board members gave their money instead of their half-baked opinions."

McGarvey started to say something, thought better of it, and turned to Travelers. "Can we get on with this?"

But Perkins wasn't finished. "Sounds like it was written by some goddamn lawyer!" he growled.

Nobody answered.

"Whenever I read anything written by a lawyer, I automatically tear it up." Perkins was grinning now, obviously enjoying himself. It was not clear whether he was making this up or if this was actually what he did.

"All right, Milton," Travelers said.

"Then I send him a bill for three hundred dollars for wasting my time opening the envelope."

"Can we just please get on with the subject?" McGarvey asked again.

"We're on the subject," Perkins said. "And when the bastard doesn't pay, I take him to small claims court just to hassle him." Travelers rapped his knuckles on the table, but Perkins went right on. "Then when he sends me a bill, I wait until just before he takes me to small claims and send him half—"

"Milton!" Travelers started to stand.

Perkins put up his hand, relinquishing the floor. "Works every time," he said, winding down. "They never even bill for the second half."

"All right. Now that we know how Milton feels about lawyers, let's address this issue," Travelers said.

"I've made my point," said Perkins.

Travelers, with whom Fred had shared his idea, announced, "Fred here has an alternative."

Fred took over and recommended making the Pequots owners of the on-campus Collection. The solution, he said, provided not only a logical answer to a legitimate ethical question, but also an excellent public relations initiative that would support the needed enrollment growth. "We can raise money for building the extra room to house the Collection from people who otherwise wouldn't give us a dime, and I believe we can also find some money for financial aid for Pequot children," he told them. "It's a win-win; let's do it."

It didn't take long for the board to authorize Fred to put out feelers to the Pequot authorities and move forward with the plan if the Pequots agreed. There was a lot of work to do to bring this off.

"I think it's a great idea!" Alan Travelers said just before he adjourned the meeting.

"We still need to put the right spin on it, though," McGarvey pronounced. "It's great public relations if we make it very clear we're doing the right thing, and doing it right."

"I agree," said Fred. "We'll do it."

"Christ, what is this, Berkeley, California?" Perkins said. He hated both the student council's idea and Fred's for their political correctness. He was not the kind of man who spun. "You open up this can of worms with the Indians, they'll decide they don't want it in anybody's museum. They'll want to just bury the stuff, and then even they won't know about their past," he said. "What about that? You thought about that?"

"Let's cross that bridge when we come to it," Travelers suggested, and rapped on the table and called for adjournment, and when everybody but Perkins raised a hand, he ended the meeting.

But, once again, Milton Perkins wasn't finished. He stared across the table at McGarvey. "Since it's spinning you want, why give just one little bone back?" he asked her gleefully. He just loved to push her buttons! "Why not give 'em a whole skeleton? We could dig an old alumna up. Find a real big one who died years ago. She'd never know the difference. We could give her to the Indians. That would shut everybody up."

Before Perkins finished, McGarvey was out the door. She'd been looking at her watch for the last ten minutes.

"YES, I UNDERSTAND," Lila admitted the next morning when Fred told her the board's decision. "It makes a lot of sense. And Marie's idea was a little crazy." But that was the trouble: Lila really did understand. She wished she didn't.

"Lila, are you okay?" It was the second time he'd asked her. He respected her yearning for the moral purity of Marie Safford and Sara Warrior's position and would have been disappointed if she didn't. "There's a lot of pressure on you, Lila," he said, taking a different tack. "More than on some of the faculty, even."

That wasn't what she wanted to talk about. Pressure. Tension. It made it worse to talk about it.

"You could have a chat with Ms. Rugoff," Fred persisted, mentioning the school counselor. He held his breath, remembering how angry Francis Plummer had been when he mentioned counseling to him.

Lila shook her head.

"All right," he said, backing off. "It was just an idea."

"I don't need her to tell me what's bothering me," she said, lowering her eyes. "I already know."

"Well, that's good," he murmured and sat quietly waiting.

"It's hard to explain, and it sounds stupid," Lila began. She looked up, studying him to see if she trusted him enough to reveal this much about herself.

"I bet it won't sound stupid to me."

She sent a little smile to thank him for that. "I wish I could be like Marie," she said, admitting it at last. "The way she cares about what's absolutely right, and nothing else."

"Not even whether it works?"

"Yes!" she said. "Not to give a damn!"

"It's too late, Lila," he said. "You're way past that point." And when she didn't say anything to that, he asked, "How old are you, Lila?"

She frowned. Why was he asking that? "Eighteen," she said. "Why?"

"How long do you think those Pequots lived?"

"In the village that was here? Maybe forty years."

"You're almost halfway there. You'd be a chief by now."

"Uh-uh," she said and shook her head. "The chiefs were men."

"Behind the scenes, Lila. The real boss behind the boss."

"No way. I'm not going to be anybody's boss. I'm going to be an archaeologist."

"You'll be the boss archaeologist," he said. "You'll take the weight."

But he's got that wrong, she thought. *I don't take it. It goes right by the ones who really want it, which I don't, and just comes to me.* She could tell him that—if she knew him better, if it didn't sound so proud. "Well, anyway," she finally said, bringing their meeting to an end. She needed to get out of there before he mentioned Ms. Rugoff again. "Thanks for telling me. I'll tell the students today in Morning Meeting." But she didn't stand up, realizing she didn't want the meeting to end after all. She liked talking to this man; he calmed her down.

"All right." He stood, and the meeting *was* over. She was disappointed. "Thanks, Lila." He shook her hand. Treating her like a grown-up. A peer. "This is going to work out fine."

"Yes," she said. "It'll be just fine."

THE NEXT PERSON Fred told was Peggy, of course. He promised that over Thanksgiving recess, which started the next day at noon, he would begin to work on the plan. He would do some research and ask around to figure out with whom among the Pequot authorities he should broach the idea. Peggy was delighted. What she had started years ago was going to achieve its most logical and inspiring development. In her mind, she saw the new wing, a true museum, the school serving not just a private but a public purpose. "Why didn't I think of this idea years ago?" she asked.

Because you're human. He wanted to quote Rachel Bickham to her. Instead he said, "Who cares who thought of it. We're teammates."

"Yes, and I love being on your team," she told him. "You're the best thing that ever happened to this place."

LATER THAT MORNING, when Lila made the announcement, applause broke out. But when she went on to tell the students that this good idea was their new headmaster's, the applause was sparse, seemed grudging, almost disappointed that it wasn't someone else's: Peggy Plummer's, especially, or Francis's, or Rachel Bickham's, even Gregory van Buren's. So Peggy stood up, showed her true colors once again, telling the school how creative an idea this was, how inclusive, how much it pleased her; and the students, corrected, supplied a little more applause.

The twenty or so students who remained unpersuaded sat on their hands until the applause ended. They did so for themselves and for Sara, who wasn't there to get this news. She had called her parents the previous evening; they had arrived in the morning and took her home. They would bring her back on Monday when Thanksgiving recess was over. That way she didn't have to be there for the turkey the school would serve tonight, the pumpkins, the corn: Indian food white people eat to say thank you to their god for helping them steal the land. Thanksgiving was not for Sara at this school, where a remnant of one of her people lay in a display for all to gawk at.

AFTER THE THANKSGIVING dinner, Peggy again went to her library for the evening instead of coming home. Levi went with her, leaving Francis alone in the apartment thinking about Fred Kindler's solution to the issue of the Pequot Collection. He had to admit it was a marvelous idea to invite the Pequots back to the ground on which one of their villages had thrived for centuries. So it didn't surprise him that he thought right then of the papier mâché model that Siddy had made in the sixth grade of that very village. It was stored away in the attic. Up there with all the other nostalgia that neither he nor Peggy could bear to throw away.

He climbed the stairs. Under the naked lightbulb that hung from the rafters, he found the model just where he had placed it years ago on an old table. What he noticed, which he had not seen as sharply before, was the familiar shape of the ground that Siddy had modeled—his son's loving imitation of the ground on which he had grown up, the place in the world he'd known best. The revelation filled Francis with longing for his son. Staring at the model, he remembered that Siddy's teacher had told him that this was perfect research. "Everything we know tells us that an Indian village very much like this one existed here on this very spot for years and years and years. On this very spot!" she repeated. He remembered loving her for being so proud of Siddy.

For a few seconds he knew he'd been in the village, way beyond mere visualization, its every part familiar, and suddenly he was so lonely for his son he missed a breath, remembering that years ago when he and Peg were very young and they had just brought Siddy into their lives, they would wake in the middle of the night and go into his room just to watch him sleep. Siddy had chastised him once when he couldn't have been more than seven years old for cutting down a small tree in the backyard that was casting shade on the garden. "There are millions of trees in New England," Francis told the boy. "They are like weeds."

"But Dad, it's *alive*!" Siddy had said.

THAT NIGHT HE dreamed: in the middle of a starlit night the students stood in semicircular rows in front of the library staring at him. Somehow he knew that he had called them there. He heard drums. The library loomed behind him in the dark.

One of the girls stepped forward. She looked like Lila, but he knew she wasn't. She handed him a torch, which a second before had not been in her hand. He turned. The library was a dark cliff in front of him. He reached toward it with the torch, and it burst into flames. He realized, strangely, that he had been smelling smoke since before the flames began. He kneeled and wept. When he rose finally and turned around, all the girls were gone.

He was still dreaming that he was weeping when Peggy shook him awake. She was staring at his face. "Wake up!" she said. He sat up. She handed him some clothes. "There's a fire," she said. "The library's burning." Her words were a monotone—as if it were someone one else's library, on the other side of the world.

WATCHING THE LIBRARY burn, all Francis could think of was that the smell and the crackling sound reminded him of campfires. He thought of marshmallows, their skins wrinkling, turning black. He stood, watching, behind the students, who had arrived there first. Everybody had to stand a long way back. Peggy stood to his right. Soon Margaret Rice joined them, standing to his left. She reached for his left hand, and he took hers. No one spoke. Finally, the fire department arrived and sprayed streams of water into the orange glow. The firefighters in their heavy coats were dark silhouettes against the flames.

He stood on tiptoes and found Lila Smythe in the crowd of girls. She turned toward him then, and their eyes met. She left her friends, moving through the crowd toward him, until she stood in front of him. Peggy moved two steps away. "Well," said Lila. "It isn't how we planned things."

"It's too bad," he said. "It was a beautiful library." Just then the building collapsed, the roof melted. There was a shower of sparks against the black sky. Someone screamed.

"Fire purifies," Lila said. Her eyes were shining. "It will work out. The insurance will rebuild the library, bring in some more artifacts, but it won't rebuild the bones. They're safe. It's a sacred fire." Her eyes were alight with more than the fire.

He didn't answer, just stared at her face. She looked right back. *Ashes to ashes*, he thought, *the bones at rest.* Then he felt a presence behind him, and he turned. Fred Kindler stood there, not ten paces away, staring into Francis's face just the way Francis had stared into Lila's.

Seventeen

"Don't come home," Peggy said to Francis as soon as Lila went back to her friends. The words surprised her. As if someone she didn't know were saying them.

Francis pretended he didn't hear. He was not even looking at Peggy. He was staring at the fire. The flames were lower now that the walls had collapsed but still fierce enough to eat the water streaming from the firefighters' hoses. The sodden smell of ashes floated in the dark. Some of the students were crying.

"Don't pretend you don't hear me," she told him. She couldn't believe she was saying this, for she could see he was grieving too. But Lila Smythe had stood two feet away from her and told her husband that it was a sacred fire, and he didn't say a thing, didn't even argue!

He stared straight ahead, but in the glow she saw the shock of her words register on his face. Margaret Rice heard them too. She turned to Peggy, then quickly looked away.

"Just stay away, Francis," Peggy said. Margaret looked at Francis, who gave her a little shrug that seemed to say, *Don't worry, she doesn't mean it*; then Margaret stepped away into the crowd. Francis turned to Peggy, reaching for her hand.

"Find some other place to live," Peggy said. She took a step away.

"Peg!" he called after her.

She whirled around, facing him again. "A sacred fire!" she said. "I hope it keeps you warm!" The crowd of watchers made room for her as she moved away.

THERE IT WAS, big as life, her first reaction to the library's burning down: she wanted him out of the house. She didn't even ask herself how long she thought this feeling was going to last. So at five-thirty in the morning, she packed Francis's underwear and socks, his shirts, and khakis in the same ugly duffel bag he'd taken to California, putting his shoes and shaving gear in a backpack. There was a Dewey decimal system for this stuff too, departing fragments, that Francis would just throw in all together if she were to allow him into the house long enough to pack them for himself. He'd come in an hour or two, after he'd finished moving around the campus talking to the students, comforting them. She was sure that's what he was doing. Otherwise, he'd be there right then, convinced that she didn't really want him out of the house. So she'd locked the door from the inside, a door they'd never locked in thirty years. She made neat piles in the duffel, squaring the edges. In the smell of wet ashes pervading her house, she had more need for order than ever.

At six-thirty the phone rang. It was Fred saying he wanted to see her in his office. "So we can get started," he said.

"Started?"

"On the new library, Peggy."

You're crazy! she almost said. The fire had only been out a couple of hours. Then she realized it wasn't crazy, wasn't crazy at all; and it was typical of him to know this was exactly what she needed.

"I knew you wouldn't be asleep," he said.

"Give me thirty minutes." If Francis came home before she was back from Fred Kindler's office, he'd just have to wait to get his things.

She carried the suitcases and the backpack out of the bedroom, across the living room, and placed them next to the front door, divining what Francis would see when she opened the door and allowed him only that one step into the house to pick up his things. Her eyes went straight across the room to the mantelpiece where, between two candlesticks, a framed black-and-white photograph sat: her father and her mother, Ada Louise Boyer—the loveliest name in the world, she thought. On the front lawn, sprinkled with October leaves, they gazed past the camera at the bright future they still believed was theirs. The photo was the first thing Francis would see when he entered the house, but he wouldn't notice. *They're dead,* she said to herself, looking away. *He never knew them.* Next to this, another picture sat, in which she and Francis stood, bride and groom, side by side. In his rented black tailcoat, grinning, Francis came up to her shoulder. She went to this, plucked it off the mantelpiece. Francis's grin was aimed right at the camera. She was looking past the camera, out of the picture, to where Francis's father stood. She placed the picture on top of the backpack.

She vacuumed, she dusted, she turned on the kitchen fan, trying to get the ashy smell out, pulled down the shades on the side of the house toward where her library had been, and when she was finished, her house as clean and neat as she could get it, she locked the door to the dormitory then went out through the front door, locking it behind her. The key felt strange in her hand. When Francis would come and find the front door bolted while she was away, he'd stand there for a little while not believing—she could hardly believe it herself—before giving up and going away. Then he'd go to Michael Woodward's house. When he would come back to try again, she'd stand just inside the door, guarding her house.

"I'VE ALREADY CALLED the insurance agent," Fred Kindler told Peggy. "He's coming right out. He says not to worry; it was completely insured."

What he didn't tell her was that he hadn't been sure it was insured until he'd called Alan Travelers, the first person he informed. He knew he was being overanxious.

"Of course it was insured!" Alan had exclaimed. "You forget what I do for a living." And then, "Oh, my God! You thought Marjorie and old Vincent were that unbusinesslike?"

Fred hadn't answered.

"Okay, I won't go there," Alan had said and then changed the subject. "Don't let this get you, Fred. Think of it as an opportunity. We've got a chance to build an even better library." Alan's voice had been full of energy. It almost sounded optimistic, and Fred knew that his board chair was trying to keep him pumped up. "Nobody was hurt. Concentrate on that."

"Well, I hope that softens the blow for you at least a little bit, anyway," Fred told Peggy now. "And I promise you this," he added. "The new library's going to be even better than the old one. You won't lose a thing."

She shook her head, a very slight motion, like a hurt boxer clearing his head.

"I'm sorry," he murmured. "I didn't mean to sound—"

"When do we get started?" Peggy asked. She didn't want him to have to apologize for trying to keep her spirits up.

"Right now!"

"Thank you! I don't know what I would do if I had to wait till Monday."

They started to work. He asked her to make a list: "Everything you'd want to preserve and everything you'd want to change if your library hadn't burned down and we had all the money we needed." *You can't replace a person*, he wanted to say. *You can a library. And you can make it even better.*

While she made her list, he made one of his own of everything that had to be done, starting with how to handle the newspapers. As soon as the faculty and students got enough sleep after being awake most of the night—it was still only seven in the morning—he was going to assemble them all. They would need to be together, all in the same space, after such a disaster; and after they talk a while, he'd ask them to send all newspaper reporters and phone calls from reporters to him. In the meantime, the phones were on the taped answering system that would tell people the switchboard was closed until eight o'clock, and if there was an emergency to please call a number that would ring right there on his desk so he could answer it himself. Even though later in the day the parents would be arriving to take their children home for the Thanksgiving recess, he'd divide the list of parents among the faculty and ask them to call and give exactly the same message to everyone: the library burned in the night; no one's hurt; the cause is unknown. "Emphasize that too," he'd tell them. "Don't speculate with anyone about the cause."

When Peggy handed him her list, he wasn't surprised that, except for a few minor details, it described the library that had just burned down. A few days later, he'd ask her to think some more.

"Thanks," he said. "This is great."

"All right," she said. "What now?"

"Keep making this list. Everything we can think of that needs to be done. We'll put it into sequence later." He stepped into Ms. Rice's office. Peggy waited alone, then watched him return a moment later with a big pad of easel paper. The two of them ripped the sheets off and taped them up on the walls around his office. "I always feel silly when I do this," he told Peggy, speaking as if to himself. "Too 'with it' and groovy. Like a consultant instead of a guy with a real job, but it works."

That's when she started to cry.

At first he ignored her, pretending he didn't see she was crying. Then he reached for her hand. Peggy didn't offer it and stepped a little further away from him. That small shake of her head again. "I'm sorry," she murmured. "I'll be okay."

"Look, I'd be crying too."

She made a small dismissive gesture with one hand, wiped at her eyes with the other, and forced herself to stop crying. "Okay," she said. "Let's get going."

He turned to the sheet he was working on and wrote *appoint a committee to decide on the architect.* She watched him write that, and on her own sheet she started writing the names of people who might be on the committee.

After they had worked for several more minutes, she suddenly put her marker down, turned to face him, and said, "Who did it?" She'd been trying not to think about this, but she couldn't put it off any longer.

"I don't know." He was still facing his sheet of paper, still writing.

"Who do you think?"

"I don't think," he said, still facing the paper.

"I think you should."

"Most people would," he admitted.

"Most people would be right." She felt anger rising. How can he not want revenge?

He turned to her then. "I have other priorities. I'm not going to wreck this community by investigating people, playing detective. I'm going to leave that up to the fire department and the police. They're outsiders. They can be the ones to hold suspicions."

Marie? he wondered. *Lila?* How terrible that would be! He hated himself for even thinking of them. Thank God Sara had gone home a whole day before the fire. At least she was not a suspect. He shook his head to clear it. This was exactly what he'd told himself he wasn't going to do.

"I'm going to need to know," Peggy said. "I'm not going to be able to let it rest."

"We'll know soon enough."

"All right," she said. "I hope so." Then after a pause: "Anyway, you need to know—"

"Peggy, I don't need to know anything."

"That you only have one person running our dormitory now. You're the headmaster. You need to know that. Francis is going to be living somewhere else."

The sharpness of his disappointment surprised him. Not just for her, but for Francis too—that's what surprised him. "This makes me very sad," he said.

"Me too. I can't believe I'm doing this."

"I understand," he said.

"The truth will come out someday," she said, because she needed to change the subject back to the fire. "It always does. I just hope it wasn't any of the students. That would hurt too much." She started to cry again.

"Maybe it just happened," he murmured. Which he knew was crazy. But he had to admit that if he knew who did it, he would know whom to be grateful to. For like wars to failing presidents, this calamity provided a chance for him to shine. He was going to manage the crisis, build an even better library, bring the Pequots in to establish a more extensive Collection, and house it there. The new library would be his accomplishment; it would give him power. He was surprised to discover that he was not ashamed of these thoughts. But he was not about to admit them to Peggy.

"Nothing ever just happens," Peggy said, struggling to stop crying.

"I know," he said, and turned back to his work.

Eighteen

In spite of Fred's determination to downplay the investigation into the burning of the library, he realized as soon as the students returned from the break that he was in charge of a school in which the only thing anyone could see was the empty space and blackened foundation that loomed in the center of campus, where the library had been.

Who did it? That was the question on everyone's mind. And even more painful for some: *Does anyone think I did it?*

That question haunted Lila Smythe, who thought she caught a certain expression, half fascination, half embarrassment, in the sidewise glances of some of her peers. She was sure that at least a few students—and who knew how many faculty?—had overheard her when she told Francis Plummer that the fire was sacred. She caught herself every once in a while feeling guilty, as if she actually had caused the fire. Even Sara Warrior, who everyone knew didn't do it because she had been home with her family, felt estranged because she knew that she was the first person everyone thought of—as if she could imagine doing something so terrible! Marie Safford also wondered how many thought she did it.

The lead investigator was a somber man in his forties, already bald, a weightlifter in a crisp blue uniform and shiny badge. He wanted to give a speech to the students about fire safety in the dorms, which Fred prohibited, angering the man and hurting his feelings. He didn't understand that his face, associated with suspicion and mistrust, should be as invisible as possible.

When the investigators finished examining the ruins, they reported that they'd eliminated natural causes such as lightning. Fred wasn't surprised. Of course it wasn't lightning; it had been a clear November night. They didn't tell him any more than that since, officially at least, he was a suspect too.

Fred pushed the investigators to work as fast as they could, and he wouldn't let them interview the students on campus. He rented an office off campus and insisted the interviews take place in this neutral space and in the company of Kevina Rugoff, the school counselor. Some parents retained a lawyer to accompany their daughter to the interview. Most of the parents of the interviewed students were angry and hurt. Over the phone and in person in his office they railed at Fred. He let them tell him how angry they were at him, sometimes several times, assuring them each time that he understood their feelings before he ended the conversations.

FOR THE STUDENTS, one small light in this darkness was their excitement over the secret they were for the most part managing to keep—especially, they incorrectly assumed, from the new headmaster—about the research Karen Benjamin was conducting on the sex lives of the seniors. The students didn't know that last summer Karen had warned the headmaster about the article. If they did, they would have been even more convinced that they'd never see it in the *Clarion*. They expected it to appear sub rosa, Xeroxed and passed around. In fact, they might be disappointed if their new headmaster hadn't forbidden publication. They expected him to confirm what they already knew: how much less daring, how much less heroically committed to the truth he was than their beloved Mrs. Boyd had been when she was the headmistress of Miss Oliver's School for Girls.

Karen's research focused as much on the girls' attitudes as on their actual activities or lack of them. For instance, what, short of actual intercourse, qualified in their minds as sex? She had distributed a questionnaire to be filled out anonymously. The first section elicited objective responses to questions about what actual activities starting at what age, how many partners, and so on. The second section, more subjective, probed the motivations, such as:

> *Why do you refrain from sexual activity (if you do)? Check any answers that apply:*

(A) Religious or philosophical beliefs.
(B) No desire to engage in sex.
(C) Lack of opportunity.
(D) Timidity.
(E) To avoid disease.
(F) Other.

Or:

Why do you engage in sexual activity as you have defined it?
Check one:
(A) Peer pressure.
(B) To stay in a relationship.
(C) Pleasure.
(D) Curiosity.
(E) Generosity: desire to please.
(F) Other.

After each section there was a space in which the student could write anything she wanted.

Karen knew how easily the students could turn her project into comedy. She could have done a fair job herself of lampooning it, and she giggled when she imagined the seniors filling out the questionnaires together, agreeing to claim orgies with gangs of sex-crazed people of both genders and all ages and shapes who snuck out of a local prison and invaded the dorms each night, and cooking up a sexual life at home on vacation that featured practices so grotesque they required positions which could only have been achieved with the aid of chiropractors and only induced by drugs. Well, if that was how the seniors would react, that's what she would report, but she didn't think it would happen, and she was right: the seniors trusted Karen's skepticism and her detachment, and so most of them filled out the questionnaires as accurately as they could.

She decided she needed a partner in evaluating the questionnaires, someone less virginal than she, to assure a balanced interpretation. So she enlisted her friend Claire Nelson, a senior colleague on the *Clarion* staff, who was poised beyond her years, long legged, raven haired, and so beautiful that people's eyes were always on her. Nothing had happened yet to Claire to dissuade her that the power her beauty gave her to project herself on the world was something she deserved rather than merely a stroke of genetic luck.

Karen stored the answered questionnaires in a safe in the *Clarion*'s office, to which she'd changed the combination so only she could open it, and on an evening in early December she removed them and carried them to Claire's room where they could work more privately than in the *Clarion*'s office. She didn't ask herself why she chose Claire's room rather than her own.

Karen sat at Claire's desk with half the questionnaires, and Claire, languid on her bed, read the other half. As they finished each one, they handed it across to the other. After a while Claire sat up on her bed, swinging her feet to the floor. "Upper East Side," she said, handing a questionnaire to Karen. She knew it was wrong to try to identify the participants, but that was not what she was really trying to do. Her remark was simply her way into a conversation. She wanted to talk, to *really* talk.

"What?" Karen looked across the room at her friend. She thought it would be a distraction to be so beautiful. Besides, she knew that there was always a bottle of vodka hidden in Claire's bureau right there in her room. She worried that Claire was an alcoholic. But Claire didn't consider herself an alcoholic. She just drank because she liked to. Whatever Claire liked to do, she did.

"New York," Claire said. "It's obvious. I can tell. I used to live there, you know. I can tell by the bragging tone."

Karen knew Claire had lived all her life in Manhattan until last year, when she moved with her father to London. And she knew Claire's mother had deserted the family when Claire was eight, but she didn't know that the real reason Claire's father, a vice president of an international investment bank, had managed to get himself transferred so suddenly was because his daughter had been caught having sex with a young teacher by none other than the headmaster of her well-respected independent day school in the city. Claire's father had wanted to get her far away from that scene, so he moved to London and enrolled her at Miss Oliver's because he traveled a lot and needed to put her in a boarding school. He'd learned from his daughter's recent adventure the value of a school's acting in loco parentis. Besides, he reasoned, at Miss Oliver's there was a dearth of young men with whom to go to bed.

Claire had been caught because the headmaster, much admired by his board of trustees for his thrifty management, made the rounds at the end of every day to make sure the lights were out, and on a Friday evening had found Claire and her paramour in flagrante in the faculty room. The headmaster, who might have been in his job a few too many years and who'd never believed the stories he'd heard about this kind of thing, had assumed that the teacher, a year out of college and thus five years older than his victim, was the predator. Or at least the headmaster pretended to, for no one knew how well the headmaster knew Claire, though he did tell his wife, who was also good at keeping secrets, that what had surprised him the most about the scene that confronted him when he opened the faculty room door was that the teacher was more naked than Claire—and Claire was on top. He fired the teacher immediately, of course, glowering and quoting the school's lawyer at anybody who wanted to know why. He was this secretive to protect Claire's honor, a word he'd learned the meaning of long ago while studying English novels at Yale, where all the males in his family always went, and where he belonged to Skull and Bones.

"RICH KIDS," CLAIRE went on. Her voice was filled with contempt. "They do anything they want, but they don't do it because it's fun. They do it because others do."

"We're not supposed to be guessing. It's supposed to be anonymous," Karen said.

"I know, but it's so childish, it's hard not to know. Look at how she's marked it." Claire wanted Karen to see how bold and large the marks the kid had made to affirm how wide ranging her sexual activities were and how, just as enthusiastically, she'd marked only *Pleasure* as the motivation. Claire didn't think anybody did it just for pleasure.

But Karen wouldn't look at the questionnaire. She handed it back. The girl who had filled this out could come from Toledo, for all they knew.

"I don't want to be a voyeur any more than you do, I just wanted to talk," Claire said, surprising herself at this confession. It gave her power away to reveal how lonely she was.

"I'm sorry. I didn't mean that you were," Karen said. She wondered why she'd been so slow to understand that Claire's beauty and worldly charm didn't bring her friends; they set her apart. The way she never talked about herself created an aura. For some of the girls their world would be less exciting if that aura ever melted. They'd rather be paparazzi to Claire than friends. Karen knew it was Claire's fault, that Claire made plans, created her aura on purpose. But just the same, she felt she hadn't been a good friend.

"Hey," Karen said, "if you want to talk, let's talk. We'll finish this later." She started to reach across the small space to pat Claire on the knee, but Claire drew away from the gesture, retreating back inside herself.

"Some other time," Claire said.

And an hour later, as they finished, Claire said, "You left a big one out when you made the questionnaire."

"What did I leave out?" Karen felt just a little defensive.

"Power." Claire said. She looked intently in her friend's eyes. She'd added *Power* in her own handwriting on her questionnaire as her motivation, the only one to do so, and had marked the kind of sex she had too. But nothing about the teacher. Nor that she had been a virgin until her affair with him. Those were still her secrets. "Now you know which one is mine," she said. "I really wanted you to know. I get lonely sometimes."

Karen was touched. "You know, I'd kind of figured it out myself," she admitted. "Because you'd marked all those things and I knew how—" She paused. She didn't want to say "active"; it sounded too clinical. She started again. "I knew how busy you were," she tried. She paused again, and then she said, "But I don't think you could be so mean. You wouldn't do it just for power."

"I made him do it," Claire heard herself confessing. "I made him want me so much he'd do the worst thing he could do, even though he knew the second it was over he'd wish that he hadn't."

"What?" Karen asked. "Who?" She was fascinated.

"A teacher. That's why I had to leave the school, that's why my dad got transferred. It's why I'm here."

"A teacher!"

"He cried every time we did it. Right after we were finished he'd start to weep. The only time he didn't was when we got caught."

"A teacher did it to you?"

"More like the other way around," Claire said. "I made it happen. *I* fucked *him*."

Karen winced. The word, used that way, made her think of guns. "What happened to him?" she asked.

"He got fired," Claire said and got up from her bed and went to her bureau and opened the drawer.

"I don't want any," Karen said. She was thinking about the teacher getting fired.

"Oh, sure you do," Claire said. Her tone was very matter-of-fact. She crossed the room with the bottle in one hand, two glasses in the other. She put them on the desk next to Karen and poured vodka into each. Then she handed one to Karen.

Karen shook her head. Claire took a drink. "I didn't mean to get him fired," Claire said. She could see the teacher in her head. He was very tall and thin, his hair as black as hers, and his thin chest naked, moving in and out with his sobs. "I'm really sorry about that part," she said.

"I know you are. I know you're not mean, but just the same—"

"Yes, just the same," Claire said. She picked up Karen's glass and handed it to her. Karen shook her head again, and Claire put the glass back down.

"I don't drink," Karen said.

"You never break the rules, do you?" Claire said. "Why are you so nice?"

"I guess I just don't want to break the rules."

"Of course you do. Everybody does. You just don't think you should. Somebody told you not to, and you don't think you should. Good for you, but I read an article in some magazine saying that kids who never do drugs or booze or sex frequently have big problems in their adulthood. What do you think about that?"

"You just made that up," Karen said.

Claire hesitated. She really had read it in some article, maybe in the *New York Times*; she wished she could remember where. Maybe she would find the article and make Karen read it.

"Don't ever do that again with me," Karen said. "You don't need to. I like you just the way you are."

There was a silence then, while Claire thought about that. And then she heard herself saying, "Yeah, I was just making it up." She faked a giggle to cover her lie.

Karen giggled too, the tension dissolved. "It really was pretty funny," she said.

Then Claire said, "Please. Do me a favor. Just join me in a little drink." She slid Karen's glass across the desk toward her.

"Because we're friends?"

"Yes, because we're friends."

"Or to prove I'm not timid?" Karen thought about Claire's made-up article. Even though it didn't exist, it could be true.

"We're friends," Claire insisted.

"All right, because we're friends." Karen picked up the glass and looked at Claire. *How beautiful you are!* she thought, and took the whole drink down in a single shot. And winced. She hated the taste.

"Thank you," Claire said, and slugged down her own. Then she got up, capped the bottle, and crossed the room with it to her bureau and put it away. "Well, that's all for tonight. I hope you'll come again."

"I will," Karen said, standing up. "We'll have a little drink to keep each other company."

AT EIGHT O'CLOCK the next evening, Rabbi Myron and Rachel Benjamin, Karen's parents, who were hosting a recruiting meeting, opened the door of their home in Brookline, Massachusetts, to Fred Kindler, Nan White, and Francis Plummer. The rabbi, tall and thin like his daughter, was bald and wore a worn sports coat. He shook hands with the three of them. Rachel, dark haired and shorter than her husband, smiled at Nan and Francis and took Fred's hand in both of hers. "Our daughter tells us you're very brave," she said, then she kissed him on the cheek as if she'd known him all his life.

The room into which the Benjamins ushered them was big and

lined on every wall with books. The guests were already seated, eleven teenage girls among them. Eleven potential students!

They had a good plan: After the rabbi introduced them, Fred would focus on the culture of Miss Oliver's School as a life-changing experience. He would describe what he had witnessed in his visits to the school as a candidate, and show how he had been drawn to the school, how he had fallen in love.

Then Francis would focus on the excellence of the teaching at Miss Oliver's School for Girls. He'd know when he stood up and looked at the faces in the audience what examples to use. Perhaps how in science the students discovered the truth before they learned it rather than the other way around, maybe history as research, maybe for English he'd teach a poem. Something short and succinct, like Richard Wilbur's "Two Voices in a Meadow" to show how charged language can be.

Yes! He'd recite the poem, then start by seeing if any of them heard how the structure of each verse mirrors the other, and go from there to get the girls thinking and talking, drawing the parents in too. Don't talk about teaching and learning, give them the experience instead. Then tomorrow, he'd mail a copy of the poem to each of the families and ask them to talk about it together. That would keep the school in their head, that would draw them in!

But when Myron Benjamin finished introducing his three guests, he didn't sit down and give the floor to Fred. He went on talking, though it wasn't really a talk, it was a meditation in which he discovered—as if he'd never known—why he and his Rachel were willing to part from their beloved daughter at a time in her life they could never have with her again. First he listed the teachers' passion for their subjects, mentioning in particular Gregory van Buren, who had engendered in his daughter a love of language and a desire to write, and went from there to claim that because the teachers expected so much of his daughter she demanded even more of herself, reminding himself out loud that the other word for *subject* was *discipline*. He meditated aloud this way for a full twenty minutes or so, never once speaking of the value of single-sex education for girls.

Near the end it came to the rabbi that great teaching was an act of love, a love that was disciplined, chosen, and that had nothing to do with whether or not the teacher liked the child. "Not like the love of my Rachel and me for Karen, our daughter. That we can hardly help, for she's our own flesh and blood," he said. "So when you choose a school, don't think so much about preparing for the future, getting into college," he told them, leaping now to their misguided obsessions. "As if your children were squirrels hoarding for the winter. Look for that passion instead, that adoration of life. Tell me, would you withhold an education from a child who you knew was going to die before she was old enough for college?" Then he stopped, coming out of his meditation like a man waking up, a little sheepish for having wandered from thought to thought and being so personal.

What could Fred say after that? Whatever it was would be anticlimactic. Besides, two talks would be enough, three would be redundant. So, though he was disappointed not to give the talk he had been so eager to give, he decided that instead of following the rabbi's talk with one of his own, he'd prove the truth of the rabbi's praise of the school by showing these people how committed the headmaster of Miss Oliver's School for Girls was to its great teachers, how much he revered them and supported them, how much he trusted them. He introduced Francis Plummer as Miss Oliver's most celebrated teacher, who embodied the school as much as any one person could. So much more empowering of himself publicly to give the floor to the little creep than have him steal it like he had in San Francisco!

As Francis stood up, it didn't even cross his mind that he wouldn't talk, as planned, about great teaching at Miss Oliver's School for Girls. But when he opened his mouth to speak he knew he would not. He saw on the faces of the audience that they were thinking about the rabbi's talk, building on his thoughts, making them their own. Francis was disappointed. He wanted to give his talk, he wanted to teach this poem he loved so much! But he was much too good a teacher to know that what was needed right then was not for him to talk but for him to invite questions about the school in which Myron Benjamin had caused so much interest.

When he began, it was soon obvious to him that some of the questions were best answered by Nan, or Fred, or even the Benjamins, and so he directed them to the appropriate person. The result was that the questions were answered well; the guests, already inspired by the rabbi, were satisfied that the school was managed judiciously and saw how well Miss Oliver's people worked together. When Nan finished her slideshow a few minutes later, the audience applauded, and before they left, several families asked Nan for an application. Clearly, the evening had been a success.

After the guests left, the Benjamins invited the three recruiters to sit with them at the kitchen table to drink coffee for a few minutes before the drive home. Francis was delighted with this lingering: a chance to savor his satisfaction over his part in the evening's success. He'd been a good teammate to Fred Kindler, felt the beginning of his redemption. He leaned back in his chair, sipped the coffee, felt his muscles relax.

"You did a wonderful job," he heard Fred Kindler say, and for an instant thought Kindler was talking to him, but then he realized that Kindler had directed the comment to Myron Benjamin, sitting close to him on his right. "Coming from a parent rather than a staffer—"

"It was a pleasure," the rabbi interrupted; he didn't need this praise. But Francis did. His disappointment was a surprise. He waited now for Kindler to acknowledge his work too, his decision not to give a talk, his deft handling of the questions.

But that didn't happen because now Rachel Benjamin was explaining that she and her husband would have started recruiting for Miss Oliver's three years ago, as soon as they saw how Karen was thriving there, if they hadn't heard the rumors that the school might have to close. "That's right," Myron Benjamin agreed. "We didn't want to entice families into a school that might not be able to stay the course for them. But then the changes were made," he said, looking right at Francis and choosing those neutral words on purpose, "and that was the sign for Rachel and me that the school was going to make it."

"Yes!" Nan said. Fred said nothing, and, for a different reason, neither did Francis.

The rabbi, who could not have survived for fifteen years in his position merely being a man of God and not a politician too, went on. "It was typical of Marjorie Boyd that after having built this wonderful school she had the grace to step aside," he said, and watched Nan's face, and now he knew that was exactly what Marjorie hadn't done. So he turned toward Fred and said, "I followed in the footsteps of a longtime charismatic person just as you have. It wasn't easy." He waited for one of them to say what needed to be said so he wouldn't have to, and when no one did he went on. "But I had an assistant who'd been here almost as long as my predecessor, and he said all the right things."

"Like what?" Nan asked, and Francis heard the fierceness in her voice.

"We didn't have any meetings like tonight, where nobody except Rachel and me remembers Mrs. Boyd," Myron Benjamin said, as if he'd already answered Nan's question.

"Like what?" Nan asked again.

"Like telling everybody who remembers Mrs. Boyd that the new headmaster is exactly the right person. That has to be the point of every recruiting meeting, doesn't it? Since everybody who remembers Mrs. Boyd already loves the school." And then he turned to Francis and asked, "That is the kind of meeting you'll be having from now on, isn't it?" When Francis didn't answer right away, he added, "Where lots of the people will remember her?"

"Well, is it or isn't it?" Nan said. But Francis still didn't answer.

Rachel Benjamin turned to her husband then, put her hand on his. She knew when her husband should stop. "Dear, we need to let these people go," she said. "They have a long ride home." Myron sent her a little look of thanks and stood up to help his visitors with their coats and ushered them out and into their car.

On the drive home, Francis burned. *It's one thing to support the man, but to have to lie, to have to get up in public and praise him when I think he's absolutely the wrong guy for the job?* When he had made up his mind to fulfill his responsibility as the head's right-hand man, he hadn't thought of that. *I didn't choose Fred Kindler*, he told himself. *I would have known better.* Up front Fred drove and pretended to listen to the radio, and Nan pretended to sleep.

The bastard! Francis thought. *The manipulator!* He thought of how Karen's father worked the conversation so that he could nail him. But his anger was hollow, he knew. All the rabbi had done was tell the truth. "All right," he said at last, to the back of Fred Kindler's head, "I'll do it."

"Do what?" Kindler asked. Francis watched him looking in the mirror to find his face.

"What the rabbi says," Francis answered. He couldn't bring himself to put it into words.

Kindler didn't answer, just kept driving on through the dark

"Well?" Francis asked. "Is that how we're going to do it, or not?"

"It's up to you," Fred said. He was damned if he was going to beg Francis Plummer for praise!

And for the rest of the drive neither of them spoke again, and Nan White kept on pretending to sleep.

LATE IN THE afternoon of December 13, the investigators reported that every suspect student's name was cleared. The best evidence they could gather suggested the cause of the fire was faulty wiring. The next morning before the school broke at noon for winter vacation, Fred announced this fact to the school, going on to tell them how optimistic they could all be when school began again in January "after we've had a rest and the work of choosing the architect for the new library will have begun." There was a visible relief among the students, but Fred knew, and so did they, that once the insult of a suspicion has been made, it takes a long time to melt away.

Soon after the students filed out of the assembly, some of them got on a bus to be taken to Bradley Airport. Parents started showing up on campus to drive the others home. One of these was Mavis Ericksen. Before even speaking to her daughter she went directly to Fred's office, getting there before either he or Margaret Rice returned from the assembly. She was sitting in one of the chairs in front of his desk when he arrived.

"Oh, hello!" he said, failing to hide his surprise and irritation at her barging in like this. She didn't return his greeting, just crossed her legs and waited for him to sit—as if it were her office, not his—and despite himself, his eyes wandered to those amazing legs of hers. He could tell she'd caught him looking. She'd gotten this little victory already.

"You told me you were going to evaluate Joan Saffire in November," she said. "Well, it's December. Have you fired her yet?"

He hesitated, trying to decide whether to explain to her—as if she didn't already know!—that it was none of her business.

"Well, have you or haven't you?"

"Fired who?" he said, putting his hand to his ear as if he hadn't heard her.

"Why are you resisting me? Who do you think you are? You heard me. Joan Saffire. Have you fired her yet?"

"Oh, Joan Saffire!" he exclaimed. "That's who we're talking about." Then, stroking his chin, he said, "What was the question again?"

"Have you fired her!"

"No."

"No?"

"As a matter of fact, I just promoted her," he said, a great big lie; he hadn't done anything of the kind. He didn't even evaluate Joan Saffire. Dorothy Strang did that. "Gave her a big fat raise too," he went on. "Biggest raise I ever gave anyone." He was amazed at himself, he'd never acted so crazy. But it was the first real fun he'd had in four frustrating months. He was not sure he would regret this later even when she paid him back. "I think I'll hire her sister too," he said.

She was staring at him now

"Anything else you want to know? I have an appointment."

"Who do you think you are?" Mavis asked again. This time it was not a rhetorical question. She really wanted to know.

"The headmaster," he said, standing up. "I do the hiring. And I do the firing. And you don't."

A look of surprise flited across her face. She had graduated from Wellesley, her husband had an MBA from Harvard, they owned a big house in Old Lyme, and her daughter would get early admission to any college she wanted. Everything had always come out just the way she'd planned.

"Oh!" she said. "Oh! Oh!" Then she was out the door, her high heels raining on the floor as she crossed Margaret Rice's anteroom.

A minute later, he was in Ms. Rice's anteroom too, on his way home. He'd promised Gail they'd drive to the shore together, spend the afternoon walking on the beach. "I'm through for the day," he told Ms. Rice.

She didn't answer. But she smiled at him—a surprise, until he realized why: Margaret didn't have any more use for Mavis Ericksen than he did. Mavis was one of the ones who had helped get rid of Marjorie, one of the leaders of the pack. He returned Margaret's smile, then left the office to begin his winter break.

Book Three: Winter Term

Nineteen

It was very cold, and new snow sparkled in the sun as the winter term began. The occasional storms that replenished the snow and the days of sunshine in between preserved this loveliness all through a January that Fred Kindler would remember later as the time when he had been most convinced he could save the school.

In the first week of the new term, three of the families who had attended the recruiting event at the Benjamins' home visited the school, liked what they saw, and promised to apply. The school they visited wasn't sick anymore with the suspicion that someone inside the community had burned the library down, for now that the charred bones of the library foundation were covered in virginal snow, the memory of that grim time before the students' names were cleared had receded. The committee to select the architect had begun its work, and the belief that the new library would be even better than the old one spread across the campus.

Most important, Hannah Fingerman's two-million-dollar pledge, which the board had made public as soon as the lawyers assured them it would be fulfilled, had much reduced the fear that the school would close, and thus one of the reasons for not applying had been removed. Accordingly, Nan White was able to report an increase in the rate of inquiries and of visits to the campus. Though the numbers were far short of those needed to reach Fred's goal of twenty-six new students enrolled for next year, the two million dollars would underwrite the shortfall and provide more time for the marketing efforts to take effect. Even with no increase in enrollment, the school could survive for at least another year, thanks to Hannah's gift.

The beauty of the winter brought no joy, though, to Francis and Peggy Plummer, who were still living apart, Francis continuing as the guest of Father Michael Woodward in the rectory and Peggy still mothering their dorm alone. They were so dreary and lonely that they lived in a state of continual surprise that they were still apart, and this surprise made them so angry with each other and themselves that it grew more difficult each day either for Peggy to give in and invite him back or for Francis to insist on returning. If Francis had banged on the door, Peggy wouldn't have refused him—especially if he'd brought with him a sincere belief in the rightness of Fred Kindler's leadership and a relinquishment of his pagan yearnings, two issues that in Peggy's troubled heart had melded into one. But all she really needed was for him to insist on coming home—and then insist some more. When you kick your husband out of the house, he's supposed to try to come back.

Father Woodward, who true to his promise continued to pray for them both and couldn't bear to see them apart, would have loved to say to them that their marriage vows had nothing to do with who was loyal to whom at Miss Oliver's School for Girls. But Father Woodward, a dreamer, unversed in politics, who would never be elected bishop, would have failed to convince Francis. Even more than when he came rushing home from the West determined to redeem himself in Peggy's eyes by redeeming himself at school, Francis believed he needed to help Fred Kindler save the school before he could reclaim his marriage. When that was done, he'd bang on her door and wouldn't take no for an answer.

Father Woodward would have also liked to tell Francis not to give up the spiritual questing that was one of Francis's motiviations for going on the archaeological dig. *Don't do that to save your marriage. That's too high a price to pay.* But that was not how Michael Woodward worked. He thought people should figure things out for themselves.

In fact, Father Woodward needed to apply this theory to himself. For he was so unselfishly focused on the needs of others that he hadn't figured out yet how closely his own spiritual yearnings had begun to mirror those his friend was determined to ignore. He did know how his heart went out to Francis when Francis told him about his abortive sojourn in the Nevada desert: how grace would not come, and he fled in his car to a plastic motel in Winnemucca. Father Woodward could see himself staying in the desert much longer than

Francis did—his own version of the forty days—breathing the spirit that inhabits the earth and quickens all. But he was not ready yet to understand that within a year or two he would no longer be able to so constrain his beliefs that they can be summarized by anything so human centered and so specific as the Nicene Creed.

But he did know that he wouldn't much longer be Francis's host in the rectory. He would not be co-conspirator with Peggy and Francis in the destruction of their marriage by providing Francis this sanctuary. So if Francis didn't soon decide on his own to return to live with Peggy, Father Woodward would make that happen by refusing to let him stay any longer as his guest. He'd kick Francis out of his house just as Peggy had kicked him out of hers. If necessary, he'd put Francis's belongings on the front porch and lock the door and tell him to go home.

A very painful moment in these first weeks of the winter term came for both Francis Plummer and Fred Kindler early in a recruiting event in West Hartford, when, as Myron Benjamin had told him he should—and as he promised he would—Francis declared that Kindler was exactly the right person to head Miss Oliver's School for Girls. Francis hated himself for his hypocrisy, but he forced the words out, going so far as to list the same qualities the board had listed in its letter to the community announcing Kindler's appointment: absolute integrity, passion for single-sex education for girls, appreciation of great teaching, skills at managing finances and marketing. Francis made this short speech with considerable aplomb.

But he only did this once. As he spoke, he watched Kindler's expression. It was all the poor man could do to keep from squirming in his seat while Francis talked. Kindler simply didn't have it in him—he wasn't that good a politician—to hear words of praise delivered in public by a man he didn't trust. *Well, that's all right with me*, Francis thought, his small admiration for Fred Kindler grudgingly rising one notch. And so without saying a word to each other, they made a pact: never again.

Nevertheless, that recruiting event and the two that followed in January went quite well, and Fred's spirits continued to rise and were still flourishing on a morning a month later in mid-February when he looked up from his desk to see Peggy Plummer in his office doorway.

He jumped to his feet and came out from behind his desk to greet her.

"Can we talk?" Peggy asked, closing the door behind her.

"Of course we can talk," he said, motioning to one of the chairs in front of his desk. He was puzzled. They'd always been able to talk.

"I mean, *really* talk." She remained standing in front of her chair.

He moved to the chair facing hers, but since she hadn't sat down yet, he didn't either. "I hope I've never been hard for you to talk to," he said.

"Not yet."

"Well, then test me this time," he said and smiled. Peggy sat down then, so he did too.

"I don't like any of the architects in the competition. Not one of them!" she said. "All their ideas seem so wrong to me."

"All wrong? Peggy!"

"Why change so much?" she asked him. "Everybody loved the old library. Some people even called it the new library."

He hesitated, remembering how long her list had been under *preserve* and how short under *change*. He should have paid more attention.

"You haven't answered my question," she persisted. "Change isn't always good."

"Peggy," he began, "I understand how you feel."

"It's not that," she exclaimed. "Don't tell me it is!" She was about to go on, to insist there was nothing wrong with her judgment, she was perfectly open to change—which of course everyone says when you ask—but there was a knock on the door, so she stopped talking, and Margaret Rice stepped in.

"Yes?" Fred asked, letting his irritation show. The last thing he needed was an interruption. He needed to focus on this. Even Peggy Plummer wasn't going to talk him out of the opportunity to create a better library.

"It's urgent," Margaret said, pointing to the phone, and right away he knew the bad news he was about to hear.

It was a Mr. Singleton, Hannah Fingerman's lawyer, telling Fred that Fingerman's ex-husband had decided to contest her right to the funds. Whatever weaknesses Fingerman's former spouse had as a businessman, he seemed to have considerable resolve as a litigant, according to Singleton, who told Fred that Fingerman's ex had hired a very substantial law firm to work on a contingency basis. It would be a long time before the case was resolved. In the meantime, the funds were not Fingerman's to give away.

"How long?" Fred asked.

The lawyer hesitated. "A long time; maybe years."

"How many years?" *One? Ten? Twenty-seven?* Fred wanted to ask, but controlled himself and didn't.

"How do I know? It could be five." Singleton sounded exasperated now. "After all, you gave them a great angle to work with, and they found it right away."

"I don't understand." Fred tried to keep his face blank so Peggy wouldn't know what this call was about. Alan Travelers should be the first to hear this news.

"As you know, Ms. Fingerman put very specific language into the gift declaration," Singleton explained "It stated that the gift was in honor of the anthropological thrust that distinguishes the curriculum of Miss Oliver's School."

"Oh, I see," Fred murmured, because now he did, and it was all he could think of to say. He knew what Singleton was going to tell him next.

"And then to make matters worse, Ms. Fingerman provided the precise ammunition her ex-husband's attorney needed by specifically stating that this distinguishing curriculum emanated from, is based on, and is still inspired by, the Pequot Collection," Singleton went on, his voice rising exactly one note with each of this triad of phrases.

"Oh, damn!" Fred said.

"I quote," Singleton said. "Those are the exact words."

"Yes," Fred agreed. "They were."

"I believe she wanted to honor the school librarian, a Mrs. Plummer."

"I guess so," Fred said.

"So, when the Collection went up in smoke—"

"All right, Mr. Singleton, that's enough. You don't have to explain."

But the lawyer was too amazed at the stupidity of others to stop. "Without that specificity in the language we would have a slam-dunk case," he complained.

"Really, Mr. Singleton? Well then, where in the world were you?"

"Not involved, I assure you," Singleton answered huffily. "Ms. Fingerman has fired her attorney and engaged me. And I can't resist pointing out that your school attorney was also careless."

I doubt that he knew the library was going to burn down, Fred wanted to say; but of course he couldn't, not with Peggy there.

"It's important to be prepared for every possible contingency," Mr. Singleton lectured, as if reading Fred's mind. "If that had been the case, the school would be receiving these funds in a few weeks from now at the most."

That was all Fred could take, he was about to burst. He cut the lawyer off; if Peggy weren't there, he'd be standing up and yelling into the phone at this pompous twerp. He'd be quoting Milton Perkins on lawyers. "Thank you, Mr. Singleton," he said instead, "keep me informed," and hung up abruptly.

"You okay?" Peggy asked.

"Yeah," he said, and she knew whatever it was, he didn't want to talk about it.

"So where were we?" he asked.

"Later," she said, starting to stand. "You've got something heavy to deal with, I can tell."

He waved her back down. "It can wait a few minutes."

And then it dawned on her. How could it have taken her so long to guess? She'd seen how his face had fallen. "I think I know what you just learned," she murmured, and Fred moved his hand in front of his face in that dismissive gesture that she knew drove Francis crazy, letting her know that she had guessed right and that he was not going to talk about it. He had never really counted on the gift coming through anyway, he told himself. Always felt a little dishonest for pretending that he thought it would. *It was just a teaser, a promised rescue waved in front of our eyes to make us happy for a few short months, and then yanked away*, he thought. Yet, God, he was disappointed!

Besides, he was determined not to put Peggy off. She was going to grieve even more when she found out that the library's burning down was what delayed, maybe even canceled forever, the gift that would have saved the school "Peg, I'm going to be honest with you," he told her, changing his mind about gentling her. The time to be assertive was now, it was the kindest way. "We're not going to base our decision on which architect we pick—"

"You don't have to tell me you're going to be honest. You could never be anything else."

Now she was worried she was going to cry. But not in front of him, she wouldn't do that to him. She hated it when women used tears for leverage. "I'm out of here," she said. "You've got enough on your plate." She fled through Margaret's office and went straight to her apartment. She needed to be alone to think.

Maybe it was the shock of learning there wasn't going to be any two million dollars to save the school that kept her from seeing that she was acting just like Francis. Her emotions were all a jumble. She didn't want things to change. It wasn't only nostalgia for her library that made her want to beg Fred Kindler to replicate it. When the library had been standing, she and Francis were together. How could she ask Fred to fix that?

One thing she was clear about: she wasn't going to sit around waiting for something to happen to fix her marriage. She was going to do something, and do it soon.

AFTER LEAVING A message for Alan Travelers, Fred stepped out into Margaret Rice's anteroom. "I'll be back in ten minutes," he told her. "I need a little walk."

"Have I guessed right what that lawyer fella told you?" she asked.

At first he thought she must be gloating. Then he knew she wasn't. Despite the grudge she harbored, she wanted the same thing he did. "No comment," he answered.

"Damn!" she said.

"Yes." he said. "Damn."

"Well, take a good walk. You deserve a break," she said, to his surprise. "I'll take care of Gregory until you get back," she added, reminding him that he had an appointment—another one—with the head of the English Department. "Maybe while he waits for you he can explain to me why *Moby Dick* isn't as boring as everybody but English teachers knows it is," she said, surprising him even more with a hint of a smile.

After his short walk, while Gregory still waited in Margaret's anteroom, Alan returned his call. It didn't take long. Alan was not the type to spend time bemoaning events he couldn't control. "I'll call an emergency meeting of the board for the day after tomorrow in the afternoon," he told Fred. "That will give us time to get as many members as possible together to decide what we should do, and we'll do it in our New York offices. That's the easiest place to gather trustees from around the country at such short notice."

"Good," Fred said.

"And Fred?"

"Yes?"

"I can't tell you how glad I am that in times like these we have you to be the boss."

"Thanks, Alan. I'll have a recommendation ready for the meeting."

"No, you won't, Fred. Let us do that."

"That makes me feel like a chicken, Alan."

"So be a chicken. We need you around."

"Well, I'll think about that."

"Don't think about it. Just do it. It's an order."

Fred didn't answer.

"And in the meantime, just hang in there, my friend," Alan said. "Just keep going as if nothing's happened. I know you will." Then he hung up.

Fred stood up as van Buren entered, but he didn't come around his desk. The last thing he needed right then was to have to pretend he was interested in one of van Buren's legion of worries. But hadn't his board chair just reminded him that it was his job to keep on as if nothing's happened?

Gregory van Buren sat in one of the chairs facing the desk. "Good morning," he said, and drew breath for small talk.

"Good morning," Fred responded, and glanced at his watch. Van Buren looked disappointed and let out his breath.

"Yes?" said Fred.

"I've come to report on *Clarion* affairs," Van Buren told him. "As faculty advisor," he added.

"And?"

"Thus to facilitate your decision."

"My decision?"

"Yes. It won't be difficult once you've heard what is in the article."

"Which article?"

"You haven't heard?"

"The head's the last to hear certain things, Mr. van Buren," Fred said. "But I can guess which article." *Well, here it is at last*, he thought. He'd been waiting for this shoe to drop since his talk with Karen Benjamin in September.

"Karen Benjamin's done research," Van Buren told him. "Lots of it. She's given every senior a questionnaire about sex. She's written an article."

"About sex?"

Van Buren made a face, a stagy gesture that irritated Fred. "How many are sexually active and how many are not."

"Really?"

"It's quite detailed, I'm afraid."

"Really? Is it a good article?"

"Of course not! I think it's disgusting!"

"Disgusting? You mean it's pornographic? Explicit?"

"No, it's not pornographic. It's just not the kind of thing—"

"That should be in a school newspaper?"

"That's right." Van Buren was beginning to look confused.

"Especially a girls' school."

"Oh, yes, especially a girls' school!" exclaimed van Buren, his face brightening.

"Well, then, tell her she can't print it."

Van Buren's face went pale. "Me?"

"You're the advisor to the *Clarion*, Mr. van Buren." Fred was beginning to enjoy this.

"The headmistress, uh, Mrs. Boyd used—"

"To make all these decisions," Fred finished van Buren's sentence again.

Gregory van Buren nodded.

"Which you thought was kind of dictatorial, I believe. And you didn't agree with her when she let the kids print this kind of thing, am I right?"

"Yes, but—"

"Well, I'm not a dictator, Mr. van Buren. I'm a delegator. You've told me, rather often, that you like that about me. And you're the advisor to the *Clarion*, and you don't think that Karen should print the article. So here's your chance."

"But—"

Fred stood up. "Just do it," he said. "Just tell her your decision. Make sure she knows it's yours. And make it stick." He put his hand on van Buren's elbow, ushered him to the door.

He had to admit he felt a little better now.

Gregory went straight to the *Clarion* office to see Karen. He was so nervous he needed to get this over with.

Karen was sitting at her desk. She looked up at him when he entered the office. "Good morning," she said. "I've been expecting you."

Her greeting sounded like a challenge to him. Moreover, she was sitting down at her desk in her office, while he was standing up, like a supplicant.

"Karen—" he began.

"Could you sit down please, Mr. van Buren? You make me nervous standing there."

"Sit where?" Gregory huffed. "All these chairs have papers piled up in them."

"How about that one?" Karen answered brightly, pointing to the chair nearest her desk. "Here," she said, reaching for the papers Gregory had picked up from the chair. "Actually, you look nervous too." She knew what he was there for, and she was going to make him pay!

He didn't answer.

"I like it messy like this, don't you?" Because she knew he was a stickler for neatness. "When things are messy it means people are busy."

"No, it doesn't," Gregory finally spoke. "It just means they're messy."

Karen shrugged. "What can I do for you?"

He drew breath, started to answer; she cut him off. "How'd you like my article?"

Again, he didn't answer

"It's good, isn't it?"

"It's inappropriate."

"But I asked whether you thought it was good or not."

He hesitated. She wasn't about to give him time to frame his answer. "You know it is," she said, smiling. "It's everything you taught. Well organized, great quotations, a subject everyone is interested in, everything substantiated—facts, figures."

"Karen, you know very well it's not appropriate. This is a school."

"Just tell me, is it good or isn't it?"

He nodded, started to speak.

"It tells the truth, doesn't it?"

"I don't know whether it does or not," Gregory hedged. "I don't really want to know about the students' sex lives."

"That's my point," Karen said. "It does what good reporting does: tells the people who want to keep on not knowing what they need to know about what the people who are written about already know."

Gregory hesitated again, taking in her comment as he did in his class when somebody made an interesting point. "All right," he finally conceded. "You've won that point."

"It's a model, isn't it? If it were for a magazine, not a school newspaper—"

"Yes, it's very good."

"Thank you. That's what I wanted to hear. From you. If you told me it wasn't good, I'd write it over. Anybody else, and I'd tell him he's wrong."

"All right," he said. "I've told you. It's very good."

"And you're here to tell me the headmaster says I can't print it."

"No, Karen, not the headmaster."

"It's not surprising."

"You didn't hear me, Karen. I'm telling you."

"No, you aren't," she said. Her voice was neutral. There was no anger in it; she was just telling a fact. "You're not telling me. Because he told you to tell me."

Gregory looked stunned, as if he'd been slapped in the face. "How do you know?" he challenged.

"Hey!" she said. "Big Momma's gone. The new guy wants everybody to grow up. And you tried just now. But it was too late, wasn't it? Because you'd already gone to him." She could see by his expression that she'd guessed right.

"You're being insolent," Gregory warned.

"If I were the advisor to the *Clarion* and some kid wanted to print an article I didn't think should be printed, I wouldn't go to the boss about it first," Karen said. "I wouldn't even tell him. I'd make my own decision."

"You're being very impolite," Gregory repeated.

"Sorry. I didn't plan to be impolite," she said. "It's just that it's true, that's all," she added with a little apologetic shrug. She felt a small sadness taking the place of her resentment. It was not the first time this year that she'd had the sense she'd caught up with him, some of the other teachers too, ex-heroes. She didn't need them anymore; it was time to graduate and say goodbye. "Really," she said. "I apologize."

"I accept," Gregory answered, his best tactic at this point, and added, as if he were still in a position to dispense comfort, "I know it's a disappointment not to print it."

"Hey, forget it."

There was a silence then they both found embarrassing, which he had the grace to end by standing and moving to the door. But at the door he turned back to her because he couldn't resist. "You really ought to clean this mess up."

"Okay, I will. And guess what?"

"What?"

"I could print it anyway, you know. Underground. Just Xerox it and hand it out."

"I hope you won't."

"I won't," she said, remembering her conversation with her new headmaster about this issue, how straight he'd been with her, how clear and realistic. How authentic. "You can count on it. I won't sneak."

"A wise decision," Gregory said as firmly as he could. "A very adult decision." Then he left.

THAT NIGHT WHEN Julie snuck out, Clarissa didn't bother to pretend to sleep, and Julie made only a little effort not to be seen as she ran across the campus to the spot where she expected Charley to be waiting for her in the Subaru. In the back of her mind, she knew she wanted to get caught so she'd be kicked out.

"We're going to blitz tonight," Charley had told her on the phone. "Party city!" Why was he talking that way? He'd never talked that way before. But he'd hung up the phone before she asked. It was not the party she cared about. It was the chance to talk with Charley, to be alone with her brother, for the half hour it took to get to Trinity.

Fifteen yards from the car she could tell even in the dark that it was Robin, not Charley. She walked the rest of the way and got in the car beside him.

"Hello. I thought you'd like a real date," Robin said.

She knew he meant a date with a brother wasn't real. It was a huge disappointment. *He's not my brother anymore*, she wanted to protest. "Well, okay. Thanks," she said instead. Robin seemed surprised by her halfhearted response, maybe even a little bit hurt. They had very little to say to each other on the way to the Trinity campus.

Inside the fraternity house, the room was crowded with dancers. The rock band was across the room from the door, playing so loud it was impossible to talk. There was a big, shiny aluminum beer keg in each corner of the room. Julie looked for Charley, couldn't see him anywhere. Robin took her hand, and they squeezed further into the room and began to dance.

She liked moving to the rhythm. Her unhappiness lifted and flew away. It got hotter in the crowded space; bodies bumped into each other. "I smell weed," she shouted at Robin. "Get me some." But he shook his head. *All right*, she thought. *I've got all night.* She let herself go, swaying her hips, rolling her shoulders, waving her arms above her head. Opposite her, Robin was graceful for such a big guy, dancing just as hard as she was. But there was a serious look on his face, a frown in his forehead, as if he were concentrating to avoid mistakes, and suddenly she didn't want to be with him anymore. She wanted to dance with someone uncaged and crazy. "I need a beer," she yelled, but he shook his head. She danced further away from him. She was dancing alone now. Or maybe she was dancing with everyone, she didn't care which.

A few minutes later the band stopped to take a break, and she pushed her way through the crowd to one of the kegs. There was a puddle of beer at her feet. She didn't like the smell of it. She filled a plastic cup and chugged it down, then filled it again and chugged that too.

"Careful," she heard behind her and knew it was Robin. She ignored him, took another slug. She didn't really like the taste any better than the smell. She'd just get a little loose so she could really dance.

She turned around. "Where's Charley?"

"I don't know," Robin said. "Making out someplace, I guess." He took the cup from her.

She reached for it. He moved his hand so she couldn't get it. "You're my date," she said. "Not my father." The band started up again, and she didn't hear his answer. He took her hand, led her to the middle of the room, and they started to dance again.

While she danced she watched the front door. People kept coming through it, crowding the room even more, but none of them was Charley. It was hotter in the room now, and she danced even harder. Robin grabbed her hand, tried a fancy move, spun her around. He was frowning again. "You're trying too hard," she yelled over the music. "This isn't a job."

He spun her again and let go, and she pretended to think he wanted her to dance with someone else and moved away from him. Next thing she knew she was dancing with a boy who was half Robin's size. He was short and pudgy, but his eyes sparkled and she liked his smile. He had black hair and a film of sweat on his face over acne scars and danced much better than Robin. He was in the zone, on the beat without thinking, and she moved with him. Some of the dancers nearest them stopped and watched. The crowd hooted and cheered, and, lost in the music, Julie was as happy as she'd been for weeks. When it stopped, the boy put his arm around her waist and pulled her to him. "Hey, hey, hey!" he said. "What a great dancer!" Their hips touched; she felt his sweat. Her own too, her blouse soaked through. "That was great!" the boy said and let her go, moving off.

She headed back to a keg. Near it a girl was passed out on a sofa. Next to her, a boy sat stroking her hair. The sofa was ripped, the innards showing. Julie filled a plastic cup and chugged it. The boy on the sofa got up and stood beside her. "Where'd you come from? Who robbed the cradle?" he asked. Julie filled her cup again, turned to the boy, looked him in the face, and chugged the beer down.

"I can do that too," the boy said. He filled a cup, faced her, and chugged it. "Now, what else can you do?"

She gave him a little smile, filled her cup again, and very deliberately poured the beer on his head.

He grinned while the beer ran down over his hair and onto his shoulders. Then he filled his cup and, just as deliberately, emptied it on her head.

She didn't move either while the cold sticky beer soaked her hair and ran down over her shoulders into her blouse. Then she filled her cup and poured it on his head.

Now a little crowd gathered to watch. They cheered with each pouring.

This game seemed to Julie to go on forever. The group of watchers got bigger, the cheers louder with each pouring.

Suddenly she was dizzy. She felt her lips twitching, her eyes rolling in their sockets. "Oh, shit!" she heard the boy say. "She's going to barf." He dropped his cup, escaped back to the sofa. Julie turned away, got out the door, and threw up on the lawn.

The next thing she knew she was sitting on a bench on the lawn, shivering with the cold, and Charley was standing over her. A girl stood next to Charley. "You passed out," Charley said. His lips were red with lipstick and the girl's lipstick was smeared. "Robin's getting the car," Charley said. "Bringing it as close as he can so you don't have to walk. He'll drive you back to school."

"No, you," she said.

Charley turned to his date.

"That's fine, Charley," the girl said. "I don't mind. But I'm going to drive. You're a little drunk."

A minute or so later, Robin brought the car up into the driveway. "We'll take her home," Charley said to him.

Robin frowned and shook his head.

"I'm driving," the girl said, and Robin smiled and got out of the car. After all, who wants to be with a girl who's throwing up? He helped Julie into the backseat. "You'll be all right," he said. "Next time be more careful."

Julie was sick once more on the way home. She just had time to get her head through the window. She made a mess on the outside of the car door.

"That's all right," Charley said. "I'll just get a hose and it'll be fine."

"Don't worry about it," the girl said kindly. "It happened to me once too." Julie realized she didn't know her name. She was too tired and sick and embarrassed to ask.

When they got back to school, Charley held her arm while they snuck across the campus. He left her by the window to her room. This time Clarissa didn't pretend to be asleep. "It's three o'clock in the morning!" she said. Julie didn't answer. "You smell awful," Clarissa said, sitting up, and turning on the light.

"I'm sorry."

"I'll help you with a shower so you don't fall down and drown."

"No, I'm all right." Julie went into the bathroom, turned on the shower, and got under it with her clothes on to get the smell out. When she got back to the room, the light was still on, and Clarissa still sitting up.

"You're going to flunk out if you keep this up," Clarissa said.

"I know I am," Julie said. She had a history test in the morning she hadn't studied for, and a paper due for Mr. van Buren the day after that she hadn't begun. Clarissa turned the light out, and Julie got into bed. She wanted to think about Charley and that girl, both smeared with lipstick. But the room whirled around and around, and she couldn't think about anything. Finally, at dawn, she fell asleep.

"CLOSE HER DOWN then," Milton Perkins muttered two days later, thirty stories above the street in New York City. "She's run her course. Just close the old girl down."

"Well, that's the question, isn't it?" Alan Travelers asked in a somber voice. "Well, isn't it?" he repeated.

Two chairs to the right of Perkins, Sonja McGarvey reached across Barbara Tuckerman, a rigidly erect silver-blonde in her fifties, and lightly laid her fingers on Perkins's hand. The red of McGarvey's fingernails flashed against the starched white of Perkins's cuff. "Please, Milton," McGarvey said, her voice as quiet as if she and he were the only people in the room. Perkins turned to her, his face registering mild surprise, and Barbara Tuckerman slid her chair back from the table, as if escaping from a scene that should take place in private. "A coed school is better than no school at all," McGarvey said. "I really want you to believe that." Perkins didn't take his hand away, and he did keep his suddenly gentle eyes on McGarvey's face. But he moved his head from left to right and back again, as if rejecting a gift.

"Oh, come on, surely there's another alternative," Tuckerman exclaimed. This was the first meeting she had attended since Fred's appointment. "I believe emphatically that we should simply soldier on as Miss Oliver's School for Girls," she announced. "And I repeat, *for Girls*. We've been doing it for years."

"You got two million dollars?" Perkins asked her, and McGarvey just looked away and rolled her eyes. Fred wanted to yell, *That's exactly the problem: you've been doing it for years!*

Instead, he used the excuse of Barbara Tuckerman's naiveté—which he guessed was fake—to sum up the situation all over again. Some of these people have been drifting so long, he needed to stick it between their eyes. "We need twenty-six new enrollments for next year," he reminded them. "We can hope for fifteen, but I can safely predict only ten. Now without the Fingerman gift to tide us over, if we do only get ten, we'll run out of cash around the beginning of next year's winter term. If we get lucky and get fifteen, we can last about two weeks longer. We just won't have any more money!" *There!* he said to himself. *How's that? Do you understand that?*

"Oh, our poor school!" Charlotte Reynolds moaned.

"This is what we get for letting Marjorie do our job," Mavis

Ericksen declared, and when no one responded she said, "Well, it's true, isn't it? Why do you think John and Charlotte and I got ourselves on the board?" she said, pointing down the table at John Williamson, who had joined the board the same time she and Charlotte did. "If the alumnae knew how the rest of you let that ridiculous Boyd woman go on and on, they'd sue you."

"All right, Mavis," Alan tried to interrupt. "Let's not go there."

"They'd take you right to court and get every penny you've got—if they didn't shoot you first."

"And they'd be right!" Charlotte said.

"But I'll be goddamned if I'm going to vote to let boys in!" Mavis finished.

"So I move that we close the school at the end of this year," Perkins said. His voice was calm, resigned.

Silence.

"Well?" asked Perkins.

"Let's not go quite so fast, Milton," Alan said, though he knew they had reached the moment of decision. He didn't want anyone even to suspect they hadn't studied everything, examined every possible way out of this. So in the way of most boards when faced with such a calamity, they spent an hour and a half going over all the numbers again as if they didn't already know everything the numbers could possibly tell them. As expected, they learned nothing new; and so they turned to the concept of operating with a skeleton crew, and Fred explained once again what they already knew about critical mass: how, since foreign language teachers didn't teach math and math teachers didn't teach English—and so on—a certain number of teachers was needed, no matter how few students there were to support them. Finished with this, with hopes even more rapidly descending, they examined the possibility of closing part of the campus, even renting some of the buildings out, the theater, for example, to the local amateur repertoire company, which happened, McGarvey informed them, having already looked into this at Fred's request, to have the use of Fieldington High School's auditorium for free. She and Travelers and Perkins and also new member John Williamson had examined every possibility of creating revenue via use of campus—including the tax implications—and even selling timber from the many acres of forest the school owned, extending from the edge of the campus to the river. They went over all of it again with the rest of the board, and at the end no one contradicted McGarvey when she summed it up as a pipe dream to think that any of this could save the school.

In the ensuing silence Perkins said again, "I move we close the school at the end of the academic year."

No one said a thing.

"That gives the kids time to find another school and the faculty to get hired someplace else," Perkins added. "We should make the decision now; it's only fair."

"Is there a second?" Travelers asked.

Silence again. Fred and Alan looked at each other. Alan made a tiny gesture with his eyebrows, acknowledging the moment.

"I move we accept boys," said McGarvey.

"Just a minute," Travelers said. "We have another motion on the table."

"Yeah, well it's not getting any action, is it?" McGarvey said.

"Why isn't it?" murmured Perkins. "What's everybody afraid of?"

"Any second to the motion to close the school?" Traveler asked again. He looked around the room.

Silence.

"The motion fails," Travelers announced.

"I move to accept boys," McGarvey repeated.

"Second?" Travelers asked.

"Hold it. I'm not through yet," McGarvey said.

Travelers waited.

"And change the name to the Oliver School."

"Get rid of *for Girls*?" Barbara Tuckerman exclaimed.

"Right. No more *for Girls*—and gear Fred's marketing campaign to a coed school. Use all the same strategies he's using right now. You know damn well that'll work. Coed schools are turning kids away in droves. So the students have signed a pledge not to come back if boys are admitted. So what? Half of them will change their minds and come back anyway. We get some boys, and we enter the much bigger market of girls who want to go to school with boys. You know damn well we could get twenty-six more students in that market. Hell, just with the boys, we'll get twenty-six—"

"Second?" Travelers interrupted "Then we can discuss."

"I abstain!" Barbara Tuckerman blurted.

Alan Travelers looked at her for what seemed like minutes. "We're not there yet, Ms. Tuckerman," he said at last.

"Let's call the question," said McGarvey.

"We can't," Travelers said. "We don't have a second." He looked around the room again. "All right," he said when no one offered a second, "I'll second the motion—just to get it on the table so we can at least discuss it."

"I'm not sure you can do that," said Meg Updike, the alumnae representative to the board. "Can the chair second a motion?"

"I'm doing it. Discussion. Please."

"Oh, goody!" McGarvey said. "We can discuss all the details while the school goes broke. Let's start with the price of urinals."

"We can start with the fact that the boys we take won't be the best students," Beverly Monroe challenged. Monroe had recently retired from a long career in admissions work in independent schools. "I just want to point that out so it can be part of the consideration."

"Is that really why you're bringing it up?" McGarvey asked across the table. "Or is it just some more bullshit?"

"Careful, Sonja," Travelers warned.

Monroe blushed. "Well, it's true."

"I agree. It's true," said Charlotte Reynolds. McGarvey stared at her. "Well, it's *probably* true," she said.

Mavis Ericksen turned to Fred. "Mr. Kindler, is it true or isn't it?"

"It's true," Fred said. "The best will go to schools that have been coed for years." He hated this topic. Talking about kids as if there were a "best" and a "worst."

"You mean second-line? We're going to take second-line boys in?" Tuckerman asked.

"Beggars being choosers," McGarvey muttered. "Jesus!"

"Any other discussion?" Travelers asked. No one answered. "Really? No questions, no thoughts? All right, then, we'll call the question. All in favor, signify by raising your hand." McGarvey put her hand up. So did Travelers—obviously with reluctance. Everybody else's stayed down. Travelers looked surprised. "Both motions fail," he announced.

"Big surprise!" McGarvey said.

"Scaredy-cats!" Perkins growled.

"I said I abstain," Barbara Tuckerman said. Several people nodded their heads. "See?" said Tuckerman. "People are abstaining. They're not ready. It's natural."

"This is no time for abstaining," Travelers declared.

"I won't accept—"

"Alan, let's go around the table," Fred suggested. "Ask each person to say whatever she or he is thinking right now."

"I think we ought to hear what you think," Barbara Tuckerman interjected. "You're the headmaster. What's your recommendation?"

"The board's supposed to make these decisions," Alan Travelers said. "You people need to do your damn job!"

Now there was a big silence in the room. "That's right," said Sonja McGarvey. "Time to step up to the plate." Milton Perkins nodded in agreement.

"We're not leaving here until we decide," Travelers declared. "Does everybody understand that? We're staying right here." Now it was even quieter in the room.

John Williamson turned to Travelers. "There is a question that we should ask the headmaster," he said.

Alan frowned. Either way, he clearly didn't want this decision to be pinned on Fred—especially if the decision was to admit boys. He didn't need a head whom everybody hated.

"It's a question for the educator," Williamson said. "The professional. It's not about which way he'd vote if he could."

"All right, ask it," Travelers said.

Williamson turned away from Travelers and faced Fred. "Haven't we learned enough about how to educate girls at Miss Oliver's that now we could apply that knowledge to the benefit of girls *and* boys in a coed school?"

"Of course we can," Fred said.

"Of course we can what?" Mavis said.

"Of course we can apply—" Fred began.

Mavis cut him off. "You traitor!" she hissed. "You son of a bitch!"

Travelers stared hard at Mavis.

Mavis stared right back. She started to say something.

Travelers cut her off. "Sonja, make your motion again," he commanded. And Mavis started to cry.

McGarvey put the forefinger of her right hand on the thumb of her left. "Admit boys," she said over the sound of Mavis's sobs. She moved to the forefinger. "Change the name to the Oliver School."

"Eliminate *Miss* too!" Charlotte exclaimed.

"Yes, eliminate *Miss*, why the hell not?" McGarvey moved to the second finger. "And continue with the present marketing strategies but geared to coed."

"Second?" asked Travelers.

"I second the motion!" Williamson said.

"You too?" came from Mavis, crying.

"You promised!" Charlotte said.

"Discussion?" Travelers asked.

"We got you on to get rid of Marjorie, not to let boys in!" Charlotte said, leaning across the table at Williamson.

Travelers rapped his knuckles loudly on the table. "All in favor of the motion, signify by raising your hand."

Everybody except Mavis Ericksen, Milton Perkins, and Charlotte Reynolds raised a hand.

Alan Travelers hesitated, looking straight at Fred. Then he moved his eyes around the room. "The motion passes," he announced. "This is an historic moment. Thanks for doing your job."

Mavis Ericksen got up from her chair, leaving her papers on the table, and charged out of the room, slamming the door behind her. Fred was sure she'd go straight to Sandra Petrie. "This meeting is adjourned," Travelers announced.

LATE THAT EVENING, back at the head's house after the drive from New York City, Fred heard a message left on his answering machine and knew right away that if Gail had thought to check for calls, she would have deleted it and he never would have heard the enraged and drunken voice stumbling over the wires: "You . . . you Quibling. Quidling. Quisling!" It was Barbara Tuckerman's voice. The prim, erect, perfectly dressed Barbara Tuckerman, who had moved graciously back so Sonja McGarvey could lay her hand on Milton Perkins's hand, was saying, "Thadz wha you are a fugging quisling, a real pansy, weak . . . weak." Big sigh then. Fred imagined her running a finger down a list of epithets and thought he heard ice tinkling in a glass. "Sonabitdch," Tuckerman chose from her list. "Knew the minud Mavis tol' me you didn' have tha guds to fire that Saffire bidch we had tha wrong person." Then in the background he heard a man's voice, obviously her husband's: "Honey, please." The voice was gentle, and now Fred felt very sad. He knew he should hang up. But he was fascinated. "Don't. You're making a fool out of yourself," the husband said, but then Tuckerman's voice got even louder, drowning him out. "Shid! We'd a been better off if we'd stayed with Barjorie Moyd. At leasd she wasan a man!" Fred heard her draw a new breath; she was thinking what else to say, she was going to start all over again. He hung up the phone.

"And I didn't even make the recommendation!" Fred said to the empty room. Then he pushed the delete button and headed for bed.

TWENTY

At eight-fifteen the next morning, the entire school was in the auditorium, the big doors in the back were closed, and Fred Kindler was stepping toward the lip of the stage. "Good morning," he said into the silence. There was almost no response. The students sat warily silent, and most of the faculty stood along the back wall near the doors, ready to retreat. If news couldn't wait for a regular Morning Meeting at the usual time, it must be bad. Fred nodded his head. He agreed: it was much too tense in there for pleasant greetings. He introduced Alan Travelers then sat down on a chair onstage, and felt a small relief when all the eyes came off him and on to Travelers. The board chairman stood and calmly began to talk.

"Yesterday the trustees resolved that beginning next September, male students will be admitted to this school," Alan Travelers said, and then he paused. He was not going to rush through this; he'd stand here and absorb the anger, take the heat. But the response was silence and staring eyes, so he went on. "This was the board's decision," he declared. "It was not the headmaster's, or the faculty's, or the alumnae's; it was the board's." He paused again. The auditorium was silent, so he finished explaining the factors that compelled the decision, citing the numbers twice to make sure they were understood. He accomplished this in less than three minutes. He was clear, firm, and wholly unapologetic, and when he'd finished, no one said a word and no one stirred.

Then Fred got up and stood by Alan's side. It would be his job now to control the riot.

But there wasn't any riot. For a few seconds that lasted forever, the students sat, and the faculty stood by the closed doors in the rear. Then Fred saw Francis Plummer turn, open one of doors, and bolt across the frozen lawn. Then the other teachers followed Francis, and the students began to move down the aisles, and then the auditorium was empty except for Alan Travelers and Fred Kindler, side by side on the stage.

"Well," Alan murmured, "that was a strange reaction."

"No, it wasn't," Fred said. "I should have predicted it." For this was exactly what had happened at Mt. Gilead when it was announced the school would close: the students fled to their dorms.

Outside the auditorium, moving away from it as fast as he could, Francis stopped in his tracks. For a crazy instant he thought he'd turn around, rush back into the auditorium, tell the crowd that was coming out the doors to turn around too and take their seats again. Then he'd climb up onto the stage, push Travelers and Kindler aside, and declare the decision void. Who had a better right than he?

But of course the fantasy dissolved as soon as he tried to think of what words to use, and he tossed it away as the absurdity it was.

Why wasn't he gathering the faculty to organize a strike, he asked himself, why wasn't he leading a demonstration, engineering a coup, instead of turning suddenly into a mere well-adjusted, practical man? Then it dawned on him that he'd been trying hard for the last six months to become a practical man who could adjust to the facts—and besides, he was living apart from his wife, and maybe he had only grief enough for that. So he headed for a dorm to comfort the students. Before the day was over, he'd go to all the dorms except the one he wanted to go to the most. For this would be the worst time, he thought, to force himself on Peggy.

What he didn't know was that Peggy waited for him there. Foolishly perhaps, for after all, she was the one who'd kicked him out. When he didn't come, she went through her dorm alone, spoke to each girl, and had never felt so lonely.

Fred wanted to hide in his office but made the rounds of the dorms, showing his face, taking the heat. A few girls told him they understood that this really was a board decision; most were too angry even to speak. Some were simply numbed by the discovery that the world was a treasonous place. He explained the board's decision over and over, trying hard to be as factual and unapologetic as Alan Travelers had been.

That morning, Mavis Ericksen telephoned Sandra Petrie. She

had needed the time since the board meeting to design a plan to present to Sandra. Otherwise some of the ideas in the plan might turn out be Sandra's, and Mavis wouldn't be in control. Though Mavis could never admit it to herself, the real reason for her enmity toward Marjorie was not the way Marjorie had run the school; it was that Mavis couldn't control her.

The conversation was awkward. Mavis and Sandra hated each other. Sandra was fiercely loyal to Marjorie and resented this newcomer who had worked so hard to get rid of her. But that was the reason that Sandra could ask Marjorie to lead the alumnae to rebel against the admission of boys and Mavis couldn't.

"All Mrs. Boyd needs is to have people like you invite her back," Mavis said.

Sandra hesitated. She had been beaten up pretty badly the last time she tried to fight back. She wasn't sure she was ready for another battle. She reminded Mavis that Marjorie was in Europe and wouldn't be back for a month.

"I know that," Mavis reassured her. "There's plenty of time after she gets back. And we can get the word out to some of the alumnae that we're doing this. They'll be ready when Mrs. Boyd steps in to lead them. And I'm sure Barbara Tuckerman will go with you. I haven't asked her because you're much more persuasive than I could ever be, and you should talk to her. And anyway, I really couldn't call last night, could I?" She knew that Sandra would understand; Barbara was usually drunk in the evenings.

A moment of silence passed while Mavis held her breath; then Sandra said, "Okay, we'll do it. I'll call Barbara right away and as soon as Marjorie returns, the two of us will pay her a call."

"Bless you!" Mavis said. "Let me know what I can do to help."

By noon, almost every student in the school, and about half the faculty, showed up wearing T-shirts with the word *NEVER!* emblazoned in red letters across the front. And that afternoon, placards began appearing on walls and other surfaces, including the trunks of trees. Some were hand printed, some computer produced, some obviously created in the art studio. All of them said *FOR WOMEN ONLY!*

THE NEXT MORNING, Gail Kindler got up early to join her husband on his morning run. This, before his day began, was the best time to be with him, to get his attention off the school and on to his family, though it was really not a family anymore, it was just a couple. When they have a child—or was it *if*?—there'd be three, a family again, and he'd have to pay attention.

While he had one more sip of coffee, she went outside to wait for him and almost tripped on the little modeled bonfire, unlit, piled with books and sticks of kindling and little logs. She could feel the hostility of this insult that someone had snuck out of the dorms in the middle of the night to build on their doorstep, but for a few seconds she didn't know what it meant, and then of course it came to her. It was about the article he'd squelched.

So he's a book burner, a Nazi, because he wouldn't print an article about teenage sex? *Well*, she thought, *he'll never see it*. She kicked the wood and the books off the side of the steps into the laurel bushes by the side of the house. Just in time. When he came through the door, eager to run, he was already looking straight ahead, in the direction they would go: across the campus and to the path that went along the riverbank where he loved to run.

She knew he was running slower than he usually did so she could keep up with him. Her hips hurt. He chatted easily, pointed out a flock of geese grazing on a field across the river, speculated about why they didn't migrate south in winter anymore, commented on the hardness of the frozen ground. She didn't answer because she was breathing too hard; if she weren't, she would have been crying.

They circled back to their house, and he went straight in, so intent now to take a shower and get to his office that she thought he wouldn't have seen it if it had been still on the steps actually burning.

That afternoon, Gregory van Buren tried to persuade Fred to outlaw the T-shirts and have the placards removed. "I'm not the Gestapo, Mr. van Buren," was Fred's weary response. He didn't even bother to point out that for every placard removed, several others would inevitably appear in the night, and he chose not to confess that besides, he admired the students for their resistance. Why should they give up?

Though the letter to parents, alumnae, and friends of the school announcing the board's decision to admit boys had come from Alan Travelers as chair of the board, the majority of the responses was addressed to Fred. It didn't surprise him that the board was still considered mere decorative support for a royal head. But the heat of the letters, especially from alumnae, was a shock. These assaults on him were so personal! Hate, he discovered, was just as intimate as love. Reading the letters, he felt soiled, as if the contempt and rage expressed in them were a filth that would stick to his skin, and yet they fascinated him. He had to struggle not to read them twice before he threw them away.

By one week after the board's announcement, most of the alumnae had canceled their pledges, totaling almost six hundred thousand dollars over the next three years—unless the decision to admit boys was reversed—and all but fifty-seven reenrollment contracts—a number close to matching the number of undergraduates who did not sign the Declaration—were withdrawn, leaving behind the five-hundred-dollar deposit.

Nevertheless, Fred, who was still wondering what Mavis Ericksen and Sandra Petrie were going to do, didn't give up. Sticking to the plan, he called alumnae and parents in each of the cities from which Miss Oliver's drew its students to ask them if they would host gatherings at which he and Alan Travelers would explain the decision. Each of them refused.

Only then did he begin to confess to himself that he was running out of ideas.

TWENTY-ONE

In an afternoon in the middle of March, three weeks after the announcement, Francis hurried to be with Peggy, who waited for him in a coffee shop downtown. She wouldn't have been there at all if it hadn't been for Eudora, who the day before had given her some advice she really needed. "Peggy, don't be an idiot. Tomorrow's his birthday. At least take him to lunch."

"You take him to lunch," Peggy had answered. "You and Father Woodward. I'm too angry."

"More confused than angry, I bet," Eudora had murmured, and when Peggy didn't answer, said, "All right, then at least meet him for coffee. One of you has to make a move." Eudora remembered what it was like when there's no move you can make and you have to wait for time to melt regret. She was angry enough with her husband for going away on a reserve Marine Corps training exercise just two weeks after their marriage and then getting himself killed on it! After that, she fed her anger and grief a relentless diet of huge peanut butter and jelly sandwiches and hot fudge sundaes, all the goodies she'd been refraining from to snare a man like him. She grew so round and smooth that he wouldn't have recognized her if he had awakened from the dead and returned to her.

Now Peggy was glad for Eudora's advice. She couldn't bear not to be with Francis on his birthday. All she knew was that she still loved him; she wouldn't have been so hurt and angry if she didn't. Just the same, she hadn't the foggiest idea how she was going to act when they were together.

She kept her eye on the door and saw him before he saw her. And then she did know what she was going to do: ask him to return to their house. That was the move she'd been waiting to make! She wouldn't go on with this sadness one day more.

Nevertheless, she didn't want to wave to him. The least he could do was find her for himself. She knew that was stupid, but she still didn't wave, and then she saw his eyes light up and stay on her face as he moved toward her and sat down with her at the table.

"Hello, Peg," he said and touched her hand.

"Happy birthday," she said. But now she knew that what she had wanted was for him to bend over her and kiss her cheek before he sat down.

"How are you, Peg?" He was still touching her hand.

"I'm okay."

"Peg, I miss you," he said. And she waited for him to say more. But he didn't, because he wanted her to admit she missed him, and then the waiter showed up.

"You want some coffee, Francis?" Peggy asked, taking her hand away. "I'm going to have some coffee. Two coffees, please," she told the waiter. "One decaf for me, and one regular for my friend." The word surprised her, though she didn't mean much by it. It was just a little dig. Just a little revenge, and then she could forgive him and ask him home.

"Friend!" Francis asked. The waiter, looking embarrassed, hurried away.

"Well, you are my friend," Peggy said mildly. "Aren't you my friend, Francis?" She knew it was crazy and couldn't help it, and was amazed to learn how much she needed to punish before she forgave.

"I don't do that to you, Peggy. I never do that to you."

"Do what? What do I do to you, Francis?"

"You know! You know damn well!" Francis's whisper was getting loud. He'd come here full of hope, and the first thing she did was insult him, and now he was too furious to care how loud he was. "Sarcasm, that's what! Not saying anything straight. Hiding behind your rhetorical questions. That's what you do. Hit, and then pretend you haven't."

"Not so loud, Francis. Everybody's listening." She kept her face bland, expressionless, as if she were commenting on the weather.

"See! See what I mean!" he barked. He wasn't even trying anymore to disguise that they were having a fight. Nor did he care how stupid this was, how much they'd regret it later.

The waiter returned with the two coffees. Peggy pointed across the table at Francis. "My *acquaintance* there gets the regular," she reminded the waiter, who put the two coffees down and fled. Francis stared at her across the table, and she could see the hurt all over his face. Later she'd remember that look and know this was where she should have stopped; she'd punished him enough.

"You ran away!" she heard herself saying. What else could she do but hark back to the summer? Otherwise he got away with it. *With everything!* she thought, her fury mounting. "For a whole summer," she told him. "You took a powder. Is that a rhetorical question? Is that straight enough?"

"Peg, this is nuts!"

"And what about him? How do you think he feels?"

"Who? Who the hell are you talking about now?"

"What do you mean, who are we talking about now? Who do you think?"

"Kindler? What's he got to do with this?"

She stared across the table at him. "Ask that again," she said. "I dare you. Ask it again." When he didn't, she added, "It's your fault that we had to let boys in."

"Don't say that!"

"I'm saying it."

"That's the worst thing you've ever said to me."

"Pay the check, Francis," Peggy said, putting some cash on the table, then standing up. "I need to go."

By the time she went through the door, she realized she wasn't angry anymore. She was amazed at how fast it had happened. She would give a billion dollars to do the last ten minutes over. She would ask him back before he even sat down. Now she couldn't ask him back at all. She didn't remember ever feeling quite so sad.

AN OLD MAN at the table closest to Francis caught his eye, then lifted his chin, pointing it toward the door where Peggy had just exited as if to say, *Follow her. Don't let her get away!* Francis acknowledged this with a faint smile, but he didn't move. He was not about to chase after her, begging forgiveness. Besides, something was worrying him at the back of his mind, something that brought relief along with this sadness. He needed to sit there and figure it out.

It's your fault that we had to let boys in—the worst thing she could have said to him, that was true.

But boys aren't going to be admitted. The alumnae won't stand for it, he imagined himself responding. *Neither will the parents.*

Dreamer! he heard Peggy answering. *When are you going to grow up?* But the words were true. "They won't stand for it!" he said again, discovering another reason he hadn't started a riot when Travelers announced that boys would be admitted: "I knew it wasn't going to happen," he said out loud this time, and the man at the next table sent him another worried look.

Francis put a ten-dollar bill on the table—a big tip for his own good luck—and stood up. The old man smiled, relieved that Francis was going to rush after his wife after all. But that was not why Francis was moving so fast, almost tripping on a rug to leave the restaurant. He was going to rush back to campus, go straight to Fred Kindler's office—and tell him how to save the school.

"Really? You want to see him?" Margaret Rice asked. Francis nodded in assent, ignoring her surprise that he was here of his own free will. "All right," she said, gesturing toward the open door to Fred Kindler's office, the signal that anyone was welcome. "Go right in." Then, to his back as he stepped toward Kindler's office, Francis heard Margaret murmur, "Try not to have a fight this time, okay?"

The remark surprised him. Since when did Margaret want to keep things peaceful for this guy? He stepped into the doorway and waited for Kindler to acknowledge him. But Kindler, who couldn't possibly not know that Francis was there, kept his eyes on some papers on his desk; so Francis had to knock on the wall beside him.

At last Fred looked up and stared. "Yes?" He didn't even try to keep the animosity out of his voice. He stayed behind his desk, didn't stand up.

"I have an idea," Francis said.

"Really? What is it this time?"

Francis stepped into the office and started to close the door behind him. "Leave it open," Fred Kindler commanded.

I don't particularly want to be in the same room alone with you either, Francis thought, and walked across the rug to the two chairs in front of Kindler's desk and sat down in one of them. Fred watched.

"I don't know why no one thought of it before," Francis began, striving to sound relaxed.

"Well, I'm sure I'll be able to tell you why," Kindler said.

Francis sat and waited. He was going to hold his temper.

Kindler looked at his watch. "I don't have a lot of time, Mr. Plummer."

"How many more girls do we have to enroll for next year than we did this year to break even?" Francis asked.

"Is this a quiz, Mr. Plummer? I thought it was going to be an idea."

That was it for Francis. He jumped to his feet "If you don't want this idea, I'll take it to the board and they'll tell you to do it. How's that? You want it that way or this way?"

Kindler leaned back in his chair, put his hands behind his head, and stared at Francis. "Isn't there something I should do first? Before I tell you which way I want it—as you so gracefully put it? I mean, shouldn't I be running to the auditorium now?"

"What?"

"To see who's starting a riot this time."

Francis was about to explain that he hadn't known any more than Kindler did that Sandra Petrie had been on campus. But once again he found that he couldn't. Who was he, Richard Nixon, that he had to explain he was not a crook? So instead he accused, "You actually believe that I would do that, don't you? You think I'm low enough that I could set you up."

"Can you give me some reasons why I shouldn't?"

"Yeah, I can. But I won't. You can believe whatever you want."

"That's right," Kindler said. "I can."

"And so can I. But I have an idea that will work, and you are the headmaster."

"All right, I'll listen to it," Fred relented. He was feeling just a little chagrined now, unprofessional, to have been so ruled by his feelings that he could accuse without any facts. Every time he even got near this guy, he screwed up!

Francis sat down again. "Obviously, if we could recruit enough girls to make budget, we wouldn't have to admit boys," he began—a neutral remark to cool things off.

"Mr. Plummer, please! That's what we've been trying to do," Fred said, exasperated all over again.

"Yes, and it hasn't worked."

"Your point, Mr. Plummer? Today! Please."

"It hasn't worked because we haven't given the problem to the alumnae and the parents."

"What do you think I've been trying to do?" Fred was surprised by how defensive he felt. "I'd give my eyeteeth to find a way to explain why we have to have boys."

"You didn't hear me," Francis said.

After a little pause, Fred murmured: "No, I guess I didn't," because now, with just this little hint, he was beginning to get the drift of this idea—and, like Francis, wondered why in the world he hadn't think of it months ago.

"You've told them what the options are: one, admit boys; two, close the school. You've announced to them that you've chosen the first option. They've rejected both of them."

"No. They've chosen the second option, Mr. Plummer." Though he'd caught Plummer's drift and knew it was right, Fred couldn't resist arguing and wanting Plummer to be wrong. "The alumnae have withdrawn their pledges, and the parents have supported the Declaration and refused to enroll their daughters. They've chosen to close the school."

"No, they haven't. That's just how it looks. They can't even imagine this school's not existing anymore." Francis paused, studied Kindler's face. He could tell: Kindler was taking it in. "They could imagine it if it were their problem. But you're still holding on to it, you haven't given it to them. So it's still your job to contemplate a world without Miss Oliver's, not theirs." Now Francis was in his accustomed role again, giving advice to the head. He felt the rightness of it and knew too—a more pressing feeling—a huge regret. That he'd given this up!

"All right, I get your drift, Mr. Plummer," Fred began.

But Francis wanted to make sure—after all, there was a lot

this guy didn't get—so he explained some more. "You go to the alumnae and the parents, and you tell the girls too, just how many girls we have to have enrolled next year and the year after that, and how much money we have to raise by what time if they want to save the school as a school for girls only. You give them very precise goals: how many girls we have to enroll, how many dollars we have to raise by a specific date each year, and challenge them to go out and raise the money and recruit the students within that time." Francis rushed on, explaining. The strategy was so powerful and encouraged him so much that he failed to realize how much easier this would go down with Fred Kindler, and how much it would help his and Peggy's marriage if he gave this idea to her and had her take it as her own to the headmaster—who wasn't listening anymore because he'd understood the strategy from the first minute that Francis Plummer had begun to talk and knew it was perfect and wished he could focus on the joy of it, this gift that would bring him everything he wanted, instead of his resentment that he was not being given it by Alan Travelers, or Peggy Plummer, or Rachel Bickham, or even one of the kids—Lila Smythe, for instance—let alone thinking of it himself. Instead he had to sit here and get it from *Francis Plummer.*

"We tell them we can't do this by ourselves," he heard Francis finishing. "We need you. It's your school, and if you love it as you say you do, then get out there and tell everybody you know to send their daughters here, raise the money, do it. And they will, you know," he added. "They will, and we'll have Miss Oliver's School for Girls forever. Because they'll never stand for letting boys in here."

Yes, Fred said to himself, *and if they don't get it done by the deadline, we'll have no other option than to let boys in and they'll just have to shut up about it. And it won't be my fault, I'll still be able to lead!* "All right," he said aloud. "It's a good idea. We'll do it."

"Fine, I thought you'd like it," Francis said, not sure whether he meant to be sarcastic or not. He started to get up.

Kindler motioned with his hand in front of his face in the gesture that Francis hated so much. "Sit down, please, Mr. Plummer," he said, and Francis sat down again. "Why did you wait so long to come to me with this?"

Because you're the wrong head, Francis longed to say. *Completely the wrong style for us.* But he held his tongue and told the truth instead. "I just thought of it half an hour ago." Later he would wonder if he would have thought of this months earlier at the beginning of the summer if he hadn't gone west instead.

Fred sat very still, his eyes full on Plummer's face. "All right," he murmured, "since I didn't think of it at all."

Francis shrugged to show he didn't care whether the headmaster believed him or not.

"I'll call the board chair this afternoon and tell him your idea," Fred Kindler said.

"Don't make it my idea." Francis corrected. "You're the head. The alumnae and the parents will need to think it comes from you. They need a strong headmaster."

"Which in your opinion they don't have?"

Francis didn't answer.

"All right, Mr. Plummer, we won't go there."

Francis still didn't answer.

"But I will act on your idea."

"Good," Francis said and stood up. He started to reach across the desk to shake Kindler's hand, but then decided he wouldn't. He didn't want to watch Kindler force himself to accept the gesture. So he turned and headed for the door.

"Mr. Plummer?"

Francis faced back. He saw that Kindler had caught him deciding not to shake hands. *This is what Kindler will remember about this*, Francis thought. *That I wouldn't shake his hand.*

"Thanks," Kindler said. "It's a good strategy. It will work."

"Yes it will," Francis answered, "thank you for listening," and moved to the door.

"Close the door after you, please," Fred Kindler said. "I have a phone call to make."

IT WASN'T UNTIL he got home that Francis realized that not only would the strategy he'd invented save Miss Oliver's School and its single-sex mission, but it would most probably also save Fred

Kindler's headship. In the first place, it will work, he said to himself, and even if it doesn't, it will be the alumnae who have failed, and they won't be able to blame it on him. At first he was stunned by this realization; and then he was surprised to be not more disturbed by it than he was, and then it came to him that if he was right and Kindler was the wrong person for the school—which Francis was sure he was—then he'd figure it out for himself and go away on his own. The guy was not a phony, there was not a dishonest bone in his body—and then for the second time this day, Francis wondered why he'd been so slow to understand the obvious. *Oh, well,* he said to himself, *if Peggy knew what we've just done, she'd say I was growing up.*

But Peggy was not going to know. Or anyone else. It was his and Kindler's secret.

Twenty-two

One week after Francis brought his idea for saving the school to Fred Kindler, Marjorie Boyd's tour of Europe came to an end. She was surprised to be so disappointed to be home again.

Marjorie had been looking forward to establishing her life in the Hartford apartment she had rented soon after she was fired and knew she would have to move off campus. It was a fine apartment: new, painted in colors she'd chosen herself, with a view of the river, and far enough away from Miss Oliver's for her to be out of Fred Kindler's hair while close enough to feel at home. But as she unpacked her bags, she knew she didn't want to live there.

Almost as soon as she had arrived, her phone began to ring. Old friends welcoming her back. She wished they'd wait a bit. She needed time to think, to discover why she was disappointed.

"Marjorie, welcome back," a voice on the line said. "This is Sandra Petrie."

For an instant Marjorie couldn't remember who Sandra Petrie was. She'd been expecting Francis and Peggy Plummer.

"Marjorie, are you there?" The anxious voice jogged Marjorie's memory.

"Yes, I'm here, Sandra."

"Oh, it's so good to have you home!" Sandra gushed.

"Thanks, it's good to be home." Now Marjorie was on her guard.

Sandra understood Marjorie's tone. The old headmistress had so much integrity she wouldn't come to a meeting to hear complaints about Fred Kindler. But she'd come to a lunch with loyal friends. Once there, she'd hear what was happening and understand that she was the one who had to save the school. "I'd love you to come to lunch tomorrow at my house," Sandra said. "I'll gather Barbara Tuckerman and Harriet Richardson. We'll have a nice intimate lunch, just the four of us. We're dying to see you again and hear about your trip."

Marjorie hesitated. Just thinking about being with these people depressed her. She remembered Sandra and Barbara as students. She educated their daughters. Harriet Richardson had been a friend for years and a dutiful trustee. But now she didn't want to see them.

"Please come. We've missed you so much," Sandra said, speaking the truth.

Marjorie had no desire to offend and didn't want to lie that she had another appointment. She hadn't had to bend the truth for anyone for months. "Well, thank you very much, I'd love to come," she said.

"Oh, wonderful!" Sandra said. "It'll be such fun!"

EARLY IN THE morning of the next day, the last full day of winter term, Fred Kindler, Milton Perkins, and Alan Travelers bounced across Long Island Sound to East Hampton on a little commuter plane to visit Mrs. Jamie Carrington, president of the Alumnae Association. She would be the first to hear of the new strategy.

Jamie Carrington sent a chauffeur to meet them at the airport in a dirty, beat-up 1960 Plymouth convertible, and though it was a cold March day, she sent it with the top down. The chauffeur, who introduced himself merely as "Jack," didn't shake hands. He wore jeans, moccasins with no socks, and a cracked leather jacket.

"This is what we get for saying we're going to let boys in," Perkins said, grinning at Travelers as they got in the backseat, and Fred sat up front next to Jack. "But it ain't too bad. I was expecting a hitman." And just before Jack started the car, Perkins leaned forward. "Jack," he said to the back of Jack's head, "it's kinda cold. Maybe you could put the top up."

"I can't; it's broken," Jack announced to the rearview mirror.

"No, it isn't," Perkins said mildly. "It's just your boss dicking around with us."

"Hey, it's broken!" said Jack. Then, apparently losing his resolve, he softened his voice. "I'm sorry, sir. It really is broken. I was going to come in the Mercedes like always, but Mrs. Carrington, she told me no, take the little one and stay in my old clothes from changing the oil—so I did."

"Yeah, well maybe after she hears our plan she'll send us back in a hot tub," Perkins said.

"It happened once before," said Jack.

"Oh, yeah?" said Perkins.

"She didn't trust the guy her daughter was dating," said Jack.

"Well, nobody said she was dumb," said Perkins.

"And I was going to meet him at the station. He was coming from New York."

"We going to get a punch line, Jack?" Perkins asked. "We're freezin' our balls off here."

"She told me to tell him to hitchhike. So that's what I did. I drove to the station just so I could tell him to hitchhike. The guy thought I was joking. But when he tried to get in the car, I just drove away." Jack was laughing now at the memory. "You shoulda seen his face!" he said.

"Really?" Perkins said. "So we're not doing too bad here." He put his hand on Jack's leather-clad shoulder. "Drive on, Jack. We'll just sit back and pretend we're Eskimos."

Twenty minutes later they stood on Mrs. Carrington's big front porch, shivering from their ride. Travelers rang the doorbell. "Remember, you speak first," he said to Perkins. "You can let her figure out you never were for letting boys in, you got outvoted. That'll warm her up. We save Fred here for last."

"Yeah," Perkins said. "Good."

They heard footsteps approaching the other side of the door. Travelers put his hand to his left to touch Perkins's elbow; to his right he touched Fred's elbow too. Fred had a sharp sensation of the three of them joined. "Here goes," Travelers whispered. The door opened.

Mrs. Jamie Carrington wasn't anything like what Fred had expected. He had expected "cute." Why else have a name like Jamie? What he discovered was anything but cute. In her mid-forties, the woman frowning at them was tall and stiff-backed. She was dressed in a blue silk shirt, tight jeans, and high heels, her dark hair streaked with gray.

"Good morning," Alan Travelers said, putting out his hand. "This is—"

"I know who you are," Jamie Carrington said, refusing Travelers's handshake. Her voice was a surprise: dark and low, like an angry man's. Without another word, she turned her back to them and started to walk away. They followed her down a long hall to an office where she sat down behind a desk.

There were only two chairs next to the desk. There was a long, silent moment in which Jamie Carrington watched with apparent scientific interest her three visitors make the discovery that one of them was going to have to stand up. Fred started to point this out; she shrugged, and then he saw a big armchair way across the room in a corner. He crossed the room, picked up the chair, hugging it to his chest, and wrestled it across the room. He put it down next to the other two chairs and sat down in it. Travelers and Perkins sat too, pretending to ignore the insult.

"I have fifteen minutes," Mrs. Carrington announced.

"You owe us more than that," Milton Perkins said.

"Fifteen minutes," she repeated.

"All right, Jamie," Perkins's voice was soft. "You owe me."

"You!"

Perkins nodded. "Me!" he repeated.

She looked away from him.

"We've been down a long, long road," Perkins said very quietly. "We've given lots and lots of bucks. Both of us. Me even more than you." She started to say something. He put his hand up. "I'm the only one who's given more than you."

"Yes!" she blurted. "Precisely! The only one. You matched me every time and then some. Precisely."

Perkins hesitated, frowning, trying to understand. Then a dawning: "Oh," he exclaimed. "That's what you thought!"

"That's what I knew! The minute I heard what you had done, I knew. Why else?"

Perkins shook his head back and forth. "Not for that reason," he murmured as if only to himself.

"You traitor!" she said. "You sneaky old crook!"

"Just a minute," Travelers said. "I can't tolerate—"

Perkins put his hand out, placed it on Traveler's shoulder. "Hold it, Alan. We're about to get to the bottom of something."

Carrington turned on Travelers. "Yes, hold it. I don't have the slightest intention of conversing with you."

Alan stood up. He'd had enough. "Well, then, we're leaving," he said. "This meeting isn't going to get anyone anywhere. Fred, Milton, let's go."

"Sit down, sit down, you're rocking the boat," Perkins said.

"All right," said Travelers, still standing. "You tell me why."

"Yes, why?" Fred asked, standing too, already thinking of other alumnae to approach.

" 'Cause now we know," Perkins said. "This lady thinks I gave more money than she gave so I could win, so we could get away with—"

"Well, didn't you?" asked Carrington. "Didn't you? Well, it's not going to happen. No boys! Do you hear? You bastard!"

"Oh, for Christ's sake, Jamie, shut up," said Perkins very quietly as if he were asking for a cup of coffee. "Close your mouth and open your brain."

She just stared.

"The way it usually is," Perkins said, "when you're not so excited." Then after a little pause: " 'Cause we're here to tell you were not going to let boys in the old place. You're the first to know. We've got a plan, and you're it, Jamie; that's why we're here."

"A plan?" she said. "That's why you're here?"

"And don't try to tell me you can't give any more. You've got lots more, and you're going to be giving it, just like me. You could sell this castle you've been getting lost in since you were born, and the house in Baja, and the one in Vermont. People like us only give what's left over."

"You're not going to let boys in?"

"That's right. No boys."

"Never?"

"Jamie, get a grip."

"Oh!" she said.

"Let Fred here explain," Perkins said.

Travelers and Fred both sat down again, and Fred explained the scheme. He started with the reasons for the first decision, but when he saw the frown begin to return to Carrington's face, he zipped through that part and focused on the new plan. He watched her face grow more and more relaxed, saw her nod in agreement, repeated the idea in a different way and concluded.

Carrington took her eyes off him the minute he finished.

"So," Travelers said. "The idea is that Fred as head, you as president of the Alumnae Association, and I as president of the board will send out an invitation together to the alumnae to attend meetings at the school and in our major cities, where we will put the challenge to them."

"All right," she announced. "I'll sign it."

"And we hope you'll communicate personally with key people to urge them to come."

"Okay! Okay! I said I'll do it." Carrington put her hand up, cutting Travelers off. Then she turned directly to Perkins. "I'm sorry for what I said, Milton."

"Hey!" Perkins said. "It's over."

"It's a good plan," she said.

"You bet," he said.

"I'll do it," she repeated. "I'm yours."

"Thank you!" Travelers exclaimed.

"Wonderful!" Fred said.

But she didn't look at either Fred or Travelers. It was as if they were not in the room. She reached across the desk and shook Milton's hand. "You're right." she told him. "We've been down a long road together."

Perkins looked embarrassed.

"So I'll sign the letter, call some people, and then I'll get back to you."

"Get back to Fred here, not me," Perkins said, his hand finally released. "He's the head."

Carrington shook her head. "I'll get back to you," she said, looking directly at Perkins. Then she stood, still refusing to look at Travelers or Fred. "Jack's outside waiting," she said. "He'll take you to the airport now."

"In the Mercedes, right?" Perkins asked.

She smiled at him. "For you? Of course."

Alan got up out of his chair. "Thanks for supporting our plan," he forced himself to say, and put out his hand to shake. Jamie Carrington just looked at him.

"Yes, thanks," Fred murmured, standing up too. But he was damned if he was going to offer to shake her hand. Nor was he going to say goodbye. He headed directly for the door. Travelers followed.

Perkins lingered for a moment, and Fred heard him say, "Wise up, Jamie. You're blaming the wrong people."

"If you say so," she said.

"I say so," Perkins answered.

PERKINS SAT UP front this time in the big, warm Mercedes. Jack tried to start a conversation, but no one wanted to talk. Finally, Fred said, "I guess I know what kind of signal I got from her."

"Me too," said Travelers.

"Forget it," Perkins interrupted, turning around to Fred. "Choose the signals you want to see, not the ones you don't. You're the boss."

"Milton's right," Travelers said to Fred as Jack pulled up to the entrance of the little airport. "You're the boss, and you brought us this great plan. It will energize everybody, and you're the one who thought it up."

"Yup," Perkins said. "You've saved our bacon, Fred. And the next time we come back here, Jamie's going to be so happy that the school's full and with no boys in it she'll send Jack here to get us in a—" he hesitated, then turned to Jack. "In a what, Jack?"

"I don't know," Jack said, grinning. "Maybe a yacht?"

AS FRED KINDLER, Milton Perkins, and Alan Travelers were boarding their plane on the other side of Long Island Sound to come home, Marjorie Boyd got out of her car in Sandra Petrie's driveway and walked around to the back of the house to look at the view. She held her hand on the bun she wore at the back of her head to keep the wind from blowing it apart. Down the hill, a little to the north and on the other side of the river, lay the campus of Miss Oliver's School for Girls. In the distance the white clapboard buildings glimmered in the sun. Girls, tiny in the distance, walked the paths, and the lawns, brown from the winter, swept to the edge of the forest that lined the river.

Once again, she was surprised. It was not nostalgia that overwhelmed her but disbelief. "I used to be the head there," she said aloud into the wind.

She walked around to the front of the house, hoping that Sandra and her guests weren't watching her. When the door opened to her knock, it was not just Sandra who greeted her but Harriet and Barbara standing in the doorway, three pairs of expectant eyes staring into hers, and she wanted to step back away from them.

Each of them hugged her, gravely. "I'm still devastated," Harriet Richardson finally said. "For you and the school. So angry I can hardly speak."

"Please, ladies," Marjorie said. "I hope that's not what we are going to talk about."

"Of course, not!" Sandra exclaimed. "We want to hear about your trip." She led them into her living room. "Sit down there so we can look at you," she said, smiling at Marjorie and pointing to the biggest chair. Marjorie sat in it; three other chairs faced hers as if she were on stage.

"Well, where should I start?" Marjorie asked.

"At the beginning, of course," Barbara said.

Marjorie began with the plays she'd seen in London, while Sandra poured white wine and everyone pretended not to notice Barbara put her hand over her glass. When Marjorie got to her time in Paris, Barbara asked her if she had looked up Sidney Plummer, who was still living there, supporting himself by working in a wine cave.

"No, I didn't," Marjorie admitted. "I would have loved seeing him. He's my godson, you know. But being with Siddy would bring back all my memories of the school. I took this trip to get away and start a new life."

It seemed to her that each of them leaned forward, and she realized they had misinterpreted her. They were waiting to hear her tell them that she couldn't forget, that she was angry and bitter and still wanted to be the headmistress of Miss Oliver's. Well, she did feel that way sometimes—but less and less, and anyway she wouldn't talk about it. She resumed talking about her trip, how exciting it was, how refreshing, and saw their disappointment. They asked a few more questions and told their own travel stories because they didn't know what else to talk about.

But Sandra didn't give up. "It's time for lunch," she announced. "We'll go into the dining room now."

As soon as they were seated at the table and Sandra had served the salad, she turned to Marjorie and said, "Do you know what's been happening at the school?"

"I know the library burned down," Marjorie answered.

"Oh, my dear, that's the least of what's happened," Harriet said.

They waited for Marjorie to ask what happened, but she didn't.

"They are going to admit boys!" Barbara announced.

"I thought they might," Marjorie said mildly.

Everyone stared.

"Maybe they had to," Marjorie said, as if she were making an offhand comment. "Maybe they had no choice."

"Of course they had a choice," Barbara said, clearly bewildered.

"Please, Marjorie," Sandra said. "I know you're trying to be diplomatic."

"I'm not trying. I can't help it," Marjorie said. Maybe that would shut them up. She was just as surprised at how angry she was at them as they were by the way she was acting.

"I understand exactly how you feel," Harriet said. "I experienced what you are presently experiencing. But the very reason for the school's existence was at stake, and then I realized that it had been planned all along and they had brought in this Kindler person for the express purpose of bringing in male students, and I finally decided it was a higher ethic—"

"What do you want?" Marjorie said. "Get to your point." She couldn't believe she was being so impolite to Harriet Richardson. "Ladies, just say it," Marjorie said when no one answered Because she knew they couldn't just say it. They had expected her to get angry to hear boys were to be admitted, and say it for them: that she would lead a revolution, stage a coup. "I know what you want me to do," she told them. "And I won't. You should have known I wouldn't. So let's change the subject."

There was a lengthy silence. None of the women looked at her. They felt a more painful betrayal than when she had been fired.

"I think I'd better leave," Marjorie said, and stood up from table. She started to walk away. Sandra got up to beg her to stay. But Marjorie said, "No, that's all right. You stay here and talk." When she got to the dining room door, she turned back to them. "They wanted me to change, and they were right. But I didn't want to, so I didn't." She put into words what she was at last willing to admit. "If I'd understood what was happening, I would have simply told them, 'No, I don't want to change.' I would have resigned before they asked."

As she drove home, she made a decision. She would break the lease to her apartment, get away, find a very different place to live, a larger scene. New York City! She still had lots of time for some new career there, she was only sixty-three. She wasn't about to ruin her memories by living in them.

When Sandra got home, she called Mavis to tell her what had happened. "Well, then, we'll have to try something else," Mavis said.

TWENTY-THREE

Julie Lapham spent the last afternoon of spring vacation with her parents, nailing shingles on the roof of a studio they were building for a Dartmouth professor. She was proud of being so sure-footed on the sloping plywood. To the west she could see across to the Vermont side of the Connecticut River to the hill where her family's house was hidden in the trees. She couldn't imagine her parents living anywhere else, doing any other kind of work, though she knew, because she'd made them tell the story over and over again when she was a little kid, that twenty years ago they had moved up here from New York without the foggiest idea how they were to make their living. Well, this was what they chose to do, she thought proudly: build post-and-beam buildings whose frames didn't have a single nail in them and were solid as a rock and beautiful. She knew how hard they had worked to learn this specialty and build this business. Now they had more offers for work than they could accept.

Maxwell Lapham, Julie's father, climbed up and down the ladder to bring the shingle bundles up. A big man with a red beard and red hair under a floppy fedora hat, he wore an intense expression and lifted the bundles easily. Tracy Lapham was much smaller than her husband, less tightly wired, and, Julie noticed, nimbler on the roof. Her hair was black, shining in the sun. Julie was proud of how well she teamed with her parents; she knew what to do without their telling her.

They worked until it got too dark, and when they got home, Julie went to her room to pack for her return to Miss Oliver's in the morning. Her parents went to the kitchen to make dinner together.

In her bedroom as she began to pack, Julie was already homesick, and her desire to stay home felt overwhelming. If she could stay home with her parents and be their only focus now with Charley away at college, she could prove to herself that she was no less beloved in her their eyes than he was. And after that happened she would dare to ask her mother and father who her biological parents were. When she first had learned she was adopted, she didn't want to know. It would have made her feel as if all her life she'd been living in someone else's home. Now she wished she'd gotten up the nerve to ask the question during her vacation. There was no way she was going to ask it tonight and then have to leave and deal with her feelings about it alone. She needed to be at home.

She packed dispiritedly, grabbing her clothes from her bureau drawers and closet and tossing them into her suitcase, shirts and shoes and skirts all jumbled together, making an even bigger mess than she usually did because tomorrow when she would transfer it to her room at school, it was guaranteed to piss Clarissa off.

And while her daughter packed in her room, Tracy Lapham looked up from her work to gaze out the kitchen window at the Connecticut River flowing south toward where her daughter would go tomorrow. "I feel like we're selling her down the river," she said to her husband, who was scrubbing potatoes at the sink. Miss Oliver's School for Girls could insist until it was blue in the face that it was an independent, not private, school, but Tracy would continue to think of all such schools as private, antidemocratic havens for the privileged, who should be supporting public schools. And a boarding school to boot! Why would anyone who loved their children even dream of sending them away when they're still so young? It was lonely enough with Charley away at college.

"Well, it's hardly selling when the one going begs to go," Maxwell said.

"We should never have given in," Tracy answered.

"Hindsight is easy, Tracy," he said. "Forgive yourself. You remember how disturbed Julie was when we told her she was adopted."

What Tracy remembered then was saying to Charley, "We thought you'd like a little sister," and seeing the look on her daughter's face that said she'd always thought she *was* Charley's little sister, until that instant when she found out she wasn't. "Now that we know how much she hates it at that school, we should let her stay home."

"She's never told us that she hates it."

Tracy ignored his remark; he was just being stubborn. Julie wasn't going to admit that she was wrong, that she was wasting her parents' money, that she was running away only because she hadn't known what else to do with the way she felt. "There's no fiat from heaven that she has to go back," Tracy said.

Maxwell left the sink and put his arms around Tracy. "Please, dear," he said. "We've been over this so many times before. She needs to finish what she started."

In his embrace, Tracy didn't answer. She knew he was right. That's what they'd always taught their children: no matter how hard it got, you stayed the course.

Book Four: Spring Term

TWENTY-FOUR

First thing on the first day of spring term, the whole school assembled in the auditorium at Fred's request, and while everybody was wondering what the bad news was this time, Fred stood on the stage and announced, "I have great news. The plan has changed. Boys will *not* be admitted to our school." And then he rushed on to explain before the roar of gladness drowned him out. "The board, at my suggestion"—for Alan Travelers had commanded him, several times, to put that in—"has challenged your parents and the alumnae and, yes, each of you to go out there and talk about this school and recruit and recruit and recruit until we're full again. And if everyone works together—and I know everyone will—then we'll never have boys at Miss Oliver's School for Girls!"

There was a moment of silence, as if no one was breathing, and then a roar even louder than he had expected, and the students were standing up and hugging each other and in the back two teachers were dancing with each other. Halfway back on the aisle Francis Plummer was standing too. Fred looked him straight in the eye. *You told me to pretend it was my idea*, he wanted to say. *Well, that's what I'm doing*. Plummer returned the stare, but he was the first to look away.

"Isn't it great news?" Fred said to the school, when at last the noise died down enough. Because, by God, he was going to celebrate too! "Isn't it wonderful?"

Suddenly there was very little noise. The cheering stopped, and the students stared at him. *Why are you celebrating?* they obviously wanted to know. *You're the one who tried to let boys in.*

He stared back at them. "I do think it's wonderful," he said bravely. "And it is a great way to start spring term." Silence again. He could see how restless they were. They wanted to celebrate—but not with him. "I'm proud of you for signing the Declaration." Silence again. They didn't believe him. "I really am," he said, and still there was silence.

So he dismissed them, and they trooped out of the auditorium, buzzing with the news. Then he left the stage and walked down the aisle and followed them out. It was warm outside on this early April day.

The students and the faculty gathered in clusters on the lawns. They talked loudly, laughing, celebrating. He stood on the steps of the auditorium watching them. From one of the faculty clusters, Rachel Bickham looked across the lawn to him, smiled, and gave him two thumbs up. Then he walked alone to his office.

He spent the next few days waiting to see how many people responded to the invitations and checking the enrollment data—especially the reenrollments. Very few came in. He persuaded himself that these undergraduates and their parents were waiting to see how the alumnae reacted to the challenge before they committed. And he continued to spend a good deal of his time walking around the campus to make himself visible, show his face. For that's how one built trust: through personal connections—like he had at Mt. Gilead, where the students had hung out in his office so much, telling him things they'd never tell their parents and kidding him about his funny clothes, that it had been hard to get his work done. But now at Miss Oliver's the students kept their distance even more than before. Nevertheless, he showed his stubborn side, never stopped trying to reach out to them.

The members of Sam Andersen's spring term dig for Pequot artifacts on the Oliver campus was one group with whom Fred's reaching out was successful. Lila Smythe and Sara Warrior were among the fifteen students who showed up each afternoon at the fraction of an acre they had roped off to begin with on the northeast corner of the campus. They welcomed him each afternoon when he stopped by to say hello and were especially glad when he had the time to put on some old clothes and join them at their work. Lila was always glad for a chance to be in Mr. Kindler's company, and

Sara was grateful to him for giving his blessing to the agreement Mr. Andersen had made with her father that any artifacts they would find would be brought to him so he could make the legal arrangements to make them the possessions of the Pequot Nation.

At the end of two weeks, Nan White came to Fred's office to report on the progress of the new strategy. She seemed nervous. Normally he met with her in her office—on her turf—but she had insisted this meeting take place in his.

"Out with it," he said.

"It's just not happening."

"How many for the meeting here at school?"

"So far, exactly seventeen."

"Didn't we figure there were at least eight hundred alumnae within two hours' driving range of the school?"

"We did."

"How many for New York?"

"On April 17, there were eleven—if you count spouses. On April 28, three."

"Philadelphia?"

"Zero."

"Zero!"

"Zero. Evidently they all got together to refuse."

"All right," he murmured. "I guess I don't have to ask about Chicago, Cleveland, and San Francisco."

"Pretty much the same. Altogether we have fewer than a hundred."

"Well, well, well," he said, trying to smile. "I hope American Airlines will give our money back."

"Don't give up yet," Nan urged.

"You don't sound convinced." When Nan didn't answer, he said, "What does Jamie Carrington say?"

"She doesn't say."

"What do you mean, she doesn't say?"

"I talk with Mr. Perkins, not with Jamie Carrington. I don't care what she thinks, or Mavis Ericksen, or anybody else says. I don't work for them. I work for you!"

"Thanks," he said. He had to turn his face away for an instant. *Mavis!* he thought. Of course. Revenge. He'd give anything to know what passed between Jamie Carrington and Mavis Ericksen. He could only guess that Mavis had called people up to urge them not to serve as hosts, but he didn't really believe that even if she hadn't, the results would have been much better. Mavis was only a small part of this.

Then he felt as if maybe he was wandering too far from where he needed to be. "You don't work for me, Nan," he reminded her. "You work for the school."

"Sometimes I hate this school!"

"Me too," he said. "Funny, isn't it?"

Outside, through the French windows in his bright sunny office, the campus flowed with girls going to classes. The lawns had turned a deeper green in the last few weeks. Buds were swelling on the maple trees. "Well," he said. "It's pretty obvious what my next move has to be."

"Don't you dare!"

" 'Long as I'm the head, it isn't going to work."

"Not another word! I don't want to hear one more damn word like that!"

"You know, I got the signal right away at Jamie Carrington's house. I did my best to ignore it. I'm associated with the move to let boys in. I'm tarred with that brush. So they won't follow me in the other direction. That's all there is to it."

"It's just not fair!" Nan said.

"No. But it's the truth, isn't it?"

Nan didn't answer. She didn't take her eyes off his face either. She was struggling not to cry. He appreciated that. He really didn't think he could handle it if she started to cry. "It's the truth, isn't it?" he asked again. "Come on. You're a professional. You need to say what you really think."

"All right," she said very quietly. "I think you might be right."

He had to work hard now to keep the hurt from showing on his face. After all, he'd asked for it. "So," he said, standing up, "I'm going to think about it. Very seriously."

"If you do, I will too," she exclaimed, her voice breaking. She saw the hurt, plain as day around his eyes and in the thinness of his smile. "I leave here the minute you do!"

Don't do that, he started to say. *The school will need you more than ever.* But he couldn't get the words out, it was too much to ask. "I'm going for a walk," he said. "I need some air."

When Fred came back from his walk, he found that Nan had left him a note. *Please don't make that decision yet*, it said. *Promise me you'll try one more thing first: get Francis Plummer involved in selling the new strategy. I'd hate it if you didn't try* everything*—even this!—before you make that decision.*

TWENTY-FIVE

Fred swept Nan's note off his desk and into the wastebasket. *How in the world can you ask me to do that?* he imagined asking her. Then he leaned back in his chair and stared out the French doors at the campus. It was not just having to ask Plummer for help that swelled his resentment so. It was the knowledge that people would follow Plummer's leadership and spurn his! Now he wondered if he could even look Francis Plummer in the face.

He got up from his desk and walked restlessly around in his office. He knew what he had to do. "Try everything," he said to himself, repeating the words in Nan's note. It was a comfort to know from her underlining that word that this was just as distasteful to her as it was to him. Then he opened the door to his office. "Get in touch with Mr. Plummer, please, Ms. Rice," he said. "Tell him I want to see him in his next free period."

THIRTY MINUTES LATER, Francis was sitting in a chair in front of Fred Kindler's desk, staring at the Mickey Mouse watch and the monstrous exclamation point beside it and thinking about how surprised he was that the goofy watch on the wall didn't insult him anymore. Instead it made him sad, sorry for Kindler, and he wanted to explain how off-key it was. But you didn't talk about style with this guy. He was all substance.

As if substance was ever enough!

"We need you to do something for us," he heard Kindler say, and took his eyes off Mickey Mouse and shook his head to clear his thoughts. He knew Kindler would say "I need" to anyone else.

"No?" Kindler said, misreading Francis's head shaking. "You're telling me you won't do what we need?"

"Wait a second," said Francis, very flustered now. "I mean, no, I didn't say I wouldn't—"

"You're sitting there shaking your head!"

"Not for that! I was just clearing my thoughts."

There was a long awkward silence. Francis still didn't know why Kindler had summoned him. For a minute it looked to him as if Kindler couldn't remember either, or, more likely, he was so disgusted that he'd just say the hell with it—whatever it was—and cancel the meeting.

"We need you to send a message to the alumnae," Kindler said.

Francis waited for Kindler to explain. He was embarrassed to see how much it pained Kindler to admit he needed Francis's help.

"Because they still think you're God almighty," Kindler said.

Francis turned his face, looked out through the French doors. He thought maybe he'd just get up and leave.

"Sorry," Kindler said, quietly, "I didn't mean to descend to that. They think of you as the fine teacher that you are. That's what I should have said."

Francis listened for sarcasm in Kindler's tone. He didn't hear any and felt even more embarrassed now. Praise from Kindler, however reluctant. That was awkward. And—he had to admit—a little welcome too.

"It really is something to be proud of," Kindler said.

"I am," said Francis almost under his breath.

"Good," Kindler said, and nodded his head, and sat perfectly still behind his desk. Francis sat still too, returning Kindler's gaze.

"Our strategy's not working," Kindler said at last.

Francis still said nothing.

"At least my part in it isn't exactly turning people on. To them I'm the guy who wants to let boys in. Among other things." There's that damn self-pity again, Fred Kindler thought, and wished he could have the words back. But it was too late, and Francis Plummer had heard them. As if he were trying to tease pity, maybe even mercy, out of him! He'd rather die.

But Francis heard no self-pity. He was too busy thinking about how he wouldn't be in Fred Kindler's shoes for a million dollars if anybody asked him—which nobody who really knew him would.

"So we want you to write a letter to all the alumnae, telling them you are behind this idea a thousand percent and you want to see them all at these meetings," Fred said. "We want you to be there at every meeting. You have more clout than anybody else around here. It's as simple as that."

Out of what had become his habit, his knee-jerk reaction, Francis spent a lively instant seeing himself refusing. He had the power now. He could do anything he wanted.

"Mr. Plummer?"

"Of course," Francis said. "Fine. I'll do it."

"At your invitation, they'll come. We all know that," Fred said. He leaned toward Francis, studying him. "And you are going to open each meeting, introduce me, tell them you think I'm just a *dandy* head. Right?"

Francis nodded.

"The rest of us will do the real work of running the school. You just do the selling." Kindler's remark wasn't meant to be an insult. He was just describing the facts.

But that was exactly why Francis took it as an insult—and was almost proud of himself for ignoring it. "All right. I understand," he said. "I'll do it."

"Thank you," Kindler said. "This whole plan was your idea, and it is a good one. Your part in it will make it work."

Francis was grateful to Kindler for saying this. "We'll make it work," he said. "Both of us. It will save the school."

Kindler nodded his head, agreeing. "I believe it might," he murmured. And he added, "Please go to Nan White's office the first minute you can. She has the details." Then he stood up. It was clear he wanted this meeting to be over.

"I'll go right now," Francis said, and stood too and offered his hand. This time Kindler took it and they shook. "I wish I'd thought of this before," Francis said again.

Fred didn't answer. What could he say? He hadn't thought of it at all.

THE ATMOSPHERE IN Nan White's office was so icy, it took Francis completely by surprise. He'd always felt comfortable with Nan—that is, when he'd been aware of her, a mere administrative functionary, miles away from the heart of the school where he resided. Now, as he entered her office, she loomed large.

Nan studied him for what seemed like forever without saying a word, and when he tried to start the conversation by acknowledging why they were together in her office, she cut him off and ran through all the details of the plan. "That's it," she said. "That's the whole plan." Her expression was rigid.

"You're not going to ask me how I like it?" he joked.

"No," she said. "I don't give a damn."

No one talks to me like that! he started to say, but checked himself and said nothing.

"Why didn't you get behind Fred Kindler in the beginning?" Nan stared at him. "It was all up to you, and you didn't do a thing."

And before he could answer, she said, "If you're thinking of telling me it's complicated, don't."

Francis checked himself again. He was not going to waste his time by giving in to his anger; he was going to write the letter, just do his job. He started to stand up.

"That's right," Nan said. "Go write that letter. Bring it back to me, and I'll correct it."

"Correct it!"

"Yes. Correct it."

On his way out, Francis closed the door gently behind himself.

Later it would occur to him that checking your feelings, holding them inside where they burned, was what a leader must do. Every day.

Twenty-six

Several days later, when Lila Smythe arrived early at the dig, she was glad to see Mr. Kindler dressed in his old clothes. She approached him while he was talking to Mr. Andersen. Mr. Kindler turned to her and smiled, obviously glad to see her.

"I need a partner today," she said, handing him a trowel.

"Well, now you've got one," he said, happy for her invitation. "We've been partners all along."

She smiled, acknowledging this recognition, and Sam Andersen's gaze traveled between the two of them. "It's true," Sam murmured. How much these two have made happen! Every new direction, every critical event, found them at the center. It was natural they would gravitate to one another.

Kneeling beside Mr. Kindler as they troweled the earth, excavating carefully, Lila felt the same calm trust in him she did that day in his office when she confessed her ambivalence, how she had longed for Marie Safford's vehement moral purity and chose compromise instead, and he'd told her she'd always have to live with such ambiguity because she'd always be a leader. She remembered how much she wished that meeting wouldn't end. *Partners!* she thought, savoring his remark. *Peers!*

Near the end of the session, two students in another part of the dig found several artifacts: a bone fishhook, a shard of pottery, a notched stone hoe whose handle rotted away long ago. That evening, Sam Andersen phoned the good news to Sara Warrior's father. He was delighted to receive it.

The next morning, a week before the series of meetings for explaining the new strategy was scheduled to begin, Nan White reported to Fred in an email (cc to Francis Plummer) that Francis's letter had produced only four additional acceptances. Fred wasn't surprised at these sparse results. He knew the reason. *If I just went away they'd come in droves*, he told himself. But Francis was surprised—and angry. *When I invite you to come to meetings to hear about how you can save the school, you goddamn better come*, he fantasized shouting. *Who do you think you are?*

For the next three days, while the buds on the big maples turned into leaves, only two more people accepted, and this failure weighed on Francis. His frustration mounted until he finally decided to write another letter, much more strongly worded—and more than that—to make a very strategic list of fifty people and get on the phone with each of them. He went to Fred Kindler's office to tell him of his plan.

Francis heard no anger, only resignation, in Kindler's mild "good morning" as he sat down across the desk from Kindler. The breeze coming through the open doors brought the smell of clipped grass from the first mowing of the year, and across the lawn Francis could see the gray foundation walls of the new library. When the construction workers arrive at eight o'clock, this silence would end, and the exhaust of their machines would pervade the air. That was fine with Francis. The sooner the new library was up, the sooner Peggy would stop grieving the old one. Then he realized that this must be what Kindler was thinking too.

Fred followed his glance. He was proud of himself for convincing the board not to use the insurance money that had resulted from the fire to prop up the school's desperate finances instead of for building the new library. "This is a time we need to be bold," he had told them. Not to replace the library would have been a clear signal that the board was sure the school would fail, a self-fulfilling prophecy. "It's coming fast," he said now to Francis, thinking that if he resigned, the new library would be the only visible mark he left behind—and he wouldn't even be here when it was finished. "They're right on time. They don't dare not be. They know I'd shoot them," he said.

"I bet they do," Francis said, making sure his tone made clear he meant it.

"This fall, she'll cut the ribbon," Fred Kindler murmured. He was not looking at Francis. He was still gazing across the lawn at the construction site.

Francis knew Kindler meant Peggy would cut the ribbon.

"I appreciate that," he said. He was very embarrassed. "Instead of some big donor," he added.

"Perkins would be the one," Kindler said, turning his attention back into the office—but not really to Francis. "He's given more over the years than anyone." What he didn't tell Francis was that Milton Perkins was also anonymously funding the architects' fees. "But Peggy's cutting the ribbon," Fred Kindler said. "It was Perkins's idea as much as mine."

"Well," Francis repeated. "I appreciate it."

Kindler looked at him squarely. "I have to tell you something."

Francis waited.

"I don't care whether you appreciate it or not." Still no anger. Just a statement of fact. Fred Kindler had cut his losses.

"Okay," Francis shrugged.

"It's for Peggy. It has nothing to do with you."

Francis didn't respond and kept his face expressionless. He was going to take whatever Kindler handed out. For the sake of the school. That was his mantra now. Be Kindler's partner, no matter what.

"So?" Kindler said. "You wanted to see me about something?"

"I need to write another letter," Francis urged. "They need to hear twice. And I'm going make a bunch of phone calls. Then I think more will turn out."

Behind his desk Kindler was shaking his head. "I don't think that's going to work."

"Let's try."

"I'm thinking of an alternative strategy."

"Oh? What's that?"

Kindler studied Francis. "This time, Mr. Plummer, you will not be among the first to know."

There was a little silence while Francis wondered what he was supposed to say to that—and then he knew what Kindler was not telling him. *You're going to resign!* he almost said, but caught himself. Kindler's steady eyes stayed on his face, and Francis forced himself not to look away.

Kindler was raising his eyebrows now—as if to ask him why, since now he knew, he didn't just get up and leave?

But Francis didn't move. Too much to take in all at once: this was exactly what he'd been hoping for. Then why did he feel so disappointed? "Look, I just wish we could have—" he began.

Kindler put his hand up. "Please don't."

"All right," Francis said. He started to stand up. He was surprised to discover how sharp was his regret. No more chances to be what he should have been since the day Fred Kindler came. No chance to rectify!

"There is only one thing I want from you now, Mr. Plummer: that you not repeat this conversation to anyone."

"I won't," Francis said.

"Do I have your word?"

Just a little while ago, that question would have angered Francis. Now it made him sad. "You have my word," he said.

Halfway to his classroom, Francis thought maybe he should turn around, go back to Kindler's office, and urge him to reconsider. The idea shocked him. Kindler's leaving was everything he'd wanted for a year. But he kept on walking. He knew he wouldn't be urging Kindler to stay for Kindler's sake or for the school's, but for his own. To give him another chance to redeem himself. Well, he'd had his chances, and they were gone. Besides, Kindler wouldn't listen.

Not to him, he wouldn't.

TWENTY-SEVEN

Fred stared at Plummer's back as he went through the door. Then he stared at the door, not seeing it, until long after Plummer had disappeared.

How unseemly that Alan Travelers, the chairman of the board, for God's sake, was not the first to know! How grotesque that Francis Plummer found out first! Before even Milton Perkins, the other board members, before Rachel Bickham, Peggy Plummer, even Lila Smythe!

Nevertheless, he was not surprised that Plummer had figured it out. It was as if Plummer had wanted his resignation so badly he could read his mind and find it there. And then that look of regret when he finally he'd gotten exactly what he'd been hoping for—and wondered if he wanted it after all. That's what Fred Kindler thought about as he sat very still at his desk, staring at the door.

In fact, Fred realized, Plummer had found out even before Gail did. It wasn't until Plummer guessed it that Fred realized he had made the decision. Right up until he'd said he was thinking of an alternative strategy, those words were true, and the minute he'd said them he knew he wasn't merely thinking about resigning anymore. He'd made up his mind.

Last night, he had told Gail he was considering resigning. He wasn't surprised at her neutral reaction. She'd already lost the place she loved the most, the one that felt like home, when they'd left Mt. Gilead. No other move would hurt that much. "Here I go again," he'd told her last night, "dragging you around."

"Please do," she'd said.

Now in his office, he got up from his desk, went into Margaret Rice's anteroom, and asked her to cancel his appointments for the day. Then he'd go straight to Alan Traveler's office to submit his resignation.

"Everything all right?" Margaret asked softly.

"Everything's fine," he lied. He was still surprised she wasn't his enemy anymore.

He reentered his office, closing the door behind him, sat down at his desk, turned on his computer, and wrote his resignation letter. He was surprised at how fast it came. As if he'd already known the words.

Dear Alan,

After much thought ["and much prayer," he wrote and then erased; what he chose to pray about was his private business] *I have regretfully come the conclusion that it is in the best interest of the school that I resign effective at the end of this academic year.*

I think you know how much I have always admired this school and how much in my short tenure here I have come to love it in a very personal way. And let me put in writing now what I hope I have conveyed to you in our many conversations: that I am deeply grateful for your leadership and support. While the sadness of leaving will subside in time, my joy and satisfaction in the partnership you and I and other board members have enjoyed will be permanent.

My sense is that the school has made some steps toward maturity during my time here. I'll leave the judgment of that to others.

I have no doubt, however, that the recent decision to retain the historic commitment to single-sex education for girls, and the inclusion of the alumnae and parents in the drive to bring that commitment to fruition, is precisely the right one. I am just as strongly convinced that this critical initiative requires a school leader who comes fresh to the scene, in no way associated with our recent short-lived consideration of admitting boys.

This is the single reason for my offering you my resignation. It is compelling. Therefore, please accept it.

Sincerely,
Frederick Kindler, Head of School

Then, as he read over his letter, his statement that the school had taken some steps toward maturity under his leadership seemed off-key. He deleted the sentence, and the one after that. For though Alan Travelers would agree with this claim, this letter would be published to the whole school community—which would not agree. Instead the community would take the statement as his ungraciousness in failure and an insult to Marjorie Boyd. No one wanted to hear him imply that Marjorie's school was immature.

But when he read the revised version, the deletion stuck in his craw.

Being gracious meant he would have to be disgraced; he would have to pretend he hadn't gotten anything done and just slink away? He couldn't bring himself to do that. He was the one who had brought the truth out about the finances and forced the board to deal with the realities, instead of drifting. That was something. And then the little interior changes, unrecognized by most—which showed how much they were needed—like sending the message that people needed to be successful or be fired by firing the beloved but incompetent business manager, and resisting the personal agendas of powerful people by not firing Joan Saffire; and insisting that people be on time; and replacing Francis Plummer with Rachel Bickham and Peggy Plummer as wise counselors. If he didn't make some claim to at least a little success, his resentment would overwhelm him. So he typed the sentence back in, changing *steps toward maturity* simply to *progress*, printed the letter, slipped it into an envelope, which he put in his inside sports coat pocket, and headed for his car.

"No," said Alan Travelers a half hour later in his office. "I won't accept it. It's as simple as that. You've got a three-year contract. You're stuck with us; we're stuck with you." Then he crunched the letter into a ball and tossed it in his wastebasket. "That's that," he said. "Time for lunch."

But in the restaurant Fred insisted. "It's not going to work with me as the head."

"Shut up and read your menu," Alan said.

So they ordered and talked of other things, and the waiter

brought their meals, and then they tried to eat and couldn't.

"Suppose we bring Perkins into this?" Fred said after a while.

"Milton? Why?" Though of course Alan Travelers knew. He'd been Perkins's friend for years.

Because he's a cynic, Fred wanted to blurt; then, still inside his head, corrected himself: a realist, remembering how unsentimentally Perkins had been willing to close the school rather than surrender its mission. He was sure that Perkins loved Marjorie Boyd, admired her, and was grateful yet had been willing to push her out the door. Out loud he said, "If Milton doesn't agree with me, I'll consider changing my mind."

"Consider? That's pretty vague, isn't it? How about tearing up the letter and going back to work?"

"Let's see what Milton thinks," Fred said.

"All right," Alan conceded. "I'll invite him to lunch tomorrow. Meantime you go back to work, get all excited again, and change your mind."

"Nope. Call him right now. I don't want this thing left hanging. Besides, he's bored as hell sitting around that club. You call him now, he'll be in your office before we get back."

Alan threw his napkin down on the table and stood up. "All right, but he's going to have a fit," he said. "You better be ready with the CPR." Then he headed for the phone.

Fred was right: Milton Perkins was waiting for them in Alan Travelers's office by the time they got back from lunch. He turned from the window where he'd been standing, watching the river, as Fred and Alan entered. Fred felt Perkins's eyes on his face and wondered if he'd guessed.

"Let's sit down," Alan said, pulling one of the chairs out from a table in the center of his office. "Otherwise you're going to fall down when you hear the news."

Perkins sat down, keeping his eyes on Fred.

"Fred here wants to resign," Alan said.

"*Wants* isn't the right word," Fred said, still standing.

"Sit down, Fred," Perkins said softly. "Tell us about it."

Fred sat down, and so did Alan.

"He's just a little discouraged, that's all," Alan said. "Who wouldn't be?"

"No, Alan," Fred said. "That's not the point."

Without taking his eyes off Perkins, Alan cut Fred off. "We're not going to give up, do you hear? And I'll not have this man destroyed. I'm not going to let—"

"Hold it, just hold it for a minute." Perkins leaned forward. "You just said that Fred wants to quit because he's discouraged? He wouldn't do that. You know him better than that."

"I'll give you that," Alan conceded after a pause. "I take that back. You bet. But he can have a dumb idea once in a while, just like the rest of us."

"Milton, the numbers just aren't there." Fred said. "No one's accepting the invitations."

"That's not your fault!" Alan interrupted. But Perkins, sitting very still, didn't take his eyes off Fred and waited for him to finish.

"The strategy isn't going to work with me as the headmaster," Fred said to Perkins. He was weary of this; it already felt as if he'd been over it a thousand times.

" 'Cause they put you with letting boys in," Perkins finished.

"That's right," Fred said.

"And with them losing Marjorie," Perkins added.

"That too," Fred said.

"Well, Jesus! Talk him out of it, Milton!" Alan said.

"I can't," Perkins said mildly. "He's right."

Alan stared at Perkins, speechless.

Then Milton turned to Fred and said, "You're a hell of a guy, Fred. Most everybody else would have to be told."

Twenty-eight

Even though the light was not on in Julie's side of the room, Gregory van Buren saw at first glance that that was not Julie in the bed. It was a laundry bag stuffed with clothes under the covers made to look like a person sleeping. He'd seen this many times before on his nightly check and probably been fooled by it once or twice. But he'd never seen it so carelessly done as this. It looked exactly like what it really was: a laundry bag stuffed with clothes under the sheet. He understood right away that Julie wanted to get caught.

"Where is she?" he asked Clarissa, who was studying at her desk on the other side of the room. Her desk lamp was the only light that was on.

Clarissa shook her head. She didn't want to tell.

"On campus?"

The look Clarissa gave him let him know that Julie was not on campus. She understood the reason for his question: if Julie was on campus, partying probably, doing booze or drugs or both, she was in big-time trouble with the school, but at least she was safe. "All right then, she's off campus," he said. "I'm going to call her parents and notify the police." He turned to leave the room.

"She's with her brother," Clarissa blurted.

He turned back. He looked at his watch. "Well, then, I'll wait one hour. If she comes back before that, tell her I want to see her right away."

Gregory was surprised at himself. He'd always been a stickler for the rules. But then there was another thing he was a stickler for: not giving youngsters what they wanted just because they wanted it. The child obviously wanted to be expelled. So that's exactly what wouldn't happen. Just the same, he was nervous as he waited in his apartment. Who knew what she was doing? He looked at his watch again. The hour was almost up.

Just in time, she knocked at his door. He felt a huge relief. She was here! She was safe! He'd been imagining terrible things. Drunken sex with some friend of her brother she didn't even know, or bleeding to death in a mangled car her brother crashed into a tree. Now Gregory was angry at her for making him so worried, and he didn't stand up. He'd be the king on his throne, she the frightened subject. "Come in, Julie," he told her through the door.

He saw right away she was perfectly sober, another relief. "You're home early," he said sarcastically. And yet it was only midnight. She could have stayed out till dawn.

"Come in and sit down," he said, pointing to a chair facing his. He could tell by the way she held her shoulders and by the calm look on her face that she was not the least bit afraid of him, not at all ashamed of what she'd done. She thought she'd gotten exactly what she wanted by getting caught.

"Have you called my parents yet?" she challenged.

"No. Should I have?"

"You haven't?"

"No, Julie, and I probably won't."

"What, then?"

"What would you like to happen?"

She didn't answer.

"Do you want to go home?"

She looked surprised. "You haven't even asked me where I went," she complained.

"Forgive me if I'm not curious. You're here now," he said. "And safe. That's what I care about."

Oh, I thought all you cared about was books, she started to say, and stopped herself. She wouldn't have said it as an insult, merely as a statement of fact. But she was surprised he cared about her. She didn't believe he didn't want to know where she'd gone that night. "We went to a rock concert. My brother drove. He had a date," she said. "He got me one too with a guy I danced with another time I snuck out," she added to make sure he knew that tonight was not the first night she should have been expelled. She didn't say how bored with each other she and the boy who'd been so great to dance with were.

"Tell me about your brother," Gregory said.

That stopped her for a minute. "He goes to Trinity," she said at last.

"I know he does," Gregory said. "It's in your folder."

"He's not really my brother," she said. "I'm adopted, and he's not."

Gregory nodded his head. He knew that too. Julie started to cry, and Gregory understood that Julie's problem was over his head. "I think you should go see Ms. Rugoff in the morning," he said as gently as he could.

She shook her head, still crying.

"All right, see someone at home."

"How can I do that if you don't kick me out?"

"Julie, this is a school, not a prison," he said, but she shook her head, so once again he tried another tack. "What do your parents expect?"

She was frowning now. *Why is he asking me that?* "They expect me to finish this year and come back next year and graduate."

"I see," Gregory murmured. "And do you plan to spend all next year attempting to get yourself expelled?"

She gave him a little grin through her tears.

"Well, then?" he said.

"Well, then, what?" she said, feeling stubborn.

"Julie, please, fill in the blank. When you don't want to attend a certain school, the alternative to being expelled from it is—"

"You mean I should just quit?"

"*Resign* might be a more appropriate word. But either word would indicate you're not a victim, and you're not being devious."

Julie thought about that for a little while. "I'm sorry if you think I was being devious," she said.

"Oh, I don't know if you should be sorry," Gregory mused. "You thought you didn't have a choice, and now you think you do. That's hardly an occasion for regret."

"Well, all right," she said. "Maybe I'll call my parents and ask them."

Gregory gave her a questioning look.

"All right, I'll tell them," Julie said tentatively. She saw that he was not satisfied and realized she wasn't either. "Yes, I will. I'll tell them!" she said again, firmly this time. She'd stopped crying by now.

"A wise decision," Gregory said. "Will you finish this year?"

"Of course! I'm not crazy enough to waste the credits. There's only another week of classes, and then I'll go, and I won't come back next year. I'll graduate from my high school at home."

"Another wise decision," he said.

"I'll call my parents tomorrow. Thanks for not turning me in."

He shook his head.

"I mean thanks for helping me make my decision."

Gregory smiled and stood up "I think you've had a very productive evening, and I've enjoyed our conversation."

She stood too, amazed at this teacher. He'd seemed so pompous and stuffy before, and boring. She stepped forward, put her arms around him, gave him a hug, and felt his body stiffen. How shy he was, how scared of his feelings! She stepped back, thinking she'd made a mistake. Then she saw he was glad she had hugged him. She felt a rush of compassion and knew she trusted him. Except for Clarissa, he was the only person she'd made a connection with at Miss Oliver's.

A few minutes later as Gregory lay in bed, it came to him that in Marjorie's time he wouldn't have made the decision he'd made tonight. He would have turned Julie in to Marjorie, and she would have decided her punishment. That punishment would not have been expulsion. Marjorie would have persuaded Julie to stay. *Well*, Gregory said to himself, *Marjorie was wrong about a lot of things.*

Twenty-nine

In the last week of May, Francis got a message from Alan Travelers's secretary: he needed to drop whatever he was doing and come to Travelers's office right away to meet with the executive committee. She didn't tell him why, and Francis didn't ask.

Maybe I'm going to be fired, he thought as he drove north along the river's edge toward Hartford. Maybe Kindler changed his mind about resigning and was going to get rid of him instead. Francis wondered whether Peggy knew he'd been summoned by the executive committee; she, too, would guess that he was about to be fired. If he were living with her, she would know, and they would talk about it. They always told each other their worries and comforted each other, he told himself. He shook his head. *Liar!* he thought. He knew damn well the problem between them hadn't started with Marjorie's dismissal and Fred Kindler's arrival. Those events had just brought their troubles to the surface.

Then he realized the board wouldn't do the firing. Heads did that, not boards. But it was no consolation.

A homeless person sat on the sidewalk holding a *God Bless* sign near where Francis parked. Impulsively, Francis gave him ten dollars—a ten-spot offered for propitiation to God. "God bless you, sir," the homeless man said, as if reading his sign, and Francis, feeling a sudden intimacy with this derelict stranger, had a strong desire, which of course he squelched, to tell him everything that had happened lately at Miss Oliver's School for Girls.

Five minutes later he was twenty stories up, entering Alan Travelers's office, and found Travelers, Milton Perkins, and Sonja McGarvey sitting side by side, Travelers in the middle, on the other side of the conference table in the center of the room. Francis moved toward them like an actor moving upstage into the lights. Travelers was pressing his hands together, making a narrow tent in front of his mouth. He was frowning. Perkins was the only person to stand up. He was smiling. "Good to see you," he said. "How's the teaching business going?"

Before Francis could answer, McGarvey said, "Please, let's just skip the bullshit. Let's get this over with." She didn't look at Travelers when she said this; her eyes bored into Francis, her expression full of disgust. Francis felt his nervousness leaving, anger rising in its place, and stared back at McGarvey. He was no more ready for bullshit from her than she was from him. He sat down across the table from the three of them.

"You got any idea why you're here?" Perkins asked, sitting down again. The gentleness in his tone surprised Francis.

Francis shook his head. The idea persisted: they were going to fire him.

Travelers reached for a stack of papers. He took the top one off, slid it across the table's polished surface to Francis. "Read this," he said.

"Yeah," McGarvey said. "I'm sure you'll be surprised."

It was two pieces of expensive paper, joined on their left margins to make a four-page booklet. On the top page he read: *An Important Announcement to the Oliver Community*, and Francis knew what he was going to read inside. He'd seen so many of these! Marjorie used to pin them to the bulletin board in the faculty room when they came in from other schools. "To keep everybody informed," she used to say. But everyone knew what she was really saying: "Look! Heads roll everywhere. But *I'm* still here!"

He lifted the top page, opening to the two inside pages. On the left, a letter from Fred Kindler. On the right, Travelers's response. He read Kindler's letter three times before he moved his eyes to Travelers's letter:

Dear Fred,

It is with more sadness than I can ever convey to you in one short letter that I accept your resignation.

As you know, when you first tendered it, I refused to accept it. The idea of our school's losing a leader of such integrity was more than I could fathom.

But when you insisted, I had at least to consider your offer—because, Fred, it was you who was insisting, you who described your reason as compelling. I have so high a regard for your leadership, your wisdom, and your dedication that what compels you to make a decision for the good of the school you have served with so much honor compels me to its consideration.

Therefore, after much consideration, I accept your resignation. I wish you and Gail much happiness. The school to which you journey next will be most fortunate.

Yours in admiration,
Alan Travelers, Chair of the Board of Trustees

Francis kept his eyes on the letter. "You win!" he heard McGarvey whisper. "Congratulations!" He looked up at her. But he saw the words on the pages he'd just read more clearly than he saw her face. "Don't even think about trying to pretend you're surprised!" he heard her say. "You've been working for this for a whole fucking year!"

"Sonja, let it go!" Travelers commanded, and McGarvey shrugged and looked away.

Francis made no answer to her, surprised he didn't have her by the throat. In fact, his huge regret, grown even more painful now that he'd read these confirming letters, left little room for anger, he could only feel so much at once. He turned away from her as if she were merely a nuisance and asked Travelers, "Have you mailed them yet?" If not, there was still some hope. But as soon as the question was out of his mouth he wondered why he'd asked it. Kindler was not going to retract.

"Not yet, it's incomplete still," Travelers said. And then shut up. He studied Francis's face.

And then Milton Perkins did the talking. He leaned across the table to Francis, white shirt cuffs shining at his wrists against the blue of his suit coat. "Awful late in the year for this to happen," he observed.

Francis said nothing.

"Isn't it?" Perkins asked, smiling now, and waiting for Francis to agree.

Francis still said nothing. He had no idea what was coming next.

"Too late to find a permanent head," Perkins said. "We need an interim."

"That's you," Travelers said to Francis. "You're the one. We need you to run the school."

THIRTY

If you spend one more second pretending you're surprised, I'm going to barf," McGarvey said, and this time Travelers didn't object. Francis Plummer had sat there like a stone and hadn't said a thing for so long that Alan was sure he was faking. But in fact, Francis was in shock.

Yesterday Sonja had at first refused to go with Alan and Milton to Fred Kindler's office to tell him that Francis Plummer would be the next headmaster, if only for a year. Of course it was the right and courteous thing to do: tell Fred Kindler before calling Plummer in and appointing him. But *Plummer*! "How can we tell Fred Kindler that?" she had asked, though she agreed with the decision. The alumnae would follow him, it made a lot of sense. She didn't want to see Fred's face when they told him.

But of course she had relented. Sonja McGarvey didn't get where she was by ducking the hard jobs. She remembered how Kindler had turned his head away and looked out through those big French doors in his office yesterday when Alan said the name: Francis Plummer. Then Kindler had turned his head back, and she could tell he wasn't surprised. Bitter, yes. Crushed. Humiliated. But not surprised. She admired the way he'd kept his face blank. But she saw his shoulders stiffen.

Alan had seen it too. "I know this must be hard," he had said.

"I understand," Fred had said. "It makes a lot of sense." He didn't tell them he'd already been through this once, when he had had to ask Francis Plummer to write those letters—for exactly the same reason that this decision made a lot of sense. He wanted to ask whether the decision was unanimous or whether there was argument among the board members, but of course he couldn't.

"It was a reluctant decision," Alan had said, as if reading Fred's mind. Almost the truth. He wasn't about to go into it. Because most of the reluctance was in the executive committee, his and Sonja's and Milton's, who nevertheless knew what would work for the school.

Near the end of the meeting Sonja had said to Fred, "I wish you'd fired the little prick," and realized she was about to cry. Sonja McGarvey shedding tears, that would have been a sight! She was grateful to Milton Perkins for rescuing her—and Fred—from that grotesquerie by standing up to end the meeting. He'd seen what was about to happen.

"Try to get a little distance, Fred," Perkins had said.

"Thanks," Fred had said, standing up and shaking each of their hands. He had meant *thanks for your good advice*—which it was still much too early to be able to follow—and *thanks for telling me first*, but mostly *thanks, Milton, for ending this meeting.*

Now, a day later in Alan's office, Sonja took her eyes off Plummer and turned to Alan and said, "Alan, tell Superman here why we chose him." She was going to get this much revenge at least.

"Because the alumnae will follow you," Travelers said.

Francis waited for more, but Travelers's mouth was shut. All three were watching him.

"Well?" asked Travelers.

"If that's the only reason—" Francis said, then shut his mouth.

"Well, it *is* the only reason," McGarvey said.

Now all Francis could see in the room was McGarvey's face. He leaned forward into the table, and this time he could imagine himself reaching across it and squeezing her throat. "Maybe it is," he said. "But I am surprised. Whether you believe it or not, I didn't plot for this." *I'm a teacher, not a head*, he wanted to yell. Besides, he didn't give a damn what she thought, he just didn't want to hear her talk. "Don't open your mouth one more time," he told her. "Do you hear? Just keep it closed." McGarvey stared back at him, then looked away.

"All right," Perkins said into the silence. "You didn't plot. That clears the air. That's good."

"Fair enough," Travelers said. "We assume you'll accept."

"I need a day to think," Francis said. His own words surprised him. He needed a day to think? Was he crazy? After being told, as if he couldn't figure it out for himself, that the only reason for the offer was that the alumnae would follow him—and only till they found the one that's right!

"We hoped for an answer today," Travelers persisted. "The school needs the certainty."

All three watched intently as Francis considered. "You'll get it tomorrow," he answered at last. "I'll consider it very carefully, and if I think it's what the school needs, I'll accept."

"Don't you think we can decide what the school needs?" Travelers asked.

"Not as well as I can," Francis answered mildly, standing up and moving toward the door. "I've been working here for thirty-three years." He didn't wait around for Travelers to respond.

Thirty-one

Less than halfway home it dawned on Francis: there was no way he could say yes to Travelers! Even if he wanted the job. Even if he thought he was right for it, which, of course, he didn't. How in the world could he tell Peggy that he was going to take Fred Kindler's place? *For the good of the school?* he could hear her ask. *The good of the school would have been your helping him. And now you're taking his place?* He would never even tell Peggy what the board had asked him to do. Nobody else either, of course. And he'd call Travelers this afternoon and refuse.

But first he'd tell Fred Kindler. He should be the first to know. He hurried to Kindler's office.

"Why not?" Kindler asked from the other side of his desk. "You scared?"

Taken aback, Francis didn't know what to say. "Forget I said that," he heard Kindler mutter.

Francis didn't respond. He was still trying to let Kindler know he could say anything he wanted.

"You'll have plenty of help," Kindler said. "There's lots of *good* people."

"That's not the point," Francis said, ignoring the sarcasm.

"Lots of good people. Rachel Bickham, for one. And your own wife."

Francis shook his head.

"You've been asked to serve!" Fred Kindler's voice was hard. "You can let them really run the school. You can be the figurehead. It's the *image*, you know." He pronounced the word as if it were a disease.

For all his intentions, Francis bristled. "If I did it, I wouldn't be a figurehead!" he said, and Kindler raised his eyebrows. "I'd do the goddamn job!" Francis blurted.

"Then, do it!"

"No. I'm not the right person."

"I'll give you that!" Kindler said. "Finally we agree on something." Then after a pause. "Who is?"

"Rachel Bickham. You know that." Francis's words surprised him. He'd never thought about who should do the job—only that he shouldn't—until just then when Kindler had asked the question. "We both know that," he added.

Kindler leaned forward, put his eyes on Francis. "Yes," he said. "We do." He swept his hand across his empty desk. "But she's new. Only been here five years. Nobody calls her Clark Kent, and besides, she didn't take sides."

"That's one of the reasons—besides being who she is," Francis urged and added, "Comes fresh to the scene. You said it yourself in your resignation letter that's what we need. Five years around here is pretty fresh."

"So?" Fred Kindler asked.

"So that's what I'm going to tell Travelers. I wanted to tell you first."

"You'll have to tell Milton Perkins. Travelers has resigned." Fred Kindler's tone was matter-of-fact. As if this news were inconsequential and not surprising.

Francis felt Kindler's eyes boring into him. He made himself look back. Kindler was sitting there waiting for his reaction, but he didn't have any; he'd hardly spoken ten words to Alan Travelers. Then it began to dawn. "Oh!" he said. "He's associated with admitting boys too."

"You catch on fast," Kindler said.

"The same way you are—"

"You catch on to some things faster than others."

Francis ignored the remark.

"Alan Travelers is a wonderful person," Kindler exclaimed. "He deserves better!"

"So do you," Francis blurted, and Kindler looked surprised. "That's the other thing I came in here to say," Francis added lamely.

It wasn't exactly true; he would have liked to put it a different way, but this was what came out. Across his desk Kindler stared mildly at Francis's face.

"I'm sorry," Francis finally said. "I could have helped you more. Maybe we could have made it work." He didn't say that he still thought Kindler was the wrong person for this school. That was not for him to say. Never was. All he wanted to do now was to acknowledge his own failure. "I regret my actions," Francis forced himself to say. He was going to speak slowly, say it all. "I apologize."

But Fred put his hand up in front of his red mustache, like a traffic cop, cutting Francis off. "Part of me appreciates your wanting to get your feelings off your chest, but another part says to me that maybe you shouldn't get them off so fast. Maybe you should live with them for a while." He stood up. "And that's the part I'm going with for now." What would his struggle be worth if Plummer got off so easy?

But he was already acknowledging to himself his resentment that by identifying Rachel Bickham as the best person to be the interim head, it was Francis Plummer—again!—who had come up with the right idea.

"All right," Francis said, standing up. He turned, walked across the office toward the door.

But Kindler discovered he didn't want this meeting to end, not yet, and had to call Plummer back. Damnation! "Mr. Plummer?" he said to Francis's back.

Francis turned.

"Thanks for refusing the offer," Kindler said. He wanted to acknowledge that Plummer was putting the school ahead of himself.

But Fred Kindler should have known that the only way Francis would interpret his thanks would be as one more insult to go along with all the rest. What Francis heard was his gratitude for admitting that he wasn't worthy and would ruin the school if he were its head.

Nevertheless, Francis said nothing as he turned away again, and closed the door behind him.

"Well, I never push a job on a man who doesn't want it," Milton Perkins said to Francis, who had just phoned to tell him he wouldn't take the position.

"Rachel Bickham?" Perkins said a minute later when Francis told him who should be the head. "Fred thinks so too?"

"Yes, he does."

"Well, he ought to know. And we know she's a star. We'll talk to her."

"Good. She's perfect for the job."

"Nobody's perfect for anything," Perkins said. "But we'll talk to her."

Francis nodded his head as if Perkins could see him.

"You're going to keep this under your hat till we get it squared away, right?"

"Of course," Francis said. And hung up.

THIRTY-TWO

Out of the blue that afternoon Rachel Bickham got a call from Milton Perkins telling her he wanted to see her as soon as possible. He didn't offer the reason, and she knew better than to ask over the phone. It was obvious something big was up. She'd find out what when she got there.

Of course, by the time she was halfway to Hartford, she'd guessed: Perkins was going to tell her that Fred Kindler had resigned. The realization made her very sad—and not a little angry—that the good man deserved much better. But she was much too aware to be surprised. It was clear to her that no one—certainly not a man—who directly followed the thirty-five-year tenure of any head, let alone the charismatic Marjorie Boyd, could possibly succeed as the head of Miss Oliver's School for Girls. The person to follow Marjorie would inevitably be the sacrificial buffer between the past and the future. She wished she'd seen that more clearly when Fred Kindler was interviewing for the job. She would have told him.

Of course he should have known himself. But that's another thing she admired in him. That he was no politician. But a man of faith. And hope.

Now she thought she knew why Milton Perkins was singling her out to hear this news before the rest of the community: Board Chair Alan Travelers, along with some other board members, must be interviewing Francis Plummer for the interim head's position, while Milton Perkins took her aside to test the waters in case Francis refused. It just went to show you never knew what was going to happen next.

And yet, however amazed she was—and sad for Fred Kindler—at how fast everything was happening, she was not surprised that she was the one the board would choose if Francis Plummer refused.

You couldn't have as much impact as she had, be as natural a leader, without knowing it.

Milton was waiting for her in the foyer when she arrived, and led her out to the terrace overlooking the river behind the club. "More private out here," he said. They sat in deck chairs facing each other, his back to the river, she facing it. Over his shoulder she saw the glint of the sun on the water. "I don't suppose you have any idea why I've asked you here," he said, studying her face.

She didn't answer. That was up to him to figure out.

"Fred Kindler's resigned," he said.

Even though she'd already guessed, she was shocked to get the news. Milton was watching her. "That's terrible news," she said at last.

"You think so?"

"Yes, I do. It makes me very sad. And very angry."

"Good, I thought it would," he said. And waited for her to speak.

But she didn't. *Your move*, she thought. *Not mine.*

"We need an interim head," he said. "To run the school next year."

Rachel answered, "Of course you do."

"We need one right away," Milton said. "Like tomorrow. We need everyone to know there's a boss. That there's someone in charge. With a plan."

"Yes, we do," Rachel said, beginning to feel impatient.

"You need to know that Alan Travelers has also resigned."

"He has? Why?" And then, before Milton could explain, she figured it out. "Oh, of course."

"Yeah, pretty wacky, isn't it?" Milton asked, smiling a little and shaking his head, and she could see the sadness in his face "You'd think a school could be free of politics." And Rachel thought, *Really! A school! How could you think that*? And Milton, seeing the look on her face, said, "Don't worry, that's what I wish, not what I think."

"Well, that's a relief," she said.

"Anyway, I'm the chair now."

"That's also a relief," she said.

"We want it to be you," she heard Milton say. "We want you to take the job," and she waited for the rest: *if Francis Plummer refuses.*

But Milton said nothing, just watched her face, and then at last he said, "We asked Francis Plummer first."

"I thought you would," Rachel murmured. It sounded a little dumb, she knew. She should have been answering him. But in spite of her knowing this could happen, she was shocked and it was all she could think of to say.

"Just so you know. From me. Now. Not later from some jerk."

"Thank you."

"He turned us down. Doesn't think he's the right one." And then, as if talking to himself, he said, "Somebody tells me he's not right for a job, I always agree, who the hell am I to argue?" And when she didn't answer—because what can you say to that?—and she was wondering if she'd have to give up all her teaching, Milton said, "He says you're the right one."

"That's good, I'm glad he does," she said. She knew she'd have to answer soon. She already knew she was going to say yes.

"So does Fred Kindler."

"Well, if Fred Kindler thinks so, I do too!"

Milton smiled. "So you're accepting? You're going to run this fun house for us?"

"Yes, I accept!" Rachel said. "Assuming the board approves."

"They'll approve," Milton answered. "Unless they want to find a new chair. It's not as if we have a lot of time." Then after a little pause, he added, "Besides, I'm the guy with the money," and broke into a grin.

"Well, then, if that's how it is," Rachel heard herself say. If Milton Perkins could do whatever he wanted, so could she. "You want me now, you keep me." The words surprised her as she said them. The idea had just come to her. It was outrageous and she loved it.

"What?"

"I'm not going to be your head just because I'm convenient," she announced. "You've got to want me enough now to want me permanently." There were only twenty-two people of color—her mom would say "colored people"—who were heads of school in the whole National Association of Independent Schools. This time the arrogance was going to come from the other direction!

"Jesus!" said Milton. "I'll be goddamned!"

She started to say, *If it doesn't work out, I'll get out of your way before you have to ask, just like Fred did.* Then thought better of it. That's a promise she'd make to herself; she didn't owe it to anyone else. "You don't want to be picking a new head every year," she said.

"Jesus!" Milton said again. He was smiling, his face lighting up. Rachel Bickham was right. The school wouldn't survive a whole year of not knowing who was going to be the permanent head. Make a bold, decisive move right now—forget all the fancy bullshit process stuff, asking everybody what they think. He didn't give a damn what anybody thought, it's what he thought that counted. He stood and stuck out his hand. "You're a hell of a lady!" he told her.

Rachel stood too to take Milton Perkins's hand. "You obviously agree," she said. This was actually happening!

"You bet I do!" They were standing face-to-face, her hand in his. "You think I'm going to announce that we don't know who's minding the store when I can announce this?" Then he let go of her hand and took her elbow, and they walked side by side, he in his blue suit, she stately in her summer dress, to her car. In a world where people didn't have to think about the color of skin, one would have thought they were a father and daughter walking across the lawn.

"I'm going straight to Fred Kindler's office," she told him when they got to her car. "I want him to be the first to hear—and from me."

Milton Perkins nodded, smiled, and opened the door for her. "I think he's going to like your news," he said.

FRED WASN'T SURPRISED an hour later that it was Rachel Bickham standing in the doorway to his office. It would have to be either Rachel or Milton Perkins—they were both too classy to let anyone else know what had been decided before he did.

"Well, aren't you going to ask me in?" Rachel said, smiling.

"Of course! Sorry to be so spacey." He didn't know how to tell her that his head was so full of all the feelings brought up by what he was sure she was going to tell him that for a minute he couldn't focus on the simple act of inviting her in.

Just inside the door, she put her long fingers lightly on his shoulder. "I'd space out too," she said. It was just what he wanted her to say, and he was grateful.

He watched her sit down in one of the chairs in front of his desk, stretch her long legs out in front, put her arms up on the back. He sat in the chair opposite her. "I think I can guess what you're going to tell me," he said. "I hope I'm right."

"You are," Rachel answered.

"Oh, Rachel." he said. "Congratulations!"

"Thanks. From you that means a lot." She took her arms from the chair back, pulled her legs in, put her elbows on her knees, and leaned forward. "Are you all right?"

"I'm all right."

"You are?" she asked, studying his face. "Because I don't think I would be."

Her questions made him feel shy all of a sudden; he had to make a conscious effort not to look away. "It hurts a little," he admitted.

"I bet it does!"

"But your news makes it better."

"Good," she said. "Thanks. I could have worked for you," she went on, looking at him even more intently now. "I could have worked for you for a long, long time. I felt good working for you," and before he could thank her for saying these words, which he knew she meant, Margaret Rice put her head in the door.

"I think this is one you better take," she said, pointing to the phone.

"Later," he said, but Margaret shook her head and he remembered the last time she insisted that he interrupt his meeting to take a call. He picked up the phone.

It was Hannah Fingerman's lawyer again. "You have no idea how lucky you are," he said.

"I don't understand," Fred said. He thought the lawyer meant that he was lucky to have quit as head of school. Well, he didn't feel lucky at all. *How does he know?* he wondered.

"We threatened him, and he called off his suit, and so we win," the lawyer said.

"Threatened? Who?"

"Mr. Fingerman. Who else? I mean, he was the one with the

motivation, wasn't he?"

"Wait a minute," Fred said. "Are you telling me that—?"

But Mr. Singleton was too proud of himself to wait. "The police let him off after one or two interrogations," he said. "Even though he would get two million dollars out of it. They were convinced he didn't do it, that he's not the type to run around hiring arsonists. Particularly since there's no evidence of arson. They think it was a wiring problem that started the fire, but they aren't absolutely sure, right? So we were able to convince Mr. Fingerman that we could put a lot of pressure on the police, stir up a lot of trouble by letting the media know how much money he'd be able to keep because the library burnt down. They'd have to haul him in again, and maybe he'd end up in court."

"Oh, come on, you know he didn't do it," Fred said. What he really meant was he didn't believe any of this. He couldn't afford to.

"Of course I don't think he did it, Mr. Kindler. But I believe we could make an awful hassle for him, and I know he's a softie who doesn't like to fight. Otherwise his ex-wife wouldn't own all the businesses he started, would she? But when I absolutely knew we won was when Mr. Warrior called me to tell me that you've found some artifacts."

"Oh!" Fred said. "He did?" He'd already guessed what was coming next. "But we've only found a few," he said.

"So what? If you look long enough, you'll find lots," the lawyers said, "and that's another reason to persuade Mr. Fingerman to capitulate. Because you're obviously going to make another Collection, which will provide the same distinguishing element to the curriculum its predecessor did. Thus the basis of his case collapses, doesn't it? Besides, maybe he still loves his wife. Anyway, you've got your two million dollars now. Congratulations."

"Whose idea was this?" Fred asked.

"I was the one who convinced him the new Collection destroyed his case," the lawyer said, but Fred guessed it was Sara's father's. He wondered if it was Milton Perkins who had laid the threat of suspected arson on Hannah's husband. And then decided he didn't want to know.

"Persistence pays, Mr. Kindler."

"Yes, it does," Fred said.

"So now the school will get the gift," the lawyer said. "It'll take a month or two, but it's going to happen. There's nothing in the way now. It's certain."

"That's wonderful news," Fred said.

"Yes, I thought you'd think so."

"Well, thanks," Fred said. "Thank you very much."

"Is something wrong? You don't sound as happy as I thought you would."

"Everything's fine. It's extremely good news. Thank you very much."

"Fine, we'll stay in touch."

"Yes, we will," Fred said, and hung up.

"Anything wrong?" Rachel asked the same question the lawyer had. She could see the shock on his face.

He didn't know how to answer even if he thought he should. Besides, his instinct was telling him she shouldn't know—or anyone else—not until after she was officially appointed interim head. If she found out now, she'd think he had another chance to succeed and change her mind about taking his job. "Everything's fine," he said, and when she didn't answer he knew she didn't believe him, so he added, "Really. It's good news, actually."

"Well, that's good," she said as brightly as she could. And then, as much to get his mind off whatever the bad news was as to tell him the exciting news about herself, she said, "Fred, guess what: I'm not the interim! I'm permanent! I'm the *real* head!" She told him about her conversation with Milton. "He didn't have much choice," she said. "I had a pretty good hand to play."

"Rachel, that's wonderful!" he said after he got over the surprise. He wanted her to know how glad he was for her, how right for the school the boldness of this stroke. "You're exactly the right person at exactly at the right time," he said. But in an instant another thought arrived: she had his treasure, and she had it with a security that he never had, and in spite of his regard for Rachel, he was crushed again. Now he wanted to be the headmaster of Miss Oliver's School for Girls more than ever.

Later, thinking back on this moment, he would be proud of how forcefully he set aside this grief so he could be gracious to Rachel. "Exactly the right person!" he said again, repeating this truth. "How clear it all is."

"Nothing would have ever gotten clear if you hadn't come along to define the issues and stick them in our faces," she said, standing up to go. She reached, took his hand, pulled him up out of his chair, and hugged him. "You need to remember that."

"Thank you, Rachel," he said, hugging her back. Her words were a blessing, and he was glad for the school that she would be the head.

Just the same, he envied her. And she was a friend! It was exactly how he didn't want to feel.

THE NEXT DAY the board unanimously approved Perkins's recommendation of Rachel Bickham. They were relieved by the handy and worthy solution she provided, just as he had predicted they would be.

And besides, if it didn't work, they could always fire her.

On Thursday, one day before graduation, the package of letters went out: Fred's resignation letter to Alan Travelers, Travelers's regretful acceptance, and from Milton Perkins the announcement that the brilliant, young, and *female* Rachel Bickham would be the headmistress. To show how fortunate the school was, the newly appointed board chair, celebrated for his steadfast loyalty to girls-only education, also sent Rachel's stunning curriculum vitae.

Before classes that same Thursday morning, Fred Kindler got the word around to the faculty that he wanted to see them in the faculty room. As soon as most of them arrived, he told them of his resignation. He made it standing up and didn't wait for their reaction. Instead, he turned and left before any of them could think of what to say.

Then at Morning Meeting he told the students. A few of the girls broke into smiles, and several made silent gestures of applause. A few others, surprising him, frowned, shocked and disappointed. But mostly there was silence. Then Milton Perkins stood. He didn't say anything in praise of Fred Kindler, didn't say how grateful the school should be, what a hell of a guy he was—because Kindler had made him promise not to. He simply announced that on July 1, 1992,

Rachel Bickham would become the headmistress of Miss Oliver's School for Girls. There was an instance of silence. And then the girls stood up and stamped their feet, and cheered.

Before the cheering was over, Karen Benjamin discovered she was walking up the aisle toward the stage. The decision was made so fast she felt as if she'd had nothing to do with it, as if it had arrived like startling news from another land.

Peggy Plummer watched Karen move toward the stage. She guessed Karen was going to do the right thing by Fred Kindler. *Good for you, Karen*, she thought. If Karen didn't, Peggy would.

Karen climbed onto the stage and stood in front of the podium, then looked down straight at Fred Kindler in the front row. "Mr. Kindler, come up here," she said.

Taken by surprise, and filled with dread, Fred didn't move in his chair. The last thing he wanted was to be onstage again.

Karen beckoned him. He shook his head. "No. Please don't," he said just loud enough for her, and the people nearest him, to hear. He wanted to melt away, out of sight.

Karen walked along the lip of the platform to the steps, climbed down, crossed to Fred, and took his hand. For an instant, he resisted. But how churlish it would be to refuse her gesture! He let her tug him to his feet. The next thing he knew, he was walking hand in hand with her to the steps and then up them and onto the stage, and everyone was staring at them. *All right*, he thought. *I'll just get through this.*

Karen let go of his hand, stepped away from him, and stared out over the audience. "Stand up," she said. At first only a few stood. "Up!" she commanded. People began to stand, some immediately, willing to do what's right, others slowly, resentful for being bossed around. "Good," Karen said when everyone was standing. "Thank you. Now we're going to do what we should have done before. We're going to thank Mr. Kindler for being our headmaster." She turned to Fred and clapped her hands, applauding him.

Peggy Plummer, of course, had leapt immediately to her feet when Karen said to stand up. She cheered loudly now and clapped her hands, and so did Rachel Bickham, Eudora Easter, and Father Woodward. The applause of Gregory van Buren, Francis Plummer, and yes, even Margaret Rice, was also clear. Lila Smythe clapped her hands loudly, a grave expression on her face. The girls near enough to her to see her applauding followed her example, convinced that if Lila applauded, they should too. But from most of the school, the applause was merely polite, and a fair number refused to applaud or even to stand. The overall effect was dispiriting: a community failing to be gracious when graciousness was most needed. Many would look back on this moment as one of the lowest in the year.

Now Fred knew even more clearly how few friends he had and how many enemies at Miss Oliver's School for Girls. It was a brutal message. He couldn't get off the stage fast enough. He turned to Karen. "Thank you, Karen," he said. He wanted to tell her how much more her respect for him mattered than the contempt of all these others. But this was for her ears only, and he couldn't say it because the meager applause had died to almost nothing, and the whole school would hear. He wouldn't demean himself by returning the insult he'd just received.

He saw that Karen was trying not to cry and wanted to soothe her. *It's all right, this is just what happens*, he would have liked to say. But he couldn't say that either in front of all those people. He went down the steps and took his seat.

Fred was right. Karen was so furious she could cry. She stayed onstage. She was not about to let it end this way! She thought back to the riot that the hysterical Petrie woman had started that day in September—it seemed like years ago—and how the next day Fred Kindler had walked across this stage in his funny suit and disappeared behind the podium because he was too short while everybody mocked and laughed. And then he'd stepped out front, red mustache flaming on his face. He just stuck his face out there! Braving them. And they shut up. He took the weight. She wanted to be like that.

"You people need to grow up," she said. "This whole school needs to grow up. You don't have the foggiest idea what's going on. But he knows." She was pointing to Fred Kindler. "That's why we blame everything on him." And then the example she would use to prove her point came to her. "Take that article I wrote," she said. "Remember that? You thought he was the one who banned it. Well, just to show how dumb you are, he wasn't. I was the one who decided not to publish it." *It's not a lie*, she told herself. *Just doing this makes it true.* She saw Mr. van Buren three rows from the front. He was staring at her. In the front row, the headmaster was staring at her too. She thought she saw him start to stand up, then change his mind. *Sit down*, she wanted to tell him. *I can do this. Let me honor you just this much. Let me show how right you were that even I could understand.* Then she watched the headmaster turn his head to rove over the audience. He was looking for Mr. van Buren. *This is complicated*, she thought. *This is really complicated!*

"It was my decision not to print the article about our sex lives," she told all those faces out there staring at her. "So if you want to be mad about it, be mad at me," she added, raising her voice. "Or at yourselves for being dumb enough to think an article like that should be in the *Clarion*. But not at Mr. Kindler. Why be mad at him? He's the best thing that ever happened to our school."

Gregory van Buren put his hand up, but she ignored him. "It would have been bad for the school, so I killed it," she said. "And I threw it away," she added, thinking, *Now I* am *lying*. "I should have told you then. It would have stopped your bitching and moaning."

Gregory van Buren was standing up. "What?" she said.

But Gregory wasn't talking to Karen; he was talking to the students. "It was the right decision," he announced. "If Karen hadn't made it on her own, I would have made it for her," he told the students. No one said a thing. No one dared. Because he was staring them down. He'd got his face right out there in front of them, just like Kindler did. And he was staring them down.

And Fred Kindler was watching—watching and smiling.

ON FRIDAY MORNING the calls from the alumnae started to come in to Nan White's office. *Yes*, they said, *we'd be delighted to come to the meetings, you can count on us to recruit for the school, we'll never let it die. For now, with the right person at the helm, and two million dollars to give us the time we need, how can we possibly fail?* In Friday afternoon's mail, the reenrollment contracts started to arrive.

It took Nan White a long time to find the heart to take this news to Fred.

Thirty-Three

In the splendor of the noontime sun, Fred Kindler walked across the dais to the microphone to begin the graduation ceremony. The graduating class sat in the honored position to the left of the dais, their white dresses glistening in the sunshine. And in the faculty section, Francis and Peggy Plummer sat next to each other, their sides almost touching. To sit apart at such a time would be an affront to tradition. Three seats away in the same row, Eudora watched them and was encouraged. "We save the school, we save everything," she remembered telling Peggy. It seemed like years ago. Soon she'd know whether she was right.

As Fred Kindler began to speak, Francis reached for Peggy's hand, as he had done for thirty-four years at this point in this occasion. She let him hold it but didn't squeeze back, a tentative grasping to match her indecision. She was not weeping now as she had a year ago, sobbing all through Marjorie's final speech; she was wondering what it would be like to follow Fred Kindler, to work for him at whatever school was lucky enough to land him as its head. It was only when she realized how far these imaginings could take her away from Francis—who she thought wouldn't even consider teaching anywhere else but Miss Oliver's—that she began to weep.

And Francis had none of the anger that last year had made him squeeze Peggy's hand so hard it made her wince. He could only feel regret that he hadn't done better for Fred Kindler and sadness that he couldn't weep with Peggy for his parting. It didn't occur to him that that was not what she was crying about, nor did it occur to him to tell her that he was the one who had saved the school with his idea to give the responsibility to the alumnae and parents. He wouldn't do that to Fred Kindler—or to Peggy's opinion of him. He had accomplished that much at least. So now he was free to try to save his marriage.

Fred's graduation speech was even briefer than Marjorie's used to be. He had no desire for the last word. When it was over, he sat down to mild applause.

For the next two hours the faculty conferred the diplomas in the sacred way. Karen Benjamin was the first in the order, her name having been the first to be pulled last night from Daniel Webster's hat. Gregory van Buren called her name, and she bounced across the grass to stand while Gregory said the memorized words. They boomed through the mike:

Only where love and need are one,
And the work is play for mortal stakes,
Is the deed ever really done
For Heaven and the future's sakes.

And then Gregory handed Karen a scrapbook. It contained every article she ever wrote, pasted in order of their appearance in the *Clarion*—and also the one that was never printed. Karen hugged Gregory long and close, then trooped back to her seat, holding the scrapbook up like a sports trophy for her parents to see.

Fred's being chosen by Lila Smythe for this special moment in her life would be among the warmest of the memories he'd take from his time at Miss Oliver's School for Girls. When he called her, the last in the order, he introduced her as the "author of the Declaration, the staunchest one of us all," and handed her a photograph of Gail, himself, and their daughter, who was identified by the note appended. "So that you know us," the note went on. "So you'll stay in touch." Lila stood in the sunlight looking at the picture of the girl, two years younger than she was. Tonight when she would be alone, she'd cry for Fred Kindler. Right then, she smiled and stepped into his hug. "Always," she said. "Wherever we go."

Near the end, Milton Perkins went to the mike and asked Fred to stand next to him. Fred felt a huge reluctance and hesitated. When he finally stood, the sun seemed piercingly bright, the faces in the audience were hard to see. So he didn't know that all alone in the audience, Myron and Rachel Benjamin, Karen's parents, were standing up to show their respect. And though he felt Perkins's hand on his shoulder and knew that Perkins must be praising him and thanking him—and God knows, praise from Milton Perkins was praise he treasured!—the words didn't register. They would later, after he was gone and had time to reflect. That's the way it always was. All he was aware of then was how eager he was for the end.

Perkins finished to polite applause. When Fred sat down again, he felt a sudden relief. It was over. The line that marked the end had been crossed.

FATHER MICHAEL WOODWARD was sitting on the steps of his front porch when Francis got back to the rectory.

"Oh!" Francis said. "You're not at the church."

Father Woodward raised his eyebrows. "And you're not at the graduation luncheon."

"No. I'm not," Francis said.

"Well, that's a first,"

"I came to get my things."

Father Woodward flushed. "Oops!" he said. "I made my move too early." Then Francis saw his suitcase and his backpack behind Woodward, on the porch by the door. "Eudora helped me pack them," Woodward said. "She knows I'm as much a slob as you are." Then he stood up, crossed the porch, picked up the suitcase and the backpack before Francis even took a step, and handed them to Francis. "Find out why she loved your father so," he said, breaking his dictum to let people figure things out for themselves.

Francis put his things in the same dented yellow car he took out West and drove across the town to Peggy's house. He was too realistic to think of it any other way. She'd still be at the graduation luncheon when he got there. He'd put his things in Siddy's room instead of theirs—as if for this beginning to come only halfway home—and wait for her. When she found him there, she'd be glad.

But neither of them could know whether they would heal their marriage.

He only knew how he would try: he'd confess he didn't need a parent anymore and try to learn why she had loved his father so, and then he'd beg her to broaden her vision enough to include his pagan spirituality, his totemic connection. He'd try again—a thousand times if he had to—to tell her his turtle story. For she needed to earn a broader view, having spent her life at Miss Oliver's, a hermetic, tiny scene. Maybe he could help them both broaden their views. After all, he was the one who'd been on a vision quest.

"LET'S GO DOWN to the shore tonight," Gail said in the afternoon sunlight of the back lawn of the head's house, surrounded by the empty tables. Just seconds ago the last guests of the graduation luncheon had departed. Yellowjackets buzzed around the little mounds of strawberry shortcake left on the plates, and the wind picked up some paper napkins, strewed them across the lawn. She wanted to be alone, with him, in some other place than this.

They left in the early evening. They took the smallest, most rural roads they could find. "Let's imagine we've already left," Gail said. "We're in a new place." During dinner, which they ate outdoors on the deck of a restaurant that looked out on the mouth of the river, that was just what they did. Over martinis, they located the fantasized new school in Italy, on the shore of the Mediterranean, to which Fred had been called with much fanfare to found a brand-new international school. By the time the lobsters and the bottle of white wine were gone, they had described the head's salary as beginning at three hundred thousand dollars with mandatory two-month summer vacations and a huge travel allowance. All the students were brilliant and charming, and there were no pathological geniuses on the faculty. "Like you-know-who," said Gail. By dessert they were speaking in broad Italian accents and calling the waiter Mario.

After dinner, driving back to the bed-and-breakfast, Fred said to Gail, "I think Maine would be more reasonable. Or North Carolina. Maybe Rhode Island?" He was trying to say, as humorously as possible, that his spirits had suddenly descended, the buzz of the wine faded. Next to him, Gail patted his knee. "Let's take a walk on the beach," she said. "A nice, long walk in the dark with my very resilient husband."

A little while later, in the empty parking lot of a state beach, they stepped out of the car into the smell of the sea. The sand blown off the dunes onto the macadam was gritty underfoot. They shivered, took each other's hand, and walked toward the dunes, pale hills in the dark.

When they reached the crest of the dunes they were a little out of breath. Below them the beach was a wan ribbon, and beyond that the little waves coming out of the dark made a rhythmic hissing. The moon made a river of light along the black water. "Beautiful!" Gail whispered. She put her arm around his waist.

They descended to the beach and stood with a dune just behind them. The waves hissed louder, the sea smell was even stronger, and the moonlight touched the phosphorescence stirred by a school of minnows in the thin water at the beach's edge. "Oh, the glory of it!" Fred murmured, "the glory!" and felt a lightness. The leadership of the school had just lifted away and opened his eyes to the world.

Gail pulled him closer. "This is as good a place as we'll find," she said.

He knew what she meant and turned to her. *Yes! this is it*, he thought. He could already imagine the new life springing in her, and they lay down together, like impassioned teenagers, with no other place to go.

Acknowledgments

I am grateful to:

The Graphic Arts Books team for their belief in the Miss O's saga and their professionalism.

Tom Jenks for his brilliant guidance.

George Eckel and Dick Bradford for reading draft after draft—and sending me back to do another.

Peter Tacy, Rick Childs, Diane Sampson, Rachel Belash, Jessie-Lea Abbott, Rod Napier, David Mallery, Jim and Cindy Ware, Joanna Lennon, Steve Weiner, Joanna, Wendy, John and Sally Davenport, and all the others who dared to read and comment on the manuscript: What would you have said if you had hated it?

Peter Buttenheim, the king of loyalty, for keeping my spirits up.

And finally, all those who work in schools, for spending their lives the way they do.

WestWinds Press Book Club Guide

Saving Miss Oliver's

Stephen Davenport

Discussion questions for *Saving Miss Oliver's*:

1. What is the culture of Miss Oliver's School for Girls that brings the alumnae and students to love their school? How does their love of school enhance the students' growth and learning? If you presently attend school, or are a graduate of a school or college that you love, what are the reasons for your feelings?

2. Most of the characters in the book were upset or even angry when threatened with the possibility of the school going coed; why do you think they reacted this way? What is your opinion of the value of single-sex education for girls, whether it is for elementary school, high school, or college?

3. Marjorie Boyd is seen in only a few scenes in the book, but it seemed like her presence loomed everywhere. What did Marjorie Boyd leave behind after thirty-five years as headmistress? What aspects of her leadership style brought positive results, and what aspects negative?

4. What should the board have done to prepare the school for new leadership after they dismissed Marjorie Boyd?

5. Four teachers are featured in *Saving Miss Oliver's*: Francis Plummer, Eudora Easter, Gregory van Buren, and Rachel Bickham. What do they have in common? What made Francis Plummer especially powerful in the school?

6. The last sentence of the scene in which Francis Plummer teaches Robert Frost's "Home Burial" to a class is: *No one in this class will ever be the same again.* How are those students different after the class? What makes Francis so effective in this class? What personal characteristics? What strategies?

7. What are Fred Kindler's strengths and weaknesses as a leader? Given what you know, having read the novel, would you advise him not to take the job? What leadership skills are needed to succeed as head of school following Marjorie?

8. Imagine that you are a more experienced leader than Fred Kindler and that he thinks of you as a mentor. He calls you asking for advice after his first day in office when he gets all that bad news. What are three or four steps you would advise him to take?

9. If you were on the board of Miss Oliver's and were faced with having to decide whether to admit boys or close the school, which choice would you make? Why?

Q&A with Stephen Davenport

Q: You wrote *Saving Miss Oliver's* after a long career in schools like Miss Oliver's School for Girls. Why did you decide to write a novel instead of a memoir?

A: It never crossed my mind to write a memoir. I didn't want to write about what happened to happen to me. I wanted to write about the universal—about what always happens. What happens in *Saving Miss Oliver's* happens over and over again in organizations, and always will. To watch how it unfolds in a specific organization is to glimpse human nature.

Q: Besides its universality, what is it about the natural resistance to change that fascinates you so much that you put it at the heart of the novel?

A: As I begin to answer that question, a memory returns: It's July. I'm on the staff of a ten-day workshop designed to impart wisdom and understanding to independent school professionals who have just been made head of a school. In the middle of a discussion which I am facilitating about pace, how speedily a leader can expect an organization to adopt to new ways of operating and new goals, one of the new heads, a woman in her thirties, bursts into tears. The discussion stops. Concerned, everyone turns to her. "I've just learned there's no way I can succeed," she says. "I'll be gone by June." She was right. She had no more of a chance than Fred Kindler had.

One of the reasons she had been chosen for the job, over several more experienced candidates, is that she had sagely pointed out to the school board what they should have known before they began the search: that significant changes needed to be made for the school to thrive. This woman had been so excited by the prospect of leading the school toward those changes that she hadn't realized they were changes in the culture of the school, traits, ways of doing things that its members rally around, not just because "this is how we've always done it," but because those things expressed the nature of what they had created. But the board expected these changes to be made right away.

Q: How did the characters come to you? Are they modeled on people you know?

A: None of them are modeled on people I know. Marjorie Boyd came to me when I was trying to craft a charismatic woman, and she fully emerged when I imagined her declaring that the graduation ceremony would start exactly at noon. I saw her then and knew that she would never invite some celebrated outsider to make the graduation speech.

When I started writing the novel, the only things I knew about the new head who would replace Marjorie was that he was male, younger than his predecessor, both a good educator and financial manager, and he had a limited time to turn the situation around to save the school. I didn't know whether he was savvy enough to understand the odds against him, nor if he would succeed. I didn't even know his name. I had found that out by writing the story.

It wasn't until I had him stand next to Marjorie that I thought Fred seemed like the right name for such a man, and I put him in a very un-preppy polyester suit. Then the other characters slowly revealed themselves to me as I built Fred's story.

Q: A good part of the plot takes place miles away from the school—Francis's trip westward, his experience with the aborted archaeological dig, and then his return. Why?

A: To show Francis Plummer only on campus is to show the reader only those qualities that Fred Kindler can see. I wanted to put Francis out of Fred's sight, into a much larger, unconstrained world than the hermetic world of Miss Oliver's school that has consumed every minute of his adult life. I wanted the reader to understand and appreciate that the failed archaeological dig on Mount Alma on the other side of the continent is, for all of its absurdity and failure, Francis's legitimate, even admirable attempt to fulfill a vision quest at the same time as it is a sneaky escape from the responsibility to stay at the school and show Fred Kindler how to avoid the rocks and shoals that will otherwise surely undo him.

Q: I understand that the only type of independent school you didn't work in was an all-girls school, and yet you set the novel in that kind of school. Why?

A: I wanted to charge the narrative with an extra dose of passion. So I gave the school a mission that inspires passion, the empowerment of young women. The name of the school is Miss Oliver's School for Girls. That's the reason it exists. It is a feminist organization, at war with systemic male dominance, where the operating slogan is "anything a boy can do, a girl can do better." Anybody who messes with that idea is the enemy, and here he comes in the person of Fred Kindler, a male, from the outside, who everybody suspects will try to save the school by admitting boys, thus eliminating the reason for its existence.